A Fifth of November

Also by Paul West

Fiction

The Dry Danube*
Life With Swan
Terrestrials
Sporting With Amaryllis
The Tent of Orange Mist
Love's Mansion
The Women of Whitechapel and Jack the Ripper
Lord Byron's Doctor
The Place in Flowers where Pollen Rests
The Universe, and Other Fictions
Rat Man of Paris
The Very Rich Hours of Count von Stauffenberg
Gala
Colonel Mint
Caliban's Filibuster
Bela's Lugosi's White Christmas
I'm Expecting to Live Quite Soon
Alley Jaggers
Tenement of Clay

Nonfiction

The Secret Lives of Words
Master Class
My Mother's Music
A Stroke of Genius
Sheer Fiction – Volumes I, II, III
Portable People
Out of My Depths: A Swimmer in the Universe
Words for a Deaf Daughter
I, Said the Sparrow
The Wine of Absurdity
The Snow Leopard
The Modern Novel
Byron and the Spoiler's Art
James Ensor
The Spellbound Horses

available from New Directions

A Fifth of November

·

Paul West

A New Directions Book

Book design by Erik Rieselbach
Manufactured in the United States of America
New Directions Books are printed on acid-free paper.
First published clothbound by New Directions in 2001
Published simultaneously in Canada by Penguin Books Canada Limited

Library of Congress Cataloging-in-Publication Data
   West, Paul, 1930–
   A fifth of November / Paul West.
   p. cm.
   ISBN 0-8112-1467-2 (alk. paper)
   1. Garnet, Henry, 1555–1606–Fiction.
   2. Great Britain–History–James I, 1603–1625–Fiction.
   3. Gunpowder Plot, 1605–Fiction.
   I. Title.
   PS3573.E8247 F54 2001
   813'.54–dc21   00-066840

New Directions Books are published for James Laughlin
by New Directions Publishing Corporation,
80 Eighth Avenue, New York 10011

A Fifth of November

Cannot we deceive the eyes
Of a few poor household spies?

BEN JONSON

There is such a profound and hidden power in sacred words,
as I have learned by trial, that to one thinking upon things
divine and earnestly and diligently pondering them, the most
suitable of all musical measures occur (I know not how) as
of themselves and suggest themselves spontaneously to the
mind that is not indolent and inert.

WILLIAM BYRD

As flies to wanton boys, are we to the gods;
They kill us for their sport.

King Lear

Part One

I

FATHER GARNET SHRINKS from the Renaissance outside his bolthole, not because he trickles and gurgles with sudden eruptive swaggers of his tripes, but because the huge polity out there bellows Death To Jesuits, as if any one label sufficed to evince this polymath, baritone singer, adroit mellow speaker, earthy Derbyshireman still close to the loam that bore him, his little knotted soul all chirps and cheeps, weary of going on being careful even as he reminds himself that memory is the pasture, the greensward, on which the mind can disport itself most ably, molding everything to the shape of heart's desire. On a sailor's grave, he recalls, no flowers bloom. He wonders where he heard that, and why, able here to summon all his mental moutons into one flock, baa-ing the gospel according to Saint Garnet, that not too gaudy, too precious, stone. Doomed to practice it day after day, even to the extent of dipping his nib in orange juice to make the words invisible, he has fallen in love with secrecy.

Once again he hears the noise of himself, squirreled away here in a priesthole made by a maimed dwarf of a carpenter who also happens to be a lay brother. Saved by woodwork, and a little tampering with the original masonry, Garnet languishes in the bosom of a vast country house, or rather in a thimble carved within a nipple, waiting for daylight, unable even to stand in the space allotted him. Why, he moans, are we hated so? He sneezes, once, twice, pressing his nose hard to quell the seizure, each time murmuring the time-honored formula, *Bless You*, that saves the soul, angelic silver skein, aloft amid the tawdry of this world, from being flung far away, never to return. You could sneeze yourself soulless. But he never will, although strictly speaking someone other than you should babble the formula. *A tes souhaits*, he knows, is what the soul-saving French neighbor says, automatic in this as in almost every other prayer. It is good, he reassures himself, to be prayed for in this way by just about anyone standing nearby. So, what does the king do when he sneezes? Bless himself or have a chorus of courtiers mumble the phrase? That is what they are there for, to keep his soul in his body in the interests of, well, not the one and only church, but the king's sect anyway. Father Garnet thinks that, for the soul to speak, it should have a language of its own, pure and godly, unknown to humankind, and therefore blessing itself in blindest esoterica. Now, there's just the kind of thought to get him damned, socially at least, hoicked out of his hidey-hole and hanged along with hundreds of other mildly dissenting churls. Father Garnet has no room in which to shrug, but his mind makes the motion for him.

This carpenter troubles him, this builder of hiding holes. He, Garnet, prefers the old-fashioned country word *joiner*. Little John Owen, the joiner in question, makes a fetish of joining priests to their mouseholes, almost as if he thinks of the priesthood as a furtive, shy calling: nothing of titles and fancy robes, but the essential spirit hidden within the rind of the planet, within all these lavish country houses. Hide-and-seek is not far from it, not when daily or even nightly life can be shattered at any hour by the arrival of priest-hunting poursuiv-ants armed with torches and dogs, probes and huge cones of bark through which they listen to the masonry, the chimneys, the passageways. Garnet chides himself for thinking ill of his savior, but sticks to his point nonetheless: hiding us away as he does, and making endless provision for ever more of us all over the Midlands and the South, he presumes to some kind of power, making us invisible and yet, at the same time, even more spiritual than ever, more abstract, more distant, more creatures of the mind than of ritual, splendor, office.

It is like being made obsolete, he tells his creaking bones, re-membering only too well the crippled joiner's instructions: "You will not stand, Father, you will have to contain yourself at the crouch, there can be little easing once you have been in-stalled. To make your little place any bigger would be to expose you." He is a priest-shrinker, as alive in his trade as the old word for plough in such a word as *carucate,* which means as much land as you might reasonably plough in a year. In a way, Father Garnet broods in his cramp, our Little John is the ideal candi-date for these cubbyholes, but he has no need, can go abroad as he pleases, more or less an upright dwarf, bubbling with good humor and perhaps more than a little amused by the spectacle of us all crouched until doomsday. He is almost a sexton, of the living, omitting only to smooth the earth over us at the last, and no doubt tempted sometimes to seal us in with trowel and mor-tar which, if we did not burst out while the seals were still soft, would encase us for ever. Between cramp and suffocation, we have a poorer life than we envisioned, far from the august

5

panoply of the high-ranking prelate. Father Garnet, the ranking Jesuit in England, tries to soothe his mind with his own
name, derived from the word pomegranate, the color of whose
pulp approximates the stone. No use. The sheer inappropriate-
ness of light hidden under a bushel, which is how he sees himself, provokes him and makes his stomach queasy, a fate little
eased by recourse to the drinking tube that enters his hideaway
from behind the wardrobe outside. A small pan, a slight tilt to
the feeder, and water can reach its priest: anything that will
flow, soup or gruel, just to keep body attached to soul. Father
Henry Garnet of Heanor, Derbyshire, indeed thinks of himself
as a light.

Now he is trying to work out which is better: being alone in
the hole or having another priest for company, Father Oldcorne, as on other occasions, or Father Gerard, as on a few.
There is certainly more talk, he decides, but of such a
thwarted nature it were better to keep still. Perhaps the pallid
patter of the inward voice consorts best with secret living, on
the run from King James's hunters. For those eligible to have
women with them, if any, it might be better, he reckons, not so
much cuddling as meeting head-on a different point of view;
after all, those bearing within them the secretest hiding place
might better adjust to circumstances and so cheer up anyone
with them. A Jesuit, he tells himself, should be able to reason
the pros and cons without too much trouble, but he finds his
mind blocked, twisted, perversely longing for daylight, sleep, a
reassuring companion voice. Instead, he hears the echo of a
refrain voiced by Little John Owen:

> *Him that can't stand it tight*
> *May never see the morrow's light.*

Small consolation, that. Imagine, then, the confessional even smaller than usual, even for the recipient, with the confessee granted room to squirm about during the painful act. What then? Should the priest freeze in there, shocked by what he hears? Should he practice in the confessional for the hole or vice versa? Has either any bearing on the other?

The very thought of all these country houses, rambling and august, is what heartens him: on the right side, the side of the angels, from Baddesley Clinton and Harrowden Hall to Rushton and Enfield Chase and Ingatestine. He has hidden in them all, there to conduct a Mass, or to have an annual meeting with younger priests, as required. Only at Sawston, however, near Cambridge, did Little John Owen manage to provide a closet-stool, for those acts of nature inevitable even for a Jesuit. The worst—could he think effectively back to 1591 (three years before the death of Palestrina)?—had been at Baddesley Clinton, a hundred or so miles from London, rented from the antiquarian Henry Ferrers by Anne Vaux, where Owen the carpenter, creating a masterpiece of adaptation, had used moat, sewer, stairways and trapdoors to produce a miracle of a hidey-hole; poursuivants brandishing swords and torches failed to find them—the only snag being that the two priests had stood for hours half immersed in marrow-chilling water. These Garnet considered the hazards of country living; it was as austere as that, and they were unprotected here by a girl child, as on another occasion, when Frances Burrowes, a mere ten, had fended off the constables, crying, "Oh, put up your swords or else my mother will die, for she cannot endure to see a naked sword." They put a dagger to her throat even as, upstairs, a priest went on with his Mass, but she resisted and finally won them over, offered a hundred pounds to visit London and meet the Bishop, she being suitably chaperoned of course. The child said no and so remained in the heedless swordsman's mind an emblem of Papist defiance. We always need such a child, Father Garnet thinks; this is no mere game, on the run while standing in cold water, stuck with our own refuse to the plank we squat on. It will have to change. Today, however, he emerges at dawn to enjoy a breakfast of porridge, boiled kidneys, coarse bread, Double Gloucester cheese, and a pot of quince jelly, making up for meals missed. It wounds him to be so dependent on fuel, he who has been Professor of Hebrew in Rome, knows Latin and Greek, and even the composer William Byrd, who often plays the organ while Father Garnet sings (or plays the lute).

What a civilised gentleman to be hard pressed by religious adversaries, soaking or bemiring himself in the interests of duty. What is worse is this: Father Garnet is a peacemaker, an affable easygoing person who has heard about the sharp remedies proposed by Papist rebels such as Catesby and Guy Fawkes, but deplores them in the interests of diplomacy. Set aside his aberrations, such as his consuming interest in the female private parts, about which he speculates like a thwarted botanist quite against his vows, or in that much more metaphysical question: his own courage and the degree of it if captured and tortured. These topics heave like dragons through his sleep, perhaps combining, and he wakes obsessively murmuring his magic word.

2

THE PROBLEM HE NOW encounters, amid his sneezes, is that the good souls about him expect him to perform as if he has just had a good night's sleep, whereas of course he has that frail, lightweight, fungusy feeling, and his breakfast is sitting none too well. Faint and giddy, he tries to go through the motions with devout precision, but his hands flutter, his eyelids tremble, his head aches, his liver gurgles. It is going to be a long day, akin to better and worse days spent at other country houses, and he begins to muse, with some undemanded-of brain cells, about his covert, erratic life so different from his calm and even days in Rome, where a priest had social weight. In this England of his, of James the First newly enthroned, he has become a squirrel, burying himself and his goods, trying to steal winter access into lofts and crannies. To maintain his dignity, to which he considers himself entitled, he has to become an ecclesiastical acrobat, steering clear of overtures to join Guy Fawkes's plot against the Houses of Parliament without seeming to suggest he will cease to pray for them. He worries about a logic that says whatever refuses to recognize me has to go up in smoke and cinders. Not a violent man, he has witnessed the ultimate violence measured out on other priests, whose final hour, from hanging to disembowelment, he has obliged himself to watch garbed in expensive robes, lavish disguise guaranteeing access to just about anything. Such events have torn his soul.

"They really have," he tells the uncomprehending Little John, who is intent on widening a bolt-hole, then disguising it as something else, possibly a hand-painted screen. "Someone has to be there to see them through it at the end. I have always wondered at the degree to which human beings like to torture one perhaps in deference to some early savagery in the history of the universe. Surely *Let there be light* could not have taken place without some rending. Or so I untraditionally suppose. On the other hand, light may have come in with a huge peaceful wave of the wand, absent one moment, present the next: no sound, no commotion, no Shakespearean knocking at the door." Little John is not listening, accustomed to the thinking-aloud of his customers, who have only to be loose for them to begin soliloquies of all kinds, as if the pressure has built up in the meantime. He knows their ways and no longer concerns himself with them, intent only on master-craftsmanship, subterfuge, and optical illusion. Besides, talk would interrupt the priestly hum that keeps him rapt, so that if he answers at all he does so by making slight adjustments in the pitch and volume of this hum, his very noise construable by an adept listener who can recognize a yes, a no, even a *not in my limited experience, Father,* this last betokened by an almost falsetto shout while he saws avidly along the grain, going through the wood without even trying.

"Brutal meaningless practices," Father Garnet tells him, not to be outdone, determined to have an answer.

"Handsome is as handsome does." A rare event, this, but it is soon over; Little John is already back in his trance, face showing no trace of his having commented or answered—his voice might just as well have come from the mouth of the gargoyle knocker on the spike-studded main outside door. Out of his own whirlwind come the sometimes obscure retorts of the champion carpenter, his mind fixed on what might save his priests from the worst excesses of royal anger. Father Garnet, reduced to silence for a while, realizes that a Jesuit need not be part of any seditious plot to be hanged, drawn, and quartered. You can be wiped out merely for being alive in the wrong place, such is the royal panic.

Very well, he can use Little John as a sounding board, off whom his remarks come bounding back to him, launched out into the world, now returning unheeded. Accustomed to debate, he longs even to be in hiding with another priest, even if only for rhetorical practice. Of course, an outsider would readily construe two priests with their heads together in the darkness (no suspicious reek from extinguished candles) as plotters getting to work. As it were, they are lit only by the caudle—tangy, sweet gruel devised for invalids—delivered to them by reed or quill. Their underground life tends to make them reckless when above: moles on beatific parade.

How rare was such a woman as the exalted widow, Magdalen Montague, mistress of a huge mansion near Battle, East Sussex, popularly known among recusants as Little Rome, so crammed was it with hidden chambers, miniature chapels, and skulking priests. The woman herself, however, a close friend of Queen Elizabeth, walked about openly with crucifixes and rosary beads in her grasp, divinely protected, as some said, but guaranteeing her own survival by sheer force of personality—so much so that she seemed a reputation in full stride; not so much a woman of quirks and charms as an older version of the irreproachable girl who had marched in the bridal procession of Queen Mary Tudor in Winchester Cathedral. Encased thus in the grandest of legends, she regarded everything subsequent as a bauble, to be trifled with and dismissed while she strode magistrally past. Father Garnet found her somewhat daunting, too much of a pope to be a lady, but right in principle, bringing to full boil the old Derbyshire saw about making a mistake: Make it bigger than life, then nobody will recognize it for what it is. This was why she got away with what, according to English law, was an offense demanding life imprisonment. Air your rosary and you were just presumed guilty. In fact, during poursuivant searches respectable ladies had been turfed out of bed lest they be hiding Papish knickknacks in the bedclothes. Father Garnet is never going to forget the trial of a priest named Cuthbert Mayne, arrested for sporting around his neck a bit of candle blessed by the Pope in St. Peter's. Treason he was accused of, and treason he died for, dismembered like (as they say in Derbyshire) a *beeast*. Once again, upon the far from dead body of Father Mayne, the point had been made: all Catholic priests were foreign secret agents committed to the overthrow of the royal monopoly. Father Garnet shuddered at the lumpish gravity of all this. To be born was to be doomed (and redeemed); to be born here was to be doomed prematurely. What a fine arena for foreigners and hypocrites, sycophants and grovelers, England had become as Catholics of all stripes sought to pass muster until the whole affair of their contorted lives went home to God.

For Father Garnet, the physical equivalent of all their prudent shifts originated in his cramped sojourns in priestholes, where, unable to stretch, flex, or twist, he had been obliged to make tiny compensatory twitches of his physique, savoring them as fully as possible before even attempting them, then noting them largely as he did them: minor easings of shoulder and pelvis, neck and ankle, all done with finicking delight as if he were a lion stalking prey but overtaken by some intolerable itch or cramp. He had long ago become the maestro of minuscule easement, always praying for a larger cockpit to wriggle around in (and one other than his own free of water), but ever reconciled to entrapment, or the sensations of it.

Would he ever be comfortable? As when he was at school, immersing himself in Hebrew, Greek, and Latin? Nowadays he felt like the dripstone head of Winchester School's founder, William Wykeham, a fifteenth-century bust that reminded Henry Garnet of a drowning man. How comfy he had been in those early years, eight to fourteen, say, before he began to vex himself with thoughts of moving on to Oxford or Cambridge, either one having a Jesus College. It had to be a *Jesus* college, he just knew; it was the natural thing to do, whereas most Wykehamites, as Winchester boys were known, advanced to New College, Oxford, also founded by Wykeham as a finishing school for his best. Somewhere in the muddle, Henry Garnet missed university altogether and was no doubt the better for it, worldlier for having gone to Rome instead, for having earned an early living as a corrector of printing press proofs in London. Is this why he has risen so high in the Society of Jesus? Not a victim of insolent pride, he nonetheless has substantial self-respect: not a creative man, but re-creative certainly, and with a Derbyshire quietness in his demeanor, betokening not the gruff intransigeance of the Yorkshireman in the county next door, but almost a diffidence, a gentle tedium that gives the wrong impression; Henry Garnet has nerves of oak. He is going to need them, he knows that; they will take him to the point at which faith, if it ever fails, does.

One outcome of his constantly being secreted is an intemperate yearning for crannies. Any slot, sentry-box, walled-up doorway, trapdoor into somewhere, gets his body rehearsing a sudden departure. He wants to inch in there and be out of sight, to dream, to fester, to pray, which is only to say that he has developed an uncommon affinity with the locked-up life: an ideal candidate for a dungeon or, worse, a punishment cell in which it is impossible to stand, or lie full length. Perhaps God has seen it all already, he thinks, and has all this time merely been training him for the grand finale. By such self-recognitions as these, he is struck the same as he once was at school, discovering that the Romans had a verb for eye-watering: *lippio,* which indicated, at least to Henry, that the winds in Rome were keen and made the Romans' eyes water. Odd, however, that during all his time in Rome, professing, he never felt those winds, which must have turned milder, weaker. The verb had not carried through into Italian. Or, he wonders, perhaps because all Romans have watery eyes, the phenomenon is not worth remarking upon. Was. He can while away many hours of incarceration with subjects such as this, in his review sometimes mustering an entire social history to make his linguistic point. In this case, though, he cannot make his mind up. Bless those cruel Romans, he thinks, they even had a word for rich-voiced, meaning a deep and luxurious voice as of someone grown fat: *Praepinquis.* No wonder his friend William Byrd wrote better music for Latin words than for English; the Romans had, well, what? Arrogant meticulousness, a brash love of detail.

No, he says, schoolmastering himself, you are missing their practical side. It was socially useful to know that eyes water in the north wind blowing down from the plain of the Po or that fat moneybags have a baritone vibrato. Romans devoted linguistic innovations only to things that had practical consequences, as if, for instance, it turned out that thin people never walk straight or people with hiccups tend to insist on a higher rate of interest when they lend. He knows he is trifling with footling, but it eases him until Byrd arrives with almost a retinue, his coach creaking and grinding like an animal saying welcome to Storton Abbas. Byrd is well-in with both Rome and the king, as Henry can divine from the retinue: one coachman coming out with the bucket of hot coals, over which the organist and composer has warmed his delicate hands during the trip, another of lesser standing saddled with the ordure bucket. Only once, Henry hears, has Byrd made a mistake, relieving himself onto the cooling coals (with attendant stench) and warming his hands above the filth bucket—a double gaffe where one might have served. It is almost an emblem, this tale, of Byrd's double nature, the epitome of loyal sedition, a stance managed by other Catholics, to be sure, but in his case carried off with a panoply and confidence that few can achieve. Byrd's main worry today, though, is to have enough voices for his *Ave vera* (Hail, Spring), which will entrance the day.

"Another year by grace of God." Byrd often begins thus, ready to launch himself into the same old muttered summary, almost in a tone of sullen complaint as if the universe were not coming up to expectations, never mind how his career prospers, and it is no use countering him in Latin, or any other

fancy lingo. Father Garnet, with the loam of Derbyshire between his toes, stands his ground and ventures something
about what has driven him to the faith: loneliness, he says, and
the impetuous lyricism of the soul, ever wanting to make the
best of everything. "Is not this a divine thing?" Garnet asks
him. "Against all odds, this desire to make the beautiful prevail, as if we were better at rejoicing than at complaining?
Witness the music of certain masters, one of whom I will not
vex by naming him. I do dwell on this push from within the
heart, to be joyous, as if the world in all its wretchedness
might be duped into siding with us."

The answer to this must be musical, rhythmic at any rate;
Byrd seems to be enacting it with his heavy brow moving left
and right in a eupeptic ague. Does he agree? Of course he
does, but his way is never to be that outright, ultimately agree-
ing only with such a gesture as a frozen man might make
when hunching over a fire. His response is evident for anyone
who labors to extract it from the mummery of his behavior.

"I divine agreement," Garnet murmurs, aware how often he
ends up saying this, having come to the same recognition all
his days, answering the temptation to rejoice with whole-
hearted impetuosity. Did he invent it for lack of something to
feel joyful about? Oh no, it happened upon him, it came out of
the divine strewn about among all sordid things. It had rained
on him in his youth, blown at him, deafened him, stoked him
up, made him dry and made his fingertips prickle. Its opposite, from the lame desire to grumble to the able-bodied one to
denounce evil, as words of complaint and disgust have risen to
his lips, has never felt so strong. His swerve has always been to
the blissful, not a rose garden tended in defiance of God, but

a little version of what it must have felt like to make the world from scratch. In this he feels a man of future centuries, hounded by the just-about-dying Renaissance, intent on whatever new fling of the wheel is ready to start. Is this feeling he has, one of being deeply implicated in thunderstruck delight, rejoicing because it feels good? Perhaps, he reasons, eyeing Byrd as the composer strides to and fro on the cropped lawns patrolled by spaniels and wolfhounds who know his smell. Airing his tunes, Garnet calls it, giving them some puff. Where was he? As if, in some unnamed society that has not discovered the wheel for practical purposes, children play with toys that have wheels, and no one gets the point, no one construes widely the impact such a miracle might have in adult and joint lives. It is something such as that, a premonition blighted, or left to rot for almost garbled centuries for lack of observation. Now, he decides, that is almost like those who listen to Byrd and see his music as only a social toy, an unguent for convivial evenings instead of, bless the mark, the body of the martyr rent asunder by a hangman not averse, certainly in older days, to leaping on the condemned's back to keep him from loosening the noose as he falls. Or was it to ease his pain, to double the weight that came to bear on the neck and thus compassionately snap it? In these days, he recognizes, the last thing they want is a *dead* man for the drawing and quartering.

Byrd, having come to rest, watches him with intense interest, at last motioning with his severely manicured hand. "Damme, Henry, if thinking does not always thicken your milk to cream. Life is good as it is, perhaps, but you make it richer by leaning on it, my dear. Is this the promised gift, the ability to ravish onself with sublime temper?" Odd to have this lyric musician asking such unanswerable things, dragging his own internal workings into the open, to have them studied by proxy and found lawful. The pair of them, exulting upward, live in the echo of each other, actually mapping out more than a slice of the spiritual main: the sung and the prayed. Their hinterland is boundless and the major piece of their being; to trap it in a stave or a priesthole is as futile as to beg them to take up whippet-racing on the downs in the interests of gambler's profit.

"I have said it before," Garnet tells him, "we think the impulse to joy comes from our Creator, but it might not; He may have felt no joy at all in that massive labor, but nonetheless created the spark that drives us on into sublimity. In other words, dear fellow rhapsodist, it's a choice between joy derived and joy underived, the one reflecting back to the fount and source, the other self-contained, yet taunting us always with the chance of being a genuine reflection of something beyond the human. How can you untrain a Jesuit? By letting the ills of the body plague him for long enough. I see no reason why all the delights of our earthly life should seem to have come from the daily or weekly round of the Almighty. Rather, I see Creation as freely going its own way, and our joy being an end in itself—not provided for us, not even derived, but as it were cropping up in a field by accident, bubbling out at us to be taken or left."

Untrained as Jesuit or any other kind of thinker (though there are rumors that he was a Winchester boy who did not stay the course), Byrd loves this side of his devout yet pagan friend, who often sounds like some fugitive ancient Greek—a flurry of Ovid among the solemn missal. "Too deep for me, Henry. Leave it alone. Enjoy it, my dear, without preaching or teaching it. What do I hear? That those who paint are the most sullen of all, the least adept with words; then the musicians, who are much more word-besotted; and then those such as you, the geometers of the ready-made universe. I do declare, sir, you are more of a heretic than I. Each time I see you, I eat and drink well, and go away murmuring your latest play on words, but worried into a palsy by your bewitching microcosm, which says no microcosm can be complete because the world is always having added to it the microcosms of unknown modelers, ergo the sum of things is always greater than any miniature maker can catch up with. Must your rose garden be an accurate one? May it not malinger as an out-of-date approximation?" This is all he usually can get out before, in a huge gust of pent-up breath that ends in a snorting cough, he moves away into the less heady company of wattmen and grooms, retainers and singers, none of whom plague their lives and the lives of others with such zealous questions. All the same, the drift and urge of Father Garnet stirs the most guarded side of him, perhaps the turbid spring from which the music leaps, worrying him that mind was provided for the purpose of reasoning things out Father-Garnet style. And not to emulate him is somehow to betray the gift of intellect. Oh, what a soft and easy pillow is ignorance! He is fond of quoting this, and he knows that to yawn in the wake of Montaigne is a gaffe. But he seeks mental refuge in the doubt about reason he finds in the long *Apologie de Raimon Sébond*, where Henry Garnet the exultant believer has preceded him, and he knows that music is the only system he can stomach. Garnet blesses him, which is to say he does it in the instant and also on a continual basis, as if music were a waterfall under which he hid, waiting for some dolphin or other.

When the singing begins, with Father Garnet robustly taking part, the house seems to change personality: less forbidding, less monumental, less inscrutable. It becomes gentler, more of a home. The music mellows it, the singers are a different race of beings, informed from afar, producing sounds casually august. Once again he notices features in the skin that he has missed before: lines, crow's feet, faults, hidden but brought into view by the grimace of glorious cantabile. Discolored teeth invisible before come into view, and without hurry. Eyes hitherto feline and sharp widen into a bulge revealing the usual amount of white. Pressed so close together, these faces share a hemmed-in, votive quality, part of their sound the result of being squeezed in on one another (secrecy of the act requires a certain conciseness in performance—you have only to imagine the ease with which poursuivants might locate a hymn of joy spread out through an entire floor or even up the main staircase). Father Garnet loves this close-knit vocale, eager to insinuate the sound of himself among those abler than he at this. Amid the gorgeous vowels he also hears the little click of muscles not used since the last time, the creak of jaws, the flurried catarrh from a cold mastered since; time passing along the staves, bidden to behave while they blend voices in choral bliss. This is better than mere speaking or chanting, he knows; the effort required to hoist the sound is noble in itself, and he eyes Byrd the combiner, whose intense, moist gaze recomposes each phrase as it emerges into the dank air of the mighty heap lodged there amid the Cotswolds.

To be sure, God's praise is never perfect, which is what endears it to Him. So thinks Father Henry Garnet, quickened by the surreptitious quality of their song, even if it happens to be arranged by a man at ease at the king's hand or the Pope's, a man facing both ways. The levels of song fascinate him even more, akin to the levels of the house, so that there is a soaring, mountaineering effect to their efforts, modest enough, but of emphatic delicacy. It can go on for an hour or two, however, easily lost as soon as born unless recaptured in the ears of a performer by some sleight of fabulous oral memory, the present phrase dragging the one just ended back into view. Today, however, because Byrd has come late, delayed by puddles and smashed-down trees, they sing for a shorter time than usual and then repair to lunch, begun with a steaming soup more solid than liquid: a filler, Garnet pronounces, ballasted with venison and halved potatoes. Were it a stew, it would be one of the most costive; as a soup, it is close to sludge and has been so for days, simmering, thickening, but almost the host in a ritual. Yes, he thinks, palming Byrd on the shoulder in grateful commendation, we sing like this before our bodies are ripped asunder to gratify the mob, who want to see if papists have bowels the same color as the rest. A different song will come from some of us on that day, not one of thanks but of fearful, unassuaged vindication. We sing because we are, presently, free to do it, and that lovely sense of being at our own disposal goes into the free-flying trumpet of the song.

Byrd the provider who publishes without title pages.

Lady Anne Vaux the host.

Divers voices mingle into a polyphony that will never repeat itself, not exactly. Unique.

Byrd is talking again, an odd sound after so much incantation, going from lofted serenity to mumbled humdrum. "Sometimes, I think we should sing everything. It would be tiring," he says, "but it would glorify the common round, would it not? We use the same musicians for faith *and* frolic."

Almost wantonly, Garnet answers, "Why not?" His mind plays tricks on him, bringing to the fore the Greek word *melismatic,* meaning an intoned word sung for its musical quality yet not a word at all: a mere noise prolonged and aggrandised by an enterprising voice. It is almost better not to mean anything but to use the voice as an instrument only. Byrd, however, does not agree, as a man habituated to writing for instruments would not: when you have instruments already, you do not want voice masquerading as one. In other words, Byrd the composer has a different sense of music from Father Garnet, to whom, even as it ascends into the empyrean of the ever-ampler holy, it remains fleshly and appetitive, both wholesome and detailed. Byrd has a wholly different view entailing some disregard of language's content, though he denies this in their lively disputes over marmalade and raisin bread, with which they mostly conclude the meal.

Father Garnet has sucked marmalade in pitch-dark holes, but Byrd has not, nor will he suffer the peculiar form of exile that seats him in three or four feet of cold water for hours, lower belly and privates numb and hidden. Father Garnet is touching on one of his favorite themes, almost a lifelong obsession that links up the names of the Oxford colleges he never went to (All Souls', Jesus, Christchurch, Magdalen, Corpus Christi) with the Cambridge ones (Christ's, Jesus, Emmanuel, Trinity, Corpus Christi), remarking harshly on their religious sheen, but then roundly separating them from the faith of Rome. How Christly they all were, not to mention those named for saints as distinct from landowners and wealthy altruists. From all that, he tells Byrd, you might have expected something better than public executions and political atrocities done in the name of the king. Byrd blinks, takes it in for the umpteenth time, and agrees. What has he to lose? Garnet knows only too well the vivid, unforgettable commemoration of All Souls' Day, when those in purgatory come most to mind, to be prayed for until their souls are cleansed of minor sins. "It is Odilo of Cluny's invention," Father Garnet says, "placing All Souls' Day after Saints' Day. After the day devoted to those already in heaven, we have a day for those aspiring. Black vestments for the day of the dead. Three requiem masses: mine, theirs, and the Pope's."

"Word-perfect," Byrd tells him. "But why inform me?"

"Because I get from the college of that name—All Souls—only the faintest allusion to its religious burden, as if pollen has fallen over it. There may be the observances, but the passionate, shuddering core of the day has dwindled into lip-serving tedium. Fancy calling a college that and allowing it to falter in ethereal quality. I must sound like a pedant of the schools, but surely something has been lost or omitted in the translation from heavenly to stone and mortar. How easily we find Jesus or Corpus on this or that street, but are they wholly symbolic? I doubt it, less so than with, say, the King's in the one, the Queen's and Queens' in the other."

"Why what a college-watcher you are!" Byrd's voice rises in incredulity.

"Those of us who go straight to Rome," Garnet says, "usually are. What we miss motivates us like a pox."

"To go forth and infect the rest of the world?"

"To stay at home and bathe the afflicted part."

Byrd tries again. "So what we have does not drive us in the least? I publish without date or printer's name, I—"

"It sways us, but not to overwhelming."

"Then we are odd victims of our disappointments."

"When we do not master them." Father Garnet is getting warmed up; he has been trained for this kind of swap.

"I am thinking, dear friend," Byrd says winningly, "of what you said once about rewards. What you said about the thing for its own sake. I am not anonymous, but I seek no fame."

"And how the glory of it blooms under your very hand, lips, mind, so much so that the reward has almost preceded the act itself. Pre- . . . anyway, you can feel it coming, and you complete the task, the feat, out of honor, since your head has already been blessed for being turned the right way. Would one ever wish a reward for being alive? Being as we are, and what, is surely the outcome of a universe that spurts us out, that squirts us, with no especial purpose in mind. God's foison spawns us. We are here for the spawning."

"Salmon, sir."

"Whales if you will."

"Henry!"

"Pray to be light, for the sake of those who carry you when you are dead."

As often as not, their spry, randomly energised exchanges end like this, stilled and amputated by a glimpse of something remorseless, not that the flow of ideas dries up; it is just that chatter's reckless bounty does not sustain them through everything. The dark side pops out and there they are, each confronting the other's guess at what troubles him most. Their levity, however, survives for further banter, best conducted with no other listeners lest the grave priest, the devout composer whose work the composer Wagner will one day echo in a string quartet, seem out of character.

* * *

With an almost bestial crash the poursuivants come through the front door demanding and scanning, swords drawn, staffs at the ready, dogs quarrelling on the leash. Only to see nothing save some untitled sheet music, now gathered by the hands of a servant who seems to be tidying it up while Byrd warms his rear at the log fire, feeling the moisture rise behind him. Father Garnet, whisked through a little closet into yet another hidey-hole, has squirreled himself away in a place no larger than a sedan chair; only after the first few hours will he begin to chafe and ache. There he skulks, behind a door disguised as a folded-up screen. He hears them ferreting about, tapping and shouting. The dogs achieve nothing, strange to say, and he wonders if a whole generation of dogs has been born without any sense of smell in his presence. Perhaps a priest, at least in the early days of a hiding, has no smell at all—none of the camphor and attar of roses he has always thought is upon *him*. In mid-song he has been put away like a forbidden book and the tiny chorus disbanded into various household destinations, with Lady Anne Vaux at her most magistral insisting on offering the "king's gentlemen" a stoup cup, some cold beef, fruit and cordial. They refuse, but waste time on smiling obeisance; she dresses plainly, but her mind is all regalia. Her only worry today is Little John Owen, due to arrive to create a superior bolthole upstairs, a sentry-box in the nursery, ideal for children to play in, but kept from them lest they unwittingly reveal it.

They do not waste time on their swoop, which is over and done with in an hour. The dogs no longer yap, the swords are put away, the staffs no longer probe or tip; all that remains of their bristling ingress, which is going to take too long to yield anything worthwhile, is suspicion. They have other houses to visit unannounced, arriving like cavalry and leaving as a cortège, all disappointment and blunted zeal. Only one search in ten yields anything, and that only in the poorest-prepared households, the ones with too much on show by way of altars and crucifixes. One day, Little John will finish his grand plan of reclamation and defense, equipping every recusant house with blatant cubbyholes designed to be found, concealing yet others designed to be found half the time – the lairs behind the lairs – which in turn conceal the most closed places of all, accessible only to the most ambitious explorer. Nobody will ever be found again. He intends to secrete in the most fastidious way possible, if only they will remember the rules: no belching, no other body sounds, no easing of the joints, no chewing during a raid, shallow breathing, and of course not the slightest sneeze or cough. He half-dreads the day when the acutest poursuivants will be able to pick up the sacred vibrations of a soul attuning itself to God during the harsh hours of hiding after the first twenty-four, with no succor in sight, no food, no close stool, no water, but only a series of haphazard raids, sometimes three within two hours, then nothing for a day, then three more: an irregular irregularity. It is no thing to jest about. To be found will usually mean prison, the rack, and quite often the scaffold. To those priests most at risk it has become a wearisome fatuity, making them mouselike, champions of scurry and lie-low, a hide-and-seek with grotesque penalties. Father Garnet shrugs at potentates who conduct their countries thus, his educated skull recalling a phrase from Tacitus: "*temptat clausa*" – he tries all the closed things.

3

THEN THE REVOLT from memory begins, once the men on horses are clear of the walls. Each voice, in its own new place, begins again, in ragged echelon, without music, but chirping in mild defiance, so that Byrd himself, still at the fire, wonders if he is dreaming: his music has never before sounded so disembodied, so incoherent, so distant; but he can even hear the stifled baritone of Father Garnet in the bolthole. Blurred and muted, the music has a threatened feel, quite without the high spirit of the first performance, but he likes it anyway, chiming in with his own authoritative tenor even as his trews very nearly blaze up behind him, and he lets out a throttled yelp, clapping his hands against his behind. In half an hour, the troop of horses and dogs may be back, having found nobody at Huntsworth or Kneberley, but it may be days. Best sing in the teeth of reprieve, he tells himself, wondering if any of his music communicates the stress and relief of being pounced upon thus, out of the day or night, no quarter given: Give us your priests and naught will be held against you. How many had succumbed to that greasy promise? He hears Father Garnet, called, coming down the stairs, no bounce in his gait, no voice in his throat. He puts the music back together again, orders his coach, has the bucket replenished with fire, and gets ready for the road, intending to spend the evening elsewhere and so, of course, become witness to the same hazards transferred.

Father Garnet is treading heavily because he is pondering Byrd's *Great Service,* music that takes a full hour: one potent uniform fluid reach of tones, utterly unfit for a troupe on the run, so to speak, just like Palestrina's four-part motet *Super flumina Babilonis*—By the rivers of Babylon. Such is the music of peace, or at least of life lived safe and secure. Life in Rome! Ah. *That* is where one should listen to these undulating, long voluntaries of unthematic sound, threatened by nothing save a rainy day. He tests Byrd alive against newly dead Palestrina and marvels at the cringing in the latter, the suffocated chirp that suggests he too had to go into hiding. He went to jail as it was, bullied by the Council of Trent: a mild fate. Yes, Father Garnet tells himself, I am using up my prime among the great elegists of our day, those whose piety transcribes itself into an unreadable language immune to the rack and the rope. Imagine composers on the rack confessing (as it were) in code or invisible ink. That surely is the way to go, not trapping ourselves with the letter of the law, with verse and chapter, easy meat for Sir Edward Coke, the king's attorney. The song that distributes our agony may well be impossible to tell from the one that blazes forth our faith. What a lucky overlap is there. Perhaps we should all have our tongues cut out before it is too late. He returns to Palestrina, in whose life, rather than in his sacred music, he detects almost intolerable repining, and has begun to slip into that mood at the bottom of the staircase when the poursuivants, having slid up on foot, hammer at the doors again.

And again they go, sullen by now, disappointed, not ingenious. Their prey, Father Garnet, Superior of English Jesuits, has a whole stock of thoughts with which to occupy himself while in hiding, uppermost today the fact that his own sisters have left the country and become nuns at Louvain, reaching far for severe privacy. In return have come the sisters Vaux, distantly French (*vaux* means valleys) but their home shall one day become become part of the town Vauxhall, site of a famous car factory. Lady Anne, so called as an honor, not because she has a title, and therefore "Lady" Anne, is actually a "maid," so-called, in other words a spinster, born in 1562. Instead of marrying, she has taken upon herself the chore of managing the life of Father Henry Garnet, code-named Missel-thrush for the bird that eats mistletoe while she herself feigns to be his sister "Mistress Perkins." To Henry Garnet, she is his "sister in Christ," and it is this he calls her when they talk alone together. It is not unknown, then, for certain conversations between Anne Vaux and her widowed sister Eleanor to run as follows: "Will Missel-thrush soon be coming to see Mistress Perkins his sister?" A slight resort, to be sure, it excites Anne's imagination and changes her face in that, having a short philtrum above the upper rim of her top lip, when she smiles her teeth form a crisp line immediately beneath her nose, giving her an eager, predatory look. Used to this, Henry Garnet flinches not, knowing his interest in all women has to be an abstract, unbiological thing. Anne Vaux, which he loves to pronounce Veau as distinct from English Vawks, has become his enabler, guardian, or as Henry puts it, a "brave Virgo become a veritable Virago." What she has managed to do over a short period is so to shade her forceful personality that it strikes Henry Garnet as brisk piety; tending towards what the age calls "stomachful" (uppity), she deals with her Jesuit as if he is the lamb of God. All her reserves of tenderness she applies to him, who bounces about in a furious totalitarian world. Thanks to the Vaux clan, Harrowden becomes known as the best Jesuit college in England, although Anne also rents Baddesley Clinton in Warwickshire, not far away, and White Webbs, on the Hertfordshire-Essex boundary. With so much accommodation at her command, Anne supervises a host of visitors, not all of them priests by any means, but members of the extensive Catholic community she deploys along her web. It is true that many a Catholic family has awakened without quite knowing where they have spent the night in order to attend a mass, and the same goes for its priests junior and senior, assembling only to spread out again into what one priest calls the underground angelical. Conceding that the presence of the faith is strongest in Yorkshire and Lancashire, Father Garnet still worries that English Catholicism is no more permanent than life and might well, one ghastly day, be snuffed out.

He muses even while playing the lute, wishing he could take it with him into his hiding places; but the temptation, even if only in his fingers, will be too great. The faintest dabble will trap him. Nothing involuntary in there, not so much (he has been warned) as a passing of gas because the poursuivant brigade has been schooled in detecting human presence in countless ways. It is like trying to beat a jungle animal at its own game. He still cannot fathom why the dogs fail to pick up his scent, but the reason is perhaps that he buries his human aroma in several others applied for cosmetic reasons, as he learned to do in Rome when professing Hebrew. Will the day ever come when all can be done openly? He doubts it, knowing now how Jews have felt in their long and punitive history, or gipsies. Infinitely curious about humankind, Father Garnet decides that the main fatuity consists in the way humans fix on what divides them rather than on what they hold in common. A simple error, this, but devastating over the centuries and of course less and less remediable as time goes on; the error has become part of an honored tradition by now, venerated by hair-splitters and compartment-makers. He yearns for something the Italians called syncretism, which amounts to the fusion of theologies: all Christian sects under one roof. But he wonders if what he really means is under the one Pope. Has he truly removed the scales from his own eyes enough to pass an opinion?

How, he wonders, uproot the personal and so make judgment unbiased? He cannot forget forgotten professional informer, Richard Topcliffe, whose evil activity began in the 1570s, late on, and went on until 1594, when he was tried and briefly imprisoned for accepting a bribe. This Topcliffe was the only Catholic-hunter allowed to maintain a rack in his own home, the more conveniently to examine prisoners. He might have been granted a scaffold too, had he worked at it, and a disemboweling-bench as well. That such people prosper sickens Father Garnet; he is surrounded by spies and black-mailers, adept at undoing both clever Jesuits and simple believers. He never forgets that the mission of the Jesuits has been to hearten and brighten the subdued, miserable English Catholics, to bring some gaiety and sparkle into their hounded lives, fresh from the Continent. The Jesuits no sooner arrive than they have a price on their heads, and English anti-Catholicism hardens its heart, eager to thwart and slaughter them at every turn. It is a kind of war declared on them, he thinks, not only waged but wagered as well, and it can hardly be terminated, except on the level of ideas and common sense. So long as there is an endless supply of Jesuits, the battle will rage, for they are the condemned whereas the population at large is merely accused. Thoughts such as these hound him from sleep and rest, make it hard for even buoyant him to maintain the *joie de vivre* for which he is well known, the sprightliness he brought from Rome.

A sudden intuition brings him out of reverie. What if the world of hiding places were from a world of private racks? And the king were out of it, the whole war having become a private feud, the rackers free to do with the captured as they think fit, and the priests to go on doing what they do. He wonders if individual enterprise on the part of the hunters would change anything. Does government sponsorship mean that much to them? Would the hunters be better at hunting if they were to do it out of sheer cruelty, for fun? He is beginning to break down, he decides: he and his fellow-Jesuits are becoming too much of a race apart, forced into a reckless individualism in a hostile country—pushed too far away from their spiritual and intellectual roots. He catches himself only just in time, recognizing that he has almost reached the point of protest, at which the persecuted begins to think about revenge: assassination, bombs, military intervention. Does the Mother Church want England that much? No, but she wants her Catholics as much as they want her. To what extent, he asks himself, is he capable of treason? Not that he already stands innocent; merely by virtue of being a Jesuit in England he has become a traitor to a cause he never joined, which he regarded as treacherous nonetheless. So why add to this helpless guilt a flagrant act, a wealth of conspiracy, merely to be hanged for a sheep instead of a lamb? It has not occurred to him before even to think of such things, but now he entertains the full idea.

Fawkes he knows about, and the others, but only through gossip; he is a man of unction rather than a man of action, but he suddenly realizes that, by doing nothing, he is committing a treasonable act. What nonsense it is that, already a traitor, he becomes a double traitor by doing nothing. How tempting it is to do nothing, to sit back and console himself that doing nothing is a violent reprisal. To counter it, he would have to bestir himself and report matters to Sir Edward Coke or someone just as lethal. He notes that, in this topsy-turvy English world, those who inform or confess are rewarded with a swift death, while those who don't receive a slow one. A poor bargain, but state hirelings strike poor bargains, he knows. And, unlike Byrd, he has no art to devote himself to; his only art is holy, and in this, as the saying goes, he cannot lose himself. In the sense that he loses himself in God, yes, and becomes completely unpersoned when at prayer, say, and returns to himself only by degrees, inching his way back from rapt self-emptying to the faintest touch of responsibility. One moment he is a Pyramid, the next he is a pillar of snow. Is that how fast, and fairly easily, one can ascend from being a prayerful believer into a gunpowder demon? Is the transformation similar? He has no idea, but foresees a whole ladder of steps between prayer and bloodshed, steps he is unprepared to take, as if his legs are broken.

4

W**HY DOES HE STARE** at Anne Vaux so much? Because, he tells himself, he is trying to sum up her features and properly express the wolfish quotient in her face. His recall during darkness, as in the hidey-hole, he does not trust; how easily she becomes mythic in his mind's eye, not so much the calm inviter to life's feast as fellow-devourer, her entire physique organized, as he sees it, around the unseen slimy fulcrum she keeps private, though he has glimpsed the bald pear of a sister's mons pubis, yet only as a boy astonished by a globe of something immature. He knows better, mainly from sniggering boys with palm against face, nose lodged in the right angle between thumb and forefinger: "the stinkfinger set" at Winchester who assembled a composite woman from a whole museum of imaginary leftovers, the net effect that of an outsize kidney with hair on it, split and bleeding. He wishes he were not eager to know this part of Anne Vaux, at least only as an expert in crocodiles frequents rivers; but some renegade part of him wants to know more than the generic, not out of desire, but what in his ribald way he calls a rude epistemology.

Well, then, Father Garnet, he whispers, it is more like a

trumpet than like a flower, although an amaryllis would come close, even one of those oblate tulips caught late in their careers, petals forced out and wide to invite the plunger in. Of course it closes up at night, unless—he halts that thought to admit something geometrical: two intersecting curves that form an inviting ellipse, found carved on the ancient desks at Winchester by boys whose first initiation may well be these crude graffiti. Scrawls limning an unknown land, these schoolboy idylls have lingered in his head like Latin roots, erratically linked with notions of something smelly, high as hung venison, rotten as a fungus stumbled upon in a woodland full of cuckoo-spit and nettles remedied only by a carefully applied dockleaf. His intellect scrambles about, scarcely knowing what he would do with such a thing if he found one. Would he even recognize it, be able to tell it from a ruptured haggis? If distance foments myth, then Father Garnet's notion of female anatomy reposes mainly on what's in front of him. The offending gash can be found in the fork of the legs, but an onion popped there, or a giant mushroom, might fool him just enough. All he knows is that his Anne of the Valleys has one, not the sort of thing you take out for cleaning, or repairing (he *thinks* he knows this), more a locus than a target, at least to him in his prison of celibate gusto, with all his natural desire dammed up, thrust back, like mother's milk turned to postassium permanganate. Will he ever know her completely without some inkling of her zone, as he has heard it romantically called? Surely all he tells her, and hears from her, will have an inhuman, angelic bias until the day he witnesses her in all her covert grandeur, aflame in the wind, open to the air, dribbling whatever she stores inside it.

Only too much aware of illicit thought, he turns contemplative to active, trying to muster from rumor the exact procedure a healthy male might adopt when seeking the favors of his Anne. Does the hand march spiderlike across her thigh? Or could there be a sudden plunge, a grab? He has no idea, for a moment entertaining the courtly notion that a budding swain might kneel before this altar, clad at its maximum, and pray for a view, a sniff. To be sure, strange and upsetting aromas have come off her at different times, but of little significance to him. Terrible tales of the vagina dentata have made their way to him, and he feels relieved that such matters remain on the fringe of juvenile horror. There has to be an etiquette, he is sure of that, and he rebukes himself for choplogic—how does a he begin to feel at a her, and vice versa? Answer: by feeling his way, surely. There is no spiritual beginning to it, or is there? Perhaps the proximate cause is the final spiritual link in the fleshly chain, when thoughts of abstract veneration yield to something much cruder, to the first intuition of it anyway. What excitement must ensue! It tickles his mind with thoughts of successive steps in a seduction, now wondering why a priest has to forgo so much, certainly on the plane of corporal knowledge, a long way from fulfilling carnal desire. Oh, he is sure of that; he is committing no act of self-defilement, no more than when, in the depths of night, that sudden slack release comes upon him and his dreaming mind clears as his body drains.

Father Garnet reveres Anne Vaux, but rarely makes contact with her physically, content to adore from several feet away, noting how her contained bulk is declared by the presence of corset and strap. Buxom, she presents herself with a narrow waist, helped into trimness by a couple of girls in waiting, who know her secrets much better than her favorite priest ever will. She knows his voice and responds to it in an almost sexual way, but her needs seem sedately transcendent; she is not one for inspecting her body, but takes it on trust that it is a machine that will behave itself into her old age. In fact, she is as virginal as Father Garnet himself, so, when they are together for Mass, meal, or concert, they attend each other in a swirl of not very assiduous guesswork, neither that much interested in the other's purity, yet not wholly bored by the subject either. They do not know that, to some others, Byrd included, they form the spectacle of two chronic chastities interacting, but marred (for them) only by intermittences of lewd hypothesis, in which curiosity and tamped-down physical compulsion (a twitch, a burn, an ache, a vacant shift) merge for an instant of sheer lust. It is easy for them to be together, these two snow pinnacles, but not for their thoughts to combine; much of their life remains unsaid, implied by gesture or mien, yet left vague enough never to be presumptuous. They cool and calm each other without conferring.

Again, from his pocket he fishes a copy of a letter written by James I in 1601, already what seems a lifetime ago. The subject is the execution of priests: "I would be glad to have both their heads and their bodies separated from this whole island and transported beyond seas." Deportation, Garnet muses: not that bad a fate for a Jesuit, but the situation is bound to worsen. He will soon become as bloodthirsty as the rest, Elizabeth included. I have not forgotten Margaret Clitheroe, put to death in 1586, being pressed to death by weights to the amount of seven or eight hundredweight. "Having made no offence," she said, "I need no trial." Nor has he forgotten Anne

Line, executed in London for sheltering priests. He is afraid to think he has become an expert on life and death, on guilt and execution, he the author of a treatise on Christian disobedience, in which he puts forth the rebellious theory that Protestant husbands have over recusant wives' souls no authority at all and over their bodies only a limited power. The vision of woman as the weaker vessel, the vassal, is not his. How ironic, he thinks, that these rebellious Catholic ladies look to Jesuit priests for succor rather than to their husbands, but then have to harbor and hide said priests, disguising them as tutors while the government damns them as spies from Spain. Amid the hurly-burly of changing roles, he finds himself become his pupil's child.

Why the hullabaloo in the house twice today quickens in him an appetite mostly scanted, he has no idea. Something comes back to life or arrives upon him from elsewhere. He has seen Byrd smiling strangely at him during four- or five-part songs, little knowing that Byrd's world of longing goes beyond poise and beneficence. A touch of malice lingers there in his noble, narrow forehead. He adores to watch the ghost of conquest past arise in the bosom of his friend the priest—not a passion for boys, but something sensual and grand, as if Anne Vaux were a meal and Father Garnet wished to devour it, just as fast however banishing the thought to the ice-land of denial. How the priest manages to shuttle back and forth between craving and abstinence, he does not know; it must take tremendous agility, he thinks, but surely, he decides, as he rattles across Worcestershire in quest of yet another Mass, it makes him more a man of the world. Father Garnet has no such idea, asking not to be worldly, but almost the opposite: a man who does not belong: to passion, to royalty, to the plot. Only in Rome has he felt he belongs, among unquestioned formulas blessed by an almost reliable sun.

Now from Anne he has to gather the news.

The ten-year-old girl who held the poursuivants at bay on a previous occasion has now been packed off to Louvain to be a nun, where his sisters already are. Too addicted to a dagger held at her throat, Frances Burrows will no longer be there to defend them.

Byrd, ever composing, has three new works, one pro-king, one pro-Rome, the other a discreet warble *in vacuo*.

"A day of alarms," Anne Vaux is telling him as she proffers a hunting-cup full of elderberry wine. "Quickening you no doubt."

"Not as the Mass does," he answers, settling for a routine response lest a more candid one drag out of him avowals he is unready for. "Certainly not with our SongByrd on hand."

"To your missel-thrush, Father."

He assents in that; he is no Byrd, but would have liked to be, everyone's ally, connoisseur of power brokers.

"Perhaps we shall not see them again for a month."

"Or until tomorrow," he answers. "What it does to the nerves is nothing to talk about, my lady. One can only rehearse by being pitched into the flames, I suppose. Just think: without the stalwart Catholic ladies of this land, we would be a headless pack by now, sent home to Rome in an assortment of bloody sacks for our colleagues in God to marvel over. On the whole, I sometimes wish I had stayed in Heanor, planting beetroot."

There comes her metallic, high cackle, a practiced irritant that now occupies the hitherto wide range of her laughter, once modulating between titter and a mellow contralto chortle. She has become more brittle with age, less courteous.

"Laugh if you must," he says, "but please do not wish us far enough, not yet. We have been here almost twenty years already. Give us a little more patience. Wait out the king, who may mellow yet. You never know. He has a surrendering side."

"And when it shows," she tells him, "I will invite him here to sing with Master Byrd."

Whatever else he may be, Father Garnet is a haunted man, obsessed still by the saga of Father Gerard, tortured in the Tower several years ago, but who escaped by means of a rope suspended over Tower ditch. Once again he tells his questioners that Jesuits are forbidden to meddle in matters of state, and that is that. He has been in prison for three years by then and told them this repeatedly, to no effect, informing them that any letters he received from abroad had to do only with financial help for Catholics living on the Continent. They ask him about a packet he received for transmission to Father Garnet. They ask him where Garnet is, but he claims not to know and denies that the Derbyshire priest is an enemy of the state. "Oh no," he says, and Father Garnet hears the bell of a human voice tolling in his own head, "give him the chance, and he would lay down his life for queen and country." They promise to torture him.

"Please God you won't," he responds. They show him the warrant required for putting someone to the torture and assure him they will torment him every day as long as his life lasts. "Where is Garnet?" With guttering candles they conduct him to the torture chamber, tiny and dark, and suspend him by the wrists in iron gauntlets, having him mount some little wicker steps, which they then remove one after another until he *almost* dangles, so tall however that they have to scoop some soil from beneath his toes lest they touch the ground and ease his plight. He is suffused with pain, which they tell him will worsen, it being the pain of the uncooperating witness. His wrists and hands above the gauntlets go numb, but he speaks to God only, and they leave him there, from time to time sending to ask how he feels, the warder mopping his face now and then. You will be a cripple the rest of your days, they tell him. Better speak up now. Each time he faints, they lift him up, but let him fall again when he begins to pray. You will stay there until you rot, they tell him. At the five o'clock curfew, though, they conduct him back to his cell, he, almost unable to walk or stand straight, but having his wits enough about him to proclaim loudly as they pass some other prisoners who seem to have the run of the Tower, "Surely they know it is a sin to betray an innocent man. I never will." Thus, in case some false rumor begins to circulate, he quashes it; he has not blabbed about Father Garnet's whereabouts. In the cell they light him a fire and bring some food, but he merely nibbles and rests. He can no longer push his swollen wrists through the sleeves of his cloak. Bile fills Father Garnet's mouth, as it always does when in his mind they reinterrogate Father Gerard, trying to scare him by referring to one man in the room (the Master of Artillery) as the Master of Torture. Once again Father Gerard faints, they take him down, seat him on a bench, pry his teeth open with a nail and pour hot water down his throat. He comes to, babbling the same old prayer. Father Garnet exhales for what seems the first time in minutes, knowing that they are going to go easy on him now, this prayerful obtuse priest whose inner resources have bested their outer ones. Indeed, the Lieutenant of the Tower, one Berkeley, resigns his post, nauseated by this performance upon an innocent man. The warder brings a message from his own wife, whom Gerard has never met, saying she prays for him all the time. Father Gerard has to learn to move and use his fingers all over again, but they remove his knife, scissors, and razors, and the whole world falls away, even the world of affliction. Father Gerard will soon be out by the grace of God, and Father Garnet, pondering his lot, will not even have begun his own ordeal.

Not far away, a French ambassador is kissing the hem of Queen Elizabeth's robe, who apologizes for not seeing him sooner, but she has had a gathering on the right side of her face. She will soon be dead, but all the tortures that go on are with her sanction. The ambassador peers into the front of her silver-gauze dress, slashed sleeves lined with red taffeta, and eyes her full bosom, the skin delicate and white while her teeth look yellow and ragged, fewer on the left than on the right, and again he looks at the bosom, noticing how wrinkled it is, not to be repaired. The fire is hurting her eyes, she says, making them smart, so she has them put it out with water, but not before he notices how her head in its reddish wig seems on fire. This courteous, dying queen's speech is blurred, but her gestures stay imperious.

A queen goes, a king comes, Father Garnet thinks, but the tortures remain the same. He cannot abide the thought that, for all the years Father Gerard—of the Lancashire accent and tall ascetic build—was in the Tower, he was nourished in hiding by sympathetic, brave women. It turns him boneless to think of it. Yet, among the new knights created by King James I at York, Gerard's brother has been prominent. He cannot work it out, this variability of favor, this wobble in the royal attitude. Why not tuneful he in the Tower instead of cheery Gerard? Is it pure luck that dictates things? Is there a scarab or a piece of amber to rub to procure sublime results? He is beginning to feel increasingly inadequate, fit neither for torture nor for the daily chores of a priest, nor indeed for ignominious escape disguised as a circus performer. Of course he would like to get back to Rome and there grow ruddy-faced like Father Tesimond, but his duties in England as head of the Jesuit mission cannot be denied.

"Dying on the vine?" Anne Vaux's ebullient temper enables her to address people in the most importunate fashion, striking to the core of what ails them in face or stance.

"Tribulations, madam, tribulations."

"The same old miseries," she croons. "Why, you are the most hidden of men; you are therefore the safest. This was a bad day, but it might have been worse. You see, the whole house reeks of peppermint, and the dogs get lost in it."

Now he understands about the dogs, which is just as well. He tends to live a seasonless, timeless life, brilliantly attuned to some radiant empyrean of the mind, a zone between music and infatuation, but drifting in and out of practical purposes, which he tends to leave to others, delegating them like a man in Rome in a golden cloak adjusting himself to the same shaft of sunlight as it moves across his desk. "Peppermint," he sighs. "I suppose spearmint would not be as pungent."

She does not respond, instead urging him to eat in peace, hovering about him like a weighted butterfly, little aware of her aromas wafting past him, stirring and bewildering as they go. Why should he worry? Was he ever designated a warrior, like Guido Fawkes, whose profession it is? Her eyes have the brown of liver, her lips the dun pink of coral. He knows about the natural world, but not about her in it, she the compassionate, clever mystery, easier for others—Byrd, Little John Evans, Tesimond—to fathom than for him, although he's a Derbyshireman brought up in London and thus made sophisticated too soon.

She has seen the poursuivants riding up, cutting the heads off chickens with their cracking whips, and she remembers one in particular, a certain Hargreaves, tall and burly, pink and glossy of complexion, much given to perspiration and gasp, a man who needs a powerful horse and whose forelock keeps dangling in his eyes, looking less a hunter of men than an overweight bookseller just arrived with a ponderous parcel of wares. Well, she wonders, must they look brutal? They tend to a blustering efficiency, but they do display some human weakness, especially with a ten-year-old. Do they have wives or lemans? Of course they do, and they receive wages just like gardeners and carpenters, the main difference being in what they carry off with them if they are lucky. Lucky-dip I call it, when they plunge into someone else's house and scratch around to see what they can find. Perhaps they enjoy it, this ferreting, or do they engage in it with disciplined aversion? We hate to be so cruel, but. . . . Some men are like that. A pack of women would never do it; you would never find women willing to sniff out priests or anybody else for that matter. We have a higher destiny, to save lives, not to end them. Are any of these poursuivants women? I have never seen one, unless this weird-looking Hargreaves is a huge woman in disguise, old sweaty-chops I call him, ever looking for Missel-thrush, or Farmer. How did he ever find out his aliases? Someone in service must have told, but who? How do you roust out the traitors in your own household? Do you listen to them talking in their sleep and so develop black rings under your eyes from all the effort? Truth told, I see no reason why my Garnet cannot last for ever, to be found only by God on the day He calls him home after a life of distinguished service, by which time he is sure to be back in Rome. He looks at me, sometimes, with an unfitting appetite I can only guess at: a longing fostered in his bolthole, I wonder. In there, do they let their desires run amok because they just know nothing will come of it? All that's lascivious comes loose in there and they conduct their yearning with private delight, growing hard or trembling, eager to thrust and lap. It must be like that at some point in every priest's life. To have sworn off is not to become a pillar of salt, is it, Anne my girl? There they go, on a parallel: florid Tesimond, that long drink of water Gerard, tuneful Garnet, individuals all with the same self-denials, dandelions refusing to flower, birds abstaining from song, squirrels refraining from the scamper. So it all backs up inwardly. Did not Gerard say that, during torture, he felt some bizarre interior feeling quite inapppropriate to what was happening? I have heard that extremes of pain prompt knife-edges of carnal delight, and I could just imagine an afternoon, a picnic say, with those gentlemen at their most unbuttoned, airing their most private selves above the tablecloth, the bread, the butter, the marmalade. Naught comes of such dreams, but the quizzy mind is ever alert for some novelty or other, especially among those of us who have sworn ourselves to purity much the same as they. What's forced back will sometimes come out unbidden like a pent-up lion, frothing for reprieve. We talk it away, we change the subject of our lives, we remind ourselves that, when these gentlemen are tortured, they permit themselves no pleasure in it. *Quel farce!* Well, I'll go to Trent: local expostulation of sheer disbelief. We are wasting our lives to embellish God. Is that all? Will we end up ghosts with fancy Latin inscribed about our necks? Or even French, beloved outcast language. *Sanz amour, tous deviennt des monstres.* Is that how it goes? That how it's spelled? My French is rusty, my placket too. It could all do with a roistering, my lads. Open me up and ream me through and through with that unused theological truncheon. Say such to him and he will faint with shock, he keeps these notions in a private attic of the brain. Now, how would it be if he had sworn off eating, say, or exercise, or blinking (hard), or rinsing out his mouth? I could never ask him, although there must have been between us at least a dozen exchanges beginning Tell me, Father, would it hurt if you—and he answers, I think, No, only we don't. Such is our penance. Or I ask him Don't you ever, I mean doesn't it ever happen that—and he answers with an abstemious nod, then says For heaven, all to come later. I have no idea what he has in mind. He is warm sealing wax without the seal. He cools, stays crisp, anonymous, does not fondle any part of anybody. Well, he knows too much Latin, does he not? Absent love, all monsters, which is perhaps more comprehensive than I intend. He will correct me when we visit together the brooks in Vallombrosa. A year, a lifetime, hence. O hence, cruel word of incessant forwardness, it's now or never.

5

LITTLE JOHN OWEN has heard that those deformed and shrunken such as he make uncommon adjustment to life's rough edges, perhaps because they know the world will never be their paradise. Not he, however, since he has become the ultimate perfectionist, never quite satisfied with his hideaway handiwork and, on numerous occasions, as if catechizing himself, spelling out to Anne Vaux, who owns or rents several of the houses he modifies, that a blank should lead to a puzzle that takes you into a quandary, and so on. His ideal cubbyhole begins with an ornate panel full of curlicues to detain the eye (as many colors as possible, but devoid of catches, bolts, latches, hooks, and fingerholes). Because he has in mind the fidgety poursuivant who cannot leave well alone, having numerous times taken more than standard interest in something innocent-seeming, he works hard on what the roving eye will find next, having swung the panel aside: a blatant door, at once conjuring up ideas of discovery, the wretched priest cowering within—but not on this occasion. The cupboard is bare. This is when, for him, Little John waxes eloquent, specifying the psychology of his technique: "At this point," he insists, "the hunter will be overcome by disappointment, but he will also surrender to a sense of something final.

Without knowing it, he closes the matter down and wants to move on. In rare cases, when you have a poursuivant of uncommon zeal, a real nosey-parker of an official, you have someone who bustles into the cupboard looking for the hiding place beyond, perhaps only as big as a cigar box with a crucifix in it, see. I like to rig up a door for him, which he manages to get open, maybe giving himself a twisted muscle to get there, and then he peeps in, saying Open Sesame – the little old bugger is in here? – but of course there is nobody, he's in the receptacle beyond, one farther than this gasping, perspiring yokel can imagine. I like always to be one step ahead with my priests. I would even, if I had time, just to mix them up, the investigators, construct a priest in effigy, even a miniature one, made of wood and canvas, putty and sawdust. I don't have time, your ladyship, alas, but I have a whole team of ideas for the next ten years or so, the Chinese-box principle with cubby-holes and the model priest that enrages them, much as some tribes in Africa make model lions and leave them out on the grasslands to torment the actual beast. My day will come. Perhaps, when all this savagery has reached an end, the king will ask me to make him some figurines of priests, so rare the species will have become. Forgive my rambling, but I so often go for days without a word uttered. The problems remain: the odor of body soil, announcing a human presence, the sounds of breath, sneezes, and other things, even the warmth given off in winter in these cold houses. I won't even mention light, heel scrapes, and debris from the nose. I want my priests perfectly schooled in evasion and self-effacement, or they will be caught, no matter how cunning the cubby-hole."

Anne Vaux knows this voluntary will have to suffice for

weeks; she marvels that the man with the squeaky high voice, fruit of undescended testicle, manages to get into the outside world at all. This fellow is like some general, she thinks, plotting a master-campaign, committed to architecture (as some carpenters can be) without sensing in it anything permanent or final; he wants to modify, adapting shelter into hideaway, although as often as not baulked by the sheer massiveness of stonework through which he cannot worm his way. On the whole, however, she fancies his reach-me-down approach, his nebulous belief that country houses are not really houses at all but masses of congealed thought which he tries to penetrate, covering or draining moats, or disguising as moats some of his cleverest root-cellars. Perhaps he has invented a new kind of building, one that he might have begun by creating the holes, then building around them. The master of perforation, she calls him, also admiring the man's commitment to priests, who might after all, as to so many, just seem uninvited interlopers bent on conversion and kudos. He walks straight out of German mythology, or Celtic, one whose full stature depends on a not easily seen mental component inherited from she knows not whom, but incontestably there, perhaps a feat of sheer self-assertion in light of his physical infirmities—even over those he defeats with chisel and hammer, saw and gouge. His very being, she decides, is a retort to the universe, and this not in the sense of a bulbous bowl tapering to a narrow fine tip to pour through. He is an answer-back.

Now he has fallen silent, but she tracks his every move up here in one of the attics, carefully fashioning a dovetail joint out of some soft white wood, almost as if he is constructing a drawer. The sharp, forty-five-degree angles of the slots and tongues delight her, much more than the common or garden mortises and tenons she has seen him make when he has been in a hurry. The essence of dovetailing, she sees, is that the tongue cannot pull out of the slot because the slot narrows as it approaches the outside edge and the tongue widens. Laced with fish-glue, this is just about an unbreakable joint, whose outlines and details he etches with a stylus that might double as a weapon (it might have to, depending on how fast he can secrete himself when inspectors show up). The house was built, she muses, then Little John Owen gave it joints. As always, she delights in the gentle taps of his mallet as he eases the tongues into their slots, forcing nothing, knowing that with him a perfect fit is certain. His eyes are good, his grip is firm. What, then, can he be making? Ah, now she understands: he rears it erect and she sees a door, which now sits behind another door, rather like a shallow coffin on its end. Behind it will be nothing but wall, a consummate dead-end intended for the over-zealous investigator whose mind Little John anticipates, knowing how to stun someone mentally, so much that the poursuivant will carry away with him to his next probing and prodding the sense of failure and frustration just encountered. Little John knows the exact ratio to provide if you want to humiliate an officious brain, maybe one in five, enough to thwart, not so much as entirely to discourage him from carrying on to the next piece of frustration. No one else has thus considered the psychology of poursuivant-blunting, and of course Little John has not been able to witness his stratagems at work. He learns the results afterward, but he knows a dead end remains a dead end: though his agile mind, ever alert to a yet finer variant of constructive deceit, toys with the idea of a dead end that somehow actually yields up a victim when one is least expected: a goat in a chair, say, or an incontinent dog asleep on a secret hearth rug. (All dogs are incontinent sooner or later, he tells himself, just like goats.) If only there were a fake priest, a nasty priest, a priest unwanted and due for removal, what a vision that would be, delivering him up to them with a clear conscience, and they would soon see that his true nature was anti-Catholic: a plant, a trap, a fraud. A mind this duplicitous belongs properly in the diplomatic service, surely, but who would ever respect a miniature freak with high pitch and bruised hands? He is better where he is, a gnome of the shadows, a creature small boys would one day hear about and ape with contorted motions, rammed-out tongues, and popping eyes: *being* Little John Owen in the school playground back in the days when the country houses of England swarmed with hidden clergy all from Rome, more numerous each year. And yet Little John has done it all, having no deputy, no imitator, touring about England with a joiner's leather bag of tools, cached when he had to be, so distinctive a figure that, if only he'd had time, he should have built a whole series of Little Johns, all the way from one wholly unlike him to one that was a double, shading the difference as he went, so that no inspector could exactly determine the point, or the model, in which he both appeared and disappeared, the former more often than the latter, and vice versa. Thus, says Anne, he might evade capture, ceding himself to an entire series of gradual proxies. The idea appeals to him, put bluntly as her way is, with vehemently intensified vowels. He has no time, though, he will have to be satisfied with his one and only body and leave it to historians to flesh him out from the tininess he seemed to the giant he becomes.

This Father Garnet says, aching to use him in a sermon, but never daring to. So Little John, adored of all as both a savior and an imp, survives as a man never invoked by name, whose handiwork they constantly gesture at.

Then Anne Vaux gets it: Little John makes so many cubbyholes because, wherever he goes—has to go—he likes to have one for himself. Nominally speaking, he is a priest too, guilty not only by association but through thinking alike. Not that he makes his own boltholes tiny, he makes them full-size and therefore useable by someone as tall as Father Gerard, especially after being stretched. She mentions it, plucking at a damp comforter, but he looks away, knowing only that a hidden person has a better chance of surviving if he is alone; with company, he will eventually yield to the temptation to talk or even laugh. So, to the endless multiplication of hiding places, there is no end. He has no disciples, though. Can it be that, as early as 1604, the trade of carpentry is fading out? If not, then why does no one follow him, indulge in on-the-job training? It must be the secrecy of it all that blocks access to this career. She has forgotten that two of his three brothers are Jesuit priests themselves while Henry, the third brother, operates a clandestine printing press in Northamptonshire, stamping pro-Catholic publications with a bogus emblem that says "Printed in Antwerp." Henry has even run a secret press while imprisoned. Henry and John have a flair for misdirection, are most at home with priests, and do not shirk the ardors of treasonable secrecy. Indeed, Little John has already worked with Father Edmund Campion and was jailed for it in 1585, learning early the kind of self-dedication he brings now to Father Garnet.

Ever an enterprising woman, she wonders how difficult this carpentry is, then asks him, although he seems to be puffing from exertion, in his hands a huge saw and a rag of chamois leather with which he wipes the teeth. He answers nonetheless, telling her that only too often carpentry takes him into mason's and plumber's domain; otherwise, he says, it repays itself, mainly from the silken feel and balmy aromas of wood, a soft medium to work in, whose detritus in the form of dust or shavings is pleasant to have afloat on one's body, weightless and pristine—though his own phrase for this is "light and new." She feels the tools, especially the sharp bite of his chisels, and the gritty teeth of the big saw, remarking on the lack of weight, which surely does not help when the going proves heavy. "True," he answers, "you sometimes find yourself leaning too hard on something, which warms things up and slows the motion. It is better to be patient and take your time. A hot saw will not cut half as well as a cold one. But this is man's work, my lady, don't cut yourself on that." She hands him the tools, excited by the detail they create, the whorls in the grain that they expose, and the aroma of sawn or chiseled wood: a peculiar scent of harvest time, with something nutty in the immediate air or a slight smell of distant paper burning. One might become intoxicated, she thinks, sawing and cutting just for pleasure, with no design in mind: no stool, no shelf, no bedside table. Surrendering to a pang she tries to dismiss as "woman's trouble" (she is in her mid-forties), she watches him in silence, envying his rapture, wishing to try her hand, then actually seizing a tool not in use and trying to work on waste scraps of wood, first scribing with an awl (faint lines in which the attic light hovers), then trying to hammer-and-chisel out a piece both oblong and deep. The wood slips, the chisel strikes her hand, and she bleeds, at which he pops a radiant critical smile and shakes his head. He means *Don't* and passes her the chamois leather he keeps by him, obviously his way of stanching blood. She wonders how old some of the blood is, dry and crystalline by now, and what infection it might carry. In the main, though, he works on undistracted, now and then murmuring something about a joist, but she cannot fathom him, not when he hums that half sing-song, never looking up. She feels as she might in the presence of a mystery, explicable no doubt but not by the man doing the job. So now she merely picks up the hammer, the mallet, the saws (dovetail and tenon, rip- and cross-grain) and makes little gestures with them, almost as if she has a few flowers to play with and is contemplating a bouquet, but she puts down all she picks up, wishing she too had a leather bag and leather apron to look professional in. He sees her look of longing, ponders her awhile, and then with an incomplete laugh asks her to come stand where he points. The door that does not resemble a door swings open and she enters the cavity no larger than a sentry-box, only to confront another non-door that opens inward and so does not open when the space is occupied. He closes the first door on her, walling her in, giving her a minor fright, so she pushes out again and marvels at his skill. What an illusion. Yet who really cares? A snare for poursuivants, this little trap amuses him more than it confounds them, or so she supposes, suddenly aware that her houses are honeycombed with such bogus entrances, doors you open only by screwing a gimlet into their face deep enough to afford some traction; then you pull. Otherwise the door stays put, a constant invitational menace, with who knows what behind it: a fall into space, another door, or a hiding place with a priest in it. Surely Little John, properly named Nicholas, is a poet of some kind, easily deploying runes for outsiders to break their teeth on. She admires the degree to which he remains his own man, not quite reduced to hiding places only, but able to express himself to the enemy through an entire range of non-functional panels. He sends them a message built with his hands, saying You may try here, but for naught, and next door to the same effect, but somewhere amid this puzzle of a house you may actually find a priest sodden, filthy, miserably aloof, sipping water and licking marmalade, sleepless and nervy. Or you may not. I am here to waste your time, to instruct you in deceptive cabinetry so that you, Hargreaves, for example, may return home at the end of a long day, or to unsatisfactory lodgings at a greasy local inn, having discovered nobody at all and having sweated, fumed, cursed, probed, tapped all day with only salary in mind. In this way, Anne Vaux decides, he instructs the poursuivants in futility, showing them how an artisan who is also an artist can choke the brain of at least a few household spies. His equivalent in writing, as a priest will be the first to say, is the man who dabbles in invisible ink (orange juice) and leaves all over the house blank sheets on which nothing has been written, in ink invisible or of any other kind. Or he is the painter who covers a cabinet with wallpaper and then paints only the paper, able in a trice to rip it off and reveal the cabinet as a piece of raw woodwork. She dreams up other kinds of fakers, from women who stuff silk scarves into their bosoms for augment, to farmers who buy produce at market in order to boast about their crops. Whatever Little

John Owen is, stunted and doomed, he rides high in his collection of country houses, imposing his will upon them during the long emergency, in a sense adding to them a dimension of the covert, likely to remain intact although unused over centuries for distant improvident strangers to gape at, wondering what manner of man conjured all this into being under what threat or during what romantic aberration: a Joseph Cornell of jails, in love with boxes and a flirt with doors.

What she does not see is how Little John tries out his protégé Father Garnet (he *protects* him) in successive holes, urging him to sit or squat this way or that, to try holding his breath or the feeding tube laid on. When he does this, Henry Garnet feels truly cared for, not as the mere recipient of civil care but someone precious to his lame little devil with so many manual skills. In a sense, he feels honored by all the craftsmen in the world, catered to, looked out for, made doubly precious in his role. A few pangs of jealousy have afflicted Anne Vaux: she always suspects the two of them have secrets she will never be privy to, a male thing, but she says nothing, supposing subordination is a woman's lot. She *has* at times seen Father Garnet's characteristic peep of the tongue, construable as a little gesture of amusement, but when aimed at a woman possibly an invitation, a promise, a desire. (Some men do this, she has noticed, to express refined amusement, instead of smiling, and she accepts the trick, but she also finds it lascivious, as if the tonguer were preparing to whistle but fails to go through with it, leaving the tip out there—a tiny, stiff, schoolboyish thing of curved cross-section—to air and flirt.) Nor has she seen Little John test himself in cupboards and cabinets already made: he is so small he can hide readily, whereas Father Garnet is bulky.

Indeed, Little John, already known to the inspectors, has just as much need to hide as any Jesuit; the mere sight of his stunted body brings out in some, not Hargreaves who is too lazy, a latent cruelty, no doubt because he looks incapable of fighting back. Little John's album of private mental retaliations includes that of a country house infested with cells entirely devoted to captive poursuivants chained to the walls and savaged by tethered rats, but he knows it will never happen, he is too busy, he has too few allies, life is too short, so is he. Yet the conceit ripens the more boltholes he builds, hiding away the part of the world he feels most pride in, setting into motion the part he most despises—the nosey-parkers paid by the Crown. Left to his own devices, just a few tools from his leather bag, he would know how to torture in revenge, mostly with saws and chisels, but also finding use for awls and gimlets, putty for the nostrils, fish-glue for the eyes, hammer for the genitals. He is not short of ideas any more than of nails and screws. His main dream, of marriage to Anne Vaux, life in Baddesley Clinton with her and a retired Father Garnet, blinds him to any glance of mutual attraction between the Jesuit and Anne; he idealizes both with workmanlike fervor, but can go no further with the concept. He spends much of his spare time, such as it is, doing with thought what he often does with a twist of scrap paper or a wood shaving, manipulating it continually for five minutes or so, making sure it is thoroughly broken up before he tosses it aside.

6

ANNE VAUX HAS the callow feeling that she has met Little John elsewhere, in some other incarnation, which is odd in that he happens to be a highly distinctive character unlikely to be confused with anybody else. If she had met him, she would remember him: nothing fuzzy, generic, tangential; perhaps she has read about him. Then it becomes hard to relate the actual John (or Nicholas) to the apparition reared up from unpronounced words, from a creature that has sidled into her head unapprehended by her senses. Not that she has read that much, too busy running large country estates to sit dreaming over pages (who reads standing up?). Little John reminds her perhaps of some demon or goblin she was told about as a child, some entity who designed and executed infernal buildings for tyrannical deities and also, in other incarnations, acted as the storyteller who, for fictional or fabulistic convenience, metaphorically lifted off the roofs of houses to reveal what the occupants were up to. Was that it? Little John the artificer, the exposer of secrets, also lame and stunted, not intended to be a paragon of prettiness. Trying to link up her recollections is as difficult as fitting someone into his own shadow; he comes to her trailing skeins of exotic fame, somebody else's pride and joy, one of the in-between people who cannot and do not explain what they are doing. Anne wishes he talked more, showed a little more passion for human contact: he cleaves to wood rather than to persons, so perhaps he is one of those old trolls of the forest, the male counterpart of a wood-nymph.

Then she admits to herself she finds unavailable people too much to bear, those who hold themselves back, refusing to take the risk of openness. Father Garnet fits this category too, although he knows much more about her, from confession, than she about him. It is ever thus, she laments, wondering if she will ever have with him a conversation in which he does not function to some extent *in loco parentis,* not exactly patronising her, but assuming a supervisory stance, forever opining on what she ought to do or think. About the confabulations of women she has no doubt: they cooperate and merge, whereas men to men, men to women, even priests, make a fetish of secrecy as if still maintaining tribal awe for future generations. She tires of the subject, trying instead to put together rumors she has heard about a Catholic plot against the king, against Parliament itself, quite different from merely snubbing or disdaining, a looking down your nose at prayerbook-bound infidels, but she has heard only a few names: Catesby, Guy or Guido Fawkes, and others, less names than flickers in the daylight. The essence of any such thing, she tells herself, is that the fewer who know, the better; but the obverse of this is that surely anyone in the know must report to the authorities, blabbing to save one's own neck. Sooner or later, she figures, someone will, so there is no need to worry, not as if she set any great store by the monarch who enforces lethal anti-Jesuit laws and then goes off hunting, having signed the warrants for torture.

Sometimes Father Garnet lends her his spectacles, most of all when she complains that she sees none too well, and then she sees better than with her own, not wholly sure he has not incorporated into the lenses some theological augment she knows nothing about. Because a priest, which is to say a seer of sorts, has used these glasses, they have magical properties, or perhaps it is the triple fold of paper they come wrapped in. He sits across the table from her, smiling at her protests as he hands them to her, saying "Try these, Lady Anne, cast off the scales, take advantage of God's good light." She accepts, certain he has graced the glass with uncanny powers.

Now it occurs to her that, all along, she has been missing the point; Father Garnet has been teasing her, and what he really means to say has been nibbed into the paper with orange juice, visible when warmed and then remaining so, or lemon juice, in writing which fades away again once the paper cools. What might he already have said? Taking a sheaf of such papers from a drawer in her bedroom, a shallow tray on runners that squeak the noise of some preposterous mouse, she walks hunched to the blazing fire downstairs and tests the sheets one by one, hoping. Nothing shows. Perhaps his messages have faded into the bowels of time, startling for a month or two, then dwindling into the huge vat that receives all used sunlight. She cannot believe it, almost as if, instead of not thinking about it, she has been saving it (and herself) up for a grand occasion, a big heart-warming read that fleshes out the extruded tip of his tautened tongue. Now the entire idea lapses back into the realm of the overlooked; he had nothing extra to say, no fond declaration half as secret as her confessions. What do people say? They proclaim their love and declare it; but it's also a confession. What a bond between them, spiritually correct, but physically neuter, and unlikely to mend itself without the intervention of some august outside power. She shudders, knowing only of monarchy and death, age and disease, recognizing that the two of them have settled down into an extraordinary kinship. Hiding her confessor all over the map, she is his protégée and he is hers. They are too much alike to be able to define themselves in the zone of each other. She wanders back upstairs to look for Little John, who is still sing-working, his hands as nimble as his face, at least until he stands abruptly beneath a low cornice (locally pronounced cornish) and bumps his forehead, letting out a child-like moan. She plants both her full, somewhat bee-stung lips right over the place, where a squiggly little vein shows, and warm-wets the wound until he quietens, urges her off him, and resumes work in a low mutter. She feels she has released something wonderful into the world, for which she is perhaps never going to receive credit. Never mind: Little John is going to go on to other *howses,* as they write it, creating a colony of his own, although it is most unlikely ever to surge up and seize power. That is one thing, whereas simply disrupting a corrupt regime is quite another. She is not going to inform on anyone, she knows, and she is prepared to succor plotters. Here in this lovely rented house, with lofty chimneys and elegant battlements, its triple-arched bridge over the moat and windows that squint into the sun, she will be safe, along with several others. It is not the Byrds of this world she worries about, who know where their butter is breaded (as she mentally couches it), it is the priests near and dear to her, her brothers in sedition, together with a certain carpenter-mason who has come straight to them from the annals of the Spanish novel. She has begun to feel exotic, proud of what hangs in her bedroom: a painting of life in a recusant household, with young Margaret Garnet, Henry's sister, sitting on the extreme left, airily deploying her arms while her chubby cheeks catch the light, before she goes off to become a nun in Louvain. She has her brother's impish, prankster look, serious high forehead to counter the levity, a well-upholstered knee in view. It is not so much a picture as a compendium of related thoughts, with here a bust, there a horse and rider subdued by a fusillade of lightning, and, far right, a slip of a girl (the other Garnet sister, Helen?) kneeling at an altar. With its figures, it looks like a sewing semi-circle.

Little John Owen believes in the laying on of hands, at least to the extent of actually testing his priests in the holes he makes. On occasion he has had to, when the poursuivants arrived without warning, bundling Father Tesimond and Father Oldcorne into their hiding places with minimum ceremony. In the main, however, he likes to prove his faith in measurements, opening up a folding rule and taking down exact numbers, sometimes even guessing with a more than practiced eye. His most effective way, he feels, is to pad himself with clothing that approximates a prelate's girth and then squirm into the space; the height problem is severer, requiring him to raise his hands to increase his height, something no priest in hiding is likely to do unless in mere exercise. A certain amount of his professional endeavor therefore resembles dumb-show, in which he relates his memory of this or that priest to his collection of overgarments and paddings, some of these garnered ad hoc from the mistress of the house. It has not occurred to him yet that a priest would want to be warm and so might require extra room in which to have blankets about him. This means, of course, he would have to pad himself twice: once for girth, once for bedding. He believes firmly that the whole of anyone's body belongs to God, even after death, so he goes along with no frippery about the soul's eventually transcending the carcass. No, the carcass becomes, always was, the Lord's, which in a way exempts him from being too scrupulous about his charges' comfort. This is no doubt why priests survive standing in deep water, contorted into postures no other human has attempted, brutally bent over; Little John allows God to provide for them, perhaps deep down put off by the prospect of too much comfort for anyone abiding by a religion that proffers rugs and jugs and candlelights. Perhaps he is an ascetic *manqué* who believes that, in their ordeals, his priests have to stomach a certain amount of inconvenience lest they emerge too smug, too comforted, too well adjusted to being saved. He goes through hell to care for them, often without sleep, so he likes to ponder their future company amid various kinds of discomfort. To an extent he is paying them back for occupying so much of his life when he might have been fashioning exquisite chairs, say, or irresistible cabinets for prodigious glassware or silverware. A whole career has been passed up to save the priests, and sometimes it exacts its meed of revenge when he is not thinking, not even looking; he is his Fathers' keeper only to the degree his hands permit, and his hands do not do his thinking for him.

Confined in an emergency, then, his priests find themselves bumping into things, unless they keep dead still during the long wait. Hemmed in, they tuck their elbows close, breathe as shallowly as possible, seat one foot on the other, changing feet only with patient circumspection, and keep their knees together like virgins on parade. If, inspired by verse, they still

continue to try to seize the day (*carpe diem*), they try to do it
by inhaling or squeezing arms against rib cage. This is not the
place for flamboyant calisthenics, but for sonnets of breath,
couplets of shrug. Little John has imagined the modus in the
cell, but his thoughts naturally go to the cell in the Tower
rather than those he has larded into grandiose country houses.
He does not think of his hidey-holes as cells anyway, more inclined to regard them as God's hives, the priests as bees. No
one knows it, but he is well informed, especially on the subject, predictable with him, of being deformed. Mentally he associates with other twisted forms, such as, on another social
plane, Robert Cecil, the first Earl of Salisbury, a brilliant brain
trapped in a twisted body, to whom, on first meeting him,
James the First had quipped, "Though you are but a little
man, we will shortly load your shoulders with business." Not
only short-legged in an era that found perfection in a silk-
sheathed male calf, Cecil, as one of his enemies put it, sported
also "a wry neck, a crooked back and a splay foot." Little John
is much the same, maybe worse, with no pretensions of pleasing the monarch as Cecil does, but he also identifies with such
as the young Frances Parker, eldest daughter of Henry Lord
Morley, so handicapped in body her father thinks it appropriate that she become a nun, being "crooked, and therefore not
fit for the world." Neither aristocratic toady nor pious basket-
case, Little John works hard with a sense of election; his work
on the hiding places is an ovation to all those stunted in shape,
and if he had his way the entire world would be similarly
stunted, just to keep the human race together in kindred misery. How he wishes the king were some sport of nature too,
matching his brutality with a thwarted exterior, but Little

John has put that thought away, contenting himself with thwarting the poursuivants and evolving, in his quietest moments, an entire philosophy of the clandestine in which to save the condemned is to shame the world, certainly rending and deforming it. Any dastardly thing prevented makes his day and adds to the illustrious sum of vice ruined. This is his moral side, which works on the world as on raw material, and he chalks up his victories—one priest saved here, another a hundred miles away—with sacred relish, king for a series of underground days, assembler of a sublime realm in which to save the skin of someone is a royal feat. In the long run, it is power that warms him, the very notion that he is not helpless like some poor soul manacled to a pillar in the Tower cellar. He makes a difference. He sometimes wonders if a hundred like him, working to upset the regime, would create a huge difference in the kingdom; he thinks so and, like a wise hummingbird sipping gently while whirring on-station, he listens to all the auguries of plot and sedition, assimilating what wild horses will not make him tell.

Where, then, does he live? He wonders, inclined at first to regard Baddesley Clinton as home, but unable to settle for that, knowing his head lies in many a foreign place. Indeed, if a man does not sleep where he stays, can he reasonably claim he lives there? If all he does is work and eat, isn't he only a day-visitor, even if he works like a madman in the night, now and then munching on bread and cheese? No, where he lives, in the technical sense of being where he comes from, is Oxford, where his parents live, where his father carpenters with rather less aggressive dedication than his son. Little John worries about this issue, suspecting that to claim he comes from where

Anne Vaux lives implies some illicit relationship with her.
Better to say he comes from Rome, which spiritually he does,
or from the troll-infested domain of wood. "Oh, from the
Tower of London," he can sometimes say to strangers to shock
them, or he says just London, or Heanor intending to imply
his link to Father Garnet. In the end he doesn't care, knowing
he hails from the kingdom of the damned, the deformed, the
stunted, which with equal indifference vomits up a Cecil or an
Owen just to make the rest of the population grateful for having been born with straight legs.

"Who asked?" says Anne Vaux, wondering if, on one of his
journeys in between country estates, he has been quizzed by
roaming poursuivants, to whom a dwarf on horseback, ur-
gently riding with a leather bag of tools, looks dangerous. Has
he ever been stopped? Has he ever said? Nothing: he is not
one for casual banter about his in-between experiences any
more than an angel en route to a wobbling cynic can be de-
flected. Little John has a map of the countryside in his head,
knows all the back roads, and passes smoothly for a carpenter.
To the suspicious, he just looks erratic and radical, as if he has
stolen the bag of tools. How could someone so broken and
small seamlessly join lengths of wood? But then indeed, how
might someone such as he camouflage an entire generation of
priests in a hostile land, not even able to design a house to his
purpose from the first? He is always having to adapt, tram-
pling over the memory of a distinguished architect of an earlier time who had no idea that an infidel improviser would be
hacking his way through his masterpieces. So far they have
witnessed Little John at work as a joiner, in the normal way,
always with a shiver of contempt at the sheer force he must

have to bring to bear to compensate for his lack of stature. They have not discerned the hideaway-maker in him: his tools reveal nothing, although brickdust, plaster dust, and even sawdust found in the wrong places would expose him fast. Anne Vaux, whenever she is involved, cleans up with almost maniacal care, even though in his way, he cleans up after himself as he goes, as if eating the afterbirth each time he works. What he does not know is that each poursuivant carries a sheaf with herald labels describing the objects of their searches and that Little John therein rates as a trouble-making dwarf, previously questioned, somehow involved as a Catholic with the Jesuits, whom he seems to cultivate with overweening addiction. They still have not figured out what this carpenter does, though it has been said he crafts coffins. The story he likes to circulate about himself is that he is the master builder of birdhouses in the Midlands and the South, always working from a careful, full-scale design (these he leaves about wherever he goes), using local wood as far as possible, and fully siting his handiwork. Gradually, over the years since his first interrogation, he has in the quietest, gentlest way transfigured the landscape of the country houses, always creating a small building to dangle from the lower branches of the biggest trees, and, such his signature, incorporating into each birdhouse a hiding place for a tiny priest, no bigger than a thumb. Left to his own devices, over the course of a century, and with unlimited resources, he will no doubt convert each stately manse into a huge birdhouse itself, aiming now at kites and eagles, or even, in his uncontrollable mind's eye, pterodactyls and rocs. Having signed just about each recusant house, he now turns his attention to those vehemently loyal to the king, wondering if he might only sneak a few hidey-holes in, here and there, utterly beyond suspicion. First gain access and then, under cover of something to do with plumbing or wainscot, install his priesthole so subtly that nobody notices, although a fleeing priest would, once admitted to the house. His mind fills with such escapades; despite bodily frailty, he is an adventurer at heart even though his forte is bringing the hunted to repose. He dreams of voles in snuffboxes, baby squirrels in amputated pipes, and tiny birds such as wrens in chamois purses borne about on the bedecked paunches of well-to-do courtiers. The seeds of revolution wait and swell within him, but he is far from violent; if he cannot do it by ingenuity he will not attempt it, although the rumors he hears from his father and his two Jesuit brothers quicken him with seditious urgency: the country is going to change, he hears, fired by an enormous outrage well planned by former soldiers back from the Continent. He longs to be part of this exploit, little knowing what it is, but vaguely suspecting that he, with his flair for enclosures and secret places, could play a useful part in concealing something, providing invisible ways in and out, hiding places for weapons and masks. The project appeals to the roguish boy in him, a reckless side unknown to Anne Vaux who sees him as a livewire conjuror, a prestidigitator whose dexterity comes right out of his marred physique—he manufactures worlds in which he can prevail, fancifully exerting power without so much as a divine right to a seemly body.

Does he too protrude his tongue, while working, say? She resolves to watch for it next time she supervises him. Would one touch it, lay a littler finger in its matt corrugation? Why does she address such a question to herself without the least desire behind it? What are these abstract speculations she gets into without really wanting to know? Mere fidgets for a thwarted mind? Could she ever, were it true, say to Father Garnet, *You had me with good-day, sir?* Not that she would utter something so overt. Had he ever, she wonders, had the slightest desire to touch her in any place, even with one of William Byrd's conducting sticks, along which inexplicable power would surge? Ordinarily she is forceful, so much so that men have shrunk from approaching her; but Garnet is her priest and confessor, a bastion from within the holy matrix, and so their mutual delicacies have been confined to spectacles lent in blank or invisibly written papers, little exercises in the poetry of courtesy, bowing and scraping, quiet meaningful chuckles about irrelevant matters, vast adoration of Little John's latest birdhouse—how beautifully it shall weather, how cosy within from the accumulated fleece, how inviting the oval door. It all helps, but not very far; they are like two of the people in her bedroom painting of a recusant household, aching to move but constrained by canvas, the adhesiveness of pigment, the old inexorable plan in the painter's head, unless, her soul informs her, we were somehow to shrink the painting to only a thumbnail's compass and so bring us unendurably close until we overlapped. We could not stand it.

In these owned or rented houses in the dormant-looking countryside, in rooms as much populated by wasps, flies, and blackclocks as by people, part French as she is, she never quite loses that pinched, weathered look of the temperate English. Her blond-silver hair she has brushed back hard as if to clear access to the almost over-candid brunt of her face; she has a potent stare and, beneath her eyes, areas of uncommitted skin neither healthy nor at risk: a vacant, helpless glade of used-up-looking filler. Her elegant neck shows to advantage beneath the sheer cut of her razored hair, and she tends most of the time to make unnecessary fumbling motions with her hands near her mouth, as if assembling or rending something. Her big, rather flat ears betoken long life rather than aristocratic lineage, and her nose, blatant but straight, without degenerating into the extended tuber of the Plantagenets, seems to have been a little broken, being not quite central. In all, her piercing direct look not without charm has awed many a man who at the same time has marveled at the youthful toss of her exquisitely waved hair all dragged back: a youthful impression although she is past her best years and, as she often complains, early into menopause, past what some of her household staff call her "ministrations." She has a bravura look, this priest-fancier, with something mellowly heroic in her features at rest. She has known passion, but has been saved for something else, though God alone knows what, as she often used to say. She says it less nowadays, hardly at all, which may mean she has come through, knows what the mystery is but leaves it in the confessional, something which Little John's Spanish demon precursor, expert at lifting off the roofs of houses to reveal shenanigans, would have been able to ferret out and flaunt. Suddenly the life she has hitherto neglected has become to her *more* an object of mystery, prone to uncommon twists and tensions, more demanded of, less a gift than a demand—no longer the prim epitome of wild promise but something installed, with a stark destiny in view, something looming big as a haystack down the road. Anyone peering back into that agate gaze, obsidian, with the steady innocence of the fawn, but blurred by her willingness to know what she does not know yet, may well duck away from it to the cascade of her fingers. On, she says, and let it happen. Her high cheekbones, sharp as teething rings, will never change, nor her challenging stance, at least until croup and bone loss bend her over for the chimney corner (if such privileges ever come to her). She is very much the mistress of her demesne, a deep in-breather during masses who can be heard even above Father Garnet's baritone, and she sways left and right with the rhythm, as lost to the brutal worldly world as an echo waning. She is nobody's, really, but her neutral cordiality inspires trust in all who meet her, suggesting a woman too rational, too of-the-earth earthy to meddle in seditious business, even as one of those benighted Catholics.

7

FATHER GARNET HAS HEARD talk of talk of assassination, but has ignored it as the sort of thing that rough-hewn military men enjoy. In any case, he decides, it would be no use trying to right the situation by eliminating the king and not Coke the attorney-general or Cecil the unofficial secretary of state. Better, if anything be done, extirpate the system that goes back through the reign of Elizabeth and now threatens to occupy James's as well. There is nothing new about anti-Catholicism and torture, or even about executions; all this is part of the Catholic secular firmament, and he sighs, longing for Rome again, for a going-on that is seemly, ordered, benign. Now, should he not as a good citizen have reported all this gossip to the authorities? He should, but he treats it as if he has heard it in the confessional, as some of it he has. He is not impetuous enough to be planning any such thing; he is more of a diplomat, except for being denied a chance to negotiate anything at all, so fierce the opposition has become. He does believe in gradual decay, however, as in nature, and trusts that bad English habits will erode themselves as the king takes an ever more serious interest in the chase—hunting. What a miracle that would be, with a monarch wholly occupied by fleeing animals instead of fleeing clergy, birds flushing into the distance, half-wits on horseback afraid not to join the royal entourage as it gallops across southern England with inane cries.

Of a plan to blow up the Houses of Parliament, Father Garnet has heard, but he dismisses it as preposterous—and hard to bring off. It belongs in the category of wildly expressive metaphors, ideal for drinking companions to mull over in their cups with vehement exclamations and much back-slapping, but as a serious project not only risky but impractical. A distant logic to the notion attracts him briefly: if Jesuits are committing a capital offense by being in England in the first place, then perhaps they *should* commit a really capital offense, just to rectify the balance, but he knows this is speculative poppycock. The risks they take are the risks they take, beginning with a surreptitious arrival at Dover, whose Mayor with his searchers makes life difficult for anyone arriving from Italy or France. Colleagues have been found wanting and therefore sent under guard to London, but he himself has been admitted, journeyed by boat upriver as far as Hythe, all under a false name, if not Farmer then Whalley or Meaze, Darcy or Roberts or Philips. In the end a man with so many aliases becomes a dispersed personality, as likely to answer to any alias not his as to his own: answering to every name uttered. It becomes hard to remember who he is. Then, no sooner moored to the quay than some anonymous man is conducting him to a friendly house in Chancery Lane where lodging awaits. He has arrived in enemy country; he is here, where some poursuivants can be bribed, such as, in the past, the chief poursuivant Adam Squire, son-in-law of the Bishop of London. To enter England was to confront an erratic world in which the law did not always apply, but sometimes did with appalling savagery; you never quite knew if a bribe would work or a sympathetic ear would end up still on your side. Father Garnet knows the ropes, of course, being responsible for almost everyone else, but he yearns for a more methodical scheme in which guarantees can be made and relied on. Even the covert Catholic life as led in the house of Anne Vaux is chancy. If Adam Squire could be bribed, Hargreaves cannot, although his joviality often persuades people, to their cost, that he is lenient and inattentive. In London especially, Garnet has found, certain penitents anxious to reach him and confess were spies. A certain Sledd, trained in Rome, had managed to reach Father Robert Johnson, a Marian priest, captured and executed. It is not only that they take their lives in their hands being here at all, but that the ordinary process of living exposes them in untold ways; unless they live in a completely circumscribed world, with no leaks, no chinks of light, they stand a good chance of being had. Every fox needs an earth, Father Garnet tells himself, and then he needs to stay there. Why, even journeying from one country house to another has its hazards; it were better to move through underground tunnels, candles at the ready, if only such tunnels existed. In this particular Jesuit mission there are always going to be losses. It is a war, with secret agents moving about under cover of darkness and praying for anonymity.

Small wonder that Father Garnet has recurring thoughts, as he calls them, that distract him from the cares of clandestine office. He wonders about, and cannot bring himself to credit, the ways in which humans actually make contact with one another's private parts. All the groping, fingering, seizing must have gone on, but for the life of him he cannot envision how it begins, how anyone can break the barrier of silence and taboo to attempt anything so intimate, which of course society and family never see. Who begins it, and how? Are there unwritten rules? This terra incognita entrances him when he looks at the populated planet and considers all the intimate grappling that precedes the act. Does it begin with words or signs? Are there specific positions known to all but priests that specify approach, demeanor, comparative tenderness of clasp? He has seen bawdy in the streets, of course, but how respectable folk launch into this mutual delicacy, if that, eludes him. He has felt his own meat rise and wondered what on earth Anne Vaux, to whom he is dedicated, bears beneath her skirts, even if stale from age and disuse. Would one ever touch it, finger it, sample it in various ways, back toward it, wondering what to call it? How indeed refer to anything in the presence of its owner-bearer? Commonplace to millions, this facet of humanity stymies him as too far within the terrain of the banned even to be thought about and best thought removed. Yet much human activity addresses it, the "zone," and it remains the prime object of many stratagems.

Divesting himself of such tantalizing thoughts, Father Garnet reviews what he knows of the developing plot. He is grateful when he can be in London, where a priest might hide, instead of in some moated grange in the countryside—a slack-mouthed observant servant might do anyone ill. The word was out that Catholic confessors gave absolution in advance for heinous deeds, a scandalous travesty according to Father Garnet. In his formal letters to his Superior in Rome, he reports how vehemently he argues and prays for peace, to him no repugnant idyll, begging the Pope to command all

Catholics to keep calm and do nothing. Wait it out, he says, ever the diplomat, the gradualist, but adding in cipher something less relaxed: if the anticipated reforms in the English attitude to Catholics fail to come about, there will be trouble, and certain hotheads will leap into action, far beyond my pacific control. He knows what he is talking about, spending much of 1604 traveling here and there to do his best, but intimately gathering what is going on in the provinces—Mass at Twigmoor at Easter in the home of Jack Wright, in November at White Webbs where Anne Vaux serves as hostess to Jesuits renewing their vows on the Feast of the Presentation of our Lady. Something violent is gathering impetus and direction, he can tell that, and divers unstable Catholic men, heroically fostered by their women, are becoming ever more decisive, prompted by frustration, heartbreak, disappointment, boredom, or plain nerves. Father Garnet shuts his ears, but knows the truth already and strokes the nettle in his sleep.

Before the rumblings began, he rejoiced in the mental whirligig he supervised, chasing truth with beauty, telling himself that a religion without beauty, eloquence, even the sumptuous, the gorgeous, was not a religion at all but merely a mode of regimentation. Worrying about art, and its absence, blinded him to what he knows deep down: that all monarchs and pontiffs profess an unsubstantiated relationship with the deity. Faith or cowardice does the rest. Now, with James the First becoming sterner and sterner with Catholics, especially unwanted immigrants, he has to recognize the political strand in the faith he professes. He wishes religion were all religion: the celebration of beauty because beauty is possible and to ignore it is to scant God's plenty. Now he is poking into revenge fired by prejudice, one earthly power denying another, both dragging in their wakes millions of committed souls. He can no longer conveniently play the aesthete, using lute and voice to beautify the earthly manger; he has to fulfill his office and stave off the wild men who are going to rough-hew any justice they can, slaughtering even their own relatives, such as happen to be in the Houses of Parliament on the selected day. This is not what Father Garnet came to England for; he came to minister to the oppressed, not defuse a pack of rebels, and he is very much afraid that the only way to sap their force is to use force against them.

Country-house life goes on as usual, he decides. Mistress Vaux, alias Mrs Perkins, can still count on the services of her servants: Jane Robinson, only fourteen and known as The Little Girl; Margaret Walker, who has been with her for three years; Elizabeth Sheppard, wife of the coachman, and James Johnson. All four are devout Catholics and do not respond well to interrogation, knowing it best to deny everything, at least at first. What interests the pursuers is the bizarre Meaze-Perkins relationship (Garnet-Vaux), either a brother-and-sister thing or something more licentious worth gossiping about. Then Jane Robinson cracks under duress and admits that, yes, there has been a Mass said by a priest "appareled like a gentleman." She still fudges a bit. Do this Mr Meaze and Mrs Perkins share the same rooms? Oh no, she answers, they are separate in everything. The officials lug James Johnson off to London with them and stick him in the Gatehouse prison to see what they might get.

Life as usual, Garnet muses in his bitter way, which means the usual atrocities go on, as during the reign of Elizabeth: Father John Sugar together with Robert Grissold his servant has been executed at Lancaster, soon after Parliament adjourned on July 7, brutally driving him into poetry at the last, as all Catholics have learned. Even while they are slicing and chopping him up, Father Sugar manages to get off a couple of lines that burn at once into the memories of those who care, even those who don't. Indicating the sun, he gasps, "I shall shortly be above yon fellow." Even later in the grievous process he comes out with something even more balanced: "I shall have a sharp dinner, yet I trust in Jesus Christ I shall have a most sweet supper." And his name Sugar. Father Garnet wonders if *he* will do half as well when tested. In spite of voluptuous distractions, the king has given orders to wipe out the Jesuits, that ancient English hobby and "divers other corrupt persons employed under the colour of religion." Recusant fines are back, arrears are being called in, and penalties assessed. The world is tightening up, and the vaunted Anglo-Spanish Treaty, ushered in by the Constable of Castile in August, has no effect at all: no greater degree of tolerance, but simply an agreement not to make war on each other. Indeed, the battle has moved inward, is being fought out on the carcasses of Jesuits. Father Garnet knows the plotters are nearer their goal, having already installed Guy (Guido) Fawkes in a small apartment in Westminster as caretaker, calling himself John Johnson: a foot in the door, even as the plotters, with their numbers rising from half a dozen to twice as many, decide now that, confronted with incessant and ever-severer persecution, they had best seek the remedy of last resort, no longer just talking about it but symbolically equipping themselves with specially made swords of Spanish steel, the blades engraved with scenes from the life of Jesus. If they kill some innocent people without meaning to, then so be it. Father Garnet shudders, wondering why he gets no support from Rome in preventing the bloodshed. He senses huge processes of life and death obliviously at work around and through him, drastic icebergs of no human temper massing to crush. He has become not a leader, but a supreme witness not careful enough to ensure that all he learns is during confession. Sometimes, as with Father Tesimond who knows too much, he listens as a confessor, then strolls out in the garden with his fellow priest, who continues to fill him in as they go, and the question remains for such an honest man as Father Garnet: Does the confessional embrace it all, or what? If caught, he will never lie, even to the enemy, because God will call him to account for it. So, lured by affability, he walks into trouble, acquiring news that is far from privileged, that he squirrels away into the dungeons of his mind, well on his way to becoming what they will slanderously call him in assorted ways: the prevaricator, because, unknown to all save a few, his notion of the truth divides into the truth he shares only with God and the truth he makes public. The two are both true, but one is wholly private. Angered by being slandered thus, and tittle-tattled about as the priest with a leman called Mrs Perkins, he suddenly lashes out at the common English folk, who all in their mediocre way have a commonplace life to be rendered in claptrap language to spite splendor, and he is sick of it and them, their blather and gabble, their slander and blind royalism. He will continue to be an eclectic, whatever the dangers.

Now he knows there is the golden truth together with a silver truth which becomes golden depending on circumstances.

And vice versa, oh yes, of course. He has to keep his wits about him as confessional shades into conversational, and what he is shielding in either case is something the king insists on knowing. So he is envisioning two kinds of refusal, really: one that depends on an absolute law, another that happens to be a matter of political preference. Is this the leaden truth? How can, sometimes, the golden be leaden as well? Only in a corrupt state whose tyrant—he stops, hesitating right on top of the word. Disemboweling people is less justified than doing the same to chickens or hogs, he is sure of that. Is there a state in which almost all would be forgiven, in which even the worst offenders suffered a public humiliation without having their entrails torn out of their living body? He knows of none, but would settle for it if it existed. He is well on the way to becoming queasy, what his Derbyshire relatives called "nesh," and he sees no relief to come. He also sees a redefinition of the word "prevaricate," which will enable it to mean prudent truth, the kind once practiced (to his cost) by Sir Thomas More, whose head his daughter kept by her in a bag as a talisman. Father Garnet strives toward a caustic forgivingness that will enable him to deal with both plotters and tyrants equally, with neither of whom can he come to terms.

So accustomed to book-learning, to calling upon it in his dealings with others, he revels with almost sceptical surprise in the way his knowledge of the plot has come from people, from confession, gossip, and chat, all its irregular fragments coming together in his tidy, mesmerized head as he struggles to take a position. Father Garnet is no gleaner from the Vatican steps, no doyen of the hallway; nor has he received much information from Rome, only little fits of guidance and warning, and faint responses to his urgent pleas. He feels very much on his own, apart from the company of fellow-priests, all of them to some extent informed, some of them dangerously so, but sealed away from pursuers and investigators in that uncorroded absolute of confidential tact that, at its crudest, says another human's heart is nobody else's business unless he/she makes it so. As a result he has to study the human sources of his facts, appraising and estimating the caliber of the confidant or informant, ever anxious to look on the bright side and conclude that these men first and foremost dwell in peace and are willing to wait it out, heedless of Catholic casualties, inspired by the Father Sugars but not driven crazy by their fate. The remedy, Father Garnet thinks, must be mental, because so is the problem; is it all not a matter of simple adjustment, accommodating the soul and the analytical brain to gruesome events?

A little gallery of dejected ringleaders lodges in his mind like an explanation. It is all in their faces. All wearing the same cylindrical-conical hats, they sport the same pointed beard, the same as Garnet himself, and vary only in expression: Robert Catesby, arch-designer of the whole plan, a look of mercurial dominance; Thomas Wintour, one of chastened sublimity; Guido Fawkes, one of rollicking good-fellowship; Jack Wright a sideways look of humiliated misanthropy. Only Fawkes seems to know the nature of joy; to him this is merely another military expedition. Guy is almost always Guido, the jaunty Italian, hardly ever the staid and repetitive Englishman John Johnson. Should not *noms de guerre,* Father Garnet wonders, at least fit the bearers? Considering his own, he likes only Missel-thrush, the one he is least known by, a nickname really, an invention of the high-spirited Anne. They all align in his mind's eye, reckless perhaps and self-willed, but not *bad* men, not criminals, not yet. There is no arguing with them; they have already gone beyond logic and rhetoric. Perhaps even in the early stages they were beyond all that, when Father Tesimond brought Guido Fawkes into England from the Continent (he being "Father Greenway") to meet Catesby, who would put him in touch with well-to-do disaffected nobles, who would equip him with horses and weapons. Even back then, the die was cast, the whole enterprise reinforced by rumors of an imminent invasion planned by Spaniards and émigrés. Was there not, in all the rumblings and twitterings picked up by diplomatic spies abroad, always a threat or promise of invasion? An island people hears of nothing else; the very idea haunts their sleep and shapes their policies. In with the rubbish of everyday apprehension come a few correct details—that Fawkes is a man to watch, Catesby (survivor of the Essex uprising in 1601) another, Greenway/Tesimond yet another. Clues abound, gossip stimulates greedy imaginations, and an occasional word let slip in an otherwise innocent-seeming letter almost gives the game away. "Fast and pray," one Catholic dowager writes, then settling for a cluster of demonstratives, "that that may come to pass that we purpose, which if it do, we shall see Tottenham turned French." Not quite literal, she is metaphorical enough to influence the mind of her recipient, except that the letter, opened by a mother-in-law, soon gets into the hands of a suspicious male not averse to mentioning such hints as come his way, not of anything so mild as a new spirit of tolerance for Catholics, as a shocking plan, the fullblooded fruit of many men's frustration.

How can they get away with it, Father Garnet wonders. The

whole of England is a sounding-board, and it is not Masses said at two in the morning in an obscure unfindable room that will reveal the plot and its underpinnings, as much as parades in country gardens to mark the Feast of Corpus Christi, say, with music and banners, stately procession and elegant finery. Ah, the aesthetic face of religion. All the spies need do is watch as we go about our sacred business in public or in secret, observed or detected by grooms, servants, well-wishers, pursuers, the whole pack of those who find us interesting.

What he discovers, only late is that, when dealing with plotters and handing out absolution, the true problem is one of boundaries. A blessing, even one made in another room, may well be misconstrued as blanket approval; understanding or forgiveness rendered at the front of a talk, or at its end, may seem prophetic or retrospective unless some line be drawn to indicate which bits of the dialogue it refers to. In a conversation in London on June 9, Robin Catesby has already asked Father Garnet about inadvertent slaughter of the innocent, and has received the standard reply: some casualties of war have to be accepted. In that cramped room in a tight lane running along the Thames westward from the Tower, Father Garnet thinks the question has to do with the war in Flanders, but Catesby, the plot's author, reads it differently, drawing from it a carte blanche that will later shock Father Garnet into exclaiming "I would to God that I had never heard of the Powder Treason!" When Father Tesimond, in deep spiritual pain, seeks him out on July 24 in that same Thames-side room, it is to confide in his Superior that he has heard Catesby's confession and now knows he is going to blow up the Houses of Parliament as soon as Parliament resits. This disheveled misery is not the Father Tesimond of before, the meticulously groomed fashion-plate from Europe, ruddy-faced, blunt, resonant of voice and bold of mind. Father Garnet has only to hear Father Tesimond's confession concerning Catesby's own confession to sink in too deep ever to be rescued. To know, as he has already realized, is to be guilty, and to know without reporting is to be doubly so. Here they are, two priests with an infernal secret, and Tesimond spells out Catesby's impatience with Father Garnet's pacific, dawdling tactics, the way he clung to certain "grave words" from the Pope, enjoining English Catholics to bide their time and leave reforms to Providence. "You have to recognize," Catesby has said in barely controlled anger, an almost constant state of his nowadays, "that those who despise Catholics for being fancy and superstitious also despise us now for being feeble-spirited and cowardly. It won't do."

Now Tesimond is no longer kneeling, they are strolling in the garden; Tesimond is still confessing, but the auspices have changed, and what he says may not be protected by the rules of the confessional. Surely, if you think you are confessing, and your confessor agrees, then you are confessing. But as soon as Garnet tries to appraise how he stands under the eye of eternity, life becomes difficult, and a priest such as he, who wants to have a perfect reputation in both this world and the next, has a great deal of anxious argument with himself to come—not too much for a Jesuit, but enough to leave him wan and stranded. He writes to Claudio Aquaviva, General of Jesuits, explaining that he has already four times stopped treason in the bud. Under the pretext of calming Welsh recusants, will the Pope—the new Pope, elected on May 29—please intervene?

Father Garnet is not so much going through the motions as repeating himself in a mood of increased panic, even asking the English Catholic emissary to Rome to back him up. Off goes the glamorous, multilingual Sir Edmund Baynham, another survivor of the Essex uprising, an enterprise that suited his hectic nature. It is ironic that, the more gestures Father Garnet makes, the more he seems to be covering up, the more he seems to have contrived a blatant way of doing nothing, or next to it. A popular rhyme captures him to great disadvantage, claiming that

> *Yes, impious Garnet for the traitors prayed*
> *Pricked and pushed forward those he might have stayed*
> *Being accessory to this damned intent*
> *Which with one word this Jesuit might prevent.*

Not exactly verse of mordant pithiness, this retrospective nonetheless identifies Garnet's powerlessness, genuine or put on, and the near-paralysis he feels about the secrets of the confessional. And, while he is stewing, James I is off hunting.

Once again, Father Garnet reviews the conspirators, as he now reluctantly thinks of them, wondering at their motives, and at them, seeking the most vibrant cause. Catesby, for instance, the ravishing six-footer of distinguished pedigree, who had gone to Gloucester Hall, Oxford, but left without taking his degree, no doubt so as not to have to swear the oath of Supremacy. A young Catholic desiring higher education is obliged to go abroad, like Father Garnet, and ever after bear the smear, supposed, of unorthodoxy. Is that the reason? To be sure, Robin (correctly Robert) Catesby has been denied a career in the country of his birth, has been fined for his part in the Essex rebellion, has lost his wife and one of his two children, has shuttled from Catholicism to the Protestant religion of his wife and now changed his mind again, winning all before him with combustive charm. To pay his fine, he has been obliged to sell Chastleton, his Oxfordshire home, and now lives with his widowed mother. He has also been imprisoned as a Catholic rebel on the eve of Queen Elizabeth's death. Is this chain of events, Father Garnet wonders as Catesby tries to reconcile the ephemeral with the metaphysical, enough to account for his fanatical mania? Or is the spark from almost a thousand Yorkshire recusants having been summoned to the Normanby assizes, as the general loathing for Catholics mounts? In the Commons, a bill has been introduced that would brand all Catholics as outlaws. Is this it? Is this the final straw? Father Garnet rearranges these events, hoping to divine the pattern that causes the final devastating blow. Reared on Latin and Greek grammar, he expects the fragments of experience to fit together perfectly even when scrambled, so commanding the suffixes are, so imperious the inflected cases: he always knows which adjective goes with which noun, even when they happen to be, as in some Latin verse, at least a line apart. No loose ends in Latin. He prefers a Latinate world. Unfortunately for him, the world is more Gothic than that, only in its chemistry is it meticulously put together. He knows this, but cannot quite dismiss the yearning for commonsense texture; the Catesbys and the Fawkeses and the Wintours should mesh together according to some law not arcane or fatuous. They forge ahead in their own directions, Catesby for one inclined to play the theologian, testing things out in the abstract against the commands of the

Church, wanting to swing into battle with metaphysical backing, knowing God is with him. In this, Father Garnet decides, Catesby is deluded, does not understand the Church at all, yet involves priests in his deadly work, asking them questions that apply as if the priest himself were preparing the gunpowder. What a shame, Father Garnet thinks, that all these young men more or less in their prime are essentially swordsmen to whom their skill is the mark of the true gentleman, but in this case passionately committed to a cause and linked to their fellow-swordsmen by marriage, and severely-dealt-with parents who have suffered much for their faith. Virtuosi of the blade, Catesby and Jack Wright and his brother Kit and the Wintour brothers and Fawkes all have a certain fame among the martial-minded. It is natural that they feel the way to put things right is through violent, expert action; their swords are their university degrees, and this means, of course, their strong suit is not debate or discussion. They are do-ers, and this troubles Father Garnet, to whom doing ranges from gardening to books. Perhaps, if there were to be no actual combat, they would lose interest in the very plot: as well as easing the lot of English Catholics, they want to prove themselves in a spectacular way, which puts them in much the same position as the medieval knight hoping to write poetry with his lance. Negotiation does not figure in their book of etiquette; they have been bottled up for too long, slighted and persecuted by successive harsh regimes. Those who can remember look back to the golden days when Mary Queen of Scots ruled, a Catholic sovereign intent upon the will of God, not upon preservation of the monarch's health through the hunt and constant delegation (to such as Cecil) of affairs of state, nor upon the disembowelment of priests as a circus for the lower orders lacking something else to do.

It is not hard, Father Garnet reasons, to shake the family tree and find a brother, a parent, executed in the most barbaric fashion; we must be dreaming to think we will ever achieve a perfect polity through such men not by violence. They come to the boil, they stay at the boil, their manhood eggs them on, they see the admiration in one another's eyes. They will go down in history, not as meddlers, or negotiators, but as men of action, latter-day knights fit to rule the country, though I doubt they would, even after a successful plot, settle happily into the positions of political power they covet. It is the old story: to achieve the result, send for the soldier, after which the soldier is of no further use, unless he be a genius or stay a soldier, having no sense of dignity. With so much death in their background, so little Oxford and Cambridge polish, so little education in the high civility of things English, they are not going to be Cecils addicted to meditation, or professional handshakers. They will always need to depend on the Jesuits for counsel, as they do now, quite lacking, for all their hearty faith, any salutary scheme of ideas in which to place their deeds. Either we will bless them and agree with them or they will go their own way, nonetheless involving all of us in the consequences of their actions. The insensate English will not pause to reflect that their spiritual counsellors did not lead them to this pitch or in any way back them. Closeted with them to warn them, we become instant accomplices, every bit as much as if I, Tesimond, Oldcorne and the rest had swords in our hands, itching to spar.

He is beginning to rid himself of an old assumption made during his early years in Rome, teaching: the bad in life comes out of the good gone wrong, or so he used to think, but now, after years of stress as the senior Jesuit in a hostile land, he realizes that the good in life comes out of the evil because there is nothing else to make it from, and making it is a monstrous feat of *force majeure* or, as said in Derbyshire, gobs of elbow-grease. Is this so preposterous an idea? He tries to work it out through examples drawn from Catesby and the rest, wondering if, interrupted at the right moment, a Catesby can change direction in spite of all the merging forces that drive him. Yet how can it be enough to seek peace from a man devoutly infatuated with violence? Has he truly got through or have all his pleas bounced off, back to Rome? It is no trick to get good from good, he ridicules this; but how about that old blood from stone trick? How do you divert a man from evil? The answer seems to be that all you can do is urge him during confession to change his ways, telling him that, once committed to a crime, a man remains so under the eye of eternity. It sounds blithe, he thinks, too much so: the idyll of a self-deceiver, omitting the strenuous conversion that must go on. What on earth is he doing, trying to deflect a handful of made-up minds while their numbers continually increase? By affecting a fraction, can he redeem the expanding whole? Even by surrendering his life, which he is willing to do, can he perform this feat? Perhaps only the English Jesuits amassed, working full time, might alter the plotters' resolution. Look how the Essex rebellion, an armed coup d'état really, foundered, with some of the very same swordsmen, who saw in Essex's attempt a way of helping the Catholic cause. Why the Earl of Essex, seeking to unseat Robert Cecil, that adroit and tireless adviser to Elizabeth, should have opted for violence, Father Garnet cannot understand; certainly it was something that Cecil himself would never have tried. Here, surely, was where Catesby, Francis Tresham, and Lord Monteagle, among Essex's Catholic accomplices, should have learned their lesson: diplomacy next time. Yet they did not, and Essex was executed for his pains while Cecil smiled. How did it go? A few things happen: at his trial, Essex slanders Cecil or mentions an unproveable truth. A book by a certain Doleman, actually the Jesuit Father Persons, wafts into and out of the trial, cited then ignored. Cecil, secretly observing, steps into view and challenges him. Cecil, the trimmer, adjusts his sights, supporting James of Scotland for two years of sedulous cultivation, secret of course—just the sort of ministration Father Garnet wants to bring to bear on the hothead plotters: gradual, temperate suasion, with Garnet the most agile cajoler ever seen.

Part Two

8

Father Garnet to Anne Vaux

"Here endeth.... I can go no farther, I have done all I can. They are resolved to go through with it."

"But, Father, is there nothing left to do? How do we reconcile ourselves?"

"In another life, dear lady...."

"Another death."

"And after," he answers. "Is that what we are looking for?"

"Perhaps. It will not be in this one. Even in the best of circumstances, nothing could happen that is not happening now."

William Byrd to Father Garnet

"The French call it a balancing act."

"The French are no better at it than you, dear sir."

"Without music at the centre...."

"Without music, almost nothing."

"From His music to mine, a tiny leak."

Anne Vaux to William Byrd

"Tergiversation."

"How would one sing that Word? Only by breaking it up,

dearest lady. To make it equivocal, indeed many-voiced."

"You are our strongest survivor, a citizen of all worlds."

"Perhaps because I am nobody at all, merely a key. I and my family are repeatedly fined for our faith."

"They say the Catesby crew mingle at the same tavern as Master Shakespeare and his cronies. Life in the open, I call it. How enviable."

"Their life is a life on the run, Anne, but know it they do not. Life is never an uninterrupted octave."

Father Garnet to Little John Evans

"A closed stool would always be better."

"Unless you are expert at holding it in, Father. Your joiner cannot work miracles."

"We have certainly enlarged our range."

"Which is worse? Standing in water or holding it in? Tell me that, Father."

"Holding it in in water."

"I am having to improvise, it's a matter of working within what's given. Impossible to design such things."

"There *is* an argument from design, Little John, which I am inclined to wonder at. Do you not sniff a surfeit of the accidental in all this, or does God's will encompass everything that happens just because it happens?"

He yields to a sound of hammering.

Little John to Anne Vaux

"Added to the list in my head. Nothing written down, ever, my lady. Nicholas is ready."

"How do you remember which house it is?"

"I never know, I just work away."

"All one big house."

"Birdhouses included, though the likes of them is seasonal. You has to watch out for non-migrating birds, though."

William Byrd to Little John Evans

"They all have swords, I hear. I wish they had lutes."

"Chisels is better."

"Soon, they tell me. I cannot believe it."

"One day I will build me a birdhouse just big enough and live in it all day, hanging from a stout branch. When I tire of being obleeging. Or you, sire, of selling music paper!"

"God bless you, my friend. Never stop."

"'Tis all Byrdhouses."

Anne Vaux to someone unrecorded

"All off to Flanders, in a hurry, as if it were a principality of peace."

Little John Evans to his helper, Ralph Ashley

"Ninety-seven houses so far. And no end in sight, except..."

Father Garnet to himself

"There are going to be many more amens. Or do I mean amends?"

Father Thomas Strange to Father Garnet

"Your Catesby is a charming fellow, after all. I had expected more of a ruffian, but Lady Anne counselled me better. He is hard to resist."

"In the end, though, you will resist him, whether or not, dear friend, you are composing in his honor a religious primer on the sciences. How swiftly you work."

"All the more so, Father Garnet, when you count how much time he and I have put in playing tennis and tunes together. *Becoming and charming*, I called him in the dedication. Too much?"

Pondering the time Catesby and his comrades have spent in the half-timbered Tudor gatehouse conducting to the huge weathered brick of Ashby St Ledgers, plotting and scheming, Father Garnet thinks in Latin but fails to comment.

What are we doing, trying to persuade such rumbustious charmers? Catesby is the beautiful flower whose lethal odors drift over us during the night, cloying and damning as they arrive.

"Father Strange," he says, "I have an uncanny feeling that you and I will eventually become *Catesbiana*."

Father Strange to Anne Vaux

"He seems to worry unnecessarily about my friendships, talking of storms and safe harbors, horrors and finales. I think so much responsibility as he has wearies and vexes him into undue wittling, as we say in Gloucestershire. I am too young to share such apprehension, and have, I am told, too much personal style to worry about being misunderstood by people in high places."

"God bless you, Father."

Catesby conversing with Father Garnet

"'Tis true, Father, Francis Tresham and I are perilous close, our mothers are sisters, and we grew up together, with me the dominant one, I fear. Never mind. I feel impelled to do what is overdue and right, not count the cost, but am reassured to know that perpetrators of violent deeds cannot be held responsible for all the consequences. Is there not a divine rubric for the likes of me?"

"There is an injunction oft wasted, to be peaceful and patient as a tree." Again he brings his magnetic charm to bear and I am a shattered plenipotentiary. May he have a bad dream about it all and forget the entire scheme, go back to Warwickshire for the right reasons.

Father Garnet and Father Strange

"You would think, Father Strange, that a man with a name such as Robin would have a gentle side, a wounded decorum. Is there not some *lingua franca* of the heart?"

"*Lingua* frankincense?" Father Strange is not yet thirty.

Sir Robert Cecil to Sir Edward Coke

"'Tis like worming a dog, is it not? They come wriggling out of the rear end by the score where you had imagined only one or two. These names—Whalley, Darcy, Roberts, Farmer, Philips, and Meaze—are these the tuppers of Mrs Perkins? Can so many Jesuits be into her placket with such regularity? I hazard a guess that these gentlemen are all the same man, a Jesuit, of prodigious energy, his hankering being to have her always in a different house, just as some men want their satisfaction now in a brothel, now on a pier, now in a rowing boat, now in the jakes of a rowdy tavern. Variety maketh. I know about Mrs Perkins and her mysteries, but who are these—suitors leaping about England with their cods at the ready? They could of course be lyrical poets, anxious to find material for their verses, but I smell a priest here, not your usual charming, urbane, Italianate one, as we are accustomed, but one with ferocious lust and even some brains. A man driven by paradoxical passions. The Vaux family has always been troublesome. I think we should ask the poursuivants to set this hunt up again on the plane of names. I must know of thirty-odd priests at large in this vulnerable land, and I can name them without being able to recognize them, but Whalley, Darcy and the rest are not among them. What can we do?"

"In the end, sir, I know we will chop the damned thing off in the usual way of state business. Give Mrs Perkins a rest."

Anne Vaux to Father Garnet

"Truly I think it might help me. Women of my age are prone to excess in a womanly way. Such a pilgrimage might work wonders on my old French frame."

So long, he muses, as the Catesby group do nothing reckless while we are away. To do anything major, in any event, they would have to have Parliament back in session, which it will not be, according to the latest, until November. Oh to breathe fresh air.

"Father Gerard says Saint Winifred was a saintly and beautiful girl. When her rejected lover Caradoc beheaded her, a spring of water welled up from the place where her head struck the ground. Then her uncle managed to reattach the head and there was only a white mark remaining to show what had taken place. It's a long way to Holywell, but it may be worth it, Father."

So they plan to go from Enfield, north-east of London, by way of John Grant's house near Stratford, calling at Worcester

(Huddington Court) and Shrewsbury (a respectable tavern) on their way to Wales. Clearly, Father Garnet reminds himself, he will have to get himself into the frame of mind needed for miracles. Anne Vaux craves a miraculous cure from a magical place, lest she become yet another of those spasmodic matrons enslaved by their private places: the hot quivers, the sessions of inexplicable weeping, the inability to whisper, none of this good in a woman as loaded with secrets as Anne Vaux, the keeper of their seditious mystery. That she expects anything at all from her visit to Saint Winifred's Well demonstrates the impressionable or gullible side of her, she the paragon of practicality, which he has some trouble in accepting. It is at her urging, however, that they depart on August 30, 1605, two days late, all feeling quite medieval, thirty or so pilgrims, as if enacting some pious quotation from old Catholic days when people lived peaceably together unfired by talk of gunpowder and accidental slaughter. That they are occupying themselves with an obsolete ritual does not occur to him, intent as he is, in some attic of his mind, on the so-called "private endeavor" he has heard so much about from Catesby. He hopes they will not suddenly deflect themselves from one plot to another, impatient for action of any kind, unwilling to wait for Parliament to reassemble. Father Gerard, however, is telling Anne Vaux and Father John Percy, these being Anne's own priests, how in one November pilgrims to the well had to smash ice that had formed on the water. "I myself," he tells them as they ride gently through the luxuriant countryside of Southern England, "prayed immersed in those frigid waters, a full quarter-hour, without catching cold, in spite of keeping my drenched shirt on under my other clothing. Clearly, something magical attends that well. Perhaps Father Bennett, back again to look after it, has fostered it so generously its influence spreads far and wide." Father Garnet, with horrors bloating in his mind, cannot believe the company he is among. Am I the only practical soul here? This far from Parliament, who can think of such horrors? Only I, it seems. I do not blame Father Bennett for sticking it out in North Wales after three years in prison, banishment, and sentence of death. He too comes from the zone of death I inhabit, whether disappearing behind a string of aliases or not. We have so much in common that I wonder if he and he alone is the true object of my pilgrimage. How little we know our aims. No, I am forgetting: Fathers Gerard and Percy have been through the mill as well, of course, tortured and humiliated. Who has not? He turns around in the saddle, feeling like a statue twisted off its base, to look at Father Tesimond and the lay brother, Ralph Ashley, with whom he is riding, and the young Digbys, Sir Everard and his wife Mary, together with their own chaplain, Father Oldcorne. He has a dismaying sense of the irrelevant picturesque as their group heads into Wales: Jesuits with a price on their heads, signs of torture on their bodies, and a company of entranced believers unwanted in this blunt, intransigent country—surely an ideal target for any gang of violent zealots skulking in the Welsh hills. But Wales, so far from the turmoil of London, runs its affairs in its own way; a loyal congregation counts for more here than any edict from James the First. On the last stage of the journey, the women in the party walk barefoot (no ice in August) in homage to Saint Winifred, who after all is a woman's saint. The open-air, unaccompanied Mass has a sketchy, punctured feel; ceremonies such as this require compression to achieve the right epitomistic drive. The participants are less aware of the seventh-century Welsh virgin Gwenfrewi, Caradoc, and the surging new spring, than of being unobserved except by those in sympathy. They feel like explorers in a virgin land, especially the ladies with wet feet nonetheless warm again. Winifred's uncle Saint Beuno does not even enter their minds as they bow to what is more traditional with them, and the homicidal ghoulish rapist has gone the way of much flesh, as he does in the original story. There remains, for Anne Vaux, in an almost gynecological trance part anesthesia and part healing, the Saint Winifred who devoted the rest of her life to problems of virginity, infertility, and menopause, and whose biography William Caxton was the first to print. Small matter to Anne Vaux, groping about for an answer to a chronic problem that only old wives' nostrums have offered to treat, that Saint Winifred was one of those popular saints demoted during the Reformation, her feast-day from 1536 onward forbidden to be a public holiday.

Father Garnet, jubilant now to be so far away from plotters, muses on the saint's name: "the friend of peace," unless he is mistaken, Old English not having been one of his languages. If only the Catesby plotters would follow *her* lead, befriending peace, sidling up to diplomacy; for him, the head that hit the ground has not released a spurt of water, has not been reunited along that white line around her neck; Caradoc the bloodthirsty has remained in view, by no means swallowed up by the earth. Where one miracle fails, others must surely follow. A talk with Anne Vaux, who has become mystical, yet not ephemeral, depresses him no end, he who to begin with had felt almost debonair.

"What is all this gathering-up of fine horses, Father? What

are they for? Who needs them? I have a dreadful feeling we are on the brink of more Essex-like behavior. Please talk to Robin Catesby about it."

"Oh Robin," he answers, "please do not worry about him. He is angling for a commission with the Archduke in Flanders, not an entirely impossible thing. His doings may seem military, but it is his career he cares about most. Why, I have even written him a recommendation that should work the trick. Do not fret, dear Anne, things are mending." Of course, without actually lying (a concept that rubs him sore), he is far from sanguine. He knows what seething world he has left behind him, several days' ride away from this pastoral retreat that evokes Chaucer or Boccaccio and those faithful they witnessed trudging from Rome to the Danube, he is no longer sure why. Reassured, Anne gives herself over to the processes of Christian faith at pagan's well, wishing she were younger and stronger, could see better, had achieved a marriage, and had a child, dimly aware of a word, *marcescence*, which specifies something moribund that has not yet fallen away.

Contemplating the ride back to London, Father Garnet feels dispirited, wondering why anyone should suspect such a pilgrimage of thirty people as a covert gathering of conspirators. Someone, *he* suspects, is bound to construe their outing thus, out of sheer anti-Catholic malice, with himself in the familiar posture of ringleader. He would not mind staying here in Wales, far from the centres of power and corruption, backing away from his job and his destiny, severed from friends, becoming for all time, after so much erudite upbringing, a lapdog of the obvious, his face like a porridge of boiled tweed. He now sees himself as having ridden away from what ailed him, taking it away with him all the same. He is unaccustomed to backing down, and why should he? Merely by association, he is one of the plot's engineers; wholly a Jesuit he is a criminal to begin with. Then why wobble? He might even be better off throwing in his lot with Catesby. At Rushton Hall, on the way back, he and Anne find a house plunged into grief, Sir Thomas Tresham having died on September 11, his widow self-exiled to her bedchamber and receiving no one. Sir Thomas, his son reports, spent his final hours tossing and thrashing about; better to be hanged, says young Francis in all innocence, clearly unaware that minimal hanging precedes disembowelment at the hands of the Crown's executioners; most of the condemned are cut down alive, as Father Garnet has heard. Yet Francis Tresham is Catesby's cousin and has a right to speculate on grave matters even if uninformedly. Francis inherits his father's enormous debts and looks onward to a life of aristocratic penury, very much his own man but obliged to create himself without an inheritance. Small wonder, perhaps, that he sees the Catesby plot as a means of proving himself to those who have always thought of him as a waverer, an ingenious user of favors. According to Father Tesimond, he is not the devoutest Catholic known and his faith has a lukewarm, easy quality not to be admired. So, his father's death both invigorates and stiffens him but also drives him in the wrong direction, he who has not long ago declared himself for the king in order to advance at court. Nonetheless he has some money and many horses, a man likely to be of use, or so thinks his cousin Robin, the holy and seductive fanatic eager to enlist as many as he can as if numbers ripened a crop. It is beginning to look as if, while Father Garnet's understanding of the future increases, the number of countervailing elements swells, wiping out his chances as a peacemaker and, in his own eyes, converting him into a sentinel for women with bleeding problems. Multipliers are at work, complicating a fraught situation already beyond the remedies of high-minded pacifists, genial priests. The number of agitated, thwarted, headstrong youngish men in their mid- to late thirties turns a quorum into a squadron and leaves the Father Garnets behind.

Meanwhile, Anne Vaux, relaxed by the friendly and uninhibited atmosphere of Gayhurst, where late summer does not yet seem to have slumped as it has everywhere else, asks Father Garnet once again if he has any control over the Catesby clique, whose presence in London, with Guido Fawkes the advance man in Westminster, looms over their return. She makes him promise to speak with Catesby, although Father Garnet surrenders yet again to the feeling that he is too late, if ever he thought he had the slightest chance of staving off anything. Something abstruse from Aristotle haunts him, a distinction between the "generally" understood version of *entelechy*, meaning one's potential, and Aristotle's version, shading-over into potential fulfilled. Thus, he seems to recall, Aristotle's *entelechy* is what Catesby has just about already achieved. There he is, erect and resplendent on the golden plain of endeavor, awaiting only recognition from the crowd. A note of disdain has been creeping into Father Garnet's usually benign view of those in his intimate circle; reluctant to judge, he is even more unwilling to rebuke, but he detects in himself the chronic stirrings of an impotent envy. He does not know that Guido Fawkes alias John Johnson and Tom Wintour have discovered that their gunpowder has begun to rot, the niter and the sulfur, even though thanks to John Grant muskets and dry powder for *them* are ready at Norbrook. Catesby and his group have already cabaled in Bath and decided to increase their numbers, in this way, surely, multiplying the chances of discovery. Extra mouths means surplus blather. Deciding that "the company being yet but few," Catesby found himself authorised "to call in whom he thought best." The most immediate chore, however, was to replace the gunpowder and add to the firewood that hid it.

Father Garnet, still mulling over the strange ways of conspirators congenitally incapable of keeping their mouths shut about anything (they insist on talking about secrecy), is also thinking how sublime it has been out in the fresh, toasty air, to be alongside Anne Vaux as if he were her chaperone-escort, their two bodies on their horses' bodies, their excessive clothing getting damper by the mile. Other smells contend with hers, of course, and his own, but he retains from her an unforgettable bouquet of heather and fried liver, certainly not the aroma of the landscape they were passing through, and this is unique to her, though he wonders if anyone else scents herself similarly but does not ask—of course. Sometimes in the kitchen of this or that house of hers, snacking in between Masses for three, four, or five voices, he develops the idea that cooking smells are better than actual food because they compose a subtler effusion, an intoxicating atmosphere absorbed in a trice rather than a chunk of some meat that makes labor for the mouth. Breath, he decides, is more precious than fodder.

How can the landscape have changed overnight, from the still-heaving plenty of only days ago to the slumped, hunched aftermath of today? He assumes he is imagining it, and looks again to make sure of the drooped, shrunken effect. How can the sun have become this much lower, making them shield their eyes? He works it out, reminding himself they rode westward into the setting sun with the south on their left, and are now heading eastward with the south on their right. The air remains warm; the angles are different whereas they should merely have swapped over, the sun from left to right, like a sentry changing station. It is as if the landscape has been inflated and now exhales, a shallower patina to trot about on, sagging and less gaudy. He wishes the season they rode up in would never end, sealing him in along with his profits and joys, his feats and failures, letting the record stand for the rest of his life, with nothing more to accomplish, no more fevered letters to Aquaviva in Rome, begging advice and action.

He must be feeling the grief of Rushton too sharply, he thinks, when they had all been looking forward to a cheery welcome from Thomas Tresham, the Catholic Moses, so-called. That anti-climax will haunt them all the way back to the South of England, but they pause at Gayhurst, home of their fellow-pilgrim, the dashing urbane Sir Everard Digby who, astonishing to recall, has been married since the age of fourteen. He is twenty-four now, the darling of all face-fanciers, James I included (who only two years ago knighted him for, well, being gracious and beautiful, it cannot be said more plainly). His marriage to Mary Mulshaw brought with it Gayhurst itself, quite exempting him from all desire for money and position; his sumptuous life depends on wife, estate, horses and dogs, and the sometimes vertiginous delights of being a Catholic convert. Digby happens to be someone of whom Father Garnet approves, identifying in him the right attitude of wait-and-see, leaving vast ructions to the impulse of the deity, the inevitable (as they both construe it) being always gradual. Father Gerard is the one who converted the Digbys, but he took them on separately, and Mary Digby had no idea that the card-playing neighbor who hunted by day was a Catholic priest. "The man lives like a courtier," she exclaimed when she found out, "he who never trips in his terms." Next thing, Everard becomes seriously ill and soon hands over his spiritual fate to Father Gerard, that agile deployer of "Saint Peter's net,"and the two of them are soon calling each other "brother," with Gerard becoming godfather to Digby's first male child. A hidden sacristy and chapel follow and Gayhurst becomes yet another country spread with a theological secret installed by Little John Owen who, tirelessly, sleepless, has left his stamp on more country houses than he can count.

Father Garnet no sooner succumbs to his pastoral reverie— crags of North Wales, wide deserted beaches whose sand has a slatey look, steady breeze wincing across the Irish Sea—than the opposite world of London intrudes again, about which he has almost forgotten. William Shakespeare, he gathers, has written a Scottish play (milking the times), encouraged by James the First's assertion that, were he not king, he "would be a University-man," meaning a play-going intellectual. A Latin entertainment put on for the king in Oxford has pleased him with its references to Scottish ancestry and the royal descent of James I from a certain Banquo (whereas from Macbeth no one descends; he topples like a sapped disease, neither moral nor noble). Shakespeare happens to be in Oxford at this time, observed by various Jesuits tip-toeing in lush disguise on the furnace rim. The survivors-to-be, the ones born to it as Father Garnet concludes, from Byrd to Shakespeare, who will leave a virtuous emblem on the age, are busily feathering their own nests even as the plotters replot, modify, dawdle. The volatile king, very much a theatre-man, having said his University-man's mouthful in the Bodleian Library, goes back to his falcons and dogs. Father Garnet, amidst all his tribulations, wonders, Am I a University-man or not? No fear, but a playgoer I would be were it safer to be under such scrutiny.

Much as certain breakers of the ocean, slamming and pitching to extraordinary degrees of likeness, the contours of Saint Winifred's Well, like faces, landscape, animals at play, abide in Father Garnet's mind; not as might be expected the south view but that from the north. To him the whole place has a barricaded look, except the barricades are low, sufficient to stem the flow of the gentle spring and guide it. Trees on a hillock stand higher than the twin steeples and the tower, while the chapel has huge disproportionate groinwork, a dun ribcage catching and hiding what little light comes from the north. A crowded-looking place, it makes dark rather than light of the miracle it is dedicated to, and plausibly lives up to the echo of *Flint*, the county it is in. He takes away from it a sensation of safety, guarded by a wall in any direction, as he well might, having set out in altruistic exuberance to return a suspect, perhaps even having led his devout troop all that way to a conference on the plot. If these pilgrims are suspect, he tells himself, then we are all lost; we might as well journey to the Holy Land as soon as possible, and to Mecca, just to prove our conspiratorial ways. Now the phrase "Tottenham turn French" reaches his ears, and he begins to appreciate how imagination transforms the tidbits of idle chatter into monstrous effigies. The merest sigh will be slanderous, a walk in the garden shall be seditious, a handshake under the moon is bound to have an ulterior, regicidal motive.

Matters less public affect his mind too, sometimes moving it at uncommon speed to no conclusion, then making it repeat the empty maneuver. Father Oldcorne, a complex, various man, son of a Yorkshire bricklayer and former schoolmate of Guido Fawkes, has studied medicine, among other subjects, and, perhaps owing to his undue familiarity with defects of the flesh, has in his time scourged his tongue so much that cancer developed there, vastly impeding his famous golden elocution. To heal himself, in the full confidence of faith, Father Oldcorne actually made a successful pilgrimage to Saint Winifred's Well four years before, and has gone along on the journey just ended with a high triumphant heart bursting to say his thanks. All very well, Father Garnet thinks, but my responsibility as his superior is to save him from such scourging as interferes with his work. He needs to speak, not to babble. And he practices other forms of scourging as well. Perhaps I, in befriending the conspirators, am scourging myself almost daily. My flesh is weak, my brain is tired, my future is abysmal. Why do I associate with them at all? I was never told not to hear the confessions of plotters, was I? I walk into it with eyes open, my heart tumbling for lack of a way out. I am as James's queen, Anne, who at Oxford recently, upon hearing a speech in ancient Greek, delighted in a language she had "never before heard." *I* never heard such proposals as Catesby makes. All must go sky-high and the government will change.

9

OVERLOADING HIS MIND'S EYE with happy vignettes obstinately recalled, Father Garnet fixes on Little John Owen chortling about his nickname and how it compares to that of Father Gerard: Long John of the Little Beard. How vulnerable Little John looks on a horse, he muses, someone struck once by lightning and awaiting the second jolt. Yet all the way, this taciturn man chattered about his craft, saying he had come along only to scout out new places in which his priests might hide, checking those he has already made. Yes, Father Garnet thinks, he is a sacred termite burrowing his way across England to create a network of priestholes—say a dozen per Jesuit, some of which even centuries hence will never be found. It has not occurred to Little John Owen that traitors on the run might need just such boltholes in the event of a failed coup. With them in spirit, he does not think far beyond his Jesuits, the men from Italy, sent here to enormous disadvantage and sometimes, after emerging, rearing up in the landscape like relatives of the wood wose, the half-human animal that infests the countryside. There they are, in *his* mind's eye, paunches held in by worn-looking belts, collars worn to threads, mud decorating their inadequate shoes, eyes pink from lack of sleep, hands twittering with anxiety—he has studied them well—with a look of special helplessness; their minds are on higher things, the rest of the human exploit left to groundlings. When not spouting words from his horse in these unaccustomed forays into affability, he whispers to himself the names of houses he has worked in:

Gayhurst
Harrowden
Hindlip
Sawston Hall
Baddesley Clinton
Huddington Court
Coldham
Chastleton

Perhaps he omits a few, but his memory for handiwork is avid, and, besides, he senses in the very names not only the site of his labor but something else, almost a phonetic illumination of the component syllables, not as uneducated as he seems, being very much the brother of clever brothers. Gayhurst has a Yorkshire flavor (for Father Oldcorne too, of course), Harrowden sings to him of ploughhorses and foxes, Hindlip severely reminds him of his own disability, implying someone whose mouth is in the wrong part of the body (words flow so freely from other people, he thinks, he wonders if indeed they come from their mouths at all but from some other source), while Sawston is for carpenters, Baddesley Clinton evokes nothing at all save its own imposing pile, and Huddington Court reminds him of suet pudding served at court on silver trenchers, Coldham of the rainbow sheen on wet slices of meat, Chastleton of spelling mistakes made long ago.

Roosting among musical people so trained they need no lute to strike a correct note, he makes a melody of his very own, murmuring these names of constant resort, and many others, envisioning the whole of England south of York, say, not so much as castles and mansions as utterly solid priest-holes surrounded by insubstantial masonry that wafts away like fog: the core of his career shows through, while all else vanishes. At his most imaginative, and not forgetting his bird-houses, he sees his entire output assembled, somehow tacked together to form an extraordinary manse of his own, com-posed of the tiniest rooms in Christendom—what Father Gar-net, whom he has told of this, playfully dubs his little-big house, emptied of all priests as befits the consolidated life's work of an enclosure-builder. Little John imagines himself into and out of these places, caricaturing perhaps his lack of stature or, in nostalgic comfort, accommodating himself: the chick slithering back into the egg. What he makes is lyrical, enduring, and free (it costs them nothing, ever), and he longs for a time when, instead of confronting a permanent emer-gency, he will be at liberty to fashion even smaller dwellings, somewhere between a birdhouse and a doll's house. His fa-vorite story, gleaned from ages-old prattle, is that of the lady of the house who, true to her name (loaf-shaper from Old English *hlafdige*), walls herself in with loaves, first erecting a stack waist-high, then raising the level up to her shoulders, lacking only a roof, unable to build a crossbeam from dough. He loves the way this highborn lady's occupation names her, as if she has nothing else to do, any more than he himself has. Will the crisis ever end? Will Jesuits in his lifetime be wel-come in England's coarse and vulgar land? He has no idea, no inkling of the future, but he accepts his lot, "makes love" to his occupation, only now and then, as when riding almost *en famille* to Saint Winifred's Well, hoping to win a physical reprieve, suddenly growing straight, tall, sturdy, much as Father Oldcorne's tongue cancer gave up the ghost and, as her friends hope, Anne Vaux's female problem will clear. Little John has faith in miracles, but also in work, believing that, if he works in the right frame of mind, offering up his little rooms as prayers (ironic that he sometimes calls them jakeses or privies), good will come of it in this world or the next. He halfsuspects he has been deformed only to test him in this life for some illustrious career in the next—even if his life has been only a constant vigil of uncontaminated purity, his prayerload discharged, to his credit a score of priests saved, most of all Father Richard Blount, outliving Little John to the tune of forty years in England. All he laments is the lack of time for scrupulous, elegant design, so that he might look back on his creations with an artist's true frisson, elated almost to the point of tears that he got it right.

William Byrd to Little John Owen

After asking him to fashion a lute, nothing fancy, mind you, but replete with your holy skill, such as will grace the airs it plays: half-pear body, bent neck, fretted fingerboard, pegs for tuning. A few days, he thinks. "A few days, Little John," he says, "I don't want to keep you from your priests too long. It would be a lovely change for you, would it not, and then people will point to you for something in the open you can be proud of, not something hidden away, that hides, my dear. If only you had time, I suppose. It will never happen. I am always in a coach going somewhere, ever trying to persuade some fellow such as you to make me a thing I can use. Of course, a master-craftsman such as you would do it in a trice, but your master-craft goes in one direction only, not that we don't need—boxes—it is a matter of God's music. I am a performer as well as a composer: not the only double face in my life, I am told. It would be blissful beyond measure, given the drawings, to go away and, on my return, find something newly fashioned waiting for me. Disappointment is grievous, is it not? We have to find ways of transcending it, lest we thunder with disease. Would you build for His Majesty James? Will you construct for me? Will you vouchsafe me an answer on my return?" Is he serious?

"I will ask Father Garnet," Little John responds. "He stands between me and God's Creation."

The Squabble over the Table: Garnet, Catesby, and others
Father Garnet: "Just a few grave words I beseech you to hear with care. The Pope's express order—"
Robin Catesby: "We're weary of persecution, Father. They all say we're spineless, flaccid and feeble-spirited. It's time to change all that."
Father Garnet: "I would to God that I had never heard of the plot you entertain so warmly."
Robin Catesby: "I speak for others as well. We have a perfectly natural right to take care of ourselves, defend ourselves against any manner of violence."
Father Garnet: "In so doing, you will only increase the vehemence of the violence aimed at you. Don't, I pray you."
Francis Tresham: "Oh no, we must."

Lord Monteagle: "It stands to sense."

Father Garnet: "Now there are three of you against me. Next time there will be six. Or shall you square? For God's sake, no more rushing into mischief. Besides, the more there are of you, see how little food each of us gets, the slower you should be. You need not be unwieldy, sirs."

Father Tesimond: "Not only have we heard all this before, we have heard-it-before before. Can we please stop now?"

Father Oldcorne (resorting to a Yorkshire vulgarism quite at odds with his habitual suave demeanor): *"Eigh-up!"* By this he means watch out, something weird is going on.

Like all people unused to uninhibited laughing, Father Oldcorne creases his cheeks a little before abandoning his face to detonation, baring his teeth and tongue in a manner he might deplore in someone else and actually noting how his voice gets higher as he soars into the cackle. Once again he has Yorkshired himself, brought a few loam-laden vowels back into civilized play, setting out his stall, as they say up there, proving we shall all end up in the same bucket. This earthy finality of his appeals to Father Garnet, who has been much too serious of late. Though he hates and despises the very idea of the plot, he can also detect the weaker members, such as Tresham or Digby, knowing that it is these who will stumble over themselves and botch the enterprise; so he worries about this too, against it but intellectually deploring its weakest links, and wondering how best to be detected: laughter, he decides, belly laughter such as he has heard on his native heath or from Little John Owen in the saddle. Why, a plot run by Jesuits would surely be one of sealed mouths. They would think the thing through to success, and the rewards would be merely mental. What about Monteagle, then? He rates him well as a believer, but low as a plotter; some men, he knows, have the internal steel for it, and, ironically, those best qualified to carry it through are the ones least involved: the Jesuits. In any event, the Pope has forbidden anything to do with it, requiring gentle gradation all the way.

10

Guido Fawkes

Glad to get a word in, I wonder if a certain degree of disdain does not mar the response to Yorkshiremen, snubbing us as bluff, rude, forthright, boorish, all that, and given to curious homely expressions such as *nobbut just,* meaning by a hair's breadth. All regions, counties, have their odd little turns of phrase, so I fail to see why people at large find even those of us who have fought on the Continent both rough and stupid. We are not. We have uncommon sagacity, it so turns out, as well as courage. Who is it who supervises matters of gunpowder? It is I, custodian of the black powder. Who is it who knows the exact proportions of charcoal, saltpeter, and sulfur? I once again. I am a soldier born and bred, attuned not only to matters martial but to the slightest flicker of cowardice in our weaker brethren, the so-called plotters we never needed but who came on board in response to Catesby's worry that his ark would not be full. There is too the blithe assumption, ladies and gentlemen, that all is possible after a bang: amid the uproar you can do whatever you please. But not for long, Noah. I am not so sure of all this Catesby thinking: afterwards, the plotters will organize much better than we think they will, and the country is hardly likely to turn Catholic overnight. The English are too sluggish any-way for such turncoat stuff. So I am doing my duty with a faint, forlorn sense of doom. We shall go down in history, indeed groveling in its filthiest gutters, but we shall not transform the country. Chaos into Catholic decorum is a non sequitur fit to please even our Jesuits, those dry keepers of our earthbound souls. Guido, they prefer to call me, as if I were some child to be patronized, one of them even a fellow Yorkshireman – smooth, chubby, clammy hands; florid open countenance sprinkled with blond hair; eyes too large for their sockets, ears huge and flabby denoting long life. The son of a bricklayer, he, he gives me a wink now and then: the only winking Jesuit I have known, and this is not the wink of a fellow Northerner that says Ay, lad, we both come of Viking stock, it is the wink of the executioner who says the time has come, we have to do this together with as little fuss as possible, so if you do your part I will do mine, and then it will all be over and we'll be glad. We are mates in this. Too much depends on the whims of executioners, they have too much liberty, giving you an easy or a harsh out. Natural for me to be thinking of these matters – all we have to do is make one mistake, and they will be recruiting executioners from all the home counties at thruppence a throw. Most of them will not be, as we say up north, much bottle, meaning much good, but these days you can't be picky with your hangmen, oh no, they fumble and bumble about but manage to top you off, *nob-but just.*

Have you ever stirred charcoal with your little finger? The powdered sort? I sometimes think gunpowder was invented in heaven, the way its elements combine, long separated from one another and cleaving together with insatiable abandon. They belong together all right, just give them a chance: light them up in unison and watch for the flash. It won't work with damp powder, though, which you might use for a skin disease, perhaps, but that is about all. Odd how my fellow conspirators behave, installing me in this little room, telling me to get on with it, and then they wander far and wide, recruiting, begging horses and muskets, as if the whole affair were already concluded. I smell a tribute to my military skills, I the veteran of Flanders, but I detect also a certain gladness to be rid of the prime responsibility, my dears, my darlings, while they get on with incessant planning of the political part. When you want something savage done, send for a Tike, as we Yorkshire fellows are called. He'll behead, blow up, strangle whatever you need, and cheap as last year's hay. Some good tidings would be welcome, but news of Tresham, Digby, Rookwood, thus making us thirteen or so, is no news at all. Catesby has all along been divided against himself, arguing that he will manage to "save all the noble men whom I do respect," a pretty thought, but also that even his own son would have to die if necessary— "rather than in any sort the secret should be discovered." How can you sift the noble from the foul when you blow things up en masse, rather than pinioning them by night and knifing them to death in the boiling fog? This we might manage, only rarely butchering the wrong man. Lord Montague's is the name some of them keep on mentioning, he who has spent four days in the Fleet Prison for voicing Catholic sentiments. Then two lords, Stourton and Monteagle, ancient warrior from the Essex uprising, friend of Catesby and Wright. Why, Wintour is his scribe. What a mess, with the virtuous and the vicious so ripely intertwined you need a crochet-hook to separate them. Are these people sturdy, stout, honest, wholehearted? I doubt it, they have too much to lose: Monteagle his appointment in the household of Queen Anne, to be sure a two-face like so many of them, yet acquainted with our plans, and preoccupied with his own neck, even to the extent—'tis said—of licking Cecil's feet while in the Tower only four years ago. He has even written letters to the king, declaring himself a lifelong Protestant, as some of us pretend to be, just so that he might sit in the House of Lords. If I had my own way, I would quietly disembarrass myself of these gentlemen with the aid of the river, binding and gagging them before floating them down. With a single helper I could do it, and cut off their noses and peckers for spite. Nay, we are too linked to what we would destroy, and 'tis ourselves we shall blow up. Dear God. Lansakes, it is not Guido who trots off to Saint Winifred's waterhole in Wales, where her undrained placket dribbles forth to all and sundry. (Leave these phrases out when you talk—that's what they taught me at Saint Peter's, they are only padding, but when you have to talk to reluctant soldiers you need more than a bolt of padding; you have to give them time to pause while thinking.) No sainthole for me, sirs, I have rough manners, too rough for the goodly erudite company of Father Garnet, who just loves to get away, wishing with all his heart he could go back to Rome. I am a *teacher*, he tells us, not a diplomat, and certainly not an adviser to plotters. Puzzling to find all the right people in the wrong places, fudging and evading rather than giving the whole thing up as a bad job. Wouldn't we do better to restrict our plot to soldiers, those of us who have seen the heart bleeding and the brain oozing? A few tortured Jesuits is not enough, suitable as they may be for figureheads, and no pampered aristocrats trying to reconcile their faith with their greed. You have to be willing to give up your life in such an enterprise as this, as would Jack and Kit Wright, those silent swordsmen also of Saint Peter's. We are the true Spartans of this luscious religion. Who else would lug barrels about underground, from damp to damp, self-effacing in all ways, born to serve, to kill, to die?

Cecil to Monteagle, April 1601
"Let us get it clear what you want, sir. Your title comes through your beloved mother, to be sure, and you want to sit in the Lords at the same time as your father Lord Morley. Just so. There is no harm in families' sticking together. Perhaps you could ogle each other, and then go home to perform the deed of darkness. We have all been of two minds, of course. I see you watching my foot. Here, sir, let me undress him for you, you see he goes the wrong way at the end of a pitifully short leg. Bow now, kneel, and pay him homage. There is naught more soothing. The kiss works a wonder. Ah, kiss him again, and cleanse with your tongue in between, oh what a delightful recommendation this is. I will be asking for your services again, sir. So this is what Catholics can get up to. There is hope for them yet. Oh, a Protestant, you say. I stand corrected. Thank God you have a long leg, with a correct foot at the end of it. You know, in this very same Tower we hang chatterboxes on hooks through their tongues, which is all part of our ab-breviated communion service. I know, I know, you told the king you had changed, but were you not involved in the Essex rebellion? Were you not privy, sir? Are you not Leviathan with an hook to be drawn up? Back with you to the queen's house-hold. You are too delicate a gentleman to be all the time lick-ing toes. Go out into the world and be a brave Christian. How

is your brother-in-law Habington? We entertained him in
here for six whole years. Is he sound?"

The contorted but aggressive mind of Cecil keeps trying to
establish what is going on beyond the usual fawning and ingratiating. He sniffs corruption in everything, not only profiting
from the excellent spy network established by Sir Francis
Walsingham in Elizabeth's reign, a whole team of false priests
included: men who pose, religiose and devious, eager to bring
down the real ones and line up their aliases under one heading
through which the recorder of executions will draw a line ending in a crude cross. Perhaps there are more priests about than
usual, slipping in and sneaking upriver to lose themselves, in
the sedate network of country houses where recusants attend
Mass. The villains must be Catholic, he is sure of that, but
somehow his spies, while communicating atmosphere, run
short of facts. Cecil does not know which way to turn; he is not
even aware who John Johnson is or what conniving has gone on
to put the plotters in charge of a cellar right underneath Parliament. Somehow, though, the name Guy Fawkes slides into the
reports he receives, not much of a find; Guy Fawkes is known
in the underworld of Flemish mercenaries. But, as Cecil discovers, there is a link to Catesby, conspicuous in the Essex uprising and always worth watching. Cecil senses a web empty of
its spider and begins to keep a private list, hoping that when
enough of the right names appear together, a spark will leap.
Long before *Zeitgeist* appears as a word, he tunes in to what he
calls "the year at midnight," suspicious of it as of everything,
and promises himself an auto-da-fé all of his own.

A modern observer, appalled by the seething rot of Eliza-
bethan and Jacobean society, may well liken Cecil to Joseph

Goebbels, joining the one's physical deformity of the foot to the other's, and their short stature, their passion for accumulating and twisting facts, minus the Nazi's PhD, actress-obsession, and propensity to breed. Cecil has the Walsingham blacklists, Goebbels the Gestapo's files. Each dispenses propaganda of his own fabrication, Cecil through minions, Goebbels through electric wind. Cecil is dapper in his deformed way, Goebbels more a stumbling shrub of pathos. It helps, though, to envision them trying to outwit each other, the one gifted at bamboozling his king, the other his Führer, Cecil a connoisseur of the torture cellars, Goebbels more inclined to make trouble for someone and leave them to the SS. Of course, Cecil, as his grandeur rises like dough, has his own aliases: he is also Essendon, Cranborne, and Salisbury, whereas Goebbels's only one is that of Joseph Goebbels Intellectual. Each serves a tyrant who has written a bestselling book, King James I his *Basilikon Doron,* a treatise on the art of governing, Hitler his *Mein Kampf,* a treatise on the art of hatred. Each also serves a woman to whom breeding is a field sport: Magda Goebbels six children, the Countess of Suffolk at least ten.

Through the mists of pain, Little John Owen has seen the face of Cecil, only later realizing who this visitor had been while he dangled from the wall like broken venison. He has seen, without savoring it, the long, pinched face with the jutting pointed jaw, the whole apparition one of excruciated refinement, and without meaning to has come to the conclusion that this man has been racked: too short, he responded well to being pulled taut, then tauter. Hence that expression of his: jaundiced forbearance or a whole series, when the face is in motion, of cunning winces. Little does Nicholas Owen know that, in all his mental acts, Cecil begins with a premise and its opposite, combing through all positions in between, selecting and discarding like a gambler on the rim of hell. The fast turmoil of his thinking covers more experiential ground than anyone suspects; most observers feel a certain pity, some a fleeting disgust, even while Cecil evaluates them and, mentally, ushers them out or guardedly invites them in for use. Little John has seen this face on several noble walls, wondering why. What on earth might his Catholic connexion be? Or does the portrait appear, *de rigueur*, out of enormous prudence, ideally put just outside the door to ward off evil-doers, but invited in out of sheer self-preservation. This is the man who runs the king and queen, who rehearses daily most of the attitudes available in England of that day. In his punished gait, his pawnbroking stare, something mincing has been fought back, which shows in the tiny faltering hands, the mouth that seems a merely nominal slit, the nattily brushed-back hair behind the thin skin at the temples. Peering at this man, Little John eyes the fate of himself and all his friends. Cecil revels in the absences of the hunting king, at last having space in which to deploy himself and his own plots, finally managing to link Guido with Guy without, however, mustering "John Johnson" in the inquiry. The gullible have heard that Cecil, a man of mercurial urbanity, has been known to set an arm around a victim's shoulders, patting him like a pet even though he has already approved the torture that will follow. He has a compendium of attitudes, seeking to have them wholly at his own disposal, knowing always that, in so crucial a position as his—his very name displacing his titles—he must always let a bad situation develop so as to apprehend everyone connected with it. A man so astute should remain content with his own brain-power, not go whoring after station and ennoblement; but twisted, gimpy Cecil does, perhaps in a belief that, suitably positioned and indelibly pelfed, he will never have to surren-der to Catherine Suffolk that jewel worth one thousand pounds for—well: he will never die, his will shall never go into action; for being stunted lifelong he will out-endure them all, who have been agile and graceful. It is said that, had he been an Oxford or a Cambridge man, he would have been less lethal, but who would have tutored him, who would have been able to mix milk with his acids? If only the plotters knew that he awaited them all, having already dramatized in his head the outline of their plot, for that matter, all plots, they might have organized themselves differently, with ever fewer conspira-tors; the more minds and mouths involved, the more there is for Cecil to probe, even at a distance, picking up as he does a flicker of sedition from the air. "A stir" he calls it, among other stirs, but one that rustles more loudly than most and promises to involve men in high places. Complacent he may be, but he knows how to lie in wait, he who masterminded the king into office while others were trying to.

In a sense, the only way to cope with such an overworking mental wizard as Cecil is to have no plot at all; indeed to do nothing, while as the king hies himself to horse and falcon, fox and dog, Cecil quietly builds his arsenal of deadly ideas. Or so it at first seems. The truth, however, may well be that, denied warts to scald, Cecil will invent them, blackmailing someone in his employ to concoct a plot for his lord and master's pleas-ant exercise. He praises those who do not matter, he disdains those who do, he fawns on king and queen, and, in the private mirror that his mind supplies, his own mental reflection. Here is a man who does not look at himself but will engulf the whole world in his dismal smile.

With some justification, Cecil does not want Monteagle to go to waste; a man who has sunk so low—lower than the groveling poet Ben Jonson who composes obsequious poems to those he has offended in his cups or with tactless aspersions in his plays—could surely be employed. Cecil decides to gamble, in almost a merry mood, asking himself thus: If I think there is something to know because I have heard a stir, but know not what exactly it might be, and discern on the ground some sniveling lord who asks for more than he needs, might I not fish him out by inviting him to write a letter to me, to anyone, to himself even, in which some greater stir is brought to light? Thus does the unknown become better known. If he knows nothing, which is doubtful, then the whole thing blows away to be forgotten. Hand him this opportunity to win favor again (he wants to sit in the Lords with his daddy) and we can end up rewarding him, having claimed him as our own. And they will all accuse him of inventing things, which mayhap he did not. Am I a Lord yet? I am an earl, so address him with polish, then. "My lord, would you care to set in writing anything known that would be to our joint advantage?" He wants the Lords more than anything, so let him air what he has in his craw. Let him vomit it up in his fancy way, and we shall part friends. Why did he come to grovel? Something so big he does not disdain to lick between my toes? He must be given scope, this fatted calf, an easier task than that old one I once addressed myself to: cultivating and seducing the Scottish king over two years of sedulous hypocrisy, all by letter. Well, letters shall resurge with Lord Toelicker. Even an empty letter will bind him ever more closely to me. He wants more than to sit with his father, he wants to be let off the hook, forgiven, exempted, released from his bond. He has that putrefied look. After all, along with Tresham and Catesby he was of the Essex party and lucky to escape with his life, unlike their leader. These sorts of men will always bear watching by someone as shrewd as me; otherwise they will try to run rampant again throughout this noble kingdom, fancy titles notwithstanding. I go to the point, the nub, don't I?

"Write to me," he whispers. An oiled voice.

"To you, my lord?"

"Have some letter come to yourself unbidden, flung at you in the street. That sort of letter."

"About?" Monteagle trembles as if ready to run.

"About *about*, my lovely fellow. You'll know what."

"And then?" Legs run in his murmur, his plea is hoarse.

"Who knows. We shall seat you on your father's knee."

Now Cecil knows it: sitting alongside his father is Monteagle's emblem for something stark. Who needs flattering poems from Ben Jonson with such mysteries afoot?

He still sees the poet seated at the other end of the dining table with Inigo Jones, the designer of exotic stage-sets: quarreling as ever, eyes hooded, fists tightly clenched, not a literary-looking man at all, just the sort of fellow to smear Scotland in a play the king sees, just the sort to slander a Cecil as a user of men, to complain about being invited to dinner and finding to his horror that he is not the only guest. In Flanders was it, on his first foreign assignment, Cecil saw a flower called goat's beard or something like, a yellow thing that opened only in the mornings and had a long frolicsome appendage attached to its seed button. It is not the flower he recalls, however, but what sat ironically next to it: the flower gone to seed like some outsize dandelion, whose massive replica he found in a Flanders outhouse one windy day, wondering what on earth, only to find ensconced at its centre on the bare ground a minor mouse in its mouse's house. Fluff and floss of all kinds had gone into this transparent mushroom-shaped, dinner-plate-sized refuge. The mouse had compiled its place on earth, carefully meshing anything portable and loose, so the structure contained petals, sepals, leaves, hairs, stamens, wings, all arrayed as if in a display, each scrap contributing its share of shield and warmth, the whole structure frail as cobweb but imposing for its shape and symmetry.

That, he thought, was what his own life was like.

This is how he means to go on, piecing useful bits together until he has an almost invisible shelter, so fine that nobody can detect it when he is right there inside it. So do his successive titles guard him, Salisbury, Cranborne, Essendon. There seems no limit to them as he acquires and soaks up the whole world, which he shares with a king, of course, living down his shape and stature, yet forever having in his gait the look of one seated, as some cruel wit has observed. If ever he has to choose an emblem, will it be the mouse-house, enigmatic and slight? And will he keep its secret? Or will he settle for some crass combination of lion, unicorn, and eagle? Better a splay foot, he thinks, in the midst of a mousehouse; that will give them pause, and they will no more fathom that than they will the bond between him and the fickle Lady Suffolk, herself a Catholic of enormous yet discreet pretensions with huge political power, especially dealing with Spain through the Constable of Castile, who finds her too much of a mouthful, too despotic with bribes, indeed having a whole theory of bribery, a subject of no interest to Cecil himself and happily delegated to his leman. Have I a life, he wonders, am I a fellow? Or am I like some trained yapping dog? I proceed slowly because I have so much else in my life demanding my attention; I am not the workhorse that Sir Thomas More was, I go my own way at my own speed, willing to let things multiply and be fruitful until all the villains come into view, ready for plucking and then my sentimental heart hardens, just like my little yard, and I show them just what a secretary of state can do for the state. I will always be hard on the Jesuits, but I will yield to nobody with an organ in his or her groin.

He has already heard (part of the "stir") about the goings-on at the Mermaid tavern, Catesby and company in the presence of Masters Jonson and Shakespeare (those scrivening fellows hobnobbing with Catholics yet again), the whole affair hosted by the latter's bosom friend William Johnson. It is with this festive pattern in mind that he re-reads the uncouth letter that sets the cat among the pigeons, brought to him as instructed by Lord Monteagle, whose Yorkshire servant Thomas Ward has been accosted in the street by a stranger, "a man of reasonable tall personage." At first Monteagle, cozy in his Hoxton home, half dozing in the faded light of late October, claims he cannot read so crabbed a penmanship, so he sends for help and finally deciphers what he is at first inclined to dismiss as "some foolish devised pasquil," as he says to Cecil, who never takes anything that lightly. Is this just a lump of nonsense designed to keep him away from his work at the Lords? Within the hour, he is telling Cecil all about it, whose first thought is the bastard wrote this to himself to get himself off Leviathan's hook, whom does he think he's fooling? It will be five days before the king returns from hunting in Cambridgeshire, but he tells the Council, including Lord Worcester, a Catholic, and Lord Northampton, the Church Papist. They are aghast and ask him to do something, but he recoils from action, certain anyway that he has taken it by telling them. As always, he rebounds into images of his private life, savoring the reputation he has acquired by becoming intimate with Catherine Suffolk, widow of that conniving cormorant Richard Rich, who betrayed More. I am too, he reassures himself, the object of this flatulent poem of Jonson intended to hymn me but so evasive and derivative it has no more personal touch than does a wasp.

> *What need has thou of me, or of my muse,*
> *Whose actions so themselves do celebrate?*

Why, none, his mind murmurs, no need of Ben.

> *Which should thy country's love to speak refuse,*
> *Her foes enough would fame thee in their hate.*

This poet should have stuck to bricklaying, he decides.

> *'Tofore, great men were glad of poets: now,*
> *I, not the worst, am covetous of thee.*

This is a poem about *himself*, Cecil says, and perhaps he is indeed the worst. God help him to a finer, cruder gift.

> *Yet dare not, to my thought, least hope allow*
> *Of adding to thy fame; thine to me —*

There are four lines more of this unctuous claptrap, but Cecil cannot abide to read them again. He nonetheless keeps the poem in his pocket, folded small, as if it contained a stomach powder, now wondering if he could frighten Jonson, who has already had one stint in gaol, into sucking his toes (at least), and Monteagle into writing poetry even worse. Either, he muses, could happen. I want these Catholics branded for good. Maybe only fire will do.

So now he falls upon what Sir Edward Coke, the Attorney General, calls "a dark and doubtful letter," lamenting that the writer missed grammar school as well as university.

> *My Lord* [it begins] *out of the love I bear to some of your friends, I have a care of your preservation. Therefore I would advise you, as you tender your life, to devise some excuse to shift of your attendance at this Parliament; for God and man hath concurred to punish the wickedness of this time.*

He snorts, wondering if this kind of monkey chatter would play well on the boards of Master Shaksper as he is sometimes spelled, especially by letter-writers such as this one, who goes on:

> *And think not slightly of this advertisement, but retire yourself into your country where you may expect the event in safety. For though there be no appearance of any stir, yet I say they shall receive a terrible blow this Parliament; and yet they shall not see who hurts them. This counsel is not to be condemned because it may do you good and can do you no harm for the danger is passed as soon as you have burnt the letter.*

A pox on it, Cecil whispers, this is the choplogic bricklaying style of Ben Jonson and his tribe. God preserve us from the pretensions of the sycophantic Ben. Yet why should he bother? This is not Ben at all, but Monteagle plucking out his feathers to make a pillow for his liver. See how this poxmaster ends:

> *And I hope God will give you the grace to make good*
> *use of it, to whose Holy protection I commend you.*

Some transitions smooth, he notes, even though the general atmosphere of the letter is barbaric; such a pretence. Out M. rides, at a late hour and in gruesome darkness, to deliver to me, who of course never rest, and work in mysterious ways my wonders to perform.

So: Monteagle has feathered his nest with Cecil, got himself off the hook concerning the plot, aborted the gunpowder business, saved his father's life and other lives of Lords, kept himself in the clear with Thomas Ward and the plotters, and fulfilled the prayers of Fathers Garnet and Tesimond. Not bad for one dose of scrawl, he thinks, even if the auspices—Cecil's foot and all—were scurvy. Would we ever have gone through with it? I doubt it. Now the thing will die away. I have incriminated nobody, mentioned no date, no place, no wife, no priest. My letter has floated anonymously in like some spavined bird of paradise and I shall be able to join my father in a peaceful Lords. What more can I want? I shall still continue as a Roman Catholic and fourth Baron. If he is to believe the opportunistic, ingratiating Ben Jonson, he is right, billed as England's savior, not merely William Parker born 1575 (*see how young I am!*). As Ben says,

> *Lo, what my country should have done (have raised*
> *An obelisk, or column to thy name,*
> *Or, if she would but modestly have praised*
> *Thy fact, in brass or marble writ the same)*
> *I, that am glad of thy great chance, here do!*

At this point in his reading, Lord Monteagle leaks a tear.

> *And proud, my work shall outlast common deeds,*
> *Durst think it great, and worthy wonder too,*
> *But thine, for which I do it, so much exceeds!*
> *My country's parents I have many known;*
> *But saver of my country thee alone.*

Ben's fustian brings tears to the eyes of thousands, but Lord Monteagle's true twin will not appear until much later, when a certain Major Remer, at Hitler's command, will round up the July 20 Stauffenberg plotters in the Bendlerstrasse after the bomb has failed. Promoted colonel on the spot, out of nowhere, merely because he answered the phone at the right time, because he was available, Major Remer prospered and went on to an abbreviated career as an officer of field rank. So do sideshow artists become major players, their minds reeling for months with their sudden change in fame.

Monteagle, whom Cecil has quickly learned to shorten into Mont, has already begun to flirt with hypotheses. What he will do, in case someone asks him, is claim that, to appease Cecil, who was riding him because he had asked to be seated with his father in the Lords, he had invented a plot and then exposed it to endear himself to the public, to gain some kudos with which to counter Cecil's starkest overtures. Or, he decides, someone else, the "writer of the letter," invented the plot; after all, no names appear in the letter, no place-names, no times, nothing definite. It has all the smell of a put-up job, but not to Cecil, expert at sniffing things out, even at fabricating facts where none were previously. It in no way impedes the functioning of his mind to know that the king has published a book which the king appears to have written, but which was cobbled together from the words of others; Hitler at least combed through his own psychosis to put his pages through their paces. Monteagle or Mont, apostle of manufactured fact, is the new comet, self-appointed, liked and approved by Ben, who has made a fetish of lauding people in the news, to attract salutary attention to himself and pave his way, even as his vile temper boils over. Left to his own resources, Mont will never concoct anything else, hardly expecting to be under such pressure from the Cecils of this world, but he could, and he knows that a diligent observer, noting the cranks and quips of various participants in this or that conspiracy, such as Father Garnet, say, might easily fake a letter from him, an anonymous blatancy whose authorship shines through the penmanship of someone else. It is not hard to find a scribe who for a few coins will scribble for you something world-shaking. Mont has learned, in a hurry, about the corruptness of the world, about its appetite for pseudo-facts, and he has ingeniously, when his heart was breaking from contrary impulses, managed to tug himself out from under. He is born for the diplomatic service, Cecil thinks, although his tendency to grovel might weaken Mont's stance in everything. Best left at home, a parasite in waiting, Mont begins to figure in the hinterland of Cecil's huge desires, young enough to be malleable, ambitious enough to be of minor service. Once again, the amiable arm of Cecil prepares to descend upon Monteagle's willing shoulder, ready to encourage and use him.

One thing about him amuses Cecil: Mont quite lacks what Ben has in abundance—tactlessness and bad temper, sheathed in obsequious pleasantries, which is why Ben more or less thrives, makes his way hither and yon, blatant self-promoter and rough-tongued arriviste, ever countering his reckless side with his other, unlike Master Shakespeare, more urbane, who insinuates into his plays "facts" so mutated that nobody will ever pin him down as seditious; he merely has suspicious-looking friends. Or he is just more circumspect, as a master-manipulator of metaphors can often be.

What Mont does not know, and has not even imagined amid the froth of his hypocrisy, is something that Cecil has already allowed for and worried about: the leak from servants to actual plotters, to such plotters as there are, and Thomas Ward in particular, who knows something treacherous is afoot. Ward's message to Catesby, at White Webbs, puts the matter bluntly, and it stuns Catesby, who has actually been chatting with Anne Vaux about going hunting with the king. How odd that a Catesby is at home in so many different worlds, trusted by so many different self-promoters. Catesby's cousin Anne marvels at his sang-froid; she knows his stand on matters Catholic, but senses she is being duped: talk of a royal outing is a front for something else. Catesby's face changes. He tells Tom Wintour and they settle the blame on Francis Tresham. Tresham is weak, they say, one disposed to give in. Their threats, that they will hang him forthwith, merely send him into paroxysms of denial, all through the night. Next day, he pleads with them to escape while they can, before Cecil and Coke compile their gazetteer of who runs the plot. They believe him, concluding that anyone so vehement must be believed, which amounts to reiteration of faith in themselves: surely *they* would not have recruited a spy, a coward. Of course not. Yet, in enthusiastically exonerating him, they miss another point: it is Tresham who told Monteagle, his brother-in-law, about the plot, putting a full heart into a slack mouth, making Monteagle aware of something he has only heard rumors of.

In an affectionate letter Monteagle writes thus to cousin Catesby in September of 1605:

> *If all creatures born under the moon's sphere cannot endure without the elements of air and fire, in what languishment have we led our life since we departed from the dear Robin whose conversation gave us such warmth as we needed no other heat to maintain our healths?*

The full-blown attitudinizing is close to that of the letter, and one might almost hear Monteagle dictating, blurring sentence structure, settling for some odd inversions as one unaccustomed to dictating a written form. On he goes:

> *and let no watery nymphs* [at Bath] *divert you, who can better live with the air and better forbear the fire of your spirit and vigour than we?*

Surely in his references to air and fire, warmth and heat, he is telling Catesby something, such as "I *know.*" No doubt he has stewed about the plot for months as has Father Garnet, the suppler stylist. One can only marvel that a plot based upon a complex network of family relationships ever got off the ground; at first, you might think that nothing is more tight-mouthed than an extended family, only to go further and realize that nothing scuttles private plans more than a family's feuds and rivalries, with all those not directly involved either wishing they were or scotching the plot out of sour grapes. An extended view of this idea no doubt leads us to the thought that no group of people can hope to get away with any plot, for it is in the nature of groups to fray and break. Even the Jesuits were beginning to crack under the pressure, and the difference between them and the plotters is that the Jesuits, strangers in a strange land, began with a price on their heads. Conceivably Catesby and Fawkes, the pair of them alone, might have brought it off, commando-style, but Catesby's friends talked him into seeking reinforcements—a dozen apostles—and he was only too willing. Did he and Fawkes have the military resilience to do the deed by themselves? Probably so, but they spread themselves out, turning treason into a social club, with everyone's aunt and cousins and sisters taking a developed interest in the new order. We have only to look at Monteagle's gain—an income of 500 pounds, lands worth two hundred annually—to realize what cynical trimming went on in the head of the Essex Rising veteran (jail) who initially went to Cecil for a favor.

Cynics of that time may be forgiven for wishing to discover and expose other plots, even plots of their own confection: the fulsome preamble to Monteagle's grant, words from the heart of an indolent, vain, and twitchy king, attest to the monarch's gratitude. He is not going to be blown up with his government after all, and anyone in favor of his longevity is going to feel the warmth of his hand. By the same token, those conspirators identified and found will pay a shocking penalty. This is what the king calls "that most wicked and barbarous plot," and he takes a sharp interest in the inquiry as it advances, at last set in motion by the sanguine-seeming Cecil, doing his best to prove he has known about it all along, his sources are that good. To begin with, however, he has not yet made the vital connexion between the plot and Guido Fawkes. Nor does he know how complacent Catesby is too, contending that a letter so vague and woolly will incriminate nobody at all. So, on with the plot, he says, and, among plotters, Rookwood, Digby, Percy and Keyes go about their lethal business while Father Garnet, Anne Vaux, Little John, Father Tesimond, and Lady Digby celebrate the Feast of All Saints at Coughton Court in Warwickshire. A day later, on October 30, Guido Fawkes enters the Westminster cellar to check his preparations, and, the day after, here come Rookwood and Percy to join Keyes in London, bristling with zeal. Catesby has told them nothing of Monteagle's letter and they are looking forward to action after so much well-bred inertia.

II

November looms and after it, Cecil realizes with a practiced shudder, so does what he calls the Lord's day, after which, on Boxing Day, he suffers claustrophobic torments, feeling hemmed in by boxes and a host of things he does not want. People like to give him things because, in some way, they need to reach the twisted little boy within, as if he were the heart of a cake. They have been taken in by his fake bonhomie, the arm draped around the shoulders ready to constrict, the mere sound of affability even as he plans the downfall of someone who does not even know he is Cecil's enemy. What he needs now, and not providing a gift of any other sort, is the mouth who will guide him to the other plotters. Perhaps by sheer divination, brooding with his feet high on a velvet hassock, he will find out who; but he sends out the poursuivants (and the reserves) to listen and watch and he grills the hapless Monteagle, making lists of his friends and hangers-on, with scruffy little check marks against certain names. The hunt, he tells himself, is on, and the king, bless him, is taking a developed interest, especially in the reference to powder, which he has picked up and allowed to infest his agile, suspicious mind. He will later write about this period of stress and melodrama in the so-called *King's Book,* from which the avid reader can perhaps infer Cecil's own attitude, buried as it is among the king's self-concerned conceits. All through, Cecil has pretended that he thinks the letter's author an outright fool to see if James can find something astute in the epistolary mess, knowing that mania meets elephants, where sanity finds boredom. He wants the king to feel good about discovering the letter's true meaning, but also then to experience the special desolation of not knowing whom to blame–tough fare for a king obsessed with his personal safety (although surely a man always away hunting can be found and killed without too much effort: someone lurking behind an oak, an archer poised in the high trees). So what Cecil achieves in his ornate way is a compliment to the king neither practical nor worrisome. He means to dawdle, short of arresting everybody on the list he has compiled from Monteagle's blatherings. It is a quiet Whitehall Friday garnished with the blatant busyness informing everything if the king happens to be in residence. Cecil likes it that way, just so long as the king does not think he's a Cecil.

Far off, in what many think of as the wilds of Warwickshire if they attend to them at all, a group of Catholics is celebrating the Feast of All Saints at Coughton Court, home of the recusant Throckmorton family, most of whose males have in their time been fined and jailed, with one cousin executed in 1584 for trying to aid Mary Queen of Scots. Deep in this elegant pile, with its noble freestone gatehouse and a useful view of the surrounding terrain. Father Garnet, no more than a step or two from his hidey-hole (one rope ladder, a small piece of tapestry, a palliasse bed, within), preaches at a folding leather altar he often thinks of as a cow in contortions. His theme, culled from a Latin hymn, is, "Take away the perfidious people from the territory of the Faithful," which in English sounds stilted and cumbersome, lacking the concinnity of the Latin. The hymn comes from the Office of the Lauds, and seems no trumped-up innovation for this solemn feast, alluding as it does to the turmoil in the country. High in the north-eastern turret of the Tower Room, as they call it, Father Garnet has pondered hard what to preach; he knows and fears too much, and has again written to the Pope protesting a persecution "more severe than in Bess's time," with the country's leading judges now saying openly, "The king will have blood." Perhaps he is unwise to settle for such a blatant text, but in preaching he obliges himself to express, if not the details, at least the intensity of how he feels, torn this way and that as the Catesbys either confessing or not, plague his memory with hesitant stances, variable promises, reckless avowals. Father Garnet wearies of being a receptacle, but there is little he can do about it. Listening is his vocation, after all.

Sir Everard Digby has already been assigned the Coughton part of the plot, required to assemble horses and hard-riding men for some kind of insurrection; he is not quite sure, but his charm and startling good looks have paid off, and the assembled force is ready, needing only to be pointed, restless at being dubbed a hunting party. When Father Gerard arrives, he asks Digby about this force and the chance of there being anything afoot.

"Any matter in hand? Does Father Garnet know?"

"In truth," Digby tells him, "I think he does not. There is nothing in hand, Father, I can tell you of, nor he." Digby resents having to prevaricate thus; if he knew, he would resent even more having been told the lie about Jesuit approval of the plot.

"No violent courses in any kind?" Father Gerard remains unsatisfied; he has seen hunting parties before; and the gang mustered in the grounds, while dispersed, has a different look: armed, for one thing, and full of boisterous frustration. Digby can hardly conceal them, but he cannot have them at the ready if he leaves them scattered about the countryside on farms, in taverns, or at other country houses. His chore, of no great interest to him, except as a homage to his hero Catesby, will soon become a burden: he trusts he has the faithful behind him: he may, but he does not have the Pope's blessing. In sartorial preparation, he fills a trunk with fancy clothes, including a white satin doublet cut with purple and several other satin things heavily trimmed with gold lace. Digby is ready to make a spectacle of himself, the dapper savior, installed now in Dunchurch at the Red Lion, along with seven servants and his uncle, Sir Robert, together with Humphrey Littleton known as Red, and Stephen his tall, dark brother, not plotters but pragmatic recusants who tried only a year ago to get a Catholic M.P. into office. They quaff and trough at the Red Lion, exuberant as boys, aching to have something crucial to do, sending for John Wintour to join them since he is in Rugby, not far away. Come be merry with us, their message says. They carouse much of the night, with John Grant, Henry Morgan, and Father Hammond joining them. It feels as if the whole of Catholic England has come to their festivity. The next morning, Father Hammond says Mass and they move off toward Coombe Abbey, eight miles away, where Princess Elizabeth lives. James's daughter, not the young Prince Charles, Duke of York, nor Prince Henry the Prince of Wales, nor the fourth royal child Princess Mary, is the target agreed upon because, they think, she might be "easily surprised."

How has their planning gone, reduced to bare bones? Thomas Percy has reconnoitered the little duke's lodgings in London. Prince Henry will not be attending the opening of Parliament on November 5. Princess Mary, only six months old, cannot even be found. They wish they had enough men for the attempt on Charles, but their London force is weak. In the meantime, one Agnes Fortun, a serving maid, wonders why that man came asking about the young prince's movements.

At this point, with plotters on the move in both the Midlands and London, the two focuses being the Princess in Coome Abbey and the cellars beneath Parliament, it would be better to desist, with the plot only slightly more in progress than not. But, with Cecil and the king at last resolved to investigate, things have almost gone too far. A whistle has been blown and the conspiracy has begun feeding on itself, though all that is needed, perhaps, is a failure of nerve in Catesby to put a stop to it. Francis Tresham has several times pleaded with Catesby and Thomas Wintour to stop, but Catesby is full of zeal, wrong-headed insistence, and Percy backs him up, saying he at any rate is ready to endure "the uttermost trial." *Reculer pour mieux sauter* say the French: jump back so as to jump forward better another day. Not our plotters, or at least not enough of them, not enough of the dominant spirits. Kill the king and abduct a royal heir seems the war-cry of the hour. It is now November 4, the very eve of disaster, with various members of Cecil's Council, led by Lord Suffolk the Lord Chamberlain, poised to inspect the cellars of Parliament and above-ground too. From his home in the Strand, Monteagle, the gossip of the week, answers Suffolk's summons to join them and watches as Suffolk passes what the king calls "his careless and his rackless eye" over a heap of firewood stacked in one small cellar. Who can the tenant here be? Why Percy, who is supposed to live in Westminster, another part of the city, and rarely spends the night there. Ah, says Monteagle, he works for the Earl of Northumberland, whose kinsman he is; now we know who wrote the letter I received! Not only that: surely he is one of the plotters—why else rent the cellar and the little lodging above? Yet Suffolk and his men shilly-shally: Percy, at this very moment gadding about London on other missions that will get him and his friends into even more trouble, may merely end up as an embarrassment to Northumberland, "one of his Majesty's greatest subjects and councillors." They are, they say, "loath and dainty" about the whole thing, thinking even now that such plot as there is emanates from Monteagle's feeble brain as an "evaporisation." Not so feeble with Cecil's hungry intellect behind it. When James I hears of this pause, he threatens to attend Parliament the next day unless they conduct a thorough search. He will take his chances, he declares, so a small group headed by Sir Thomas Knevett, from the Privy Chamber, undertakes the task and, about midnight, perhaps a little after, discovers in the cellar a dashing figure in cloak and elaborate hat, in boots with spurs that augur flight, busily doing something obscure in the gloom. They identify him as a "very tall and desperate fellow," seize him and tie him up. Now they have Guy Fawkes, alias John Johnson, linked to Thomas Percy, and the plot is done for.

Ironically, while all this has been happening underground, Percy has been traipsing about London, eager to be on the move, doing *some*thing, and where should he go but to Syon House, Northumberland's mansion on the Thames, simply to ask his patron what he's heard, if anything: rumors have begun to fly. He pretends to be needing a loan, but he knows if anything is amiss he will be seized. Northumberland knows nothing and sets him on his way again, about one o'clock, little aware of how Percy the intemperate and self-willed egotist has compromised him, and indeed has got him in for it, not even warning him about the explosion to come. He never says, "My Lord, don't go tomorrow, whatever else you do. For the sake of your life. Do you never hear rumor?" All Percy has come away with is some routine question about audits of rent that Percy collects for him. Next thing, Percy has gone to Northumberland's London residence, Essex House, providing his employer with a double contamination to explain later. In all innocence, Northumberland dines at Syon, then sends for horses to take him to Essex House, without consulting anyone about it, where he intends to spend the night before going to Parliament next day. Of those intending to sit in the Lords on the Fifth, twenty-nine out of ten bishops and forty peers have appointed proxies, but not Northumberland. For a moment, afflicted by a bout of fatigue he attributes to a too-early rising, Northumberland hesitates, but then he goes, man with one too many homes, clattering across London to what might have been a fiery fate, but will now turn into a bureaucratic morass wholly the fault of the feckless Percy.

The plot goes on. Percy assures three of his fellow-conspirators that all is well, having inquired of his nephew Josceline at Essex House, where he is employed. He heads for his true lodgings in Gray's Inn Road, leaves orders for an early four-horse departure on the 5th, and settles down for the first time this day. Toward midnight, Catesby, with Jack Wright and the servant Thomas Bates, sets off for the Midlands, where the second phase of the plot will ensue under Digby's leadership. Guido Fawkes has in his possession, little good that it will now do him, the watch that Percy has provided, with which to time the fuse. More impressively, yet another of those incidental symbols or emblems that pop up during the plotting of the plot, John Craddock, a cutler from the Strand, delivers to Ambrose Rookwood an exquisite sword, one of several engraved with the phrase "The Passion of Christ." The plotters confront agony before it happens, giving themselves a doomed, forlorn aspect to begin with.

The first warrant for arrest is that for Percy, who has been flaunting himself: tall with a stoop and white hair, "a great broad beard," and "privy to one of the most horrible Treasons that ever was contrived." At all costs, keep him alive: but they hunt him in the wrong place, Essex House; it is Tuesday the 5th and the plot is fizzling out.

Of all the plotters, three remain still, Rookwood gaping in heroic wonder at his gorgeous sword, knowing exactly what to do with it, or so he thinks; has the opportunity already passed? Tom Wintour, even now brooding on the delightful conviviality he has known right here at the Duck and Drake, as at the Mitre in Bread Street and the Bull Inn at Daventry, tells Kit Wright to bid Percy be gone, but makes no move himself, like one waiting for a tidal wave to roll in. Francis Tresham is high and dry because, since urging them to halt the plot, he has heard from nobody at all; he waits for a summons that will never come, does not expect the one that will. He feels cold, adrift. The others, like particles in some ionization experiment, take to horse, uttering as they go, catch up, ride ahead, pithy summaries of what is going on:

"The matter is discovered" (Kit Wright to Tom Wintour).

"I will stay and see the uttermost" (Tom Wintour to him).

"I am undone" (Percy to a servant).

"Follow me fast. It's all up" (Rookwood to several).

It is as if Rookwood has sucked energy from that sword, at last recalling what a superb rider he is and what perfect steeds he has bought. Swordlike, he thinks. He manages to cover thirty miles in two hours, overtaking everyone else like the hero in some ancient epic ballad, first Keyes in Highgate, then Kit Wright and Percy at Little Brickhill, north of Dunstable, Bedfordshire. Now he catches up with Catesby, Wright and Bates and gives them the bad news. Catesby's exuberantly planned coup d'état, for it is no less, founders on a November afternoon, except that the defiant Catesby still refuses to give in, persuading them that "what though the field be lost, all is not lost." When he meets with Digby, he provides the full picture of both plot and flop, and Digby allows himself to be persuaded, joining in Catesby's romance of victory snatched from the jaws of disgrace, with the king and Cecil both dead. "If true Catholics would now stir," he argues, "they might procure to themselves good conditions." Like a man determined to convert an elegy into a military march, he calls the roll of places that will come to his support—Warwick, Norbrook, Hewell Grange, Grafton Manor, Wales and the West, where Catholics have more freedom and assume whatever stance they wish. Because he still adores him, Digby trusts in what Catesby says, and Catesby, the more he loses, the more he talks, substituting rhetoric for arms, cheers for men (his band numbers some fifty), an intense present for a barren future. Part of Digby's posse had heard the news and decides to pack it in, while the servants, those unconsulted perpetual bringers and fetchers, warmers and tidiers, decide to melt away lest they be taken down themselves. George Prince, servant at the Red Lion Inn, recalls hearing someone at an opened window (this in November, which attests to the inside fug) saying, "I doubt not but that we are all betrayed." Lucky he, the servant with a job quite outside the plot, able to continue his usual life, only catching wind of overheard dismay, elated heroism, the grandiosity of tipsy zeal. Their servants will not do their fighting for them, nor will the sympathetic George Princes. The mood of the day finds epitome in an encounter that Catesby has with a recusant called Huddlestone, returning to Cambridge from London. A relative of Anne Vaux, Henry Huddlestone attaches himself to Catesby at Dunstable, where Catesby's horse has to be reshod for a lost shoe. He knows the plotters and something of the plot and is amazed to see them galloping about the countryside in a sullen humor. "Go home to your wife," Catesby tells him, "there is precious little left to do. And thank you for your company." Merely by accompanying Catesby and Wright, Huddlestone has tainted himself. Off he goes, leaving the six remaining plotters to ride toward Dunchurch; Percy and Jack Wright, with a show of debonair abandon, fling their cloaks into a ditch so as to go faster, and Keyes goes off at a tangent to Drayton, there to vanish into Lord Mordaunt's house and any convenient priesthole.

The seemingly immoveable Tom Wintour, a man turned to salt, at last decides to go to Westminster to see what is happening, but a guard in King Street refuses to let him pass, giving him a crude summary of the plot foiled. At once Wintour heads for the gelding in his stable and rides away, knowing he cannot reach the appointed rendezvous in Dunchurch in time and aiming for Huddington instead by way of Norbrook, where his sister lives. Arguably, with so many blood relatives at their disposal, the plotters might be able to sink away into the landscape like water into soil: hardly a one of them does not have a hiding place to go to, but Catesby, fanning the courage of those remaining into a flame, will not desist. Yet when they meet at Ashby St Ledgers, he tells his brother Robert that the game is up: "Mister Fawkes was taken and the whole plot discovered." The more he mourns, the bolder he gets, as if all problems in life were abstract things to be solved by a twist of the mind, a fine phrase slotted into a paralyzing vacancy. Now he meets his friends on the outskirts of towns, in the darkling fields, yet continues to egg them on, commander almost of a phantom brigade who, whatever is going to befall them, will clatter through history in a permanently ennobled role. In those days, there were real men. So, they do not vanish, inconspicuous as ladybugs, unwittingly exposing themselves much as Fawkes, squeezed by torture on the king's command, begins to reveal certain details, minor ones mostly, bringing to light matters only guessed at. The rabble of London, ever eager to back a winning side, light celebratory bonfires because the king is safe, thus creating a ritual that will persist through the centuries, even when people have forgotten who was saved. Now the city gates are guarded, the ports closed; the foreign diplomats in the city prudently light bonfires of their own and sprinkle coins down into the crowds below. The mob gathering in front of the Spanish Ambassador's home dwindles away–after all, he had planned to be at the opening of Parliament and would have been blown to smithereens along with the king. Even the Dutch do the same, determined to take no chances with a country in beginning turmoil. Poor, deaf Northumberland, twice compromised by brash Percy, goes home under house arrest, but failing to hear what the Council has told him, babbling about rents and audits, certain he has won a clean bill of loyalty. Two lines of inquiry emerge, each requiring outside help: to find Percy, the only plotter known so far besides Fawkes, Cecil's Council sends for the astrologer Simon Foreman; and to persuade "John Johnson" to talk, a cooperative Catholic priest must be found. One gapes at the thinking as far as Fawkes goes, being racked in the presence of a Father Somebody, there to console him no doubt–all of them mired in practicality–while Simon Foreman, through sleight of planets, divines the countryside for a sign of Thomas Percy. In the Tower and its dungeons, the medieval world and the Renaissance, miracle and machine, combine, an assertive hunter of a king in close attendance, thirty-six barrels of gunpowder on his mind.

Under blustering pressure and needling sarcasm, Guido Fawkes tells his interrogators little, admitting to being Catholic, from Netherdale in Yorkshire, and thirty-six years old (he is in truth thirty-five and so is perhaps playing games or starting to yield). The scars on his body he claims come from pleurisy, although he has been a soldier in Flanders and known fierce fighting there. In his possession they discover a letter addressed to Guy Fawkes, which he identifies as an alias of his, sustaining enormous poise in the teeth of their onslaught and their threats. His answers seem candid: a yes, he did indeed mean to blow up the king and the Lords, he is sorry only that he failed.

"The devil and not God," he tells them, "brought about the discovery of my plot. God is on our side."

"So God is not almighty, then?" Fawkes does not enter into the proffered discussion, being no Jesuit, though this is easy meat for the Father Garnets of this world. No, he explains, he was not going to warn the Catholic peers, but he would have prayed for them. Regard me as a soldier, he says, not one of those fancy quibblers. Now the king asks him how on earth he could attempt so foul a plot against children, royal ones at that, he falls back on the stock line among the plotters, so many of them bonded together by interlocking friendships and kindred blood: "Dangerous disease, desperate remedy, your majesty." They have tired of hearing this among themselves ever since Catesby first said it to Wintour.

To cap everything, Guido even shifts into his anti-Scots mode, telling his interrogators that he despises Scotsmen and would dearly like to shunt them, the king included, back to where they came from. When they stare even harder at him for risking such bravado, they see him smile the smile of intemperate mania, pitying them because, as he says, they are not qualified to question him. He is the ultimate Yorkshireman, gruff in his nuances, able to wish away other tribes to the distance. Their only consolation is that, when they subject him to severer measures than mere talk, he will change his tune and his phobias. They have not reckoned, however, with his obtuse streak. He wants to buy as much time as possible for, as he thinks, the Catesby group to get away.

12

WHEN SHE KNEW too little, Anne Vaux hungered for more, obsessively fingering the facts and searching them for ever fuller implications. Now, as people of all sorts ply her with knowledge, some of it wrong, she cannot bear to hear, instead transferring her mind to the domain of music, lingering on something as arcane but beautiful as an eleventh-century gradual about which Byrd has told her, fixing her mind on the art of melisma, which is the accommodation of several notes to one syllable. Perhaps, she muses in her dither, this is what human life is like: you settle on one thing and, if you care for it, stretch it out and out, far beyond *Allelu-u-u-u-u-u-ia*, until you have abolished time in an instant, have defied the entire concept of language in the interests of one sound. It seems plausible, a way of cheating, no more reprehensible than her playing Mrs Perkins as Father Garnet's pretend sister. You have to take charge of your life, she thinks, even if it means you have to descend to chicanery. Save yourself. It is bound to come to that sooner or later as spies inform, plotters gallop away, disguises come off, hunters get better at their job, the king and Cecil and Attorney-General Coke sharpen their teeth and their wits in the interests of the realm. She senses what dreadful outcome there will be; but

her mind, evasive as ever, provides her with other woods to
skip through, not exactly restoring her to girlhood, before eye
trouble and chronic women's ailments, but lodging her safely
in the dimension of music, the Mass: where Byrd seems to
achieve an intimate rather than an ecclesiastical quality ideal
for private recusant chapels and tiny congregations have a
more intense response than people in a pew. The extra pull of
stress is one she knows well, and she marvels how Byrd manages to incorporate it into the very music; she recalls it not as
some quirk of acoustics or style of singing, but as urgent holiness distilled–for three, four, or five voices. No more than
that, so there is something hounded, precarious in the ecstasies delineated therein. Is she imagining this? Is Byrd that
good? He does not have to be; all he has to be is sentient
enough, to have seen often enough the vestments, the crucifixes, the beads, the folding leather altar–the things always
seized and carted away as loot–and read their full significance. And then, having participated in clandestine services,
he lards his music with the tension of it all, which the singers
receive and respond to without realizing what is going on. She
has felt it, so perhaps others have. She will ask Father Garnet.
When all is falling to bits around them, she decides to attune
his mind to matters of theological esthetics, if that is what
they should be called. This will distract him from excessive
care about Catesby and his team. The time for worry, she
knows, has gone, and now is the time for secrecy, becoming
invisible. Thank God for Little John's wormholes.

Something else in all she has heard, from gossip to rumor to
fact, disturbs her, and she wonders if some of the plotters are

not angling to be captured, if all they want is to be caught and martyred. Otherwise, why should Digby have gone off to war (as it were) as the conspicuous gallant, with lace-encrusted fancy satin garments, or even Father Tesimond, with his sense of bravura quite unspoiled, wearing his own version of colored satin with gold lace? Is such splendor, she wonders, an attempt to attract the enemy, or, almost as likely, a gesture of ultimate splendiferous defiance? Are we playing at being splendid? Is that what our Church is about? If we went about in plain habit, conducted austere services, made no fetish of ceremonial beauty, would we be the pariahs we have become in this no-nonsense country? They claim to persecute us because of the Pope, but it may go deeper than that, into the philistine English soul that keeps finery in its place. This line of thought takes her as far as the finery of Master Shakespeare, sanctioned by the state, and brings her back unprofitably. She has failed to work things out. Perhaps Byrd will know, certainly Henry Garnet.

A whole year discussing such affairs would soothe her, but here she is, obliged to obey the emergency, whose causes she only partly understands, having to piece results together from the partial accounts Catesby has chosen to distribute around him, telling some people this, other people that (Digby and Tresham, say). If you have not been privy, then you are bound to feel an obsolete resentment when plots fail. Along with the There-but-for-the-grace-of-God relief that comes with never having been a member, there comes the irritation that, if you are going to be hung, then you might as well be hung for sheep, not lamb. After all, Father Garnet is bound to suffer through association even if he has never embraced the plot.

She has hosted him under various aliases and even posed as his sister. Guilt by association contaminates faster than anything because there are no logical limits to it, as Coke and Popham the Lord Chief Justice (a fat, brutal, appalling man) are going to prove. How fast a blessing given in general to one individual or a group becomes an endorsement of some plot. Whenever one mind is neighbor to another, suspicion becomes the most persuasive art form. Anne Vaux tries to imagine a machine that will separate what is said from what is not said in human intercourse, but cannot, resting the whole problem in God's hands. She faces the fact that she, along with many other decent people, is involved. Even if all you do is stop the devil's toast from burning, you are damned.

Perhaps the role of Mrs Perkins, Garnet's mock-sister, has corrupted her into longing for some degree of incest. Now that everything is breaking apart, she has a dreadful sense of waste: what was never begun, with a caress or a stroke, will never happen now. It will not even happen as a wrong. She regrets the hours of make-believe; after all, it is not as if she were a nun, one of those about whom all manner of romantic erotic tales are told. A free woman, she has spent her freedom on a cause lost before she even began, like someone adoring basalt, chicory, coal. Father Garnet belongs to another order of beings, although the Cecils and the Cokes will surely try to persuade him that Jesuits are not exempted from the ordinary laws against criminal conduct. This gives her momentary hope; if he can be that secular in other things, might he not be worldly in this? Thus the divinely-committed soul might manage to entangle itself in the skeins of average humans, not as confessor or adviser, but as participant. How many times has she hidden him away as if he were her secret lover? Sometimes she has not even known the difference, although Father Garnet has always insisted on the proprieties, never guiding her elbow but cupping his hand an inch behind it and, on saying goodbye, putting his palms together in an almost Indian *namaste*, which he must have heard about in Rome. How she would like to escape to Rome with him, to conduct some kind of forbidden alliance there in the blessed sunlight, away from this crabbed, loutish England she does not understand.

She knows that searches have begun and that White Webbs, in Enfield Chase, judged too dangerous by Father Garnet, has yielded nothing beyond "many trapdoors and passages," as the examiners' report with some irritation said. Four terrified servants, while admitting to being "obstinate Papists," tell nothing else and claim that Mass has never been said at White Webbs – until fourteen-year-old Jane Robinson cracks, and says, yes, now she remembers a Mass of sorts said by a man in fancy clothes: Mr Meaze, she thinks, there to visit his sister Mrs Perkins, or perhaps to visit along with her. Separate accommodations, she says, and the examiners begin to wonder, lewdly dismissing the chance that Mrs Perkins may be a priest in woman's apparel, but wondering hard about the identity of the *priest*, certainly not a brother of the type specified by the witness, and someone they would dearly like to interview. Anne Vaux's blood runs cold with each gossipy, exaggerated report filtering in to Harrowden, where she has Father Gerard in profound hiding, equipped with feeding tube, continually self-catechizing herself about procedure: no candles, no taint in the air of snuffed-candle smoke. Father Gerard is an old hand at being hidden away; in one search, of a house called Braddocks, near

Saffron Walden, he was hastily shoved into a hideaway by a Mrs Wiseman, who, having in her hand at the very moment biscuits and a pot of quince jelly, gave him these as his rations for the next four days. Father Gerard's waistline shows the benefit of such rigors, and his outlook in general has become sophisticated: a true adventurer of the hidey-hole, as indeed of the Tower torture dungeons, he takes life as it comes, abler than most to live out the day, and grateful for the nights, especially after searches have abated, when he can be brought out and warmed up by the fire. One way of disabling a search, as Anne Vaux knows, is to have a not very well concealed hiding place primed with "Popish" books, which the examiners carry off with triumph as booty, partly appeased, having no idea that a priest, curled up like a worm, remains hidden in the bowels of the house. Father Gerard is grateful for the places in which from time to time he can stand, and this is not one of them; Little John Owen is not always able to tailor spaces to the needs of his guests, nor to worry himself unduly about the maintenance of work he has finished; not about moisture, leaking pipes, rotten wood, unsettled supports, mildew and mold, roof sheathing decay, condensation and cobwebs. As he sees it, he must make inroads on the domain of the searchable, and he leaves it at that, wishing with all his heart he might bring more finesse and decorum to his rescue acts.

When they arrive at Harrowden to search, under the anxious eyes of Anne Vaux, they stay for nine days, completely upsetting household routine and bring to a halt all candid talk. They go poking about in buttery and pantry, heedless of Anne's repeated entreaties couched in such formal language as "May I *suffer* you to be careful with the glassware," not said as a question at all, though sounding so.

"Have you done in here?"

No, they say, they will always do a second round.

"Then how can I manage my own house?" She makes a severe face, of the agonized *Hausfrau,* not that she knows the word. She specializes in making them uneasy, distracting them with lukewarm drinks that send them outside to relieve themselves. Anything to interrupt them, make them look the other way. Those who have any idea who she is have no idea of her links to Jesuits, and those who know her not except as Mrs Perkins-Vaux lose patience with her so much they flinch away from those rooms in which they find her, pleading, wheedling, cautioning. Does she rent or own? They have seen her in so many places they think she owns half of England by now and is merely a profiteer, renting a house only to establish its weak points with a view to purchase. She does not seem "batty" enough, eccentric enough, to be concealing priests, and the Mister Meaze, with whose name she is sometimes joined, seems never in evidence. Perhaps, they conclude, she is just a loose woman, addicted to Italianate ways of making love, not to priests, of course, because they do not indulge in such conduct. Why, Anne has relatives who, all through and even now, have sent and are sending gifts to those in high authority, game and fruit and falcons and even a standing bowl to Cecil, this not to curry favor for priests but to secure position and titles. Though Eliza Vaux has already been hauled before the Privy Council on suspicion of harboring Jesuits.

As she leaves, after a taxing session, one of the friendlier Councillors escorts her to the door saying "Have a little pity on yourself and your children," almost whispering. "And tell these fellows what they ask to know. If you don't, you will have to die."

A pungent, forthright woman, Eliza specializes in answering back, and has done so since being a small girl; she is far from whispering when she says, "Then I would rather die, my lord." Her servants, eavesdropping, begin to weep, knowing she has recklessly sealed her fate and that of everyone else linked with her. Put into the care of an alderman in a form of house arrest, she harps on being just a frail, frightened woman, and she gets away with it, easily convincing her host-spy that no one in his right mind would entrust either a plot or a priest to her haughty, imprudent ways. Nor do the examiners advance from her to Anne Vaux, little realizing the family structure, unable to see the ingenuity in the loudmouth dowager who professes her incompetence to run anything, unable to crack the sturdy woman who hounds them from room to room. Anne relaxes briefly as the examiners, having put a black mark by the weird name of Vaux, move on to other matters, despairing of stating exactly the degree of depravity the name denotes. It always seems to be something foreign that upsets the king, Cecil, and the Attorney-General, and no amount of Mrs Perkins-ing will convince them otherwise; by this logic, then, all Anne Vaux has to do to be cleared is to permanently change her name to Perkins. Perhaps the same applies to Henry Garnet, unlikely ever to change his name to Mr Perkins. Yet, in the mind of both, some shiver of pagan reciprocity endures, not to be entertained in the daylight, but there, awaiting nourishment, opportunity, expressed by cordial support. Anne Vaux thinks of what might have been, what will certainly never happen now, and contrasts their benighted lives with that of William Byrd, intently creating for himself a brilliant name that offends nobody at all, pleasing all parties with an art that seems Catholic to Catholics, Anglican to Anglicans, and, to the disabused, unconditionally spiritual.

Now, with relief, she returns to music, certain that Byrd creates a space in which God can emerge; you would think God could emerge wherever and whenever He chose to, but she does not see things that way. God has to be catered to, allowed in, and Byrd's music does this sublimely, not so much imparting doctrine as preparing the mind to surpass itself in humble assent. Is that it, the quintessence of Byrd? She learns by listening, though in the worst of circumstances, and she wonders again if, in better surroundings in another era entirely, Byrd would sound so good; perhaps stress and torment, fear and exhaustion, are important catalysts to the right reception of his Masses. It has always been ironic to her that the jocose, articulate Byrd has been able so to trim his career that no one takes offense at him, being the member of all parties that he is: everyone's friend and ally, a man of fragments rather than a man of parts, a shoal of attitudes and stances without an identifiable human being behind them all. A man so protean can hardly afford to be a failure, and that he is not, yet he is certainly no success in the business of protecting Jesuits or Papists. She repeatedly questions the way art thrives without a moral basis, transcending all agonies and sorrow, all delight and disaster, somehow lifting its exponent clear of the human ruck yet making him depend on it with fierce agility. Has anyone ever, she wonders, asked if William Byrd is a Jesuit in disguise? Who would care if he were? He simply is not martyr material, quite lacking in the love of pain that seems to animate the major religions she knows about. Without suffering, nothing has value; she asks herself why this has to be so, why euphoria and crass contentment cannot have their place in God's epiphanies, and why denial, as practiced by the Henry Garnets, appears to be the seal of holiness. Suffering prevails because it is easiest to create. Is this true?

She would very much like to know the track of music from God to human beings, wondering if God-given music takes the listener straight to God or only so far, and if an infernal composer could conduct the listener anywhere but to the devil. These, of course, are hardly academic yearnings: the wonder in them is paramount, and this succors her in the absence of anything physical. Oh, she has on occasion pushed Father Garnet on the shoulder or back while easing him into his hidey-hole, but such contact amounts to nothing; she has shaken hands, returned a bow, allowed him in his Italian way to mouth a kiss a leaf's thickness from the surface of her hand, as Europeans do, but all that is frippery. At her crudest, she tells herself a woman has three holes in her that have more effect on her thinking than any philosophy, and she is sure that the same is true, changing the numbers, for a Jesuit. Perhaps if they had never cooked up the sister-Perkins act, life would be easier for them, and the phantom of some intimate bond would not now and then haunt them, evoking the world of ordinary people, who know of no Byrd, who have no cripple on stand-by to create hiding holes in rented country houses, who do not worry about the passage of music from the deity to sentient souls standing at a folding leather altar. She feels not only doomed, but deprived, realizing that now, with Father Garnet hiding at the Digby house in Warwickshire, they cannot exchange even mundanities–spectacles, marmalades, quinces, smoky candles;

thoughts on the usefulness of Latin, the lesser usefulness of Greek, the kind of cup or mug that keeps a drink hot longest, the weather; the gossip about Cecil and his relatives; the way the presence of poursuivants in a house annulls conversation, the physical health of Little John Owen, open-air dining in Rome and the prevalence of pasta over potatoes. Many marriages have survived on more meager fare for talk, but Vaux-Garnet is a high-wire act, nerve-wracking and illegal, bound sooner or later to get them into trouble, so in this they are rather like a pair of illicit lovers who borrow someone else's room for an assignation, except that their meetings end when the door seals Henry Garnet in until they bring him out again, stiff, cold, stale, aloof, contorted and sleepless. Many a prayer she sends to heaven, requesting some way they might at least hold hands, but the prayer goes unanswered, while he, preoccupied with the plotters' inordinate demands, prays for guidance, able only to dissuade them for short spells until their hubris boils up again and they canter off toward the violent future, anxious for just about anything to do.

While they play their waiting game, events pile up around them. "John Johnson" is now being held in the king's own chamber. Catesby declares that Cecil and his king are dead: a vain hope.

The king approves torture for Guido Fawkes, writing that "The gentler tortures are to be first used unto him *et sic per gradus ad ima tenditur*—and so by degrees proceeding to the worst—and so God speed your good work. James R."

Popham, the Lord Chief Justice, "a huge, heavy, ugly man," goes after the servants of Ambrose Rookwood and generally cleans out Clopton, by the evening of November 6 already able to sit and contemplate his first list of plotters—those gentlemen he would like to testify:

Catesby
Rookwood
Keyes
Winter [sic], *Thomas*
Wright, John
Wright, Christopher
Grant

Thus far, no Digby, Robert Wintour, or Bates, perhaps—at least as far as the first two are concerned, because his information comes from Tresham, no longer in the loop, while Bates is only a servant. The real problem so far is "John Johnson," scarred and enigmatic. Who *is* he? The king himself draws up a list of questions that starts "as to what he is, For I can never yet hear of any man that knows him." Whence his French? Is he a priest?

The team ranged up against the plotters has a stark unendearing quality:

Cecil: twisted, clever, very much the son of his cunning father Lord Burghley.

Sir Edward Coke, nimble jurist, worldly and pitiless; married to one of the Cecil family, Lady Hatton. He has been Attorney-General since 1594.

Popham (Lord Chief Justice), lumbering, cruel, foul. A more savage, unscrupulous team would be hard to imagine; these men overlap in their potential for horror, and it is chastening to think of them, in power, arrayed against the Jesuits, certainly their equal in mental dexterity, but vested with no power at all save in Rome. If ever a team arose to make guilty the innocent, this one will do it. None of them is a stranger to use of the rack, whose virtuoso operator, one Thomas Norton, once boasted of having stretched Alexander Briant a foot longer than God made him. Failing the rack in the Tower, another way of extracting information is "pinching," or starvation, with prisoners locked in pitch-dark dungeons, pitifully dependent on water droplets from the ceiling. In time, the same Norton has to recant, saying he only *threatened* to do such a thing to Briant, who in fact was a priest. Among the gentler tortures are manacles such as have been affixed to Father Gerard during what feels to him like an earlier incarnation. According to the Topcliffe who tortured Edmund Campion a dozen times, mostly on the rack he kept at home, the apparition of the prisoner dangling from the wall by means of iron gauntlets around his wrists "will be as though he were dancing a trick or figure." One Jesuit, Father Henry Walpole, a veteran of the manacles or gauntlets, can no longer use his hands—a mild case compared to what, after the first days, they do in the Tower to Guido Fawkes, so maiming him that he can no longer scrawl his name even after confessing, and is reckoned by others in the Tower a broken, unmendable wreck of a man who began confident and brave, actually having a good night's sleep before being severely racked the next day. "Therefore," says Waad, newly appointed Lieutenant of the Tower, "I willed him to prepare himself." But Fawkes explained that he could not oblige, he and his fellow-plotters having taken an oath of secrecy before partaking of a Sacrament given by a wholly innocent priest. Late on November 7, he cracks and begins to talk, resuming on the 8th and 9th as they rack him further, so much so that one observer, Sir Edward Hoby, a Privy Councillor, remarks, "He beginneth to speak English," no doubt an aspersion cast on Guido's French, his evident foreignness, and his lust for the king's Scottish blood. Has he not already confessed he wants to rid England of all Scotsmen, anyway? Guido's signature, unlike Thomas Wintour's faked and misspelled by the government, decays from bold emphatic to shaky brambles with a few palsied taps of the pen on paper standing for "Fawkes."

On Guido goes, mostly telling them what they want to hear, but suppressing certain vital things, giving Catesby and his allies in the Midlands a chance to make good their escape. The planned raid on Warwick castle yields horses, but little more. The government proclaims a wanted list, the same as the Privy Council's except for the addition of Percy, and Robert Ashfield, a servant. After collecting arms at Norbrook, they aim for Huddington after Catesby sends Bates to Father Garnet with a note saying "Please forgive us our rash behavior in a good cause. Will you please assist us in winning support in Wales, where Catholics are not so easily intimidated?" Digby signs with Catesby, for what that is worth. When Garnet reads this, he is scandalised. Then Father Tesimond arrives, and in Bates's hearing utters the famous, fatal words "We are all utterly undone." No quibble about it. Father Garnet instantly foresees an end to Latin and Greek, teaching in Rome, Byrd music, the peacefulness of being the ranking Jesuit, and, worst of all, his abstruse life with Mrs Perkins. In his reply, Garnet begs them to stop and heed the Pope, but he cannot keep Mary Digby from weeping, her husband a clearly defined traitor although not yet listed.

The bad news reaches Eliza Vaux from the lips of Henry Huddlestone, her cousin, the same person who encountered

Catesby on the road; she pretends, however, for safety's sake, it came to her from one of Sir Griffin Markham's retainers, said to one of her own. Distancing oneself has suddenly become an art. Anne Vaux has been able to do this through music and well-bred brooding, but the news keeps on getting worse and now exceeds her capacity to blunt it. The worst thing happens when Father Singleton, Father Strange, and Henry Huddlestone (the bad-news bearer) set out for Warwick only to find the city full of government patrols in the wake of Catesby's raid the previous night. Trying to go around, they end up halted and arrested at Kenilworth by Sir Richard Verney and his posse. Eliza Vaux has family connexions to Verney, but they do not pay off; she sends detailed descriptions of her priests lest there be any confusion, and he blithely sends them on to Cecil, who as promptly as he can has Huddlestone and Strange sent to the Tower and Singleton to Bridewell jail. It takes little to qualify for Cecil's special attention; the Tower is filling up, and so are the local lock-ups, mostly with innocent or fairly innocent serfs. Anne Vaux, however, manages to spirit Father Garnet away, posing once again as Mrs Perkins.

"It's all horses," she tells him. "We seem to live on horses. So I always feel sore."

"Worse, we ride in circles. There seems truly no place to go to, not where you can arrive and repose, take your ease, be cordial to your friends and fellow-Catholics. I no sooner arrive, my dear, than I get bundled away into this or that hiding place. You know the expression, not that you have needed it, mostly used when threatening children? *I'll give you a good hiding.* Meaning a good thrashing? Well, your great distinction is that you give me, Father Garnet, *Henry* Garnet to you, a good hiding. You do indeed. You give me good hiding places, you save my neck. How can I ever thank you? I do have this dream of being one day able to see you in an unpersecuted city, Rome, and show you all the wonderful sights, but such wonders appear far off, and we have a pile of trouble ahead of us now. If a Derbyshireman may help himself to a Yorkshire expression, we'll eat a peck of muck before we die. Perhaps it is a Norse expression right from the Vikings. I have another thought about the shires as well."

She informs him he is being talkative today. Perhaps being on horseback loosens his tongue, she tells him. "Poor Guido," he observes, coughing in the dank November air, "has found they have other ways of loosening the tongue. He will hold out as long as he can, but he is a doomed, ruined man. I wish they had all spent their time praying, never making a move without the Pope. In any case, they never seemed competent to me: full of charm, yes, and bright ideas, and lovely ways of doing things once they got into power, but in all, clumsy, hot-headed, unprepared, uneducated. Look at the men they have been trying to undo: Cecil, Coke, Pop, that fat old tiger in his seventies already, itching to maul just about anybody he isn't obliged to. We shall see some terrible things. I wish too your relative, Eliza, would keep her trap shut; she writes tactless, revealing letters to people in power, she sends information a spy would covet; and she tries to use family connexions when they have all been nullified by somebody higher up. Why, this country even has a king who takes a pointed, personal interest in everything going on. He actually writes out lists of questions and tells them in his clumsy Latin to torture Guido in stages. He is not always hunting, is he? Hunting men the whole time."

An extraordinary thought unnerves her: she thinks, oh my, if only the innocent Henry Garnet had been their leader, in charge of their sloppy minds all through, they might have managed. Why did they turn against brains from the very outset? Is the prohibition against Jesuits really a banning of brainpower? Is that why the king hates them and Popham rages into a foaming fit at the very mention? "Henry," she murmurs as they reach a crossroads, pause for bearings, then trot on, wondering why they are not in a coach. "Do married couples ever ride thus abroad, as if showing off?" She marvels at the way Henry Garnet works his protean changes, hardly ever looking like a priest (he rarely gets a chance), but approximates all manner of other men: courtier, solicitor, butler, valet, gardener, at times even a woodworker. She laughs out loud at the incongruity of Henry Garnet trying to look like Little John Owen; he had far better try to imitate Cecil himself or some other parasite potentate, like him prolonging his avaricious, cruel family tradition. Ironic, is it not, that the one thing Jesuits are famous for is the one thing they cannot do in England: use their minds for the public good. She stares at the half-frozen ground, wondering how horses first learned to trot or gallop on spongey ice. He loves the sun, she reminds herself; any time he spends in this raw, mutable climate is a penance. Now he posts, which she, riding side-saddle, cannot do.

"My own theory," he tells her in breathy blurts as if the ride is pummelling the air out of him, but it is only the morning's cold, inducing a brief gasp. "I have thought this over for some time. My goodness, here we can speak without the least fear of being overheard. Back to my point. So many of our Catholics happen to be northerners, Yorkshire or Derbyshire people, Lancashire even, and these folk are notorious for being, well, gruff and brusque and headstrong. Even our Yorkshire priests, Tesimond and Oldcorne, have that peremptory quality in which the Viking consorts with the furious farmer. You know what I mean. If the plot had been run by suave Southerners, immune to the hot heads of the northern counties, the situation would be better. If I am at war, then I need a Guido Fawkes beside me; but if I am maneuvering during a so-called peace, then I want a Cecil to counsel me. If only this *had* been a diplomatic ploy instead of a revolution with bombs and bloodshed. They could have negotiated a tawdry peace."

He is wasting his brains, she thinks; the plot is over and done with, at least from the plotters' end. They will be the party done to from now on. I foresee a gloomy Christmas in the midst of all this: some devoutness, to be sure, if we remain lucky, but a time of appalling agitation in which it were better to talk Latin and Greek than to confide anything to anyone. I am finished with telling Eliza anything, blood be damned. Yes, music, which can never be trapped, accused, or put to analytical proof, immune to the rack, will save us yet, clearing an open channel between ourselves and God, even if only like the blood gutter in a slaughterhouse. One way or another, the Almighty will reach us, even if offering no consolation on the secular plane. I am a mature, irritable woman with a woman's troubles, all shaken up by constant riding, constant coaching. I owe it to myself to go on harboring, secreting, gathering up, protecting— all those Jesuit children of mine. How specialised I have become. He is right: we should all have *connived* more. Surely too, a woman whose mother dies in childbirth, like mine, should perhaps repay the debt by becoming a sister at Louvain, like Henry's sisters. Or is the debt the other way? Does God owe *me* something? If so, He has paid it, it comes in cryptic form: He sends me a senior Jesuit, the most peaceable man in Christendom, to whom nobody but me listens. The man of my heart is pacific, neuter.

She knows that, if she is to touch the beyond without any outside help, she has to strengthen her own resources, discovering in the merest wrinkle, ache, twitch, a wreath, a garland, a star. Perhaps she has already achieved some of this, on her way to accomplishing an intensity as deep as his. If she never does, she will be unable, she reasons, to deal with him on any terms whatever; she will always be in the position of one who hides him, a servitor, a subordinate; and she hates the very idea, having come far enough to transcend the scruffy dinnerplate correctness of a Mrs Perkins. If, she decides, we are never to be fulfilled physically, and it looks as if there is not going to be time enough, then we will have to fuse in some other way, thinking of each other, cleaving to the soul that may wobble but does not faint. If Guido Fawkes, rough and tough Yorkshireman, can shilly-shally on the rack in order to keep something most secret apart from his inconsequential babblings, then surely she, a woman whose family name occurs in a Shakespeare play, can survive and exploit the racking she must give herself. Why, oh why did we not compromise ourselves sooner? Will we never know the delicious pain of lovers that the thing most precious to them slaughters? All of a sudden she discerns, from his point of view, the vastness of space and time in which she is not going to be, has never been, and it sickens her to the heart.

The remaining conspirators have now become fugitives, shopping around in the Midlands for safe harbor, but not finding it, even from previous supporters who already have priests hiding in their homes. When they arrive at Huddington around two in the afternoon, Gertrude Wintour, stationed at a casement window, watches for the sign: a hat waved means all is well, a hat kept on means all is lost. There is no arranged gesture for a message in between. Having scratched with a diamond ring the inscription *past cark, past care* (cark is hope) on the glass, she retreats to her household duties, little aware that one day she will march along Lady Wintour's Walk, a ghost in the woods, permanently embodying the mood of hopelessness. Rebuffed at Huddington and Hindlip (destined to be Father Garnet's best refuge), apart from receiving genuine concern at Huddington on the part of Father Tesimond, who tries to give Catesby some relief but cannot alter his state of mind, all who intend to gallop away take confession in the early hours of Tuesday, November 7, and the Sacrament at Mass, then depart into the sodden gloom, thirty-six of them, hardly an army, reaching Hewell Grange by noon, where they help themselves to powder, arms, and money, trying not to respond to the locals' hostile faces, all of them swearing to a patriotism invented overnight. Ten o'clock that night, the soaked, weary group shows up at Holbeach House in Staffordshire, the home of Stephen Littleton. They try to convert the house into a fort, but are too weary to do much; their main worry, suddenly changed into a feeling of euphoria, is that someone has been following them the whole way: sympathisers have come to swell their numbers, they conclude, except they never arrive, they are in fact the vigilantes of the High Sheriff of Worcestershire: "the power and face of the county." The cheerful mood vanishes again, and they try to dry out. They put out feelers to other homes in the area, but nobody wants anything to do with them, and the intermediaries—Tom Wintour, Stephen Littleton—start back, forcing themselves not to lose hope.

The Whewell gunpowder, brought here in a cart open to the rain, is now virtually useless; they spread it out in front of the roaring fire to dry, their minds really on the failure of any sanctuary. It catches fire and explodes; it was not as damp as supposed or it has dried fast. Flames pour over Catesby, not exactly the detonation he has wanted all along, as well as over Rookwood, Grant, and Henry Morgan. Robert Wintour whispers later that he has dreamed the whole thing, "steeples stand awry, and within those churches strange and unknown faces." These are the burned faces of his friends, in agony in front of him. Word actually goes out that there has been an explosion and the plotters are dead, the bodies scattered. Now it comes to be, thinks Robert Wintour while his brother, out in the deluge, decides that, rumor or no, he will continue back to Holbeach to see what has gone on. Stubborn as ever, he declares that he will "first see the body of my friend Catesby and bury him, whatsoever befall me." The rain is still heavy. The rumor-bearing messenger has gone; so has Littleton. Back at Holbeach, Tom discovers that Digby has gone to give himself up (the only conspirator to do so), while Robert has gone to find Stephen Littleton. Bates is missing too. Among those remaining, John Grant is blind, Morgan badly burned, Catesby and Rookwood phlegmatic about their own injuries. "We mean here to die," they all say, as if in symphonic retort to the chapter of accidents that has exposed and ruined them, slicing their party ever smaller, rendering the plot less a plot than a pretext for company. Here they are, waiting for the Sheriff, making grand vows to one another as men do when they are up against it, as if brave pronouncements will bend the destiny to come, procure yet another accident that will help them out for a change. Sir Richard Walsh, just to make sure of things and not knowing how many supporters the plotters will have mustered to their cause during their long ride in the cold rain, has two hundred men at his disposal. Back in the Tower, Guido Fawkes steels himself for the first racking of the day. While his supporters pray, Catesby kisses the gold crucifix that dangles from his neck. "All for the honor of the Cross," he says, almost chanting as he test-wields his sword.

Walsh and his two hundred begin their cautious siege towards eleven in the morning, discharging their muskets into the courtyard, where Tom Wintour takes a round in the shoulder, Jack Wright another, Kit Wright next, after which the burned Ambrose Rookwood is struck. Their swords have become useless ornaments; there is no one to threaten or to slash. Only Catesby and Percy remain to defend their refuge, with Wintour, Grant, and Morgan on the injured list.

"Stand by me, Mr Tom," Catesby ambiguously says, still game for a little bluster among the sullen arpeggios of defeat.

"I have lost the use of my right arm," Wintour answers him, "and I fear that will cause me to be taken." They and Percy mount guard at the main door, where Catesby and Percy are felled by the same shot, fired by a John Streete of Worcester, who later on asks for a thousand pounds, but is told fate and chance shall inherit his prize. Stripping of the bodies begins, the men of Walsh's amateur force being none too gentle about it, ripping souvenirs away from those dying: Percy and the brothers Wright. Off come Kit Wright's boots and fancy silk stockings, now become the pride and joy of the force's ensign. This is hardly the result envisioned by those desirous of Tower confessions, show trials, auto-da-fé with the hangman presiding; but ultimately, as Cecil realizes, you cannot have a shambles both ways—if you wipe the plotters out, then there is no one to confess and nobody worth incriminating. All that remains is the beheading of corpses and the racking of their families for sport. The final scene reveals naked bodies—Percy, the Wrights, Catesby—lying on the matted crust of incinerated powder, a stench of sulfur and niter in the air, the big room full of loathsome smoke and ecstatic yells as Walsh's rabble quarrel about the horses outside. The burned—Grant and Morgan, Rookwood (also wounded)—are going to survive, as is Tom Wintour, though jabbed in the stomach by a pike. Catesby has crawled back into the house too, dead with a picture of the Virgin Mary on his chest, which the Sheriff sends on to Cecil as a sample of rebel ideology. Something wretched and inferior about this final humiliation dogs the minds of the survivors: plotters wielding swords against muskets, or rather waiting a chance to use them while the musket fire pours in. The disproportion sickens them, reminding them that history is almost always thus; there are few ties. The whole affair is one of botched gunpowder, holy delusion, and grandiose pseudo-chivalric dreams, amounting to a wisp in a scrap of a torn-off fragment. Was it ever doable? Not if over-discussed and poorly supported. They seem to have been creating their revolution hand to mouth, somehow entrusting success to the magic distilled by the Jesuits, who backed them only out of compassion. What they have invented, in fact, is the guilt-by-association machine, which will destroy many more than any of Catesby's original soldiers even imagined.

Cecil cannot be more pleased. If a pet puppy had cleaned up after itself, he would feel this exact degree of proprietorial joy. He examines the hypothesis of the plot that blew itself up and takes genuine, aristocratic delight in the thought that a few remain; you need them, he insists, for the public spectacle that sways the plebs to right-mindedness. And, besides what better way to catch a pack of Jesuits? Even if all had perished, he would make a case for pursuing evil intent along all branches of the family tree, stamping out treachery in the cradle if need be. His friend and ally Coke, the Attorney-General, needs a work-out anyway and will make a good job of it. As if planning a party for intimate friends, he scrawls up his lists of those to be invited, always chiding himself for having omitted someone without the least degree of malice:

Digby	*(Tower)*
Wintour, Robt	*(Tow'r)*
Grant	*(id.)*
Bates	*(in Gatehouse)*
Rookwood	
Wintour, Tom	
Keyes	
priests	

Next, he decides, he is going to list all those women who have husbanded the said priests, but he mourns the dead among the men, wishing always for a complete bill of complaint.

Part Three

13

A NNE SEES IT NOW. After much thinking, you find the answer by ignoring the problem. This is the journey from which not to arrive. After this side-saddle canter, all will be imaginary, and Henry Garnet will enter the dark night of rheumatism in a dank hole of Little John Owen's devising. So, they will dismount, having ignored the bleached-looking winter sun so as to lose their sense of direction, galloping now to just about anywhere, preferably no place at all. They will dismount—yes, she had reached that far. Then they will make a shelter from brambles and briars, filling in the crannies with straw blown about and leftover leaves the deer have not yet discovered. In this lean-to or hovel, they will huddle wordlessly until they freeze. November is the ideal month for this: not too cold, but severe enough to be the dark evening of the soul. She reaches out, but he is on the other horse, his back to her, two yards ahead, riding like someone well-trained but with no love for the act. It is a means, for him, of going from Mass to Mass, hiding hole to hiding hole. She has heard rumors, but knows only about the glamorous, ornate swords, made to order like prizes commissioned by competitors who prefer to make sure of winning. Her award is

Henry Garnet, what is left of him. Back to those swords: these men are not Romans, they are Catholics, so there will be no falling upon them, old-style. If they fall, it will be to go to sleep, as if on guard with their weapons awake beneath them, brands of live Toledo sparkling in the gloom. How can she resist so pregnant an image, fail to see its religious slant? As she sees it, God does not exist as people do, but is a nominal void experienced at first as nothing at all. Some *people* are that way, she decides, from Cecil to the king, both of whom she has encountered without delight, her natural faculties discovering no object worth responding to, which is extraordinary, she knows, what with the one's panoply of clout and luxury, the other's derivative power—a wasp in a bee's hive. She knows now that certain people, many perhaps, exist only to serve as hinges, clasps, doorstops, nothing grand; but at the same time they aren't trivial either. What bottle has she squeezed in her time, what leather flagon filched from Spain, only to hear in its recumbent wheeze the snuffle of a child with a cold? If you are awake enough, Anne decides, you soon discover one thing is all others, it only requires an intense enough view, which means that the teeming world is only a pretext for learning. Byrd has fanned her into this in his highest reaches for unaccompanied voices, but so too has Henry Garnet, romancing about Italy, where in his mind he lives. All this poppycock about divine right, and the vain pavilions of temporary Scottish splendor blowing apart like kilts that reveal only commonplace parts garlanded with rough Highland hair, is nothing spiritual at all. Of course. It is not so difficult for her to imagine herself where she is not, or to discern the mystical flank of a cow, the Jesuitical cast in a sheep's eye. It is a matter of pushing yourself forward past the breakwater of accepted phenomena, then taking in in an instant what you find on the other side, while the objects of sense are naked (without tradition embalming them). You have your way with God's things. It is as easy as that. She still recalls, prompted sometimes by Henry Garnet in long-forgotten conversations, seeing how three hundred years ago what was real was abstract; the word *real* was a Platonic concept. She has forgotten most of this, too busy hiding priests in suitable places, keeping a mental list of which were occupied and for how long, which required cleaning out or fortifying, in which you might not stand or stretch out. She has even tried to match priest to hole, testing physique against cavity, trying to square Little John's extempore handiwork (he creates them as the midnight mood takes him), worrying most about big hefty Yorkshiremen never designed for this kind of compression.

No wonder, then, so much of her is lost, like meat off bones. Would she ever have predicted that, with all the gifts at her command, she would spend her mature years like some frustrated innkeeper, ever fretful about the length and shape of overnight, over-week, guests; the sniffles, the coughs, the hiccups, the sneezes, the yawns, the tummy rumblings, and other noises of the human being. To survive thus, the priests (and their keeper) have been obliged to be less than human, subverting their sense of wholeness, of being anyone at all, becoming merely a part of the masonry, the woodwork, a ghost without measurements. She too, denatured as a woman, with no private life, although in its place a mighty secret one. Now, riding behind one of her champions released into open air, she again remembers who she was and is, with the November wind assembling her again, whereas it has blown others apart. If you go deep down into yourself, she remembers Garnet's saying, you will find that you already possess what you desire. So there is no pilgrimage to it, as to Saint Winifred's Well; it is all over before you deludedly begin. What you yearn for, you have already had. What a way to gnaw on futurity! What a fine demonstration of how fruitless most human activity is, certainly if it all leads to a null point. So, if you station yourself at that point to begin with—she wishes she believed it. She is promising herself emptiness. Her joy to come is not an idea in the mind of God, because God does not have a mind, not in the human sense. God is impersonal: an entity spread out, racking Himself. She drifts away from this idea, only too willing to picture God as some infinitely extended tier of clouds and stars lying along a line that goes from Rome to Northern Scotland. Sacrilege, of course, but God's nature is always open to question, is indeed that which is most open to question. She feels like someone trying to translate a text she has never read, but, lord, she is really trying, with each thump and rumble of Ginny her horse getting a new angle, a new idea, heedless of the words Father Garnet tosses out behind him as he accomplishes yet another equine chore. If he truly wished to talk, he would ride alongside.

Fact is, he is wondering about the nature of lying, of God's knowing everything, on the one hand, and your knowing only too little on the other. Why would humans not, in all their affairs, allow for lying? Call it the liar's fraction. As for prevaricate, he thinks otherwise, choosing to rescue the word (after its Latin *tergiversari*) for turning your back, or playing for time by composing distractions. *Misleading*, he decides, that is it. So, when the head Jesuit says he has been in no way involved in the plot, although he has confessed and counselled certain plotters, he is merely trying to put them off the scent. He and God know the truth of it: he has done no harm, except that to the Cecils of this world his mode of doing no harm does sharp injury to the state. If I tell God, he asks himself, need I tell Cecil?

But thought, of course, wans and palsies us, turning the bright polyvalent human firefly to soggy porridge. They halt and dismount, he helping her although she is expert at merely slithering off. They stand in the centre of a field across which many have already galloped, on the way to somewhere less enticing than Hindlip, their destination, deep in the environs of Worcester, only two miles away. They face the already dwindling sun as if expecting it to recognize them, saying not a word of all they have thought while riding. They touch hands, almost a leper's tap. Eye to eye, they shiver, she thinking friendship is a great fault, he, quite forgetting prevarication, that love is a roaring beast. They have trapped each other in their decency, which means the *fittingness* of their souls – how appropriate compared to what they have to undergo. Their souls fit fairly well, although neither Anne nor Henry feels any great pleasure in the fact. Each senses having done something right at some point not worth lingering on. They remount, then ride in a circle in the tufted, sallow field, he chasing her, she chasing him, in an endless ring. It should have been a day of unusual heat, but they cannot have everything. They go so far toward each other and then break off, she telling herself she doesn't quite see him right because her eyes are poor, he reassuring himself that his private life is over again.

In the profoundly sheltered corner of his brain that wonders about Anne's body, Father Garnet has filed away the
phrase *cleft for me,* filched from an English psalm. He will
never need it, but he has not been able to resist its prurient
sound; as if knowing he will never need the phrase in any sexual way, he neutralizes it, feels free to hold on to it without the
least trace of desire. Certain looks of hers he has been unable
to look away from, but the analytical nature of his mind has
always saved him, together with his huge regard for God's
omniscience: God always knows. His vows are his vows, but
sometimes they exist for him only as things written down to
have a signature after them; he will not break them, but he will
allow his speculative, imaginative mind to play with rumors
and small-boy innuendo—not too far, not enough to make
him feel unpriestly for more than a quarter-hour. Where one
Father nails his tongue and another birches himself, Henry
Garnet flirts with his untapped gonads, always censoring
them, but marveling at the sudden changes that can afflict an
unwitting body, of a boy, a youth, a middle-aged Jesuit. How,
he wonders, do you live all your life with that part of you as
vulnerable, as alive, as responsive, as your brain? Does one ever
learn to control it? Millions have, or so he supposes. He need
not, of course, but the phenomenon of its waxing and waning
has occupied him several times a week, and he feels like the
proprietor of a sea creature obedient to all currents.

Anne Vaux still likes it when they stop for a posset (hot
milk curdled with wine) and the innkeeper addresses her as
Mrs Perkins (she is known) or refers to her, when addressing
Father Garnet, as "your lady wife." It may be an illusion, but
she finds it a satisfying one, even if, deep down, what she re-

ally wants is some painter to come along and portray them to a standstill. She would like to be frozen in ice with him, imprinted in some sedimentary layer that no one will discover. Now she turns her attention to the speed at which they travel, doing her mathematical best to work out a pace that will bring them to a stop just before Hindlip. At best they manage five miles an hour, which she thinks of as five miles within-an-hour. She estimates a constant speed reduction all the way until they are at best crawling along, traveling through an ever more viscous element that holds them up in the sense of buoying them. By how much to reduce speed on each horse's leg, she does not know, but she can guess, and she wonders, if she tried it, would Henry Garnet notice? The horses would, and might start gallivanting about for something to do with all their unused energy. After all, Hindlip once reached, Father Garnet goes into hiding; there will be no time for casual chatter, not even time for a proper meal, a sit-down as she calls it. He is lucky that he will be taken in; since the plot flopped, people have been refusing, invoking all kinds of excuses not to have a priest on the premises. After all, a priest, as the nation is now teaching itself, may be a plotter too. So, he will be instantly secreted, popped away like a parcel, and she will have to minister to him as best she can, painfully attuned now to the various traditions in which lovers soon to be parted make vital tryst. But she and he are not lovers, except in some abstruse sense; what, then, can they do to intensify their final hours together, with only two miles to go? She silently bewails the time already spent on horseback, not even riding side by side (news of the plot's failure has turned him into a taciturn recluse). They could stop, for one posset after another, until their heads swim and they have to spend the night in some mouse-infested inn off the road, munching stale bread and moldy cheese, just for the chance of being together at arm's length. Why, she thinks, there should be training for middle-aged ladies in this kind of a swivet; perhaps convents would do it, or women of the world, ladies from court. It is a matter of love inhibited, she decides, and love postponed. Surely the pair of them merit sympathy, even as the Perkinses.

Father Garnet's thoughts, alas, do not chime with hers. He is worrying about his neck, mostly because he has so many cares of office, which of course another Jesuit might inherit; but he still wants to return to Italy, his job in England done, the rest of his life a round of study and friendship; not as a memory or a sanctified reputation. Miss Vaux, as he likes to think of her, hardly figures in these plans, but the pair of them, as allies, go back some twenty years now, enough, as one of the earthy Yorkshire fathers expressed it, to be on farting terms. He winces, as Derbyshiremen do when confronted with Yorkshire phlegm, but then marvels at the non-existence of time. Ideas and time, he believes, don't mix; intersect, perhaps, but no more than that, no more than *bel paese* and rosary beads. Perhaps, he thinks, she will aim for Louvain, far enough away for the proprieties to be obtained, but near enough for amicable rapprochement. Such a solution appeals to him, relieving him of her as a fleshly burden, who may indeed move on to interest in some other man, not a Jesuit. Something suicidal in her make-up both alarms and soothes him. Her sister-in-law, Eliza Vaux, a woman of robust temperament, is surely an influence to be reckoned with, equipping her with a disregard for bounds, yet also advising her that to love a priest is like asking God to read to her. He sighs and finds joy only in the fact, as he construes it, that she is not involved in the plot, although from Cecil's point of view she is in it up to the neck: aiding the enemy year after year. He wonders at the malleable English policy toward what they call Popery: a crime when they want to make trouble, a mere ceremonial sideshow when they want to look the other way. Look at Byrd, the Proteus of music, at home in all camps, not even concerned about the plot, to which, being sublime and insatiably practical, he pays little heed. What a technique! If you pretend something does not exist, you can hardly be involved with it. What is this? She has come to a stop at the bottom of what seems to be a sled-run for local children. This must be a cool patch in the landscape, with enough snow already for runners to glide.

He asks when they will arrive, coughing in the cold, as if he has not thought to do it before now, with the horse making all the effort.

She tells him there is no need for haste. They are close to Hindlip. He understands differently, he says. A couple loitering on horseback—

"Is one of the most ordinary things in the world," she answers. "A couple riding *fast* toward a known Jesuit sanctuary—well, you can imagine."

"It depends," he says gently, "on who is watching."

"Cecil always," she says. "He has spies everywhere, in households you would never suspect."

For some reason, he wishes he too had some kind of majestic sword, not that he would know how to use it. To brandish, to flash. Where is the sun, though? Friend to hurtless souls.

"It gets just this cold in Italy," he says, "but they say the

sun leaks into the walls and comes out in winter, like a blessing renewed."

"Then," she retorts haughtily, "we had better hie to Italy at
all speed. Where a woman is warm, she thrives."

The horses are restless although accustomed to each other's
company; they sense a meal in the offing, having done this
ride before, for the same reasons. From pillar to doorpost, she
is thinking. This is how we live. Furtive and incomplete. What
do other women do? How cope with lovers deeply embroiled
in the plot? Eliza goes in and confronts all manner of Cecils,
risking prison and torture, but prevailing through sheer force
of personality; they do not dare, ultimately, not to let her go.
She has influence, of course; she has even entertained the king
at Harrowden. Anne wishes she were more like either: less intellectual, more aggressive. Perhaps she will grow into life-
saving habits, will learn to eschew priests, her devotion to
whom, so Eliza argues, betrays an unrecognised desire to remain a virgin, although mentally she's as worldly as a woman
can be. Am I that nesh, she wonders, using a local word for
timid. I was never nesh when growing up. Now, it seems, I am
cooling down, but with my fetishes on parade, awaiting service. I know who I am, and I wish I approved of myself. I know
what: I like a priest to ratify me, to sponsor my guilt.

14

GUIDO FAWKES IS crumbling, to Cecil's delight, though he leaves the officiating and the dirty work to Waad, lieutenant of the Tower, whose wife, Lady Anne, takes an uncommon interest in the doings there—more than Cecil finds seemly. What cheers him is the absence of Thomas Howard, Earl of Suffolk, deeply involved in running down the plotters, which leaves his wife, Countess Catherine, free for dalliance with his majesty's major-domo. In his perverse way, Cecil enjoys any sexual act that produces a grimace not only in him but in his partner, something outré and demanding, and then he can relish imagining how he looks, matching contorted face to contorted body, the pain exquisite, and genial enough to distract him from his work for the king. Indeed, Cecil has arrived at that happy combination of work and play epitomised in the phrase *mens sana in corpore sano,* a sane mind in a clean body his grandest work of self-delusion. It gratifies him, and his king, to have Fawkes spouting truth and half-truth at their beck and call, unable to hold out any longer, and having a team of ghouls to do the racking for them while they go about the business of pleasure. Some have said that Cecil is dilatory, only half-interested, and the king too, but the pair of them know exactly what is going on in the Tower, hour by hour, and have no intention of not exploiting the discomfort—the destruction—of Guido Fawkes. Many men, perhaps, will not have this lust for having someone completely under one's domination, but these two, potent in their. own way (James eager for boys, as the rumor always said; Cecil corrupting Lady Suffolk), form a devilish combination, casually satanic and urbanely cruel. Even Lieutenant Waad, lingering at bedtime with a prisoner to provide a graphic account of what he will be subjected to tomorrow, the prisoner made to sleep near the rack for obvious reasons, ranks not as low as James-with-Cecil in the order of depravity. Clear: James wants to know what is going on in his kingdom, but his relish of the torture order for Fawkes has something of the stylist's schadenfreude, while Cecil's deliberate dawdling, while he goes about his opportunistic forays into Lady Suffolk's incessantly busy body, recalls Caligula, who would have profited from some of Cecil's deformity. A whole procession of the wretched will follow Fawkes (one rack requires serial torture), not so much to gain information as to exert the power of the state on dissenters, to encourage the others as the ironic French maxim puts it. After all, both the king and Cecil would have gone up in the explosion had it taken place, so they both have a developed interest in getting their own back on those insolent enough to plot against them. The revenge motif so common in the theatre of this period has one of its roots in the powder plot and its aftermath.

All the same, James is careful to maintain the persona of the jolly hunting chap, out for a romp with the boys, a clever king, a book-writer, who simply has to unwind from the intellectual pressures of the court, and Cecil still drapes his friendly arm over any shoulder he can reach, heedless of what abomination will soon be practiced on the rest of the body. To be sure, the fault is Waad's, Coke's, Popham's, anybody's; he cannot be in charge of everything, can he now, just as clever as the king, no, cleverer, and therefore just as swamped with pressure while on duty. Both men unwind as best they can, requiring only a sufficiency of victims, which the Powder Plot amply provides. Anne, the queen, is a tolerant, fertile Dane not given to critical discernment, so James goes his own way (a simple masque silences her quite fast) while Cecil's cursory household restrains him not at all, and he toys with the drastic notion of hanging himself upon his tongue just to see how it feels. He makes too many speeches, however, to go through with this bizarre self-infliction, but the conceit of it warms and stiffens him as he goes about the tedious paperwork that an abundance of traitors creates.

Anne Vaux thinks she now has it: reduce the pace of the horses by an increasing amount every fifty yards, timing the experiment as best she can. So should the fraction be one tenth, then two tenths, and so forth? A crude approximation will have to serve, together with sustained pauses for the horses to crack the rimy ice on the water and drink their fill. So long as they two never quite arrive, she says: that will do amiably, will it not? If only they could go backwards, but Father Garnet has to be hidden without delay. The very phrase makes her smile ruefully. Now she sees a gang of local boys marauding through the scanty woods with bows made of ash, aiming and firing arrows of some lighter wood, mock-killing one another with whoops and appalling shrieks. No girls in this gaggle, she observes, all no doubt home doing something useful. It is November. Is there no school afoot? Is this a mid-day adventure, then? Can civilization be that close to the pair of them? If so, Father Garnet is in some danger, certainly more than he would be in the middle of some barren Worcestershire heath among incurious animals. They move on, now side-by-side, chattering about how Father Gerard has instructed several high-born ladies in meditation, a subject Anne has delved into herself, reckoning that, whatever others call it, she does meditate for herself, uninstructed, *spurred by Byrd* (she smirks at the rhyme, recalling how Father Garnet once explained that nobody would ever fathom Byrd without knowing both he and Tallis composed a sequence of *Cantiones* for Elizabeth, each composer writing seventeen of them, one for each year of her reign—such fawning!).

Ah, Garnet tells her, letting the topic surface above a host of contending worries, true meditation requires a Catholic framework; it is no use just dreaming, wallowing, turning speechless; the whole enterprise has to be strict, preferably after a reading in Aquinas. He knows she has read *in* Aquinas, but not how much. She has forgotten, she says, but she gets his point. Mere mental sauntering will never do. Of course not. The entire procedure is a means of access to God. "Whenever I say *I*," she says, "I am depriving myself of contact with God."

"A fair start," he answers, "but the erosion of self is a gradual discipline, the problem being that you cannot accomplish it without, it seems, using the self as a tool to do it with. So, the more you use the self as if it were a chisel, say, the less you can break through to God in all your nakedness. It takes years. It took me longer."

He is boasting, she thinks, showing me how hard it has been to become Father Garnet, especially for one who was indoctrinated as he was. He was not born to this trade, and I am never sure if he's a priest or a dominie. She watches her breath billow sideways as she slowly advances, noting an increased number of cottages and farm buildings. They are getting close to Hindlip, where Father Garnet will, like Orpheus, descend into the underworld, denied the special pleasure (as she sees it) of watching servants shovel snow away from the environs of a great house. Their repeated motions, with the flash sideways of the flung shovelful, soothes and lulls her where she often sits behind glass, unset diamond in hand, lost for exactly the right phrase to leave for posterity, yet caught up in the impetus to want to make a mark, Anne's mark. God was greater, complete, before He decided to lessen Himself by creating human beings. She loves to consider the implications of this, trying to work out if a death helps God to be His original self a bit more, because of course you have to reckon in all the new lives coming into being each minute. It seems to her that God lost the bargain long ago and will never retrieve the balance. God will always be incomplete from now on, she realizes, unless all human life were to end, and even then, history will have made permenent inroads on the putative completeness of Him. What a fascinating topic for a ride with Father Garnet on a raw November day, except he seems preoccupied with Hindlip, the Powder Plot, and the fate of Catesby. She, she can see it now, has begun to drift indelibly into the zone of compensation, distracting herself with God's problems, tossing into the riddle her own halfpennyworth.

"You are far away," she tells him with a touch of acerbity.

"No, daughter, I am too close to things."

She is not sure how welcome the appellation *daughter* is; even *child* would be less inhibiting.

"If every human being," she begins, and tells him what she has been thinking about God dismembered. His answer is to wave airily at the dreary heavens above them and re-entrust the problem to God's wisdom. Not a very Jesuitical response, she decides, and returns to the point. "God uses up God in creating us. Yes or no, Father?"

He now trots ahead of her, urging his mount. He wants to be hidden, even from routine questions, settled in his quarters without light, warmth, food, not even room for a folding altar. He has heard of foldable leather bowls from which horses drink; all you have to do is take one along with you on the journey and then unfold it, just like the altar, at the right moment. How ill at ease he feels in this landscape next to a so-called city (a town with a cathedral), where little groups of locals come out duck-hunting, stopping at tiny inns for beer and gingerbread, or Islington White Pot, a custard made famous elsewhere but now sweeping the land. Angry, filthy children, orphans no doubt, exercising squatters' rights, stick their heads out of derelict monasteries and abuse all passers-by. Why are there so many buildings going unused, he wonders. Where have their occupants gone? Into town, no doubt, where life is easier. Nothing taunts him more than an empty monastery, or an alms-giving hut now open to the rain and wind. Compared with Italy, he finds his native England a triumph of outdoor living: it is too cold for the likes of him, even in the inmost bowels of a country house famed for its architecture. That old yearning for the Roman sun on his face, making him smile even as he squints against the light, makes him incessantly homesick, no matter how ravishing the company he's in. No time today for custards, beer, or gingerbread, but he wonders if a supply of all three might not be arranged for at Hindlip, especially as the national emergency is likely to endure for weeks and months. To be actually among The Wanted, although with a virtually unknown face, and amused by the appearance in the lists of his other aliases—Whalley, Darcy, Roberts, Farmer, Philips, Perkins—he suddenly feels impressed with himself, a man to be hunted down for the simple crime of listening, as a priest is supposed to do. If listening be a crime, he thinks, then breathing and eating cannot be far behind in the new Sparta of James the First. If all this is true, he foresees a more straitened life than hitherto, stretching out into long months of hiding until, if ever, the king and Cecil grow bored with him and his avatars. To have lived on purloined time has been taxing, but life on the run with a price on his head (the price unstated as yet) is going to be disastrous. He may not survive even if he gets away with it; he is likely to perish amid a cloud of prayer and starvation.

So now he sees the point of her slowing down. Why, until their brains seize up and their blood ceases flowing, they might keep on riding in a circle, given a sufficient supply of fresh horses: Witley Court to Ombersley to Fernhill Heath and then eastward to Dodderhill, then circling back northwestward again, ever stopping short of Hindlip. He thinks that is how it will go, an ellipse rather than a circle, so that the pair of them become almost a feature of the landscape. People come up from Worcester to watch them going around and around, the constantly hesitant lovers (ha, he grunts) doing the human equivalent of a dog preparing to sit down. It will never do; he has to ride in to Hindlip with her and get into position as swiftly as possible. Cheer up, Henry, he tells himself: it was built to order in the middle of last century, and it is honeycombed with hiding places, almost every room somehow equipped with a trapdoor, an annexe, a recess, a secret stairway, a false wall, and all the chimneys are double—one for smoke, the other for a man. Unfortunately for Father Garnet, little that he knows it, an old description of him is now being circulated throughout the land, citing him along with Father Gerard, and Father Greenway (Tesimond):

> *of middling stature, full faced, fat of body, of complexion fair, his forehead high on each side, with a little thin hair coming down . . . the hair of his head and beard grizzled.*

They claim he must be between fifty and sixty years old, but he is only just fifty, aged by life in hiding, and not as "upright and comely" as his description says. Father Garnet does know, however, that Thomas Habington, recusant of Hindlip, has already turned away the plotters on the run, with a wife and a newborn son to look after, as well as Father Oldcorne, his resident priest. Why, Father Garnet wonders, recollecting how he really looks (nobody in power has had a good look at him in ages), do they not refer to the bags and rings under my eyes, my perpetual look of astute disappointment? It is an old problem. The only time the poursuivants have an accurate account of a man's face is after they have captured him. Before then, it is all speculation, tantamount to gambling; so they might seize just about anybody, confining themselves to the generic. If only the literary artists of this nation assisted the hunters of men, the hunters would fare better. So the literary men, those with better backbones than Jonson and Spokeshave as I dub him, perhaps know what they could a-do about, and so do the portrait painters. In isolation, no doubt light-headed from lack of nourishment, one comes to discover all manner of clandestine truths. Let me see now: is not Hindlip so well endowed with boltholes that each priest gets a room to himself (room in the diminutive sense, as in birdhouse, say), or do they pack us in three to a tunnel? I will soon find out. What is plain is that no lady friend has access except through speaking tube or food slot, and any cravings one might have in that direction (not lasting long) soon dwindle into feathery delusion. There must be something to look forward to, other than saying au revoir to a Miss Vaux who promises to remain on the premises to keep guard. Her entire life has been like this, poorer by far than Habington's own, and he too late trying to dissociate himself from plotters. He has taken in Jesuits, and the English king sees no difference between the two: we are all Guido Fawkes, to the end.

Anne Vaux, having dismissed the idea of riding circles in pastoral paralysis, much as she now also dismisses all notions of an alias, realises how little she can do for Father Garnet—rather like Garnet himself confronted with plotters eager to confess and confide. All he has done is listen, and that is forbidden. She amazes herself with the number of passive ideas that keep the government going, from loyalty to recognition of the so-called divine right of kings. Such concepts, she decides, lie in people's brains like patches of marsh-gas planted there by politicians. We are all victimized, she decides, by what we do not question; and then, of course, when we have questioned everything and there is nothing left to hold on to, the world seems to be only a miasma of shadows and shifting shapes. Is it possible to have faith in a king? I doubt it; kings are too verifiable. The sheer idiocy of a splinter group such as Guido's trying to take over a country with damp gunpowder evokes only pity. Where did these sometime soldiers learn their strategy? In which winning battles have they acquitted themselves well? I even, now, question the need for a Jesuit, a priest, a confessor, to *listen*, which seems a main sin in this land of foxhunting Scotsmen. Why do we not have a secret passageway to Italy, along which our priests, like loaned books returned, can migrate one after another? We make ample provision to conceal them, and to get them admitted to do dangerous work, but none to get them out of trouble once the ax begins to fall. To whom tell this?

On November 7, Ben Jonson appears before the Privy Council for having tried to communicate with a hidden priest who wanted to cross the Channel. Jonson cannot help them, but has to clear his own name, suggesting, once released, that there will be "five hundred gentlemen less" subscribing to the Catholic religion. None of Jonson's relieved cynicism appears in the testimonies of many who come forward, volunteering lengthy versions of their innocence, Sir Walter Raleigh included (his wife, Elizabeth Throckmorton, cousin to Lady Catesby), who with huge conviction denies any contact with the plotters: indeed, he tells the Privy Council, he would have gladly given his life to uncover any such dastardly endeavor. They may recall, he says, his previous service to the country, so far from "this devilish invention." His more dubious friends, the Earl of Dorset among them, ask him if he knew of anything that would have kept him from Parliament that day.

Fawkes is the only talker, advising his rackers that there were only five men in the plot; what he knows most about, he jabbers, is the attempted capture and proclamation of Princess Elizabeth. Now, thanks to his own admission, he is no longer John Johnson, but Guy (Guido) Fawkes, and the very thought of a foreign alias does not go down well. Names he at last yields up are Francis Tresham, a very minor conspirator, he says, and Father Gerard, generous with the Sacrament but ignorant of the plot. Tortured on the 7th, 8th, and 9th of November, he attests to what he has moaned out, regaining as one observer remarks in Cecil's hearing "a clean breath of air for the first time in days." Fawkes has asked to see Cecil, so Cecil comes; the ditty playing in his ears is the words of James I's oration to Parliament on the 9th: "It may well be called a roaring, nay a thundering sin of fire and brimstone, from the which God hath so miraculously delivered us all." Cecil has watched amiably as his king's mood shifts from astonished relief to unsparing calculation to impulsive revenge (a late impulse; he begins by actually commending English Catholics who have had no part in the plot and roundly condemn it; this should include, of course, Father Garnet but it never will). In his speech, James begins to come to the boil, denouncing fire as the most merciless of deaths. Even unreasonable wild animals pitied Daniel. It is he, he says, who divined the true sense of the Monteagle letter, and they should notice his brilliance in this. He goes on to say how grateful he would have been, if die he had to, to die in such a glorious company as he now addresses instead of in "an ale-house or a stew." Ranging widely from the Bible to Ancient Rome, he discerns the mercy of God in all things, in his being saved, and gives thanks, in which the House of Commons concurs. Murmuring repeated ayes, vowing devotion to "the Uttermost Drop of their Blood," they now adjourn until January 21, allowing time for the conspiracy to be fully plumbed. He was delivered on a Tuesday, he announces, so let Parliament meet again on a Tuesday, his lucky day.

Now Cecil has to compose tactful letters to ambassadors in Brussels, Paris, and Spain, notifying them of what has been going on, and what to expect. He takes pains to warn them not to blame any foreign power, certainly not the Catholic ones: "we cannot admit so inhumane a thought as their involvement." Revulsed expostulations will follow, resorting to such words as "atheists and devils," while Zuniga the cointossing, bonfire-lighting Spanish envoy in London avows that the main culprit must be Thomas Percy, a Protestant, he claims and known to side with France over Spain. The French blame the Spanish in a cunning paroxysm of Gallic bigotry. A gullible person, such as Cecil never has been, might conclude the entire plot was a Puritan uprising disguised as a Catholic one; Catesby and his death-ridden crew are only camouflage. Even their deaths are suspicious, engineered perhaps by loyal Catholics. Never one to bandy words when they might be smothered in a fancy complexity, Cecil indulges all these ephemeral myths, sensing the unexpressed delight of so many heathen foreigners cruising and gallivanting about in what he sometimes, now, refers obliquely to as the Realm of Guido—in which no healthy Englishman dares set foot, but where devious plotters malignantly prepare before setting out to rid the world of their betters.

* * *

Something cold and coarse is brushing against Father Tesi-mond's eye. It has bristles and was not there to begin with. He hardly dares open his eye to see what it might be, to expose his eyeball to the threat. Why should he be so surprised, coming in here with only a gruff dock-laborer's permission? His clothes, rolled up neatly in a small satchel, are not within reaching distance; he does not want them soiled. On the pe-riphery, he has stripped before, as it were, the plunge in, and he is still only a couple of yards from the edge, having chosen the nearest cavity he can. It is cold in here, cold with the clut-ter and reek of death, the chill roosting in his body and de-clining to move away. To solace himself, he thinks of soft warm Italian bread, warm from the sun, with spread butter melting into its pores, inviting the bite, the jam, the sigh of delight. First, though, even before continuing to dream against the chill, he has to safeguard his eyes. Opening, he sees nothing; the object is too close, and he feels too hemmed in to move his head backward. After a wriggle or two, shoving his head against only slightly yielding masses that give off a pu-trid odor as if he were in some ancient sea-pool awaiting the tide, he manages to view the open eye that is in front of him, an eye that looks upside down and has long, wiry lashes he cannot even reach with his hand. How long has he been in here, in the hold? Since morning, since dawn, when the light was poor and almost nobody was about. He has actually paid money for this privilege, horrified by the prospect of London after discovery of the plot. First, his face and physique have been touted abroad: his "good red complexion," Yorkshire born and bred, and his fondness for flashy Italian clothes. Safe in a crowd, as he thought, he all of a sudden encountered a pair of eyes staring at his own, and then the redoubled stare that knows it has found its target and the target knows. The poursuivants have him in seconds (he is not that limber a man) and lead him away to the authorities. Why, this is Hargreaves of old, the one haunting the great homes of the recusants, the burly perspiring one with delicate forehead skin and hair of the feeblest flaxen hue.

"Sir, if you please, this way."

"If you insist."

It is a poor enough exchange, but Tesimond's brain is working as they traverse a dull, peaceful street; as they turn the corner he does the simple thing and runs away as fast as he can, stranding Hargreaves in a group of roaring boys. That is how, with a little haggling on land, he comes to be here, naked, in a cargo of dead pigs, all shaven, destined for Calais and the bellies of a thousand Frenchmen. His own skin, since he is more or less deficient in body hair, roughly matches that of the pigs, whose rops (intestines) have been removed. A carcass, he lies among carcasses, wondering if indeed he is not the most original priest in the world; has anyone done this before, he muses, trapped here for a rough crossing, his stomach heaving from both the voyage and the dead flesh surrounding him. Since his body has more curves than straight lines, from good living in London (sojourns in hiding holes not having thinned him out much), he makes a more than adequate dead pig if he keeps quite still, often inclined to call himself, as some investigators have, big and beefy. Well, he says, to himself, big and porky now. When do we reach Calais? When can I change languages? When do I become safe? It can't be easier than this: you just walk away from them. From Calais, God willing, I

will somehow go to Saint Omer, and so to Rome—a better way
than Stephen Littleton's, who, apprehended in his own home,
along with Robert Wintour, has made good his escape on a
gelding, but getting only as far as Prestwood in Staffordshire.
A treacherous servant has done him in, starting the terrible
sequence of trial, sentence, death, that brings him so low he
offers to cooperate with the authorities, wringing from Father
Tesimond the acid thought that those with no hope of life
should not stoop to loathsome measures to try and save it. Re-
iterated, as Tesimond whiles away the voyage, from within a
load of dead pigs. Surely, Tesimond thinks, moving from horror to plain fear, there will be room among other carcasses for
the likes of Father Garnet, Father Oldcorne, Little John
Evans and Ralph Ashley, all hidden away at Hindlip, Oldcorne now known as Hall. This constant changing of names
inspires him; their host is always larger than anyone knows,
and a man with so many turns of phrase applied to himself is
surely ideal for work with congregations. Proteus and his
flock, he thinks, make an interesting historical phenomenon:
compact of disguise and anonymity. The lack of names in the
confessional gibes neatly, he decides, with the shoal of names
around each priest. If only the priests were anonymous too.

It pains him to think of so many men dead; indeed, of a
plot whose engineers have for the most part left the scene,
leaving Cecil with only peripheral people to brutalize. This is
why so much emphasis is being put on priests, those double
offenders who, meriting death for being in England at all,
have given their ears to the plotters in half-submissive tactful
sympathy, by no means denying them access to the boons of
the Church. This, he knows, is what comes of doing one's

metaphysical duty. He hears, below, the crude suck of the sea, from somewhere above him the raucous cry of gulls; the boat creaks, wallows, almost seems to yield, with the carcasses tumbling and shifting about him, oozing blood (he can feel seepage on his cheeks), and in the mildest most fractional way beginning to rot. Only cooking will save them from utter putrefaction, although, he ruminates, surely they have all been scalded; you cannot shave an unscalded pig. He rejoices in the thought of his next bath, but worries about how soon it will come, being that odd priest the down-to-earth dandy, effete in dress, in speech sometimes fierce and always blunt. In Italian he is quite different, as if a monotony of word endings had converted him to a gentility not merely of dress.

With a series of thumps and crashes, the boat arrives and Father Tesimond delights in the flow of dockside French that leaks down into the tiny hold. How many pigs? Perhaps fifty. He worms his way out of the heap, wipes himself off with a piece of sacking, and begins to dress, now observed by a pair of incredulous stevedores who marvel at the slow assembly, from among pig carcasses, of a debonair priest who pays them not the slightest heed. There comes a torrent of commentary, all of which he understands, even as he brushes himself off, pats his chest and rump, takes in a deep breath of survivor's air, and ascends the filthy ladder leading to the deck, like someone who has attended his own birth. He resolves to write down an account of all he has witnessed, not so much for fame as to remind himself in years to come of what he has endured. He proposes to forget, his book will remind him, especially of Father Garnet marooned there among the most heroic members of the English laity. What is there to choose, he wonders, between dead pigs and more than a month amid your own mire?

So long as escape shines at the far end, he says, all is acceptable. Once they have you, he muses, you are done with, unless you run for it. If they keep you and condemn you, you may bargain with them and they may seem to agree, but when they have heard you out they will still put paid to you. They are inexorable and pagan, and Cecil is the lord of devils. Make Devil from Cecil: Decil, Devil. Easy, in two.

The two Frenchmen in their blood-stained blues are still exclaiming at the priestly apparition. Father Tesimond is gone, in one brief gesture up the stepladder arriving in the whole of Europe, where nobody, unless he is acutely mistaken, will bother him. A little hovel choked with books, old candles, ripening Chianti and perspiring cheese will see him through the next thirty years, *d.v.*, as he always tends to say, allowing God a perpetual suffix. He can hardly believe what has gone on in England, what is going on in the Tower with Guido Fawkes this very minute with Sir William and Lady Anne Waad presiding, Cecil and Popham in the gallery, Coke hovering, the dungeons filling up with vaguely suspected people whose only crime seems to have been born in Worcestershire or Yorkshire. Father Tesimond wonders if he will ever speak English again—he interrupts the thought: only with English priests, he says to himself. If there are any. In no time, all those illustrious country houses, havens he calls them, will begin to merge in memory, except for huge honeycombed enigmatic Hindlip, extolled by Father Garnet as he abandons Coughton: "They can not only suspect you are here, but they can find you; at Hindlip, thanks to Little John Owen, they may well suspect your presence, but never will they find you. *Ars celare artem,* my dears. Time to be off. Keep calm."

Father Oswald Tesimond, S.J., alias Greenway, changes his

mind, deciding that henceforth he will address Englishmen of whatever station in broad Yorkshire, a thicket of uncouth vowels the plotters might usefully have chosen, much as the riff-raff of London talks its own incomprehensible slang. This would confront poursuivants and other busybodies with some such verbal slide as *Azthagenityon, then? Ant tha? Thatmoant. Geroffooamwithi.* This means, more or less, "Have you given it to him, then? You haven't? You'd better not. Get off home with you." The obtuse, offhand, northern quality of this outburst delights him, not that you'd think anyone spoke this way or ever did; it is just that the king has not decreed it into existence. It is an English so primitive that even horses understand it. He will not miss it, but he will never forget it, any more than such an exclamation as *"Eigh-up!"* When he feels low, uncouth, angry, or corrupt, he will emit sounds like these, savoring them like a man with a mouth full of marrow. Perhaps, one day, he will indoctrinate some willing Roman in this language, warning him not to use it in London unless he desires total secrecy. Some of those old words still keep their enormous sentimental appeal, having come to him from his grandparents and parents, almost, when he used them, enabling him to pass muster in the street, he a Jesuit in the making: Italianophile, fashion-plate, go-between (he who conducted Guido Fawkes into England).

15

IF THERE IS ANY MORAL to be drawn from recusants' experiences of being hidden, it is better, if you intend to hide, not to do so on your own premises or, for that matter, in those of anyone else. Best go to Saint Omer with Father Tesimond. Or, if that proves impossible, make sure you deal with a country house that, impossibly, has no servants in it and is not located in any of the English counties. Robert Wintour and Stephen Littleton, on the run, camping out in barns, washhouses, seed stores, stables and byres, were found by a drunken poacher, whom they had to gag and bind; but in their next abode, Hagley, the country home of "Red Humphrey" Littleton in Worcestershire, they were exposed by a certain cook, John Finwood, who wondered at the excessive amount of food being sent upstairs. That Finwood receives an annual pension for his good deed goes without saying. When the poursuivants arrive, Red Humphrey denies everything after trying to block their entry. "This is our home, you shall not pass." Something Roman in his demeanor pleases him at this point. They come in anyway and receive the immediate cooperation of yet another servant, David Bate, who shows them the courtyard in which the conspirators have gone to ground.

Hindlip is not far away, readied like a fortress, although who is to guarantee the behavior of servants when they hear of John Finwood's pension and his becoming an eternal spy, before the word gets out about him grafting himself on to the domestic life of another country house in order to undo it, pay promised, no vengeance as yet visited upon him. His breed will prosper in these gruesome times, and the trade of household spy will establish itself among the poor, almost in itself a revenge calling.

Anne Vaux and Father Garnet, Anne and Henry as they are now just about calling each other, have exhausted all means of delay, even standing their horses in the fashion of a love-seat, he pointing northward, she pointing south, in fervid contemplation of each other, with no help from tradition or literature, but left to the meager resources of eye and hand to express what is forbidden. Now they change places, advancing not at all, but feeling heavy at the much shrunken extent of land between here and Hindlip, that labyrinth of lighthouses—almost, Henry Garnet thinks, like Sicily in minature. When, at last, after much dawdling (which Henry Garnet in his original way calls prevarication), they arrive at the rear of the building, he dismounts on a patch of ice, unassisted by grooms, and immediately slips backward, gathers himself to surge forward, then loses his feet altogether and crashes to the ground, in one fall slamming his knee, outside left ankle, his right thumb, and his head on the virtually invisible ice. It is a poor welcome, but he survives it, feeling shaken, a whole series of fresh pains and aches moving through his body, and in his hands a potent trembling. Anne is almost in tears at this last sight of him before the mansion gobbles him up for what? A month or more. Already, Mary Wharncliff, a scullery maid with child by her lover on a neighboring estate, Blackstone Grange, where she has walked to confront him, has returned with news that Sir

Henry Bromley, a local justice of the peace, eldest son of Thomas Bromley who conducted the trial of Mary Queen of Scots—a brash, invasive family—is on his way from who knows where, intent on combing through Hindlip from top to bottom. This leads, of course, to a further piece of wisdom which says: If you wish to move from one country house to another, say from Coughton to Hindlip, do not do it on horseback, or by any other means that entails travel between two points, lest you gallop right into the gang led by one of the Bromleys. Nor, knowing this and some of the Bromley history, should you extend too much trust to the idea that Sir Henry, related to the recusant Littletons, might go easy on certain Catholics. The schizophrenia of the times allows him to do his job without, in this case, altogether losing face with Muriel Littleton, his sister. It is simply another variant of the William Byrd philosophy, enabling the happy practitioner to face both ways without ever being damned as a hypocrite. It is almost as if opinions, tenets, beliefs, were so many silken handkerchiefs to be floated about in the wind, no more committing you to a certain code of conduct than the passage overhead of a moulting sparrow. Whence, Anne Vaux asks herself, this new breed of trimmers, people who out of corrupt self-interest trim their conduct for each situation? Is this the fabled opportunism of wolves or what Henry Garnet, rarely at a loss for classical exemplum, calls "Man being a wolf to man"? Perhaps, though, she thinks, if nobody believes in anything very much, then all persecution is going to come to an end because nobody believes much in that either, except as entertainment for the mob. It is all too much for her, being severed here and now as Henry Garnet, with no time for a meal or a drink, goes his way to join those already cached in the house: Father Oldcorne, the house chaplain, and the lay brother Ralph Ashley. Outside, by special dispensation granted to himself, Little John Owen hides in a dwarf-adapted birdhouse which, through a miracle of hydraulics known to him alone, floats in a duck pond. Or it did; thanks to the freeze, it now sits, compelling upon him all kinds of privation but permitting, as he has so often said during the design phase, fresh air galore. Crouched out there, indeed a consummate piece of the drama, the engineer, the artificer of the whole hideaway (there is room for a dozen more, should the need arise), he fulfills yet another part of his destiny, as much in charge of his scheme as Cecil of his. Simply, as he designed it, the birdhouse goes over him like a cloak; he then steps into a specially designed circular punt fashioned after the coracle, and waits, lowering the birdhouse to the coracle rim, which it exactly matches. Supplies inside abound, more or less, as if he is truly a flightless bird; the birdhouse is not round, but has a round base and this, he has assured the Habingtons, aghast at his perverse ingenuity, enables the birdhouse to move around in the water, making it the centre of a perfectly selfcontrolling motion. It spins itself very slowly, without favoring any particular direction, whereas a rectangular punt will not. As if itinerant birds had left emergency packages for later comers (the code of the distant, romantic log cabin in America), the Owen birdhouse contains in tiny compartments bits of twig called locally Spanish juice; an import like strawberries from Aranjuez; hazelnuts, beech nuts, and roasting chestnuts; tiny pastry pockets of quince jelly; sunflower seeds collected in small leather pouches that might have held rings; unicorns made of gingerbread, none more than two inches high. On the quiet, in the hours left over when he subtracted his work from his life, he baked and rolled, stamped out two-dimensional pastries and polished nuts for storage. A squirrel, in short, with a higher destiny ever awaiting him: there will never, what with the new influx of priests from the Continent, be enough hiding places. Yes, he grins, chilled in his private minaret, you can't always get a good hiding even though you deserve one. Such wit warms him when nothing else does. Attracted by the small holes de rigueur in a birdhouse, some non-migrating birds have already called on him, and he has made the reckless error of sharing his supplies with them, in the interior dark proffering what he can, a sunflower seed, say, between finger and thumb, with aviary refinement. Surely, he thinks, hardly giving a thought to Hindlip's crew of festive, garrulous servants, they will never find me here; I am too blatant. No, the birdhouse is. They will search the house, but nothing else save the outhouses and barns. This is much better than suicide with beautifully crafted swords or being shot in a courtyard or blown up by gunpowder arranged to dry out in front of a roaring fire like a drenched cat. When they come, they will bounce off, as always; I wonder why they bother. Well, it must be to earn their wages, little realizing their real wages will be paid after death, in another world altogether.

Put out by having to share a space with Father Oldcorne (this the safest in the entire house, Habington says), Father Garnet, thrown by the fall on the ice, tries to collect his wits. He feels hollow and brittle, crouched in a space he cannot stand or stretch out in: almost a torture in its own right, inflicted by friends. He tries to fix his mind on some old Roman words first discovered in childhood and treasured as jewels but they will not come, as once they did when he was in a better mood or circumstances were less drear. It is as if the shock of falling on the ice, as well as making his head ache and feel sore to the touch at one point in his left temple and upsetting his stomach too, has wiped out his memory, at least the verbal one. Come back, he says, trying an old trick to bring something to mind, catching himself in the act of identifying it before he even tries to retrieve it. But only *tuli, latum,* come, and they in severed, broken form. He is not that much of an old Roman after all, he decides; all it takes to rattle him is a patch of ice and a household in a hurry. If he weren't who and what he is, he would be inclined to say damn them all, but he refrains, wishing instead he could have an accompaniment from Byrd, of Byrd's music performed by any of them, himself included, but there is so little time. Byrd, he notes drily, feels no need to hide: why does he not happen to be on the poursuivants' list of undesirables?

Making matters worse, even as he poises on the brink of darkness at noon, there is the standard cooking smell of Hindlip, the savory aroma of beef and gravy familiar from his childhood, when he lurked by the big kitchen table with his sisters and they sampled various tidbits of the meal. A small spoonful of gravy would set him up, or, better, a square of Yorkshire pudding, crispy brown on the outside, soft yellow within, a substance designed to replace meat when meat is hard to come by. None of that, though surely it might have been prepared for him. A hot cup of almost anything would serve, he thinks, it does not have to have much taste, only be hot, so that the warmth will linger after he has descended into the hole. He gives up, still wrinkling his nostrils at the cooking smell, almost as if he could eat with them. It is later than mealtime, but who is watching the time? The absent sun is no guide, only his aching, volcanic stomach. No small ceremony, then, with a few chaste words in any language, softening the bleakness of the moment as language has the power to do, converting the worst of situations into an interpreted something. In an ideal world, "real" in the sense that Anne Vaux uses it, he would be escorted (he loves the dignity and finesse of that word) upstairs to a small quiet room with clean sheets, there to sleep off the impact and stretch out his weary body. A pitcher of hot water would be there when he woke, and sundry other things; a snack from the kitchen would set him to rights, it would not even have to be Yorkshire pudding or, if later, wondrous trifle with custard and cream, peeled almonds and sponge cake, or gingerbread drenched in fortified wine. No such perfection needed, neither ambrosia nor ichor. He is willing to go without, he tells himself; it is a mark of his courage, as one going to punishment, which is bound to come later—Fathers Gerard and Walpole have already been through that particular honor. If only, throughout this process, he could sagely sleep, putting his feet where directed, scooping himself in with the expended smile of a man shoved past his limit.

What he does feel rather than witness is a host of hands nudging and easing him, pressing him this way and that, raising or lowering, prodding him to buckle left or right, palming his head forward as if it stuck out too far, and with gentlest tiptoe of their own, urging his feet to tuck themselves in better or he will never get all of him into place. He nearly chokes, being adjusted into so strait a place, but he lifts the top of the moment off as if dealing with boiled milk, tossing away the skin that says he might better have been naked for this, and oiled even, converted into a performing animal for the sake of safety. With muscles only a little more willing than not, he inches his way into the already established, pungent gloom that clings to Father Oldcorne, always a man of no great conversation, who twists and hunches as best he can while another human pushes into his space. The special aroma of the cancer-ridden Father Oldcorne is familiar to him; perhaps it is the bouquet of the self-flogger, the man who punishes his tongue as if it were some live, lascivious beast, corrupted by language. Father Oldcorne smells of burned leather, he decides, at least in close quarters he does, but this might be an effect of brief confinement; the smell is actually that of cooking cauliflower, not a human aroma at all, but direct from the kitchen's anteroom, where discarded celeries and crozzled leftovers are put, often tempting a mouse into the open. Father Oldcorne is not his choice of traveling companion, or even for sitting still with through the dismal watches of the priestly night; the man's hangdog, punished look, not visible in here, thank Jesus, puts him off, as does his constant need for praise at having subjugated the body to a greater degree than Garnet and his free-flowing, almost flamboyant friends. Oldcorne has a dun, grievous quality that restores those who have overlooked it to the miserable side of life; no one, listening to him or smelling him, will want to live too long.

Much of this Anne knows, can divine from what Henry Garnet fails to say as he vanishes bit by bit into the architectural trap devised by Little John Owen who, thanks to the emergency of Sir Henry Bromley's squad impending, freezes out in the martin-house stuck in pond ice. Anyone finding him will turn into a purple martin. One hug and Henry Garnet is gone. She wonders how many hugs there have been: two or three, this by far the most final, seeing that once again they are gambling with their own lives and those of priests. She stands here to marvel at the completeness of the disappearance when the hiding place seems to have been sealed off, the upstairs water-tank shoved back into place by eleven pairs of hands. With so many in league, she thinks, how keep a secret as bizarre as this? Only in a recusant household habituated to such scenes can you get away with it. Perhaps we will. It is assuredly one of Nicholas Owen's most decisive inventions, with the one priest's toes beside the other priest's head, for hygiene's sake. She scoffs at the very thought of hygiene, knowing they had better hygiene in the Ark, and this is a Greek word come down from a people who, professing it, loved the word because they achieved nothing of the kind. The voice of Father Oldcorne, rattled, comes from behind the tank, which actually seems to amplify any sound they make. "A devil in hell," he is saying, always partial to the extreme view of things. Not a sound from Henry Garnet, who has never felt more like a parcel of dirty clothes stuffed into a moldy drawer by a feckless washer-woman. Henry Garnet has never made a fetish of answering Father Oldcorne, whose self-directed rhetoric implies the coldest reaches of the universe, the most fearful moments of any human life. He is not exactly a misery, Henry thinks, but one who exaggerates the dark side of the human antic. Well, when he gets out of here in a month's time, he will have cause for complaint. No, not a month, a week will do; even less, once Sir Henry Somebody has performed his sullen chase through the enormous house and gone his truculent way, his commission from the Privy Council fluttering in his hand. Father Garnet does not know that the Bromley team has been promised "a bountiful reward" for its best efforts, so when they come they will screw their gimlets into the elegantly panelled walls with avaricious zeal—wherever a priest may be hovering (a favored word of the Privy Council, whose notion of priests involves a paradoxical angelic component that makes their lives difficult until they manage to combine angel with harpie). Everyone at Hindlip is familiar with the sounds of probing as, once again, the poursuivants, some recruited only for the day, sedulously go about the business of ruining good panel work, much to the distress of Nicholas Owen. Such grinding and scraping suggests a house full of rats, which in a sense it is whenever these busybodies show up. Mostly from hovels, they delight in the spoliation of luxury, delighted to bore holes in the eyes of the faces in portraits (who would hide behind *them?*) or next to an old borehole so that the two, plus perhaps another, form a peephole. •.• By now, the house has a much-penetrated look as if musketry practice of the wildest abandon has taken place in the dining room, the bedrooms, even lofts and closets. Father Garnet thinks of Hindlip as *the punctured house,* practiced upon by dunce-doctors trying to let the blood out of it, to no purpose —nobody has ever been found here, never mind how vehement or specific the official proclamation borne in the hand of the poursuivant who leads. Nicholas Owen is far too clever for them, and Hindlip gives him more scope than almost any other country house. They might as well look for actual faces in the coats of arms proudly displayed on the walls.

Anne Vaux knows she cannot stand any more of this, so she goes downstairs, unable to believe she has just ridden cross-country to entomb the dearest priest in the world. She has not so much assisted in this as lent an ear, an eye, a heart. Now her stomach, deviously fragile given her robust-looking life, al-

ways upset by riding sidesaddle or any-saddle, begins to return
to normal. She is not that strong, she knows, what with her
eyes, womb—no, there is nothing else save the acid swilling
about in her stomach. Not because she wants the dish, but because she associates it with conventional everyday conduct,
she asks for an unusual lunch: ham and eggs, a dish often favored at Hindlip because the makings are always fresh. Gradually, overpowering the reek of cauliflower, the bouquet of
roast beef, the companionable wide-awake aroma of ham and
eggs bubbling in hot lard ascends the stairs and seeps through
the structure, reaching Henry Garnet and actually bringing a
tear to his eye; why, this is the most exquisite torture, he feels,
and surely Anne could stop it. Who on earth—no, he stops. It
is no use getting into a swivet about a wrongly-timed breakfast he would give his folding leather altar to devour. The
smell will endure for at least a day; no windows open in November. Over the decades, the house has brilliantly captured
and fused its own smells, like a prisoner inhaling himself, until there is always a fused aroma—faint smoky oversweet straw-
berry infused with an acrid spume of boiling vinegar—that
serves as background to the smells of the moment. Against
both delight and abomination, Henry Garnet decides to hold
his breath, but he can do so only in upsetting spasms, and he
soon gives up, rhapsodic and revulsed all at once.

Anyone with any appreciation for coincidence, as may have
developed after reading a great deal of Dickens, will wish Father
Garnet never to have arrived, instead circling with Anne Vaux
in some nondescript, drab field until the end of time. By the
same token, one does not want to have Sir Henry Bromley arriving within half an hour of Garnet's reaching Hindlip. As

zealots go, Bromley is fairly civilized, although his coming coincides with break of day; Henry Garnet's feeling that it is already lunchtime shows how exercised his mind has become (he's ahead of himself, as almost never), while Anne Vaux's craving for the ritual of ham and egg reveals her attunement to a daily round, a regimen that both pleases and steadies. Amid the panic of their confusion, no one is saluting the dawn except the kitchen staff, who time their work by daylight, and need only to be consulted once about, well, not so much the time as the phase of the day. Sir Henry Bromley is too eager, having risen well before four in the morning to get his posse on the road.

So here they are, a motley team, some adorned in butcher's smocks with a big tool pouch in front containing awls and spikes, boring-tools of all kinds, and little listening tubes with funnel ends. Some of them have teak mallets with which to tap on hollow-looking panels. They also have with them kindling to test the chimneys with, knowing full well that a lit fire in a fake chimney soon proves the case. Hargreaves is among them, but dragging a leg, he too from a fall on ice, but this time he kowtows to Sir Henry, who can make or break him depending on the skill with which he exposes the priests. They do not even recall who tipped them off about priests at Hindlip, but the word is out; perhaps it has always been out, as there has almost never been a time when priests were not at Hindlip. The rumor and the event match each other, but to no advantage for the poursuivants, who have found no one at all during their previous searches. As it happens, Thomas Habington is not at home when the inquisitorial rabble arrive at the main door, but his return prompts some lively exchanges between Bromley and himself.

"Do not brandish your proclamation, man," he bellows at Bromley. He speaks as a man who has already been in the Tower once. "I take your word for it. I will gladly die at my own front gate if you find any priests in here. Lurking under my roof! You will as soon find fish folded in among the tablecloths. We are who we are, Sir Henry." His vehemence cuts no ice; Bromley has seen it all before, the bluster and the indignation— he would cavort in the same fashion if *he* were hiding Jesuits. It goes with the suit, and Habington is not a "bad" man, just a misguided rebel with a taste for punishment, hence his impassioned cry about dying at his front door. There is no need for emotion, Bromley knows; either the priests are here or they are not, and he does not intend to go until the house has been ransacked, and indeed made to pay. It will take three days, he estimates, with his men rampaging around upstairs and downstairs, ignoring the protests of the Habington family and enigmatic visitors such as Mrs Perkins, whom he has met before. The grinding, drilling, boring, go on all day, with naps taken in the big public rooms, nothing provided by way of food, but the kitchen already raided so much the staff feel demented, unable to function according to the strict rules of the house. That they mean to spend the night appalls Anne Vaux, who detects in their behavior a new resolve: gone are the days of the lazy, casual gentlemanly search; this is the work of plebeians eager for profit, and she works on her disdain, doing her best with stare and sniff to embarrass those who seem intent on taking the house apart.

"I actually turned people away," Habington is telling them, then as he thinks better of it (priests, plotters; who else?) "old friends who wanted to stay the night. I have a wife with child,

I am far too busy for visitors. That includes you all."

"Quite so," Bromley says, himself doing nothing in the way of search; his servants do that for him. "I am not accusing you of being inhospitable, sir, or of uxorial coarseness. Oh no. I await only the conclusion of this business and will be happy to acquit you of any charges if we find nothing amiss. We have to be thorough, though, as your pig-scraper does, and your steeplejack. We cannot afford to skimp matters, sir. The national safety is at stake. As my father always said—"

But no one listens; he has been here before, with the same quotations, although a smaller crew. They intend to spend the night, sprawled anywhere soft, belching and grunting, drinking and quarreling, seeking the temporary oblivion the laborer needs from his hire. At such a time, Anne thinks, we might actually let the priests out, for a stretch and a snack, but there are so many of them there is bound to be a mistake. Little does she know it, but Bromley, an organized mind in an untidy life, has insisted that at least one man remain on guard on each floor, although how far any watchman can be trusted not to fall asleep he cannot know. If the priests make a move, he knows it will be by night. He resolves to stay awake until dawn, but realizes he has been on the go since today's, and readily exempts himself. Does he hope to find a priest or merely achieve the most thorough fruitless search in the world? This Habington, he muses, is a rather rash person, but manly in bearing and, if a liar, one with plausible good manners. My sister lies in the same fashion. Yet I do not worry about her: her lies are between her and God Almighty. Some of us in the highest power blow both ways: we are not without sympathy, but work is work is duty. Will I ever have to rope my sister in, merely for being a

Catholic? Never, so what's all the fuss about? If you strip away the varnish of religion, life is the same for all of us. If I were God, would I want to be prayed to? No, I would want to be left alone, lost in the lap of memory.

Even on the first day, through diligence and willingness to deface the house's interior, the poursuivants have found a grist for their mill: three simulated chimneys with planks soot-blackened to resemble the bricks, and cavities, chambers, full of trinkets and trumpery (as they say) ranging from books to rosaries, vases and chalices and huge thick candles. "I am a collector," Habington raves, "I am entitled to put my things where I want. Nothing *has* to be on view." What are these? They produce the title deeds concerning the estate, opening them up and riffling the pages amid their pink ribbons. "Are you telling me," he insists, "I have no right to put important papers in a safe place? Don't *you?* What does this signify? I am a landowner, I do not want people wiping their boots on legal papers, or peering at them to see how much I am worth." Then they inform him that, in the brickwork of the gallery surmounting the gate, they have found two spaces, each large enough for a man. Why so many open cubbyholes? He tells them in his protracted huff that all country houses have such facilties, in which to store unwanted books, vases, hunting boots– "You know, Sir Henry," he says with his most produced voice, coming on strong, "the sorts of things you don't want to part with, but cannot stand to have under your feet. Any woman will tell you that. After all, dear sir, you found nobody in these places. There *is* nobody, as I said. I dare say, if you and the loyal Hargreaves wish to stay the night, as all the signs indicate, we can surely find so-called priestholes for you, in which you will feel so uncomfortable that you will just as soon recognise that they were never intended for human occupation. They are for storage, but you are welcome to try. A severe lesson cannot be more certainly learned."

"I respect your ardor, sir," Bromley tells him, "but you must understand we will be here as long as necessary. Hargreaves will keep an eye on the house all night."

"No, Sir Henry, *I* will."

"Not the need, sir. Take your rest. I will take mine."

"Not in a priesthole, then. We do have rooms adjudged suitable for a gentleman."

"A sit-up sleep," Sir Henry tells him. "Taught me by my father." He is still pondering Habington's riposte about a country house's being so vast that you forget what you have, that you do not memorize a house by its cavities, whatever their purpose might be.

So: Anne Vaux ordered and got her ham and eggs just in time and so feels nourished for a fray in which she plays little part, now thinking of herself as merely a mouth, a tongue, likely to give evidence by accident. She keeps quiet, out of the way, wondering if music by Byrd might serve to lull the searchers, making them skimp and miss. Little John Evans, still out in the birdhouse in the pond, has done good work here, although perhaps not the best of his optical illusions. In one recently modified house he created a painting of a door opening on another door: three-dimensional until you get up close, just the sort of thing to suck in and confound a Hargreaves, but he has not done this everywhere. Another lifetime would help, she thinks. If only he had started work ten years earlier. Off she treads, out of the house, chunk of suet in hand to fasten to the side of the birdhouse in which he roosts—the side facing away from the house. It will be better than nothing, whereas cheese would alert their suspicions. All Nicholas Evans has to do is somehow help himself and try to keep the suet down. It is like wartime here, she decides, with troops garrisoned all over the house. Isn't this how they treat Jews in Europe? I am better doing this by day, in the open; they would wonder why I was doing it at night. If they keep watch, and they will. If Henry Garnet, who hurt his knee, cannot stand being cooped up, what are we to do?

In the blistering, gusty cold of that night, Wednesday leaking into Thursday, Nicholas Owen, who has been outside since Monday, cranks his almost petrified broken body out of the birdhouse, lifting it up and off him, and creeps into Hindlip through an entrance only he knows, thence into a hiding place known to most of them as Curly because it does not lie straight; and whoever is in it—in this case the lay brother Ralph Ashley also there since Monday—can only lie curved. There is little room for two, but they wordlessly share the apple Ralph Ashley has been saving for three days. It as cold in the house as it is outside, and Little John feels he has exchanged death for something worse. Ashley's body gives off no warmth. What they do next is rash, but they both feel dizzy, weak, can hardly move their legs. The kitchen tempts, the open road next. As Little John sees it, he is bound to be discovered if the searchers occupy the house long enough. Wordlessly they decide to move out, through the wainscot into a gallery. The house is still and only faintly lit. If someone catches them, they will give themselves up; perhaps the poursuivants will be satisfied with what they say, mistaken as to who they are. Out they slip, one foot caressing the other before going farther, but the house becomes an uproar; Hargreaves, on his third patrol of the night, wandering into the gallery out of boredom with no expectations at all, catches sight of two shady figures tip-toeing their way into the hall and communicating with each other in dumbshow. In a second, they have been surrounded and pinioned while Sir Henry, half asleep and blustering, to compensate for his bleariness, asks them who they are. Just servants, they answer, unable to sleep. But sleepless servants, he comments with a sniffle, do not wander through the main house at night like invited guests. Who are you? Are you Tesimond and Oldcorne, Greenway and Hall? He is wide of the mark, of course, but convinced he has caught someone, though not of high station (he knows the smell of a servant when he sniffs one, and the whiff coming off them is quite different). Rather than interrogate them, he sends them off to his headquarters, and occupies himself with the expectant mother, Mary Habington, sister to Monteagle, the savior of the hour.

"No fear, Sir Henry," she shrills, "not unless you carry me out yourself. I am staying here, where I belong. How dare you?"

Clearly he has no business trying to lug around someone so well-born and well connected; he makes no attempt to remove Anne Vaux, whose sharpened glare upsets him, so he retires again and writes a report to Cecil, waffling away about the devious ways of Catholics, hosts, country gentlemen, ladies of the house, and just about everybody not on his side. He will not sleep this night - nor will he hit on the truth - he is so eager to present himself in a good light as the finder, the exposer. Restrained enough in speech, he tends to hyperbole at the merest feeling of self-esteem, informing Cecil that "Of all the various scheming and trunculent priests, those Jesuwits, I have two of the vilest in hand, for prompt sending to you, sire, and your diligent punitations. I have one or two misgivings about who these people are, for they will not say, but truth told they have, without any airs or graces as of high-born gentleman, that bloated humbleness we all recognize as bombast in reverse. We, who have not been educated for nothing, need yield no quarter to the Roman-suckled rabble of high priests. At your service always, with intaminate pride." He can go on in this vein for hours, sufficiently launched with writing materials, like someone taking to water for the first time and hitting on the correct stroke, even were he swimming in pitch. He calls off the search, explores his conscience, wishes he had not been so swift in sending them up to London, then renews the ransacking of the house into Friday, Saturday, and Sunday, deeply conscious of interrupting a religious timetable that no one dares mention. From memory, in her diary, Anne Vaux writes as follows:

> *We have here again, for the seventh day, the same behaviours as before at Baddesley-Clinton, which I fiercely complained of, though this house be none of mine and therefore not subject to mine own remonstrances. Suffice to say, these poursuivants behave like a pack of bad boys playing Blind Man's Buff, who in their wild rush, bang into tables and chairs and walls and yet have not the slightest suspicion that their playfellows, God save them, are right on top of them and almost touching them.*

She reads this through, crosses it all out as dangerous, then tears it out, looking exasperatedly at the diary, flicks through some pages, wraps the whole thing in a fold of wall paper she picks from a minty-smelling closet, and bears the whole thing downstairs to the roaring fire, unseen in the whole endeavor, although one glimpse of her ferrying something perilous to read would have had them snapping at her heels. She realizes she is not living prudently: the constant hammering has unnerved her, given her a headache that reaches down the back of her neck into her shoulders; and the egg-and-ham breakfast seems to lie there and haunt her still, and she now agonizes at having put Fathers Garnet and Oldcorne through the miseries of aroma. Indeed, nothing she does helps them. They are not in the lower chamber that sits below the dining room, where it is possible to pass food down to them as if they were plaintive dogs behaving well at their masters' feet. They do not even have an apple between them. She stews about Little John and Ralph Ashley, seized and sent away incognito, and knows there has come an end to hideaway-building. Further torture inflicted on Nicholas Owen will kill him certainly, and the whole recusant scheme will perish. It would be one thing if the searchers, having found their prey, were gone, satisfied; but here they are still, racketing about, so much so that she twitches at every tap or rattle, every creak of the house as it settles into winter repose. She recalls having noticed in herself and others a curious habit of completing a watched motion, when someone, bracing to move an arm or a leg, curtails the movement and the intent watcher goes through with it, for the moment identified into union with the person watched. This is how she feels about the two priests in their hole, sensing all the movements they dare not make and accomplishing them by guesswork. Will it always be thus? No, she knows, it is going to be much worse. The poursuivants, having found two, want two more, yelping and scattering, heedless of a house routine destroyed. Brave Mary

Habington has refused to leave, but she finds their presence vile in the extreme; and all she can do is maintain a cool austere demeanor while her husband orates incessantly about an Englishman's home being his castle. Was he the originator of that saw? Well, castle no more, my loves, the rabble has entered its final playground and will not be contained by any code of decent manners. Sir Henry is already at odds with himself, she notes, for having not interrogated Owen and Ashley himself; whatever they said would be gold.

"The trouble is, my lady," Sir Henry is saying to her, "the moiety of this rabble we have here has not enough proper English to get someone to draw down their trews for the jakes, if you will pardon the reference. I am among apes."

"We are both, *all*, among apes, sir."

"Hence the high degree of choler among us."

He needs no agreement, she can see that; he is accustomed to silent assent while he roams in hit-or-miss meditation, hoping for a coup that will raise him even higher in Cecil's esteem. In truth he finds Worcester a bore and would love to move to London, at an advantage of course. In Worcester jail at this very moment, to save his life or at least delay his execution, Humphrey Littleton is telling all: he will tell who the Jesuits were who talked him into becoming a plotter. Why, Father Hall (Oldcorne, he explains) is almost certainly hidden away in Hindlip at this moment, "at this present," and easily flushed out. Hall's, Oldcorne's, servant happens to be in Worcester jail, and he will know all. Show him the rack. The manacles. Littleton is getting carried away with vicarious cruelty. "After all," he adds, "Oldcorne said the plot was a good thing and long overdue. *Commendable* was his word." The Sheriff of Worcester at once stays his execution to see what else this tap of a man might yield. After the top layer, there are many others, with truth at the bottom, tiny and glistening: a corm of fact.

In fact, Oldcorne had compared the plot to a pilgrimage made by Louis XI of France, in the course of which the plague erupted twice, wiping out most of his retainers the first time, and killing Louis himself the next. His enemies came through unscathed. So much, Oldcorne said, for excursions organised by St Bernard of Clairvaux. Someone flinched at the second-syllable name in Clairvaux, but no one spoke. "The principal thing," Father Oldcorne had said, "was what the expedition was for and how it was conducted. Many failures are honorable, and can only be judged by the moral good they bring about." Father Oldcorne still does not know what Catesby was trying to do. "It is between him and his God. Of course. I am against all reckless violence, sir." How easily, though, his words could be twisted into treason and treachery; between the inability to reveal what was said in confession and a general ignorance of the plot's aims, all priests were both unable to defend themselves and guilty to begin with.

To swell the general clamor, Mary Habington has her servants begin cleaning the household silver, tons of it all dun and gray from disuse, and suddenly Sir Henry feels at home in the presence of a familiar ritual, as if in readiness for some social event, a banquet, say, and his mind saunters away from his reasons for being here and starts to dream of banquets, balls, near-orgies he himself has held. Oldcorne and Garnet watch one another talk and listen to one another eat. The acrid tang of silver polish rises upstairs to the nostrils of Father Garnet, as he gags and tries not to cough. He has been here since January 21. It is now Monday January 27, what feels like years since

Monteagle revealed the plot. He thinks he is going to faint as someone outside begins to hammer and grind. Surely this will be the ultimate discovery. He has no idea of what has happened to Nicholas Owen and Ralph Ashley, and he wonders if Anne has stayed on at Hindlip, convinces himself she has not. If not here, then, who has been sustaining them with warm broth sent through a long reed coming through the chimney? Was it not she who plied them with caudle, a food for invalids, succulent and sharp? Marmalade and candy they have provided for themselves, but that is all, and with the house in a state of perpetual siege from within there has been no chance of anyone's doing better. Their past week has been an elegy for egg and bacon, the aroma now overpowered by the reek of silver polish, the high acid content rising above everything else to tickle and scald the noses of those nearest.

"Well," says Garnet to Oldcorne, "shall we? I am choking, Edward."

"If we do, Henry, there will be no turning back. You well know how they proceed."

"Eternity in a byre," says Father Garnet. "Is this a perpetual penalty or have we earned our keep?"

"Our keep has always been free."

"Just so. Do we brave them, then?"

"Another day."

"My gorge rises at the thought."

"Mine too. Shall we stay?"

"Shall we go out together?"

"To bathe and eat."

"To bathe and eat," Garnet echoes. Against their will, they take deep breaths and then have trouble uncoiling limbs. They impede each other, slithering out of that noxious narrow cupboard, Garnet coming out headfirst, his grievously swollen legs dragging behind him. He is an old lizard, that ungainly. Oldcorne follows and, for a moment, they lie side by side in the open, the old position, gasping, and weeping tears of supreme effort mingled with self-disgust. "Were you ever in the one at Sawston," Garnet whispers. "I was," comes answer. "I know why you ask. There's an earth closet there."

"Just so," says Henry Garnet, feeling like an incontinent schoolboy who has messed his pants during Latin grammar and will soon be thrashed, given a good hiding (he winces) once he has been scrubbed. "With one of those closed-stools," he murmurs, only inches from the stone floor, "we could have endured another three months. If we had only been able to get outside for an hour every so often, we could have set ourselves up in there for life, with a folding altar and everything." He feels cheated: a brilliant idea has died at the hands of crass matter. "Oh to stand," he sighs.

"Or to stretch," Oldcorne adds, rising to the kneel.

They both have a look of stunned arthritis, unshaven and wan and shattered. They are the palest priests in or near Worcester, not as pale as Guido Fawkes, but victims nonetheless of stilled blood.

"Ho," says Sir Henry, "who *are* these stinking fellows?"

The team of poursuivants, briefly dipping face into the hole, recoil, heaving and gurgling, and then move away from the two priests who stand unsteadily, in barbaric isolation. Anne Vaux, horrified and weeping, keeps her distance, marveling that a mere week can reduce a human to such an abominable pass, as Sir Henry, sensing the situation requires a summary comment, says, "They have been undone by those customs of nature which must of necessity be done. Those little vital commoners

of the body keep us all in slavery to them, requiring that we ob-
sterge the podex, ladies and gentlemen. These wretched
prelates have squatted in there with the devil himself and he
has paid them back. Who do we have, then? Do you have
names or do you just make noises? Are you well enough to answer? Shall we wash you?" Anne Vaux volunteers, but it is a
motley crew of Hargreaves and some six searchers holding
their noses who escort the two priests to an alcove on the
ground floor, to which water can be brought, and clouts can be
thrown away as infested infected loathsomes. The water-
bringing servants squeal in horror and hasten to wash their
hands and faces. Anne Vaux knows now that the rationale of
the hiding place has another side she has never thought of. It
was folly to feed these men at all or to succor them with liquid.
A weeklong sleep, she decides, next time, like that—what is it,
the polar bear in somebody's play, when I was a civilized
woman living a social life? Under the sign of the glazed bear?—
usually she will ask Father Garnet and he would know, but not
today. What does it mean? The forming of the ice? Ah, now I
remember, 'tis the snowy Bear! Her mind has eased itself a little, unable to hear any more about customs of nature, which, to
be honest about it, nauseate her at the best of times, not per se
but because the facilities impress her as primitive and gross:
wood-ash and earth shoveled on the mire of the day. Pico della
Mirandola, she recalls, says we stand in it to clutch at heaven.
Pico was right. Now they are cleaner, Sir Henry is urging them
along, he wants them in Worcester, but he seems oddly benign
in his treatment of them. Perhaps he likes priests.

Sir Henry Bromley can hardly believe his luck, but he begins to lose faith in it when he questions Father Garnet. Father Oldcorne, alias Hall, he has no trouble identifying: a man

with only one alias naturally has fewer hypocrites among his friends, but someone such as Garnet, alias at least half a dozen other men, has been brilliantly dispersed and camouflaged. Certainly this emaciated, worn, shuddering person is not Mister Perkins, nor is he any kind of whoremaster or manual laborer (Bromley examines his almost silky palms).

"Are you a priest, sir?"

"I cannot lie before God."

"Well?"

"I am a colleague of this gentleman."

"Have you been rash enough ever to submit to a name, a single name?"

Father Garnet identifies himself in a listless monotone; Anne, eavesdropping behind a door, has never heard him sound so depleted, so dreary. Now she begins to understand the impact of hiding month after month in abysmal quarters unfit for animals. She would like to start over and install him from the first in a luxurious apartment like the one they envisioned having in Rome: a room full of sunlight sheathed in gold satin. How reckless of me, she thinks. Now they know who he is, and what: quite a catch. They are bound to let him go as guiltless. Look what brought him to this. She does a dry sob, blaming herself for making of him a constant fugitive.

16

S IR HENRY BROMLEY'S offhand civility belies the mind-
    set of Worcester's Sheriff, intent on executions; Garnet
    and Oldcorne come staggering out of hiding on Monday
27 January, a couple of tottering ghosts ready to be dismissed
with a wave of the hand, but England is agog with capture and
torture, sentences of death, and prolonged executions. Fathers
Garnet and Oldcorne may not know it, but the population especially in London and such centres as Worcester is getting
ready for some ghoulish entertainment. Off go the two Jesuits
to Sir Henry's home, Holt Castle, there to mend while Cecil
makes up his mind what to do with them. To Anne, Garnet,
who has been a week away in hiding, is now away in a more
grievous sense, yet neither bound nor shackled, nor cooped up
in any kind of castle dungeon. Rather, he is being treated as a
professional gentleman down on his luck, awaiting perhaps an
astrologer to guide him, not the interrogator or the headsman.
From his treatment, no one would ever surmise that the procla-
mations brandished by the Henry Bromleys of the world an-
nounce the Jesuits as leaders and authors of the plot. It is as if
Sir Henry does not believe it, can hardly credit these two mild
and emaciated gentlemen with anything so vile. His orders are

to keep them both "strait," as he informs them, apologizing beforehand. His hypothesis remains abstract, that gentlemen dealing with gentlemen can please themselves, never mind their religious persuasion, and Bromley, quite at ease with a Catholic sister, is quite willing to apply this for these gentlemen's liking. Nothing is forced on them but food; indeed, he singles out Father Garnet as "a learned man and a worthy priest," and never mind the aliases, the notorious relationship with "Mrs Perkins," the general clamor in the land for the blood of Roman infidels. Sir Henry is going to preserve his gentlemanly demeanor, even his bumbling sense of honor, despite his slips in English. To him, Father Garnet is a find, a treasure, to be peered at and talked with. He even plans to have this novelty, his own resident chaplain, celebrate for him and his family the feast of Candlemas, the last feast of the Christian calendar before the onset of Lent, using a piece of booty from Hindlip: a huge wax candle with "Jesu" and "Maria" imprinted on its flanks. Clearly, Sir Henry is taking advantage of what is on hand, but the ambiguity of his position—jailer, celebrant—merely foreshadows the double-minded treatment in store for Father Garnet elsewhere, even in the most unlikely places. He is so likeable, so modest, so dignified, they can hardly conceive of him as a plotter; instead, he casts a religious shadow over them all, and many a regret goes unvoiced as this mellow, civil man goes along with a whole series of indignities intended for such troublemakers as Fawkes, Catesby, and the Wintours. It is not as if Bromley were some pagan Assyrian or Hun: as a practicing Christian he feels a certain sympathy for someone from the other, rival sect, showing a freemasonry of belief. What a rare gift, Father Garnet thinks, giving me hope even now that we are never that far apart, as with my dear friend Byrd, to whom the strife of contending factions is a merely a breeze disturbing his hair. This Bromley is worth talking with; I see what drives him and incites him to think both ways. After all, the test of a gentleman, the double test, is never to be surprised by anything (a sophisticate finds all familiar), and always to be able to balance opposing ideas without betraying either. We shall no doubt see, when his orders arrive from London, how far he is going to resist them; perhaps all this kindness is a covert effort to make me babble away out of sheer relief, perfecting my taste for sherris-sack, increasing my addiction to trifle, my love of a cold chicken bone to gnaw upon. This is not the terminus, this castle near Worcester, though I do hear that some will end their days here to enliven the local populace. If I am regarded as big meat, then so be it; the Jesuit's role in this benighted country was cut out for him long ago, and his life becomes a mere act. He has the oddest feeling that life as a priest with Bromley in this castle is no different really than with Anne Vaux in her country house, is perhaps what he was born to, the ideal locus of his most pious endeavors.

Now comes Cecil's usual dawdling order (he conducts the brutal affairs of the land as if attending a card-game late): Father Garnet, no matter how parlous the state of his legs, is to go to London, after Father Oldcorne (who, however, belongs more to Worcester than to London and will eventually return), given the finest mount on Cecil's express orders (Father Garnet, while grateful, groans at the prospect of more riding), and furnished the best hospitality that life on the road can offer (the king's command). So: he is to be treated as a celebrated person, not some guttersnipe plucked from the ranks who messes with underground gunpowder, like Fawkes, but a man of the world, a paragon of intellect accustomed to the best of life. He smiles at this preposterousness, whatever its aim; determined to find something wrong, just to see what will happen when he complains, he wonders which books he needs, which little luxuries. He writes a careful hand in his letters to Anne (all of which will go to Cecil, of course). They are trying to make him relax, he sees that, and relaxed he is supposed to be off his guard; indeed, he is right, there begins much fuss to find a Puritan clergyman to ride with them to London and pepper him with awkward questions about the line between king and Pope.

First, though, he has to recover somewhat from his ordeal at Hindlip, which he now for the rest of his days associates with ham and eggs frying and the tang of silver polish, the airy fusion of the two a sweet succulent pink burning smell. To an extent he is marooned in the past, and always will be; deprived of his Anne so many times in the past few years, he finds himself deprived again, compelled through some echo of the old Socratic *elenchus* to see his life as a blank with an open end through which he will slither away, his work undone, his career interrupted, his every effort travestied. I chose to become who I am, he thinks, but I have been perpetually compelled to do other things I never had in mind, as if a career in the waterfall of thought were insufficient. Now they attend the holy candle, inscribed, of enormous girth, drinking the health of King James with heads bared, as in some ironical scene from Chaucer. What he would like from life, unless it is too late, is to work hard amassing learned editions of classical texts so that the entire corpus of them may be said to have transcended him, and he in their midst only as a copyist. Yes, they should say, his legs grew weaker and weaker, not least from all that confinement in Curly and the Hindlip hole called Twist Up, but his heart grew firm. He kept saying that, if a man is to

be condemned for what he has listened to, then the only innocent men left will be those who have never heard anything.
Yes, he acknowledges, old Twist Up did me in, or rather Twist
Up on top of riding from one country house to another, trying
to go slower than you can. Now, when I go to sleep, the muscles in my calves rebel and put me through a sudden little
seizure, a hot wire running up the back of my leg, with strange
convulsions in the ankle when I tilt the foot down at a painful
angle. I am told the cure is to get up and stand on a cold floor,
which these houses and castles abound in. Surely they might
have sent a carriage for me; if I am worth a horse, easily as
good as one of Rookwood's best, then I merit something with
wheels rather then hooves. I love the modern.

As they ride toward London, through Oxford and High
Wycombe, a journey of some hundred and twenty miles, taking twenty-four hours (Father Garnet slows them down), the
Puritan minister snipes away at him, quizzing him on points
of doctrine he at first answers in Latin, getting ruder and
ruder as only a disciplined Jesuit can.

"This is not worthy of my time, sir," he tells Bromley, the
ever-courteous. "Need I answer at all?"

"I tell you what, noble sir. I will preside and let you both
speak. But, if I know my man, he will keep raving away and
you need only listen or shut him out."

When the Puritan finishes his harangue (easily half an
hour's riding), Father Garnet, stimulated by the discomfort of
the ride, puts him in his place, saying, "Obedience is the
purest thing; there is nothing purer, for it implies the total surrender of the human to the Divine, and leaves nothing for
the will to do. As is evidenced with microcosms: there is the
ever-present problem of all the other microcosms coming into

being even as you devise your own, the result being that one's is always out of date, and the only microcosm that seems accurate is prophetic, proleptic, in other words an anticipation, for a second, of what does not yet exist as, through the ceaseless play of human minds on the texture of being, all the other microcosms, themselves trying to allude to all other microcosms, try to come into being. It cannot happen. There is no way, short of the imperfectly metaphorical, of creating an adequate model of the universe.

"You can always tell when a civilization is running down," Father Garnet tells Sir Henry, ignoring the Puritan cleric for the moment, "when its theological conversations take place on horseback. They are getting their blood sports mixed up. I am glad this amuses you. Not everything in the past few months has amused *me,* such as the misuse of the word *prevaricate,* whose true import is when a man or a woman remains in touch with two opposing points of view."

"Don't you mean lying?"

"No, I don't," Father Garnet tells him. "I mean something much more complicated. The double dealer, if you wish. I bring to mind the deponent, *praevaricor,* to walk crookedly."

"Ah, *praevaricor!*" Bromley exclaims. "How I have missed it these past twenty years."

"Ah, so you know, Sir Henry, the fascination of words has never left you?"

It never did, he says, wishing he had never heard of Latin. This old boy, like the Puritan, doesn't know when to stop.

"Cicero has most to say about it," the old boy is saying, his Winchester days not that far off. "And he used it most, so it makes sense that he would have more theories about it than anyone else. Are you listening, sir?"

Oh yes he is.

"A dangerous occupation in this country," Father Garnet whispers out of the Puritan's earshot.

"If there's one thing I respect," Bromley says, "it's eradition, I do go in awe of you fellows who have read all the books and can talk to we groundlings about it."

This charitable oaf, Father Garnet thinks, is conveying me to my doom, or at least an uncomfortable inquiry. If they will only conduct it in my kind of English, they will find out nothing at all. Look at his ears, they'd say, see what has passed through them! Nothing to convict him on at all.

"Here we are, sir," Bromley is saying, "yonder the gate. I have a word for you. Watch out for Cecil, Coke, and Popham, and their clever punatations, they will trap you soon as look at you, and in front of venible witnesses. God save you, Father Garnet, sir, it has been an honor to know such a fine Christian scholar. There's many, I trow, as have never met so illustrious a gentleman in holy orders. God speed you, Father Garnet. I am for you, sir, I do not like to part from anyone so eloquent, not being much of pettigogue myself. We may not meet again, but if we do you will bless us, I trust."

"God speed you, Sir Henry, in all your endeavors." Father Garnet espies the gate at which a crowd has assembled at the mention of his name; this is the Gatehouse Jail in Westminster, and the Superior of the Jesuits has just arrived, not to be fêted but to be quizzed. Looking at the expectant faces, nay voracious ones. tilted up at him as he rides in, courteously dismounted (his gaze lowers as he descends breathing hard), he tries to bellow, not his style at all, and what comes out is a sturdy tenor voice accustomed to song—ànyone can tell that: "Are any of you assembled here of the Catholic faith?" Many are, it seems. "Then," he chants on, "God help you all! I am here to keep you company for the same cause. We are together in God, and may He succour us." One man cries out "Don't you know me, Uncle?" This is his nephew, Thomas, yet another priest formerly working under an alias, now swept up into the king's net. Father Garnet hails him, bows, opens his arms wide to receive his nephew along with a shoal of other fishes.

So it is here we have come home, he thinks. This is yet another form of church. From here, truth told, you can purchase just about anything by brandishing money through the bars of the window. Mass gets said without excessive supervision. I foresee a month of letters and messages from Anne, and vice versa, thieves and prostitutes milling about without and within in order to practice their trade. Yet this is not the famous eponymous Clink (jails are the clink in ruffians' language) of Southwark, but there is hope of entering that too, where, it is said, Catholics abound. Father Gerard confessed many while incarcerated there, which is usual. You function as if nothing has changed, whether in the Gatehouse, the Clink or bad old Newdigate itself. All meets God's eye, He the supreme listener, to whom all obedience is due. It is from Him we get our bodies back in the fullness of time. Is this a pigsty? Why, the whole of human life is a pigsty, whether sullied by Cecils or not.

What he soon learns is what he has shrunk from knowing. Only a few days ago, eight executions took place, four at the western end of St Paul's churchyard (Digby, Robert Wintour, Thomas Grant, and one Bates), the others not far from here in the Old Palace Yard of Westminster (Thomas Wintour, Rookwood, Keyes, and Guido Fawkes). So, they are cleaning house already, Garnet notes with prickling aversion. A short way of dealing with dissenters. Who comes next? The jail is agog with news, and many a minor recusant fears for his life. Are they going to make a clean sweep and slaughter everybody, getting so carried away with the frenzy of it all they even hang a few of the innocent as well? What if Popham in his frenzy (hatred, working on a choleric disposition) gets Coke to help him hang the king? Oh, what an answer to prayer that might be. The lethal three, Cecil and Coke and Popham (the king making up an even deadlier quartet) remain remote from the jails, but not from the trials, whose tours de force they are, Cecil tending to watch and listen from behind a screen, sometimes with James himself. The main thing, Garnet gathers, is being shown off after being questioned and tortured. Father Garnet thinks of Father Walpole, tortured so badly he no longer functions even as a letter-writer, and yet to what point? As he sees it, without fathoming it, torture is merely a gratuitous exercise in power, in its application and increased use. What is going on? When most of the inner circle of plotters is already dead, what can a Cecil do? Hang the rest, most of them, apart from Fawkes, minor characters? Only the Jesuits remain, and this reminds him to ask if Father Oldcorne is here in the Gatehouse, gashing his tongue with a nail long before they hang it up for him from an even longer one. Did he see him? He's not sure, and Oldcorne is indeed here, worrying, cursing, wondering what to do with his unspent political zeal. Father Garnet has known for some time that people with cancer do not shrink from monstrosities of human behavior, as if the monster within saps all teratology without. Father Oldcorne remains unshockable, just possibly having inflicted upon himself worse horrors than Cecil's crew will ever descend to. But is he here? Prisoners are fairly free to move about, Garnet finds, so he spends an hour searching and asking, and eventually discovers Oldcorne looking for him, as at a reunion by the sea in Terracina, with a warm breeze wafting the pennant flags. Oh to be—Father Garnet halts all reverie; it will unman him in this place. He still has not quite become used to the idea of being a prisoner in a jail, he the Superior Jesuit, brought down to the level of common thieves—for having listened and not blabbed. The Gatehouse doesn't square with Bromley's treatment. Did he abstain from his orders to keep him "strait"? And all that cordial treatment as if indeed he were the scholar he is. Pampered on horseback and at every inn between Worcester and London, how can he adjust to this, and why, once again, is he free to roam about, as if the entire seizure of his person were a game? This must be yet another of Cecil's greasy overtures designed to seduce him into convicting himself: make him feel at ease, unthreatened, then confront him with a copyist's notepad of all he has said. Father Garnet shrinks from anticipating the rest, but he yearns for Anne Vaux, for the cool compress of her almost truculent mind. And what of Little John Evans, whose huge dropsical jowls suggest that the marrow in his face has been allowed to fall into his neck, leaving behind the merest doily of facial structure, there only to taunt and beguile? Who would mistake him for anyone else? He cannot be here; indeed, he is in the Tower, being stretched even as Father Garnet thinks of him and his trapdoors, birdhouses, hoping Owen does not blame himself for the disgusting Hindlip fiasco when two men unable to contain themselves any longer burst out into the soggy daylight and a free ride to London. Father Garnet does not know that, at the trial of the hanged eight, the indictment read aloud began with the names and aliases of three Jesuits—Garnet, Tesimond, and Gerard—described as traitors all. Among all the names read out, including the four already dead from the shoot-out in the Midlands (Catesby, Percy, the two Wrights), only one headed a separate bill of indictment: Digby, because Sir Everard, dapper and debonair and clearly of ravenous conscience, decided to plead guilty, profoundly ashamed of having been caught in the wrong.

First, though, the Sergeant-at-Law, Sir Edward Phillips, stands to denounce the very concept of plotting: "The tongue of man never delivered, the ear of man never heard, the heart of man never conceived—" his pacing is predictable, his choice of words almost so—"or the malice of hellish or earthly devil ever practised such loathsome, traitorous intentions." On he treads, with his voice magnifying the stupefying obviousness of his preamble, contending how it is "abominable to murder the least of God's creatures; so how much more abominable to murder such a king, such a queen, such a progeny, such a State, such a government, such an august assembly of statesmen and peers . . ." On hearing him, a malicious listener wants to invest at once in gunpowder: such saltpeter, such charcoal, such sulfur, extolling explosion as an art form, a swansong from the elements. Sir Edward Phillips has not had the advantages bestowed on Coke and Cecil, so he lumbers around in the English language like an elephant in a granary, knowing he does not have to impress, only touch the right resonant indignant chord in his hearers, who have heard this speech from when they were in their cradles. Phillips bumps on.

As the hours go by, and Father Garnet becomes more or less accustomed to living in a ferment of gossip, the riff-raff in the Gatehouse try to reassure him by saying the Gatehouse is only a minor prison for minor criminals. He is not to worry. You only worry when they ship you off to the Tower for the rack. He does not know how to take this pawnbroking reassurance, which comes also from some of the more substantial personages penned up here, such as his nephew, Thomas. You fellows, he tells them, don't know you're born; you have all kinds of privileges, you can walk about, shout through the window, undertake all manner of commerce, and you have affable company. He recommends to them that open secret, the hiding place, where you begin to hate your own body and even your companion if you are lucky or unlucky enough to have one.

Anne Vaux is already in London, presently with Habington's sister Dorothy, a Protestant turned Catholic. They settle into Dorothy's house in Fetter Lane, just off Fleet Street, actually finding the emotional composure to argue over the toss about Protestant males having to pay the fines for their Catholic spouses. Clearly the mistress of Hindlip has had enough, having her country home ransacked for a week by Bromley and his squad. Indeed, she has become so accustomed to incursions from that quarter she finds life without poursuivants rather slow. Anne Vaux, attentive as she is to Dorothy's concerns, has other worries, mainly the fate of Father Garnet, spirited away in a flurry of amiable good fellowship that must be the prelude to something more sinister. She hears news of Parliament, activity on a formal and abstruse level that interests her only marginally, with Catholics now divided up into three groups: "old, rooted, and rotten," which she imagines includes her; "novelists," meaning converts; and "futurists," meaning the young and most dangerous. Catholicism, she gathers, is going to be stamped out. The newly arrived Venetian ambassador is appalled. So is Anne Vaux, to whom word of recent executions comes as a nightmare fleshed out. Pieces of events have already begun to be mythic, like the final utterance of the good-looking man-about-town, Everard Digby, who, even with the executioner's hands in his entrails saves enough for a final shout. "Behold," cries the executioner to the mob after Digby has been partly hanged, "a traitor's heart!" He plucks it out and holds it up for all to see. Everyone is shocked when Digby can be heard saying, "Thou liest." Things such as this do not fortify her or endear London to her. This, she feels, is a terminal place, and she wishes with all her heart that Henry Garnet were back in his bolthole at Hindlip.

He will soon be able to tell what happened on February 13, the day of his journey to Whitehall to meet the Privy Council –Cecil, Coke, Popham, Waad, and certain lords (Worcester, Nottingham, Northampton, and others). En route, Father Garnet, somewhat astounded by the attention he is getting, hears one wag in the crowd say, "There goes a young Pope." He feels humiliatingly flattered, as he does also when the Councillors doff their hats when addressing him, treating him with a certain respect he has not anticipated, as if this encounter were a merely diplomatic run-through. Indeed, they are treating him as they would a foreign plenipotentiary, except they address him as Mister Garnet. The only snag comes when Cecil, at last unable to restrain himself, asks about a letter from Anne he has intercepted in which she signs herself, "Your loving sister, AG."

"What," he hears, "are you married to Mrs Vaux? She calls herself Garnet. Why, you slimy old lecher, what have you been up to? We always thought that Catholic priests were immune to the temptations of the flesh. Do you have a special dispensation? Is she comely, then?" To be accused thus affronts and sickens him, but at the next meeting Cecil sets an arm around his shoulders (the fatal arm) and apologizes, saying he only meant to tease; it was all "in jest." This is the contorted man who, on a little silver disc to be found upon his desk, is quietly building a tumulus, a tiny heap of the dirt he pares daily from beneath his nails, patting the little pile into a pyramid shape and wondering what he will do with it after ten years. At least, he consoles himself, his nails are clean. Garnet, more shocked by the jester than by the slanderer, freezes where he stands, wishing that encircling arm, which reaches only to his breast, far enough. It amounts to an emblem of possession, he thinks. Cecil is demonstrating for his cronies how completely he has this Jesuit under his control. It is no use the Councillors chiming in, taking their lead from Cecil, reassuring him that all is well, he is an exemplary priest. Just as all men need to fornicate, no matter with whom or what, they need to tease as well, as if the whole of life were no more than a jape, and the poor victims on the ladder, in St Paul's churchyard next to the Bishop of London's house, waiting to be dropped with the noose around their necks, were a Punch and Judy show. He has gathered that London jewelers do not polish stones, and here he is among the most rough-cut of men, flouncing around in fancy clothes and mocking his chastity. No good is going to come of this forced bonhomie, echoing as it does the antics of the good-natured Sir Henry Bromley, fat Hindlip candles and all. Banter amid the murder-

ing, he thinks, and I the next performer. He sees it now. First re-
vile the person you intend to destroy, especially if you have no
real evidence against him. If you wish to condemn some fellow
for listening, make him out to be a whoremaster and liar, a hypocrite and pervert. He has gathered, in his innocent, unworldly
way, that he is now supposed to have been the chief conspirator,
as could be expected from a Jesuit. It is a natural enough transi-
tion, from the vaunted celibacy of priests to the libel of fast living and whoring. What easier counterpoint than that? It requires no brains, says Cecil, but merely a good deal of repetition
until the crowd hears about it and races forward with the news
of his depravity. Well, he actually committed incest with his
pretend sister. You can hide fornication, committing incest, but
is it not worse than the other? What on earth do these priests do
in Italy, where they have free rein? It is claimed they use the "unfit orifice" in all relations. They have been through it all before
with Father Gerard, supposedly swyving Lady Mary Percy, and
Topcliffe the racker confronted him with this aberration in the
Tower: "It was you who stayed with the Earl of Northumberland's daughter. No doubt you lay in bed together." Gerard
shook with anger, but what a waste of temper; everyone knows
that these priests, going for so long against the ways of nature,
can hardly hold it in any longer and have to vent their saved-up
lusts. Who should be surprised, then, if they turn to the very
gentlewomen who tend them, turning them into baggages? So,
at the trial, Waad, lieutenant of the Tower, tells Garnet deri-
sively that, when he attended a christening in the Vaux family, it
was only to encounter one of his own offspring. "Surely you
were there at the infant's begetting!"

"Such a slander is unfit for this place of justice." Garnet can hardly speak for rage and disgust.

"Nay, sire, the baby had a shaven crown, just like a priest. Born with it."

"I implore you, sir, desist."

"I implore *you,* sir, to put *it* back into your habit."

"Not so big as a garden spigot, but tap enough for certain purposes," he hears amid the guffaws. "At a stretch, it would do duty for an ordinary man." He begins to see two levels of this attack, the one crude and lewd, the other related to it but different, being mainly aimed at Anne Vaux, a middle-aged spinster beyond reproach, as he sees her.

"In twenty years of ferrying yourself up and down the land of England, with this lady in tow, did you never, never, let so much as a hand stray, sir? What face!" They mean swank, showing-off. The Derbyshire word for the kind of man they have in mind is "swankpot." They are debasing and trivialising him at the same time. One of Digby's servants has attested to the couple's inseparability, little understanding that Garnet's only role apart from friend has been to be her spiritual adviser. She has been his daughter as much as his friend. What *she* has been is his patron, his coach. He will never dream of saying it, but she has been almost a Saint Clare to his Saint Francis: the whole partnership wholesome and selfless. Who are these Councillors to understand a relationship so finespun? If they wish to tease him with a hearty snigger, so be it, but there is no way in which they can change his life with Anne, much as they both at times might have wished things different. A piece of him chimes with them: he wishes, now, in view of all this, they had had something more vigorous and sharp, worth dying for.

17

THE MORE UNSAVORY his tortured imagination grows, knowing that everything about Anne has already met Cecil's gaze, he begins to worry about a classic old punishment's being visited upon her: being dipped in honey then coated with feathers, seated nude on a mule backwards and led through the streets as a loose woman like some huge, wobbling lupin. How to stop such an event? He knows that to plead with Cecil will only egg him on, perhaps adding himself to the spectacle, strapping antlers to his head and painting his face orange with ocher mud from a nearby stream. They seem to have come to a certain pass, with no secrets left and little hope of even sustaining their old relationship. No more need for Curly or Twist Up: his life is in the open now, and so, also, soon, will be his writings. Everything he owns has been seized; but they still, from time to time, as if recalling his high status with Rome, insist on treating him with exaggerated civility, suddenly remembering the code of gentlemen, then just as fast forgetting it and subjecting him to loutish, obscene interrogations that clearly do not yield up the information they desire. What on earth do they think I know? he wonders, unable to fathom his devious shift in their minds from whoremonger and roaring boy to traitor. An immoral man, even if a priest, they say, will plan immoral things: besides, he has no business being in the country anyway. Considering this, he marvels at their capricious courtesies and waits for the worst.

Certainly, without Anne's help, he could never have accomplished his duties in England; her complex blend of mothering, concealing, and spiritual affinity has become something else neither practical nor wholly abstruse, which he needs now more than ever, in this Gatehouse, the jail where Thomas Bates was kept before being taken to St Paul's churchyard to be hanged. So this place has some caliber after all, he thinks, even if only for prisoners of so-called "inferior" rank. Servants, in other words. Doomed servants, he recites to himself, blaming innocents such as me. He does not know whether to dread being eventually moved to the Tower or to look forward to it; while the Gatehouse is no playground, it is no annex to the Star Chamber either, and Father Garnet has a paradoxical desire to be toppled by the highest court in the land, to be restrained in its most awful prison. As always, he wants things both ways—the true meaning, as he insists, of prevarication, which others think is lying. If your world has two suns, the Pope and James I, you will profit from a certain double-mindedness, thus enabled to live a decisive life under threat of death. Just look at Anne Vaux, with never the faintest interest in marriage, never deigning like hundreds of other Catholic women to flee the country and join any of the religious orders created on the Continent for expatriate Papists. The utterly pragmatic pair of Anne and Nicholas Evans has kept Father Garnet safe, although uncomfortable, for years, and it is hard for him to think that, first, their work together is done with, and, second, that it finally let him down, its principles and methods having proved too frail. In the Gatehouse there is no such provision for concealing himself from the king's cruel and canny edicts. Here you await your turn, which in Henry Garnet's case means a series of cross-town interviews of a degrading sort, to be followed by—what? He knows Cecil and his crew of savage chums are capable of the most heinous acts; why, their chosen context is that of torture and brutal executions. There will soon be nobody left except for him, kept back to stand for chronic treason, a symbol of holy bigotry to be shown off; but at least his head will not have been impaled for show on a pike.

Accustomed now to their tactics, he realizes it is also a strategy, but does not alarm himself just because thus far he cannot see the connexion between their scurrility and his treachery. In his own eyes he is neither immoral nor treasonous, but more the aloof virgin destined to bounce off major events as they plunge downward, taking with them a host of accomplices. The king, however, insists on adding this theologian to the list of subjects that vex him, but he can do this only because, through a stroke of luck, Sir Edward Coke, poking around in the Inner Temple, where he has lodgings, discovers two versions of the same book, this a treatise on equivocation "Newly overseen by the Authour and published for the defence of innocency and for the Institution of Ignorants." There are two copies, one quarto, the other folio, the former marked up and corrected in what turns out to be Garnet's own hand. What Coke does not at first realize is that Garnet is also the author of this manuscript treatise whose title he has not invisibly altered from *A Treatise of Equivocation* to *A Treatise against Lying and Fraudulent Dissimulation.* When, in the course of interrogation, it becomes clear that Father Garnet, in all innocence, is speaking as the author, Coke at once fixes on the initial title for his onslaught, scenting an equivocator– a liar–who has much to conceal and has dared to compose a treatise anticipating his need to defend himself. All his life, Garnet has been fascinated by double-thinkers such as the Pharisee Nicodemus, a Christian who practiced Christianity only at night, a certain Father Ward who, not long ago, told the Dean of Durham Cathedral he was "no priest," actually meaning mentally, through a technique called sotto-voce suffix, that he was not "Apollo's priest at Delphos," or, theoretically, a priest of Isis, Osiris, or any other pagan cult. This same prelate also swore on the Bible that he had never been beyond the seas, in this instance privately intending that he meant the "Indian seas." More than a straight lie in an emergency, this kind of surreptitious self-editing corresponds to Father Garnet's notion of equivocation as heeding "the equal voice"–in other words, opening the mind to simultaneous possibilities and deciding to protect them both. It also matters, he specifies, that when the questioner is not entitled to receive the truth, being unable to manage it, he does not deserve it, and giving it to him amounts to a severe disservice. Private ramifications tilt everything said in favor of the speaker: so that a man who says, No I am no priest, may be saying this because, in his mind, various qualifications go into the making of a priest, and one is an ability, say, to estimate exactly the weight of oranges. Such private reservations enrage Coke and Cecil, who feel they are being monkeyed with, and by a treatise, not merely by someone in the impromptu act of saving himself.

Indeed, Father Garnet points out, reluctant to cite texts but willing to do so to appease these militant Saxons, when Christ, preparing to raise Jaira's daughter from the dead, says she is not dead but sleeping, he is using a euphemism or white lie dependent on a private reason.

More devastating in the courts than the mere onslaught on lying is Coke's assertion that equivocation is the habit of wily, oily, deceitful foreigners of Latin blood: something endemic they cannot live without and therefore to be expected. "I wonder, dearly beloved," he rants in the Privy Council, putting on his most religious demeanor, "what the blessed martyrs of our own faith, Cranmer and Ridley, would make of such tricks merely to save their lives. You remember how, because his hand had offended, Cranmer thrust it into the fire first?" Warming to his theme, he half-forgets that Father Garnet, although being tested for treason, is a Derbyshireman born and bred, not an Italian at all. Indeed, in so behaving he exemplifies just the kind of double standard Father Garnet pursues in his treatise, just the kind of ambiguity William Byrd practices, as do many others. The wisest course would have been to end all interrogation on the spot, since liars were dealing with liars, to put it crudely, as the Privy Council always does. A man might steal away home to Jesus by simply saying he was going out to buy a white custard, and that is really nobody's business. And, normally, such questions would not have come up. It is only the heap of gunpowder assembled that stirs them into hair-splitting. If politicians want your head, the merest quibble will serve, as Father Garnet has begun to realize, whether the questioner be an educated or a boorish man.

Distracted from such concerns by being moved to the Tower

(the onset of serious trouble), Father Garnet lets himself be diverted by the amenities of arrival and settling in: bedding, coal, arranging for claret with his food, and buying some sack for himself and those adjoining him, such as Father Oldcorne, already ensconced. Even Waad, the Tower's lieutenant governor, strikes Father Garnet as a reasonable man, except on the topic of religion, which turns him into a raving firebrand.

The gossip in the Tower is of a graver sort than that in the Gatehouse, forming in Henry Garnet's mind a woeful assembly of last words, last looks, one day to be tabulated and deciphered for subtler meanings, but sufficient now to rob him of all cheer induced by claret or sack, or by whispering through the wall to Oldcorne, who indeed as often as not brings him bad news. All this carnage, Garnet sighs, has been watched by Sir Francis Bacon, who ought to know better. So he knows about Bates managing, from the hurdle that bore him face down and wrong way up, to give his wife a bag of money; Digby, pale on the scaffold and "his eye heavy" but still the dapper, sly courtier they all adored, hanged for the merest moment and so fully conscious when drawn; Robert Wintour quietly at prayer throughout; John Grant, unable to see because blinded at Holbeach, being led up the ladder to the noose; Rookwood with eyes closed all the way to the scaffold excepting an instant, arranged with his protectors, when he could open them for a last glimpse of his gorgeous wife who called out a fortifying message: "Offer thyself wholly to God. I, for my part, do as freely restore thee to God as He gave thee unto me." Bates and Rookwood sadden Garnet the most, for obvious reasons; he dwells on Martha Bates and Elizabeth Rookwood, inaccurately, as *their Annes,* although the most distressing calls of all come from one of Digby's little sons who cries out "Tata, Tata," meaning two goodbyes, twin dadas, or goodbye, dada, one cannot tell which. Tom Wintour, "a very pale and dead colour," receives the merest swing of the rope before vivisection. What did they tell him about Rookwood? He said all the right things about repentance, king and queen, the royal children, only "to spoil all the pottage with one filthy weed," pleading with God Almighty to make the king a Catholic. Even so, they hang him a long time, into unconsciousness it is to be hoped. Keyes does a sudden lean off the ladder, either because he wants to die at his own chosen moment, or to break his neck. The rope breaks and Keyes goes alive to the chopping block. Now Fawkes, *il Guido*, blanched and frail from torture, asking no forgiveness and crossing himself repeatedly, is helped up the ladder by the hangman; the drop easily snaps his neck, so reduced is his physical state.

All have gone, beheaded at the last, their heads black from being tarred. Henry Garnet is going to have to learn to stomach the tidbits whispered through the wall by Father Oldcorne, that tongue-thresher of old and fondler of others' pain.

Yes, Garnet thinks, it was in such an atmosphere as this, with eight men sent to disgusting deaths, that they decided to send for me from Worcester to London. Now give us Garnet to play with. We will soon have nobody left. Signed: Cecil, Coke, Popham, Waad, all the usual dainties. He knows these selfsame Privy Councillors have commanded that "the inferior sort" of prisoners in the Powder Plot be tortured, beginning with Little John Evans, Ralph Ashley, Father Strange, and James Johnson the servant from White Webbs. Into Tower manacles they go, Father Garnet observing through his nauseated mind's eye.

What he dreams of having is an exemption, meaning he will sit in some rickety chair in his cell, waiting, weeks, months, years, but they never come for him even though they have done away with everyone else. They recognize his essential innocence, cannot bring themselves to order his vivisection. So thank you one and all, you Privy Councillors, you are much better than you sound (hint of men having clever ways with jakes). He knows this will never come true, but he has speeches ready for the occasion, setting his arm around Cecil, shaking hands with Coke and Popham, bowing to Waad and Lady Anne (who somehow gets to know the inmates). One of them says, "You ought to publish it now, now that it's had such a good reading by experts." Will he really hear this? Can he be spared when dozens are not? Being a survivor, he begins to worry about living conditions in the Tower, especially the need to avoid water with meals, since Thames water is deadly, substituting beer or liquor. A man could dry up if he had no funds; he could cheat the hangman by drinking water with his meals, and perhaps that is the whole idea of being pent up here. End it all, he thinks: odd that so few have tried it. Prisoners can never shake the conviction that they will survive, even after torture; indeed, especially after torture, the idea being that they have suffered enough already and are to be "let off."

Now and then, from manacles or rack, he hears muffled sobs, but they have not even shown him the machinery yet: the first stage of intimidation. Once again, recalling Hindlip and other coffin-like enclosures, Father Garnet gladdens to be at ease in such a commodious place, with occasional trips abroad across London for fresh air and conversation with semi-educated men. Slowly the mesh of misconception is lethally unraveled about him: James Johnson, racked for a week, confesses to having served a Mister Meaze at White Webbs, Meaze, he adds, being Garnet, of course. Ralph Ashley too confesses his part in assisting Little John Evans, the priest secreter. Father Garnet pleads with Anne Vaux by letter to get some money from the Society of Jesus with which to provide, at least, beds for tortured men to lie upon; but this hardly halts the procession of victims, succoring them only when they are too far gone to know they are being succored. So this, Father Garnet thinks, is what the planet was created for. No, this is what the planet is *doing* to itself—should we not always try to behave better than this? Tapping, hissing, Father Oldcorne, already back to his old self-punishing ways (nail in the tongue again) informs him through the crack in the wall that they have tortured Father Strange, the lover of music and tennis, for reasons unknown; he never knew of the plot nor was recognized by it. Those released eventually, like James Johnson and Father Strange, go away stunted, having had nothing to reveal, having now nothing to offer the world, having had their gifts and health pillaged from them by the inexorable machine of justice. Father Garnet has never been so close to vomiting throughout the day, most of all when he thinks about Little John, a man afflicted already with hernia and a deformed leg, who should therefore be exempt from torture. A man who starts broken can be questioned only in the mild sense of the word. But those in charge see Little John as a lemon to squeeze, his head full of names and aliases, partridges to net: "Is he taken, then," asks one prominent Councillor. "He that knows all the secret places? I am very glad of that. We will have a trick for him," by which he intends the manacles, to begin with. So they hold him in the semi-civilised prison the Marshalsea, hoping that priests will try to get in touch with him there, but they have too much common sense for that. Moved to the Tower (Oldcorne again passing the word), Little John prays incessantly, just as he has done while building refuges in country houses. Out of him come two empty confessions, in one of which he admits to not knowing his own nickname, affecting to be rather peeved by it when they tell it to him. Now, after long days hung from manacles, his muscles give way and his stomach has to be patched, contained, by means of an iron platter, which hardly keeps things in. He admits bits and pieces, nothing of worth. On they drive, taxing him to the utmost, but never managing to winkle out of him anything not known already, and therefore provoking them to extremes, none of which work.

Little John dies on March 2, slandered by a story put out by the government that he tore himself open with a table knife. Lies, Father Oldcorne insists; Little John's hands were so mangled he could not even eat with them, still less wield a knife. A benign craftsman and dedicated servant has vanished from Father Garnet's limited ken, and in his bones he feels the death as his fault. Without *him,* and the likes of him, Little John would never have entered upon the covert profession he gave his life to. He would have made things he could show and be proud of, perhaps even creating objects for use at court. Still treated humanely, perhaps out of some paradoxical denatured hatred, Father Garnet soldiers on, his head a swamp of cruel memories, buttered up by Privy Councillors and jailers who actually begin to respect his Catholicism, acting as if they were on the brink of conversion, so exemplary is their prisoner: polite, contained, decorous. What he does not know is that they began in exactly this manner with Robert Wintour and Guido Fawkes, whose heads are moldering not far away, black with pitch and pecked by crows. Father Garnet, a trusting soul, has no idea what will come next, but he half-expects, on the basis of his treatment so far, to be released and told to leave the country.

For someone in the know, less gullible perhaps than Henry Garnet, whose experience with courtly thugs is limited, the situation could appear simple; it strikes him as complicated because, by and large, they treat him as *persona grata*, an educated thinker with a holy passion. To anyone else, this is all trimmings, dealt with as if it were the king's own frippery, or the queen's, or Cecil's, Coke's. Father Garnet is being sucked in by urbane insincerity, something the Councillors and even their henchmen, from warder to rackman, have been practicing for years. He has no idea that, as usual, in a certain eavesdropping room, as with Wintour and Fawkes, Edward Fawcett and John Locherson overhear whatever he says. He might have become suspicious when they offered him a cell with a talking hole to Father Oldcorne, but such is not his way. He welcomes the concession and opens his mouth. So he mentions Anne Vaux, in London, and his jailer Carey's willingness to convey to her anything he cares to write. Mistress Vaux, he says, will put them all in touch with one another once again. On he goes, saying how Anne Vaux will furnish those little luxuries that life in prison denies you without forbidding them. Fawcett and Locherson, at the other end of the speaking tube lodged in the aperture to Father Oldcorne, cannot believe their luck, hearing their prey even advising Oldcorne to endear himself to jailer Carey, the plebeian spy whose easily impressionable front works wonders with high-born prisoners used to a little deference.

Presumably, if Father Garnet had worked with the Inquisition, he might have understood better the compatibility of cruelty and charm. The piece of human psychology he has missed, being a country boy to start with and a scholar ever after, is the one that says, Even if the end has to be bad, we don't have to make the journey there unpleasant. It is too hard on us, and certainly on the victim. So, gentlemen, let's be debonair or, if unable to rise to that, at least courtly and civil, almost as if we liked the fellow. And he will tell us much more that way. So polish your suavity, put on your face of the compassionate clown, and save your resentment for his final day. Is there not something refreshing in the thought that you alone have power to impose an ending on him? You know his final day, or will. There is nothing he can do about it. Does that not make an otherwise powerless man feel stronger? So why not a little amenity to smooth the interim as the poor devil sweats out his wait?

One steady look into Cecil's eye, or Coke's, would have provided him this text, but he has been dealing with priests, a different breed, who are not without malice, of course, but lacking the crooked power mania of Cecil and his cronies. Or are they? It is hard to separate the power mania of the virtuous from that of the malign; the Annes and Little Johns have not prepared Henry Garnet for the rough and tumble of Catesby and Cecil's circus.

Perhaps responding to pressure, or because in truth he has settled in, although by no means as harshly accommodated as at Hindlip, he drinks a little more each day, achieving a similar aural blur to that experienced by the eavesdroppers when his and Oldcorne's murmuring is drowned out by the crowing of cocks. He is happy that Oldcorne remains at a suitable distance here, a communicant in the secular sense, but no longer cheek by jowl with him. They incriminate few people, possibly Lords Northampton and Rutland, and only inadvertently themselves, Father Garnet decreasingly worried about it as his consumption of sack increases, he having once upon a time said a prayer in favor of Catholic relief from royal persecution. Could such an innocent thing be misconstrued? It could, and Coke has already underlined part of the transcript in readiness for Garnet's show trial. The two priests confess each other, as on previous occasions, but little that is seditious emerges from their exchange. Father Garnet's repeated pleas for oranges tip off the warders that he is hoping to write with juice, and they gladly oblige, willing to take him, as it were, at his word. When he uses a big sheet of paper for a tiny message, they at once suspect he has written something else in invisible ink, and Waad warms the letter at a convenient fire and reads it. Because warmed-up writing in orange juice remains visible whereas lemon juice fades again after exposure, Father Garnet asks for lemons, but receives none, though a few come his way through the bars of his window, smuggled in from outside vendors. It is quite a bustling, almost euphoric life he leads in the Tower, although none of his invisible-ink letters get through; indeed, Waad, expert and devious, can by now sniff fruit juice in the paper and can always tell which letters might hold treasonable material. Most, however, and this is a release for Henry Garnet, are sentimental, letters to his nephew Father Thomas Garnet, asking to have his spectacles (enclosed in a fold of paper) set in leather and put in a leather case. "And let the fold be fit for your nose," he avuncularly says. Is he giving them away in view of what might happen later on, or merely asking for repairs? Sack perhaps explains the muddle. At any rate, the spectacles come back to him via Anne Vaux, to whom he writes regularly, counselling her as her spiritual adviser, which he has been for some twenty years. She needs a replacement for him, obviously, but he seems slow to provide one, no doubt fearing any change in their intercourse. He needs all his contacts in here; he thinks he may be in more danger than he knows, but he cannot prove it, able only to adduce to his horror the savage retribution going on outside, where Cecil and Coke have free rein, requiring only the tiniest slip orally or in writing to rack somebody now deemed dangerous.

18

KING IN ALL but name," Anne Vaux has heard people
say of Cecil; "King in effect, he rules both Court and
Crown." It makes him sound makeshift, she thinks,
but this cannot be true of a man who is such a sound sleeper,
who rests his five-foot-two frame with avid sensuality; he
made the throne as certain for himself as for James, he, a
pigmy rampant, true to the tone of his last request to the dying Elizabeth, who said, "I told you my seat hath been the seat
of kings, and I will have no rascal to succeed me; and who
should succeed me but a king." The lords attending her
deathbed shuffle and peer at one another until Cecil asks her
what she means and she responds, "Who, quoth she, but our
cousin of Scotland? I pray you trouble me no more." A Cecil
this blunt and pragmatic, Anne thinks, so deft at handling
queens, will never do anything foolish. And so, despite what
she has heard about his ruthlessness, his impersonal loyalty,
his festering secrecy, she settles for the gallant who, once again
confronting his moribund queen, tries anew: "We beseech
your Majesty, if you remain in your former resolution and that
you would have the King of Scots to succeed you in your kingdom, show some sign to us." They are not content with what

she said earlier; they are willing to trouble her further. Near death, she draws herself up and frees her arms from the sheets to point them into a steeple above her head, making for them a coronet. This man, Anne decides, will do nothing sloppy, not with his exactness, so lithe, so august. The more she thinks about him, the more she is tempted to like him. And the more he functions as quasi-king, the more he will indulge in Elizabeth's own habits, actually pardoning such as Markham, Grey, Cobham, and Sir Walter Raleigh, merely sending them to the Tower, never mind how many she has sent to the block. Why, Cecil himself, seeking common justice and yielding to the "accident of their places," has been known to utter words of compassion, conceding that such men can be undone—unfairly— by such unfortunate shifts as they engage in. Ah, now she sees it, she thinks. He has cruel Coke and unscrupulous Popham go after noble men on trial just to get them to say so much. They are bound to utter something that will save them: only in the flow of confessing, they will come up with something that evinces their essential nobility, their innocence. Only so savage and omnicompetent a mind as Cecil's will bother to pluck from the commotion of apology the saving phrase; for others it would pass by amid the mill-race of response. This is not the flamboyant Raleigh, the Hispanic-looking enemy of Spain, there parading in the very same Tower, dark-skinned as the Devil. Cecil's face is a literate mask, an arrangement of static demeanors, with his palm laid always against his heart as if auscultating himself, in order to marvel at his sublime ability. He does not blink, which is perhaps to say that bits of grit do not float his way, or his eyes do not run with the watering disease of the Romans so beloved of Henry Garnet. Yet she sees pallor and strain and the thickened skin beneath these eyes, as if all the unused blinks have collected there, bidden to form into an unheard-of stone, *cecillium,* once discerned in the ice-eyed myriad-minded English queen.

Oh, she imagines saying to him in some moment of impossible candor, thou little splay-footed crookback dwarf with dropsy of the head (only because thy carcass is too small), do not thy delicate features deceive us, and that sprightly charm? Note this rotund forehead as easily cracked as an eggshell, a touch of milady's grace in your brows, bold hazel eyes, mouth like a punctured wound that has daintily dried. O sire, of the caressing hands and constantly enfolding arms, be good with him: poor priest that did no more, ever, than listen. What aileth you most? Not the honest listeners of this globe, but the smallpox that turns the face into a straw nest. Besides, have you ever seen a Jesuit with the pox?

Then she slips out of her pleading mode, as unable to sustain faith in him as to endure the vision of his face. In truth, he is one of the most logical, rational, shrewd men in England, ever willing to pepper his utterance with such ballast as "for my own part" and "I am not apt to wonder" and "cannot but suppose," achieving a treacherous effect of self-doubting, an elegant modesty, a willingness to defer to others. He seems always to be saying too much, yet without giving much of himself away; he musters his opinions with pensive adroitness, but seems to have only just survived a mental fumble, having aired several other lines of thought scotched at the last moment. It is only too easy to misconstrue his passion for history and science (astronomy having led him to purchase a so-called "perspective glass"). He adores *things,* from jewels and currants, to all fruit and firewood. No wine-bibber he, Cecil opens his mouth wide at the blazing sun as if he will take a bite of it. As a pagan he has failed, but as a caricature of the balanced man he comes through with disconcerting sharpness, on one occasion (unknown to Anne Vaux of course) failing to extol someone who has sought his good will:

> *I think it good to tell you* [he writes] *that —— is no way toward me other than ordinary messenger, of which sort I think him as bad as any. For me to punish him, I can do it but as a Councillor, which authority I like not to extend. You are a judge, proceed as you please.*

He will hear men out although he picks up the thread of their discourse long before they have finished, his best maxim, no doubt based on many long-suffering sessions at Court or in the Privy Council, being "Send me some short abbreviates and I will henceforth be my own carver." Elizabeth calls him her "Elf" even when reviling him for something he knows not what. As he ages, early, he grays fast, his jowls wobble, his jaw-line hides, the mouth becomes a tiny portcullis, his eyelids lose their flutter. How anyone so tiny can be so haggard yet overbearing cannot be known, but he is all of that, creating in his interlocutors (or dumbfounded mere observers) a strict uneasiness: with the same impassive pout, he can clasp you around the middle or sign the warrant for your death.

Anne Vaux abandons her attempt to sum him up; he is too many in one, not connected together by either spine or faith, by tradition or diet. It would be wise, she decides after summing up her knowledge of the man, to broach him with a sneering reference to London, a huzzah to Paris, a well-tempered mention of eye-fluxions (too much paperwork), hawking (he makes careful notes each outing), and then to deplore the multitude of unwanted dogs, horses, silver cups and doormats of human hair sent to him. To his heart forthwith, she writes in her diary, with a remark about the dampness and fustiness of new walls. Loves paddocks, parks, glades. Has actually in jest described himself as "A good architectour." Most of all, unworldly enough never to carry money with him or to claim his allowances; he borrows from some grocer whom he uses as a bank. To people he wants to be rid of, he lends money, not in the way of a cynic, merely accepting human nature. Whatever else, the State comes first; he is a Company man first and last. Those who seem to thrive best financially, he declares, are lawyers and merchants and, in the countryside, maltsters, sheepmasters and graziers are the veritablest moneybags.

Unaware of being watched (as a notorious woman will be), Anne tries to pretend that all her life she has been aching to live with Dorothy Habington on Fetter Lane, not far from Fleet Street. Life is different now, she concedes, with the government hiding the priests for her. Without actually walking into the lion's mouth, she is making herself fairly conspicuous, buzzing about, asking questions, trying to muster a firm reliable portrait of Cecil and his late wife, that quiet, underspoken woman of slight build, mild disposition, in no way the intellectual helpmeet Cecil might have needed. She tells everybody what she pays for things, and the word gets out, even to Anne Vaux. In his indulgent, mildly ironical way, Cecil notes to Michael Hick, his one-time early tutor, another Cambridge man, that "she pays under three pounds ten a yard for her cloth of silver." Her brothers think she has made a strategic match, but Cecil always denies them his favor, to their mounting chagrin. But Anne Vaux has no idea that Cecil views his wife as a gentle, exotic beast extended to him for genial, uncritical care; she is so different from him that he marvels at all her ways, never having quite recovered from his first encounter with her:

"The object to mine eyes yesternight," he wrote, "at supper hath taken so deep impression in my heart as every trifling thought increaseth my affection." He brooded on her all night, only to set down further thoughts while short of sleep. Would she soon find him hideous? Will she advance to "the risk of mislike of my person"? He lets his mother do the wooing and the sounding out for him, vowing to "lay hand on my mouth" even if unable to govern his heart.

Then Anne, realizing she is in danger, comes to her senses, no longer obliviously wrapped up in what she can glean about Lady Cecil and the terra nova of the Cecils' newfound love. The lady died in 1597, overtaxed while pregnant, smarting always from the ridicule to which her tiny husband was subjected, entertaining the queen and other dignitaries at their Strand house without ever having the flair or the energy for a hectic social round. She dies virtually unnoticed, neither blamed nor praised, but just exhausted by the career demands placed on her by a husband she has too often heard referred to as "Pigmy." What Anne does discover, over miscellaneous teacups in sundry drawing rooms, is that Cecil commissioned for her an epitaph in both Latin and English:

> *Cecil her husband this for her did build,*
> *To prove his love did after death abide,*
> *Which tells unto the worlds that after come*
> *The world's concept whilst here she held a room.*

The end-stopped lines have a predictable quality, but Anne Vaux generously notes, as she pauses at the austere marble tomb in Westminster Abbey, four-square and columned with muted grandeur, the faint originality of the concluding half-rhyme, with doom implied in between "come" and "room."

Anne uncovers a woman silent, true, and chaste, wondering if her death curbed him, slowed him, or perhaps energised him in some unnatural way, relieving him of the burden to be tender and solicitous, awakening him to the continuing presence of a harsher, more glamorous world. Did all the stylish hospitalities at Cecil House tax her too far, and did he at the point of her death accept himself for what he is—a resolute dwarf intent on running the country without apologising too much to anyone? Indeed, she concludes, after her fishing expedition is done, the marriage's end restored him to himself, with no one, certainly not his plain, blunt, ambitious mother, to mellow him, and his life rippling out before him like some frayed umbilicus. He shall always be granted what he asks for because he salts the ground beforehand. Is he all bad? She feels relieved never to have hidden *him* away in one of her country houses. It is he, after all, who has put paid to Little John, racked Fawkes, had most of the plotters hanged almost as if staging a Punch and Judy show for himself alone, to distract him from the weird shape of his body, ogled by everyone else, the deadly dainty of his generation.

After all, she tells Dorothy, whose ashen face seems more powdered than ever (the *poudre outrée* as Anne privately dubs it), Cecil is a Welshman, so you have to be careful of his sparkling animosity. Who are these strong-willed Welsh, moving eastward into London to prevail through social arts, shrinking from unpleasant truths only to infuse them into covert policy, labile and mercurial, quick to emotion and out of it again, infatuated with melody and song, but full of duplicitous coaxing, whereas the English—well, she ruminates, what of the half-French English? Are they any better? They are stabler than the Welsh, she thinks, you can count on Tuesday's Englishman bearing some similarity to Monday's, if you are lucky. Henry Garnet, what's left of him, is English. Q.E.D. She leaves Cecil alone for the time being, surrounded by hearty Welshmen bellowing such oaths as "Zounds" and "God's wounds," capping it with, "This it is to serve a base, bastard, pissing kitchen woman." Among such profane, scurrilous ruffians, Lady Cecil lived her life and died, over-preoccupied with a husband whose twisted spine came from being dropped by a nurse. The twist in his daily living consists in his ever answering almost meekly to whatever raw overture comes his way, and this is the Welsh in him, what strikes some as cunning, others as diplomatic excess, yet others as reluctance to engage in combat. Cecil endures, so far, and he will endure long enough to put Henry Garnet squirming on the skewer of Privy Council questioning, or worse. She wonders if there might not be something she can do, freeing Garnet or impeding Cecil: an escape from the Tower, Gerard-style, or the classic plea from a well-born gentlewoman of another faith. Why not exile, she thinks? Banished to Rome with him does not sound so bad, and they will open up their mouths to wolf down the sun.

Yet, in this vicarious game of hate-love, she has no sooner thrown him down than she picks him up, gathering together the unconsidered trifles of his life, including his long-standing habit, contracted from his father, of compiling tables and almanacs of private and public life, a terse diarist showing himself amid the calendrical wallbars, his handwriting itself derived from the Italian writing-master Gianfrancesco Cresci, his letters done with a gracious architectonic that stations the paragraph high up, gives his signature written out in full (only later did he sign himself "Ro: Cecyll"), and the address an almost operatic flourish. Writing home as a young man from Paris, he declares Paris in August, so wearisome to Parisians, delights him a great deal, and he dreads his father's command to return: "I determine never to hold my face into the cold northern coast, when the heat of the warm sun is at my back." He is closer to Father Garnet than he can know, at least with this heliophily. He longs for the Mediterranean, but never gets there, all the while thinking he has been born in the wrong country, wishing his reward for being born stunted might be instructions from his father to follow the sun, much in the mood of certain children convinced the *sun* is following *them*. But the French, as Anne learns, call him Monsieur Bossu (Hunchback), which rather pawnbrokes his charm and gives him cause to be back among the cold, sniping English all over again, even if only to dally for a couple of years at Cambridge.

Father Garnet, already feeling somewhat ashamed about the speed with which he has adjusted to prison life, does not share her warm sense of Cecil's good side, unable to forget what Old-corne told him about the messenger from Cadiz, one of Essex's men caught smuggling: Now was the time, Cecil said, to break the knave's neck, "before he hath recovered by false humility and insinuation, a *ne noceat* from his Lordship." How, Father Garnet wonders, can a man who revels in the intellectual ferment of his days at the Sorbonne be so callous about someone else's neck? This facile consort of cruelty with mental finesse amazes and sickens him; he has already seen it applied, from behind a damask curtain, to the first eight plotters, for, to be sure, nothing happens having to do with life and death that has no approval from Cecil. There is a depression, almost a cavity, in Cecil's temple, out of which the milk of human kindness must have leaked until it all was gone. His mother had it too, and to the haunting, lurid image of wobbling dwarf it brings a touch of extra deformity, setting the mind to wonder what a piece of work the man would have been with the hole filled in. Father Garnet thinks he could lay a young carrot in the concavity, and, if the head were laid down on the right, leave it there without its rolling off. The story that circulates most in the Tower comes from 1595, recalling the fate of the Jesuit Robert Southwell, being tortured at Cecil's command. After he has watched for a while, along with other members of the Privy Council, Cecil rides away observing impasively, "We have a new torture which it is not possible for a man to bear. And yet I have seen Robert Southwell hanging by it, still as a treetrunk, and no one able to drag one word from his mouth." Cecil invokes the name of God frequently, even more than his father Lord Burleigh has done, and is fond of professing in the name of "Him that knoweth and searcheth all men's hearts." So, at times, he loves (as he puts it) to cast a stone into the mouth of all such crabs. All the same, Cecil is not coarse enough for James, although James gladly does his bidding. Cecil, also, is the subtle lover of cipher, who numbers friends and enemies, quietly reciting to himself the numbers of his darlings (3002 and 2050, for example) and his vipers. This is not far, Garnet supposes, from one of the ways he and Oldcorne used to communicate, breaking up the alphabet into a grid of twenty-five spaces, five on each side, with A at the bottom right-hand corner and Z, that unnecessary letter, omitted altogether. Thus, Cecil would become 1:3 (line 1, third square from the right), 1:5, 1:3, 2:4, and 3:2. Little does he know that Cecil, cipher-master extraordinary, knows from the first of their elementary code and thrills to find his numerical name among their verbal contraband. Garnet knows of Cecil's ciphers too, and marvels at a man who needs to number acquaintances totalling several thousand, his wife and parents and children included, and, he savagely adds, all the crabs in the sea. Father Garnet has no sense of triumph, certain he has lost in all ways, now unable even to perform his duty to someone such as Anne Vaux. He takes a little pride, though, in his perverse way, from having had so many aliases, and therefore no doubt, in Cecil's capacious numerical mind, just as many numbers, all misleading, some of them perhaps between Sir Walter Raleigh and the Earl of Essex. His capture has of course, he decides, freed various empty numbers for other malefactors, unless Cecil has kept him on the books to preclude confusion. Malicious for once, or perhaps just plain witty (or so he guesses), he imagines his number might have been 666, the number of the beast—perhaps this was Meaze's number, or Whalley's, Darcy's, Farmer's, or that of Roberts or Philips. In his most intimate moments, Father Garnet suspects, Cecil thinks of numbers, not people, thus ridding himself of unnecessary emotion in the matter of chopping off heads. If he kept a number for himself, what might it be? Which of all numbers would be best for someone as secretive and complex as he? A vulgar fraction, possibly, or the square root of minus one? This is a game Father Garnet would have liked to share with the late Father Oldcorne, supplying even more chatter for the two eavesdroppers in the adjoining cell. So far as he knows, Oldcorne's cell has remained vacant ever since he was shipped off, complaining, to Worcester and Redhill to be hanged.

Again and again Garnet returns to the enigma of Cecil, the one that will put paid to him but for a miracle. Why, he too might be sent back up to Worcester to the evil English of Sir

Henry Bromley, who will couch his death sentence in subliterate misprision. The trick of Cecil, he concludes, as ever before embarking on the problem too late, is that he is a man of parts, indeed of fragments, whose main skill consists in being able to make you think the part on show is the whole of him: hail fellow well met, or the cool paragon, or the callous egoist, or the Parisian-polished Cambridge man who venerates such national heroes as Sir Humphrey Gilbert going down in the *Squirrel,* Sir Philip Sidney dying at Zutphen, Sir Richard Grenville who went down in *The Revenge.* Pure bluff, perhaps, designed to make you think nobly of him, and rather less inspiring, Garnet thinks, than Foxe's *Book of Martyrs.* So, what remedy for this long-fingered chameleon, Cecil, who takes you in with the merest visible fraction of himself, the arm circled around you actually bearing a knife? My offence, Garnet reminds himself, has been to listen, to be told, so my redemption may amount to saying nothing at all. I can listen to myself privately, not yet a crime, and that's all. Alas, Oldcorne and I said far too much before we realized we were overheard. To them, of course, confession is a perverted thing, unworthy of respect, a hypocritical contrivance, unlike these pestilential oaths of loyalty. Father Garnet is learning how to lose his temper. Not for him, the classical scholar, this boyish adoration of stout Englishmen assaulting the pack-ice, wobbling about on top of frigid oceans in twenty-ton vessels emblazoned with no-nonsense names such as *George, William,* or *James,* all en route to the secular holy grail of Cathay. He does not slobber to prance about in mandarins' silk or to read the Bible at hordes of uncomprehending Chinese. A concordance to Tacitus would be more like it. He sighs at the completed, static beauty of the classics, calm and unruffled, at the mercy of none, awaiting only the ultimate codification done by someone as dedicated as he, and then he recognizes it: he and Cecil are not that far apart, both of them men anxious to reduce the world to order, he through etymology, Cecil through cipher, he through dictionaries, Cecil through the home-made almanac. Could this help him? Only in conversation, and even in that, dangerously—Cecil is just the man who, seeing his overlap with someone else, will sequester that part of himself to keep his originality intact. It is too late for talk, Henry Garnet tells himself: small-talk, maybe, but nothing more, top-dog to top-Jesuit style.

Now Garnet remembers his talk of the microcosm, which he hurled on the Puritan clergyman during the ride from Worcester to London. By the time you have made up your little cosm, he reminds himself, it is obsolete because in the meantime all kinds of other little ones have been added to the big one—there is nowhere else for them to go. So with Cecil, then, he decides: you no sooner think you have him than he changes, ever exceeding the grasp of any epitome. Keeping up with him, as with the macrocosm, is a waste of time; his destiny is ever to outstrip us, as if we were Spaniards or Italians, as if he were determined to best them in the search for the Northwest Passage in the interests of selling tons of English cloth. He is not to be reckoned with, only surrendered to. You do not know you are bound to lose, so competing with him is a vain exercise.

So—he cannot complete the next thought.

The energy has drained from him, buoyed only briefly by several cupfuls of sack. In the end, liquor only makes a misery of him, like some profane sacrament.

He is like one of those English sailor-adventurers, going down for the last time, crying out to the clouds that heaven is as close to the sea as to the land, crossing themselves with arms frozen stiff, trying to wet their lips with spittle that is all icicle, finally losing the haunting image of the long-sought jade. Better sacked than racked, he thinks. It must be possible to be so inebriated that one feels nothing at all, not even the slither from man's world to God's paradisal one. Ay, Father Garnet will soon be above yon fellow, the sun. Now who said that?

19

WAS IT NOT ELIZABETH the mercurial who, reluctant to sign the warrant for the execution of Robert Devereux, Earl of Essex, signed, then called it back? Then she tried again, and did not revoke it, instead appointing two headsmen: "We would first have these two persons secretly conveyed within the Tower" because "if one faint, the other may perform it to him on whose soul God have mercy." As if realising for the first time where he is, Father Garnet feels a caustic shiver sail through him. Cecil will be no backslider, nor his James. In truth, he is one of the few remaining victims, virtually alone in what Cecil, writing to Carew, the friend he sees all too little of, calls his "purgatory," with only a huge abdominal tumor to look forward to, edema, and scurvy in spite of his lifelong appetite for fruit. Father Garnet, the innocent listener, turns bitter again, remarking to himself how Cecil, the hunchback, always seems to be leaning forward like a man seated on the jakes, straining and gasping, eager to be shut of what ails him internally, the bile built up by cynical, adroit maneuvering in the interests of that fatuous blank the State, at least it seems so when likened to the kingdom of heaven. Father Garnet aims his revulsed mind toward the gardens of Vallombrosa, there to ponder how Greek *f* became Roman *ph,* and was this not retrograde, an addition where a reduction might have served? Something that analytic will calm him, he hopes, stilling the shakes that now afflict him beyond the power of his sherris-sack to curb.

Predictably, Henry Garnet, not believing he has done anything wrong, but nonetheless accused, decides to find something in himself that merits suspicion. He decides his emotions are too visible, that he is too gregarious; he should have been more aloof all along, less willing to listen to confession and confidence. It is always better, he has learned (not to his own benefit) to live in *rented* places; the modicum of money forked out guarantees a certain hold on the premises without committing you to them. You cannot always be found or pinned down, not even by taxmen and census-takers. This would make the Pope himself a wanderer, slinking from lodging to lodging, but all the closer to God with each use of a temporary home. If only I had run things on those lines, he murmurs in the depths of the Tower; now, I inhabit the house of sack and float about in its element. In the Tower, the ne plus ultra of hiding places, I can always be found, as never in the priestholes until that dreadful day at Hindlip. A man of ideas, of faith and gadabout usefulness, had better let others receive his mail, his money, his praise, turning up only on the darkest nights to claim what fairly might be his own, then disappearing into the dark again; and they not only do not know his whereabouts, they do not know his name, or what he looks like, sounds like, smells like. O to have been so wise early on, certainly a member of the Society of Jesus, but leaving social connection at that, belonging to a freemasonry of the mind in which the code for all priests is

S.J. No numbers, no names. We should all be called Father Sugar, say. This is how to confound the Cecils, whose meddling with ciphers only obscures the entire issue; his assigned numbers would no more correspond to priestly identities than to angels in motion. If only we had thought to thwart him, harnessing our social energy for self-preservation rather than giving an ear to indecisive plotters.

Then he admits to himself that, having heard a plot was afoot, he was duty-bound to reveal it. To whom? In a sense he had: to Rome. But Cecil means something else: he should have blown the whistle to the king, as a true Englishman. It is his nationality that has brought him to this, not his theological affiliation. Born here, he has a duty here, but who has control over the circumstances of his birth? Truth is, he is an emigrant, as free to play fast and loose with the lore of England as the Irish are or, not to put too fine a point on it, with a Scottish king in mind, a Scot. James's loyalty is not to his adopted country but to himself: he can shout and fart at the same time. Better anything, Garnet thinks, than two virgins confronting each other for twenty years in the interest of some abstract ethic, each succoring the other with certain knowledge of the power of language over the hereafter. *That* is where the reward will be; without this certainty they would have wandered away from each other in search of something pagan, more banal, such as marriage, lamentably unable to control the appetitive side of their natures, at least letting the ghost of desire float unsatisfied through their intercourse. Simple cuddling has never come their way, not in all those years, which leaves for them only the most distant caress, the most denatured embrace. Too late now, of course, with matters more urgent preying on them; indeed, the whole affair converted into a miserable emergency, with little time left even for their old time-honored clips, if even any of them can come about.

Thinking of the universe, God's noblest fretwork, Father Garnet reviews all the places she is not: those empty, unseen spaces, the all-encompassing not-ness that beguiles astronomers and philosophers alike, whose mere emptiness is living proof of God's existence, for He created it blank, having a strong desire to have it thus. Spaces are full of her non-presence, the sky as well, not just empty fields lying fallow between Worcester and London, but *all spaces:* she cannot be found where she *is,* not by him at least; and not where she is not. He almost whines with frustration, certain now that whatever error he has committed (fancy, Oldcorne already hanged!) derives from some haphazard cipher in Cecil's brain, the statesman in Cecil having decided that a man with numerous aliases *must* be corrupt—there is no other reason for it. Long ago he should have cultivated his enemy and joined with him, accepting one solitary number in Cecil's almanac of souls, initiating him further in the culture of the Mediterranean (for which he longs, haled back by his father Burleigh to his intense displeasure, left lifelong with Garnet's own craving for the warm breeze, the golden coast, the ever serviceable sun). Two sun-worshippers should have made better music together, two lovers of languages, two compilers of immutable records. They could have spoken together in half a dozen languages, merely for sport, shown off their calligraphy, actually devising new examinations for Cecil's children based on the old familiar questions "Where is the thigh-bone of England?" and "*It is the hope of a reward that drives people to the study of virtue.* Discuss." The

Cecil who as a youth read the Old Testament as a compendium
of power politics was the same Cecil who, in the same years, sat
at the kitchen table among the cooks, inhaling the steam and
aromas, or watched his mother and sisters (just like Henry
Garnet) busy with their knitting and needlework. Neither man
could dance, in spite of Elizabeth's hankering for the galliard.
They might have ruminated on all this, their overlap and difference, if only confronted with each other early enough. They
might have gossiped, Father Garnet decides, prattling about
the misdemeanors of other men less skilled. They might have
founded a new civilization, not to mention a friendship, based
on codes and ciphers, in which the king's number was certainly
not 1, or Cecil's 2. The entire society would be situated on an
offshore island, he thinks, accessible but selective, requiring an
entrance examination invented by the Cecil children, reared on
weird esoterica. All very well, he thinks, but his experience of
human life has taught him that, sooner or later, the best of
friendships wilt, begin to fray at the edges; the fellows on
whom you counted most go out of their way to avoid you,
merely because novelty is all. So the most he could hope for is
ten or fifteen years of stable amity, amid the earthquakes and
surrenders of power politics. In Cecil's favor, he can only think
of his virtual addiction to his friend George Carew, always
abroad, and Lady Suffolk, whereas his relations with almost
everyone else mutate along with the English weather, and he
considers all of them vipers, telling the king that he would like
him to know his mind in full, but no one else. If only, Garnet
romances, he and Cecil had met up with each other earlier;
each might have mellowed the other, given each other the euphoric pliability to be found in the faces of loose women. Yes,

married to Anne Vaux (preposterous inversion of the historical fact!), he would have figured largely in Cecil's domain, counselling and advising until the Spanish chose to make war anew.

Never before has Father Garnet been demoralised by the might-have-been; but now, as he looks back, he sees ample reason to be so, aggrieved by the way in which those he thought friends regarded him only as another pebble on the beach. He leaves his native land partly in the belief that Italian men are friendlier, less barbaric and aloof than English ones, but finds himself deluded: his fellow-Jesuits seek him out for business or ideas, but that is all, they rarely go beyond effusive attention into something stronger. Is it love he has been looking for? He doubts it, thinking more of committed sympathy, not a rare commodity, or so he has thought up to now. And what of Anne, who needs him as confessor and spiritual adviser more than as, well, certainly not lover, but something intimate. She has mothered him as he has fathered her. No more than that. It is as if all his life he has been searching for an emotion in relating to others that does not exist except as an abstraction, a desideratum fudged up by nimble, lonely thinkers. God created the Platonic form of friendship, but few humans even come to an approximation of it, being more absorbed with themselves than with anyone else. God, he surmises, must be very disappointed with us, especially in view of the fact that, as with the Cecils of the world, friendship becomes merely the rhetorical cloak for the dagger. Too often he has heard the miserable tinkle of a declining friend, one whose enthusiasm has dwindled, who is surrendering to novelty, flash, ephemera. Can it be that men have no gift for friendship, but only skill in using one another? Why, Cecil is as isolated as he, and perhaps this is the reason he treats all as vipers. There has to be, Henry Garnet thinks, an element of defenseless surrender, otherwise friendship cannot survive, and it is clear to him that so-called friends who are doing better in the world than you (even the strict theological world of Jesuits) will eventually siphon themselves off, looking for someone more compatible with whom to repine.

As best he can, he dismisses the entire subject, too late to do anything about it, cut off and pegged as a plotter. He will be lucky to survive to complain about the deficits of friendship in the new century. He longs for the boyhood trick of pulling his jersey up over his head and shutting the world out, even concealing the set of his mouth, the wateriness of his eye, the pallor of his countenance. In the Tower, deprived of "friends" now dead (was Oldcorne ever a friend rather than an unwilling accomplice?), he will be able to compose a fugue on soup and send it out to William Byrd, yet never hoping for succor from that ambiguous quarter, Byrd not even a fair-weather friend, but a fair-weather onlooker with pretty hand movements. Oh, Byrd, what a falling-off is there, he laments; it is as if music has betrayed us in a person of circumspect finesse. Over the past year or so, Father Garnet has come to know emotions as people, as characters, no longer like most obliged to finger the texture of daily living and responding, trying to make sense of all the interwoven strands; but, thanks to a good education in English, less so in Italian, he is able to specify such feelings in himself or others as, say, captious sympathy, sceptical zeal, animated enervation, and so forth—all, he imagines, taught him by listening for so long to plotters, whose emotional gamut was always narrow: a good beginning as he moved on to encounter Byrd, Cecil, even Anne Vaux, whose belated apprehension now seizes her by the throat and makes her entertain the idea of death.

For him, there is no longer the muddle of response, the spray of possible motives, but the clear motive of whomever he is dealing with – Waad and his Lady, for instance, or Carey his jailer and his unseen but reportedly sympathetic wife, for whom a pot of sack given to her might make all the difference in the world. So, he muses, what state of mind does this put me in? He knows, and calls it acquisitive condescension, whereas when dealing with Cecil in public or in private he answers to high-minded fawning. In a sense, since being en-Towered, he has grown up emotionally, with his loftiest branches grazing heaven, or so he jests to himself, unable any more to confide. Why, they have read his treatise on prevarication and know him back and forth, regarding all he says as a lie, which may mean that at some point the truth he evades makes itself evident. This he calls irony, meaning the opposite of what he says. Knowing people better, is there a strategy of conversation then? Of course; he has been schooled in it by Jesuits, but he hasn't grown naturally into it as a lamb into wool. Why, he now realizes, there are emotions restricted to lust alone, having nothing to do with any other object and defunct as soon as the deed of kind be accomplished with a grunt and a silver shudder. The male's point of view, of course, Father Garnet having been initiated to no other. He hearkens back to that favorite idea of his, about renting rather than owning: possess the interim metaphysically, with uppermost the same idea of quitting, either midnight flit or a long-planned disappearance piecemeal. When leaving, do not have a home about your neck. He feels he is on to something major here, especially for a Catholic priest discontented with his lot. Live in heaven, rent the world. *That* is what he means, is it not? Is that why Cecil, as rumored, is ever building, ever eager to spread himself out in yet another manse? Does he have enough children to make the vast spaces palatable, as if each entire home were like Italy, land of noisy children, almost a burbling surf of the innocent? Perhaps Cecil too has this sense of the uninhabited universe being exactly as God wants it, not for further or eventual use, but merely to reveal the concept of emptiness upon emptiness, in contrast with the human mind that is never empty. Such is the Godlike way, he thinks, akin to the hangman booting you off the ladder for a swing or two before hoicking you down for the rest of it.

Has he, then, altogether given up hope of getting off, getting away with his supposed crimes? He cannot see how, but a piece of him persists in hoping. Yes, he tells himself, an optimist has a persistently hopeful habit of mind whereas one can be now and then hopeful without ever approaching the outright outlook of the optimist. I never thought I was an optimist, but, if you manage to go on hoping when there seems little chance of prevailing, then an optimist you are. Hope in spite of everything. Does this mean faith in God or just a lucky chance? God supervises all lucky chances, he knows, so if he survives it will be God's doing. And vice versa. Yet if, like he, a man dissociates himself from good deeds, out of modesty or severity, does this make him an optimist or none at all? He can feel the arguments of his mind beginning to burn and crumble, faced with too many paradoxes. Shall he then settle for being a modest optimist? Why not? The phrase has a cautious sound, on the brink of optimism whole-hearted, but he yields once again to modesty, not wishing to categorize himself as too fierce, too energetic an anything. Had he really been a plotter, the plot would have worked better: if only they had incorporated a few Jesuits into their cadre, not as spiritual counsellors but as shrewd manipulators, the king and his children would have gone sky-high long ago. He is far from sentimental about James or any of the lords; but since the execution of the first eight a new harshness has come upon him, knowing that where his own neck is at stake so should be all of theirs. Somewhere he has heard it said that the best judge of a murderer will be a murderer, so would a plotter judge plotters aright? He does not know, or care that much, but he resents being indicted for listening, for lending an ear as the phrase goes, and he thinks an honorable monarch should take his Jesuits on trust as decent (docent!) fellows committed only to ephemeral affairs concerning the beauty of God's universe. You listen to all that comes along, he reassures himself, and you do not become involved with either side. There is always much to be desired—he loves this expression, fusing as it does sheer plenty and desire's intensity; it also means we are unsatisfied; so it means three things, perhaps his triple view of the world: foison, zeal, and dissatisfaction. At last, he feels, even on the brink, he is beginning to understand himself. Or should it read "Leaving" much to be desired, which has an elegiac flavor, robbing the phrase of adverbial intensity while strengthening complaint as if it were a sardonic end-of-term report on the performance of a schoolboy: *his work is both untidy and ill-couched, leaving much to be desired.* Yet the phrase also has cruel resonance for one condemned, with its daunting omission of the word "behind"—leaving *behind* much to be (that remains) desired. Ah, he sighs at the behest of language as applied to the afterlife, a favorite notion of his. No man loves to leave it, not even a priest.

Then, with no preamble whatever, he imagines it beginning to happen, inspired by his occasional gift of sherry to Martha Carey, who then eggs on her husband the jailer to be nice to that Italian gentleman who likes to drink the day away. By night, it would have been more prudent, but by day it becomes more daring; there is suddenly a stout rope stretched out slanting down between his window and the bollard opposite across the moat. The rope is there to dry out, to weather, to ripen if need be, having been washed and re-oiled. All Father Garnet has to do is loosen some bars, two at most, carefully treated beforehand by Carey, who has done this kind of thing before, then slide hand-over-hand like a rat from the sinking ship, and walk away, an odd sight to be sure in his clerical habit. Should he lie along the rope, then, or hang from it—*depend,* he calls it in his mind? Can he support his own weight, softened up for the event by sherris-sack? Too many questions obsess him. He could always climb out and sit upon the sill, awaiting the next event, ecstatic, in a funk, but where will that get him? He goes, scrawming out, in a long white nightshirt, assailed by Tower ravens that at first size him up as an adequate meal coming over to them. He slithers, then stops, knows he cannot sustain his weight even as the rope sags bringing him nearer the water, then becomes something useful as he dips into the freezing moat: it keeps him above the waterline, so he ends up walking in water, his chin at the surface, his feet treading away, the rope at full stretch (badly calculated by Carey) and a true life-line. Father Garnet is laboriously moving through London water to a hot ale on the other side, straight into a tavern like a drowned rat, where, perhaps, new plotters are already getting to work. No one notices how wet he is; in London they always assume it is raining and so are never surprised by the arrival of a sodden human, thirsty and craving a severe dose of the huge fire in the parlor. He has of course not even noticed Father Oldcorne slithering along his own rope a few yards away, able to go hand over hand without touching water and mouthing an uncouth phrase, half of triumph, half of warning. Father Garnet is so afraid of drowning he forgets his dread of being caught, hauled back, made to pay in a sackless lightless dungeon within earshot of the rack.

None of that. On he goes. Any fool can advance from this auspicious beginning to lying naked among a cargo of dead pigs headed for Belgium; he simply has to find his way to the docks, a mere matter of ten minutes waterlogged walk humming something august from Byrd so as to seem nonchalant. On he goes, finds the right boat and vanishes amid the pork, all of this rehearsed for him by Master Carey, whose prisoners often escape thus while the Careys grow rich and pretentious, inching their way into an area of London that smells better. I could have done this earlier, he thinks, it was only a matter of saying one two three, go. How lucky to find the weekly boat, how expert of Carey to know all about it. No Waad intervening, no master at arms directing musket fire at him in the water, not even Lady Waad shrieking the alarm: a Jesuit is going out to infect a city. It has all been so seemly, so quiet, and even Oldcorne, nail through his tongue again, has managed to lose himself in the crowd. It must be ten in the morning, no heat in the sun, no solace in the wind, no recognition in the eyes of passersby. Londoners must be used to the apparition of maltreated, disheveled priests treading across the river from the Tower, no hue and cry, no pursuit, no dog collars floating on the Thames like ivory garters sucked from the ecclesiastical calf by the potent tide. Father Garnet is pleased, knows now that a similar transit might be managed from dungeon or scaffold, from chopping block and pillory. All one has to do is decide to make a forceful go of it. "Eigh-up" indeed. This is better than skulking in a hole at Hindlip surrounded by—well, it was all too much for them both, and by those standards of incarceration the Tower was a pleasure, clean and commodious. I could have been at my ease in the Tower all the time, Garnet thinks as his nightshirt steams away at the fire and his limbs begin to thaw. I could have hidden out there; what better place to secrete yourself in? *Start* with the Tower while they search Hindlip in vain. No parting word with Oldcorne, however, which is just as well because, with the nail in his tongue, he can hardly speak.

But of course the Carey who helped him out is really Little John Owen, master of priestholes and birdhouse hideaways, accomplishing his masterpiece after many years. And now in his mind it is he, not Oldcorne going along the other rope, ably as an ape, only to vanish for ever in the teeming streets of Southwark whereas Father Garnet has headed for East Smithfield. Of course he has it all wrong and would have succeeded better trying to disguise himself as a Winchester goose (prostitute) in that district. His fellow-escapees are dead men, his keeper Carey would never risk his head for a length of rope, and

Waad and his men patrol the cells with rigor—this is not the Clink in Southwark, Liberty Hall to some, where the bishops run the brothels and prosper on the proceeds. Father Garnet goes back to sleep, or rather to inert eye-shut worry, wondering why he has not been put up in, say, Beaufort Tower, whose prestigious and luxurious apartments have a good view of the private executions on Tower Hill. Perhaps they chose to humiliate him because he brought no servants with him; but would bringing a retinue really matter? He doubts it. Arriving at the Tower with such riff-raff would instantly get you condemned and relegated to the vilest quarters. Of this he is sure, but *who* went out over the two walls and the reeking river? All that was needed, really, was a quiet threepenny boat at Traitors' Gate. Father Garnet knows how he will leave this building, of which in his self-punishing way he has become quite fond of thinking, and yet he tries not to linger on the prospect. He will wait and try never to sleep again.

Yet fragments of chatter remain with him, Oldcorne in his slur teasing him about who has longest to wait, then improvising silly questions: "Shall we walk on water, then?" To which Henry Garnet answers "Only on Sundays. And in one direction." "Oh, then," Oldcorne responds, "it will all depend on how much we have eaten that day. You have to be light to walk on water." Garnet longs for the Red Sea lapping at his window, then savoring the irrelevant thought, adds, "And alone?"

"Do you mind eating alone, Father?"

"I am never alone when I am with food." It sounds like the latest of Father Garnet's rhetorical triumphs, the riposte of a frightened man whose wit calms him in a bear-garden or lions' den. Father Oldcorne never laughs, but he knows how to nod, and when unseen, his grotesquely impeded tongue dangling out in front of him for relief until, as sometimes, he slips a finger on either side of the impaling nail and tugs the tongue forward as if to exercise it through stretch. This is Oldcorne's way of suggesting the pensive, and he adores to do it in much the same frame of mind as certain wearers of an eyepatch like to pull the patch away from the eye and thus shock those watching with a vignette of eggwhite and crusted blood, a mere hole behind the pupil. Father Garnet has lost his companion, his code colleague, and Waad has not sent him a replacement, not even nephew Thomas; it is as if they have overheard all they need and would prefer Father Garnet to lapse into silence, at this point having perfectly convicted himself out of his own mouth.

20

FATHER GARNET'S FUGUES are getting riper, no doubt under the pressures of the Tower. He remembers what some alienated Jesuit of old once told him in a fit of worldly pique: beyond a certain point, you live your life in the past, translating recent pain or joy into something stored up from childhood. We are duty-bound. Father Garnet decides, to become gluttons of nostalgia. He has noticed it in himself, not so much in dreams as in daydreams, especially when squirreled away in the Hindlips of the world, shoved up against unthinkable physical extremes, cleaving to the days when, with sisters destined to be Belgian nuns, he romped underneath an ancient peasant-woven laundry basket through whose cracks a reluctant but adequate English sun entered. There they lay, pretending to be dead or unborn, hoping to be discovered, their hands joined, their breath sometimes held, wondering if spiders or caterpillars were already walking on them. As ecstasies go, it was not much, he supposes, but it was a beginning, certainly for closeness and novelty. How many times they did this he does not recall, but it might have been a dozen, with increasing amounts of conversation as the thrill wore off and the outside world seeped in. To be, as then, responsible for almost nothing, protected from the hurly-burly even his parents endured, with the hinges of life creaking around them only at an enormous distance, was greater than any pleasure and took remarkably little arranging. They just swooped outside without a word and popped under the inverted basket, except when it was in use by Florrie, who came to pound the week's clothes in a wooden tub with something called a poncher. Ponchers squeezed the dirt out, hence granting (he used to think) a new start, almost a reprieve, and he watched her for hours, her muscular oddly brown arms pounding away as if to the rhythm of an old marching song filched from the wars. Something hypnotic held him; he loved the spell of someone else's working rhythm, knowing he had no part in it but could remain a besotted watcher for ever. Florrie's motions connected him, he thought, to the motion of the world—not only to ancient wars, but to the filth amid which they all save the children slaved. Was it this that sent him packing, away from things English to the esoterica of a Roman intellectual? And was it he who inspired his little sisters to depart for Belgium with both parents dead and gone in the fashion of the day? Children, almost grown-ups, bound to make their own way in the world, shadowed and jostled by uncles and aunts, thank goodness, who in the gentlest manner imaginable coaxed the children to become independent. They became devout, he thinks, so as to have somewhere to go, some basis for their amputated lives. Had it not always been thus? Was this not, as Byrd was fond of saying, how children became choristers and acolytes, the orphans among the ones with parents still? So, he muses, there was a link between purity of sound—of voice and mind—and being orphaned. Surely the purest tones came from those who had no worldly bond remaining, so when they sang they were singing with all their heart, upward and outward, to wherever they were not yet. He likes this idea of a flock attuned to distant glory, having no cuddle to return to at the end of a morning's hard sing. It was always the morning, was it not, when they performed, locally at least, because in the morning the throat was rested, the muscles had eased themselves, the body was ready for its most exquisite toil. What a lovely voice he has, he remembers hearing about himself; shall he not be trained? He was, yet not for long, soon evolving into a word-person, one who professionally *thought*, more thrilled by the old *tuli-latum* conundrum than by melody, and eventually deciding (caring this much) that the old verb *ferre* changed its form so suddenly because another verb with a different form became mixed up with it. He loved, still does, the eruption in its history, that sudden swerve in so many minds and mouths from the almost babylike *f* sound, blowy and sustained, to the *t* and the *l*, a stutter and a palatal. Trying to make sense of his career thus far, he draws the line from orphan through song to language, and then from language to the Society of Jesus, and then from being a Jesuit to becoming that fatal thing, a good listener. Yea, a man habituated to, skilled in, confessional is bound sooner or later to flower as a merely secular auditor, ever willing as the phrase has it to lend an ear. He thinks he sees it now: an expert hearer, he has sanctified the very act of attending to others in mere conversation, which surely from the Latin amounts to an effort to "convert" the other, to "turn" him into the way of your expressed mind.

No wonder he got into trouble. He should have remained under the osier basket or gone with his sisters to Louvain. Instead, his recent life seems to have consisted of hearing out upset plotters and listening to the late Father Oldcorne through the Tower wall or confined at close quarters in country houses.

Yes, it's too late for the plotters, mostly gone, the dirt punched/ponched out from the nation's dirty laundry. He sees now that he should have talked much more than opened his ears; if you never shut up, can you be accused of hearing at all? When his intake of sherry has been high, he hears voices of people not there, but wholly unidentifiable. Who can these voices-off be? Were there ever, are there, people to match them? Or do voices float about in the empyrean merely to tantalize him as less obvious speakers? Are there voices at large, for hire, available to those who have spent a lifetime being dumb? Are these voices those of dead plotters, at last free to opine and complain, or are they those who have long suppressed their thoughts, coming to him from highborn prisoners in Beaufort Tower in this very prison, weary of the beautiful view accorded them of beheadings down below? His mind, ranging hither and yon, has begun to torment him with unmanageable hypotheses, as if a geometry master had been obliged to conceive of a two-sided triangle. Things will no doubt be worse, helped on by Cecil, Coke, and the Waads, mitigated only by the hypocritical Careys, but it will be none of his doing, nor of Anne's, lodged in London on the most fruitless quest in the world, hoping to see a man whom nobody sees, trying to communicate with him whose letters are never private, whose mind fills in the blanks with borrowed plainsong.

Father Garnet decides he has never been prepared for life such as this, not even by being hidden away. Poised on the raw edge, having no notion of what will happen next, beyond insult, spying, ridicule, irate interrogation, he longs for some gesture that will reassure him, something not concealed in juice of orange or lemon, something mercifully banal. What are they going to do with him? They are waiting an eternity to do it, so perhaps it will be something unique—a forced marriage with Mistress Vaux, perhaps, so as to make amends for all his uncommitted sins of the flesh? Someone, maybe Carey, will tip him the word, give him an inkling with the next flagon of sherry. Exile he more or less hopes for, and settles for that, knowing nonetheless that the Cecils of this world will not send someone to cities they cannot visit themselves.

"O that I might see you" are the words that occupy Father Garnet's clouded mind even as he writes a bread-and-butter letter to Anne Vaux, acknowledging in ink the things his "loving sister Alice" has sent him: a Bible, a black nightcap, some socks, sheets, and handkerchiefs. Mundane enough stuff but, in the Tower, fabulous treasures from the Orient. In orange juice (they allow him an occasional fruit) he cautions her about the imminent seizure of other priests: the more voices contending in the turmoil of post-torture interrogations, the worse for all concerned. "Take heed," he warns her, "no more of our friends come to danger. It will breed new examinations. Father Anthony Hoskins shall take my place as Superior. I now release you from any obligation to me as your Father Confessor, for obvious reasons. Should you wish now to go to Flanders, I understand, but you will be best off in England provided you manage to attend Mass and Communion. Do not in any way draw attention to yourself."

The letter never gets through and Anne Vaux, agonizing in unpropitious Fetter Lane with Eliza, has to improvise her life as never before, wondering (yet knowing) why Father Garnet never answers her. Is he still alive? In the Tower? Or where? Cecil is getting used to their correspondence, to orange-juice aroma and pretended appellations. Just what he himself might have tried, he thinks, although there must be other ways. Why, he who ministers to a vast network of spies at home and abroad knows the ropes and naturally thinks in not only concise, limited cipher but also in ciphers large as a page, in which a simple overt statement about clouds and wind have a complex secret meaning. Motif disguise, he calls it, wishing he had time to couch it in French or Spanish, but he has not. The case of Father Garnet is not advancing as it should. We have waited a long time for this gentleman, he thinks, and we should jolly him along as best we can; eavsdropping on his lost loves is hardly worth it—one can guess at what they find themselves deprived of. One taste of my toes might liven him up, even a lick at my heel. These fellows are so high and mighty, so genteelly aloof, you would not think they were human with daily droppings to dispose of. He is wrong, of course: after his many years in hiding, Father Garnet knows better than almost anyone in the worst dockland slum the earthy side of life and does not enjoy it. He is too confident, Cecil concludes: an ideal time to ride him further, just as he concludes we have nothing major against him. He presumes we have only presumptions against him, lacking all evidence, and will have to surrender him to his Anne. A touch of the manacles will brisken his spirit for a while, and he so orders, having an aghast Father Garnet hang on the wall for a few hours like venison improving. This strategy works better than he expects, and Father Garnet makes the first of two declarations, admitting them in an alcoholical blur (his hangovers blend into one another, and even the last one before being manacled hangs on for most of the afternoon). Tesimond walked in the garden, he tells them, and explained about the plot, yes. For more news, they keep waking him up from his foggy sleep, with the result that, when Father Garnet appears before the Commissioners, he is unhelpfully woozy, too much so for them, in an exhausted dither that yields not information but a comatose subject. Cecil cancels the sleep disruption order, substituting for it reduced rations, but keeping the sherry and wine to soften him up.

When he is compos mentis, Father Garnet shows some fight, telling the Councillors it is unjust to torture someone over and over for information he does not possess. "No," the Councillors affably inform him, "this happens to be a case of treason, sir, aimed right at the person of the king, which therefore involves the royal prerogative." Again he writes to Anne, telling her he is to be tortured yet again, but he might just as well write direct to the smiling Cecil, glad to watch this long-sought worm squirming with an empty belly. He writes to Tesimond as well, but the letter goes into Cecil's capacious mailbag. Written by daylight and orange, Cecil thinks, ready even to identify the man's prose style, blithely assuming that Father Garnet's letters will end up in the Records Office for another generation to read: anguished, oblique, courteous, they show a hand resolved not to shake, come what may.

At his trial, which abounds in redundancies in view of all the questioning so far, Father Garnet admits he has been well-treated in the Tower: "You have been as well attended for health or otherwise *as a nurse-child?*" He has hardly felt any such thing, if what they mean is like a child being nursed, but he plays along, answering Coke "It is most true, my Lord, I confess it." This appeases them; things are going normally now, and they can extort from him the kinds of answers they want, often implying in their questions the responses they want, which he dimly recalls as an echo of Greek, in which various particles in the sentence do much the same thing. On March 8 he makes what to him seems a confession, admitting that he knew about the treason plot but kept it to himself. Misprision of treason they call it, and they beam at him as if he were a well-briefed schoolboy. At last they have the rabbit from the hat, without which they would be hanging someone uncooperative. Now he fits into position in their world and cannot waggle sideways into an alias. Father Tesimond's words are coming home to settle him at long last, for so long shielded by the code of the confessional.

"Inviolable," he explains haltingly.

"Not when the king is involved," they tell him. "You, Derbyshire-born, have an inviolable duty to His Majesty."

"No, only to Rome," he protests.

"No, you cannot be beholden to two masters." Now one of the more searching questioners asks him with an almost apologetic air (for seeming to exact a tassel from him after so much insult), "Why admit it now, to save yourself, perhaps, rather than earlier, to save the king and the peers of the realm? What is the point of such timing?"

They do not understand when he explains that one cannot break the seal of the confessional without the express permission of the penitent. Yet Catesby, anticipating disaster, had freed Father Garnet to tell all to save himself, if he had to; but the priest, obtuse in this or not taking him literally, holds on to the seal as if his life depended on it, as it now does. In effect he is taking his stand on something Catesby had the good grace to dismiss, which means Father Garnet is clinging to ritual, to an abstract invention mostly his own—*equivocating,* as they love to call it when he might have (he alone can muster the suitable verb) *univocated.* He has been all through this before when questioned about his treatise on lying. They do not understand, as later generations may, that it is possible to live wisely and effectively while serving two masters, while heeding mutually contradictory ideas. Not lying, but vacillating. He tells them again, but they dismiss him with the noise oft written in those times as *Pshaw!*

"It matters little to me, the king, the Council, or anyone," Cecil now goes on to say, "whether you live or die. The damage is done. What matters most is that we all discern the corrupt, treacherous tendency latent in all Jesuits, and never mind their fealty, often professed, to the Pope, God, Jesus, or anyone, anything, else. You and Guido Fawkes corrupted the noble workman, the artisan, John Owen into becoming a Popish lackey. It is bad enough to scant the king, but almost as bad to twist some poor malformed journeyman such as he into being a traitor. It is on your hands that his death rests. You demanded intolerable things of him and his body gave way."

Father Garnet knows it is useless arguing, as with Southerners who mock his pronouncing "Derbyshire" to rhyme with sherbert, as Derbyshiremen do—they never say "*Dar*bishire." With some things they will have to live; they have at least damned him, degraded him. "I could not sleep for worrying about it," he says.

"What a pity you did not wake up when you could not sleep."

Now the king sees the signed confession or admission, finds it not to his taste: "Too dry," he says, "squirt some orange juice into this treacherous Jes-wit. Have him testify as to which lords were involved in the plot, the ones who were going to ignore the next meeting of Parliament to save their skins." In the end, Garnet babbles a few names – Rutland, Arundel – but this is feeble stuff, hardly what James wants from him. "Catesby," he tells them, "felt so badly about what was to come that he went out of his way to avoid Lady Derby and Lady Strange, though he loved them above all others – just because they would have been there to be blown up."

Cecil writes to his master-spies abroad that Garnet has claimed the plot was just, but Garnet has said no such thing. This is misprision of utterance, and Cecil knows it, ever glad to mold a statement until it fits perfectly the rigors of the situation. They are quietly shaping Father Garnet into being the consummate conspirator: the head Jesuit and arch plotter, the presiding spirit, the conduit from abroad, the devious regicide wolf cloaked in the lambswool of mild counsellor. Oddly, Father Garnet finds, this in early March, he has done enough; they expect no more of him. He is shut of it, as they say in his native county. Now he can sleep, drink, and eat, all long-lost marvels, and he has even provided the king with the emotion, the local color, the monarch wants, ever glad to pretty up the confession of a man whose powers of language surpass his own. Father Garnet comes to rest, in both senses of that phrase, thinking he has written to Anne Vaux as much as possible, thus consoling her perhaps, whereas she has heard nothing, and her own frantic missives to him have ended up in the same lost-letter box as his. Deceitfully, they ask for her soon after, tempting her with a rendezvous arranged by Carey the jailer: but when she arrives, wondering about Cecil and his honesty, she sees guards everywhere, men who seem glad to see her, and she at once departs, going not to her lodgings but to Newgate Prison, ostensibly to visit its Catholic inmates. If everyone else could go see them, why not she? They arrest her and dispatch her back to the Tower to be interrogated: a fine sight, the only woman in the prison, and a fine gentlewoman at that.

"Ah, milady," he begins, "No, we don't do that, do we? We don't need to say that. Does he roist your cleft well? I imagine these Jes-wits save it up for one big push." She has a private audience with him, almost as if he were king, which inscrutably he is. "Now, Mrs Perkins," he resumes, "how nice to meet you at last. You have led us quite a chase, whoever you are and have been. Don't upset yourself needlessly, and so provident of you to bring a handkerchief. In my own life, alas, the alias has proved a hindrance. How would *you* like to have been Saint Gobbo, Bumbasted Legs, Elf, Pigmy, Roberto il Diavolo, Microgibbous, Bossive Robin, and the rest, including Monsieur de Bossu, this one coined by one of our own secret agents?" This copious madman, she thinks, is the one who laid out plans for the search at Hindlip: he knew every cranny, every one of the hidden passageways and every one of those angled tiny rooms. He must surely have had an informer. It is the same man to beware of as always. It is he who has hideously mutilated and then beheaded the plot's survivors who could have proved Henry's innocence. Look where we are now.

He is racing on, delighted to have an intelligent woman to talk to, whereas by and large most women have cold-shouldered him except for his plain mother and his insipid late wife. All he has to live for is further twists to his spine and extra corpses from the gibbet. Anne Vaux, rough-handled outside

Newgate prison and bundled back to the Tower, sits now parallel with Father Garnet, perhaps as close as they will ever again be. There is an odd resemblance between the flirtatious but sagacious lewdness with which Cecil confronts Anne and the high-minded, boys-out-together quasi-intellectual romp with which the king himself occupies Father Garnet. Cecil can hardly keep his roving hands off her (just a few handclasps actually), and the king likewise, like a would-be suicide groping after poison, adores to begin a disputation with the tired Jesuit, swiftly moving into matters of treason and theology. Soon, surely, it would be Cecil again with Garnet, and the king with Anne Vaux. Why, she thinks, they must be running out of victims. They will be seizing children and horses next, just to weight the load.

"Others will be asking about that," Cecil tells her, "and we would very much like to know. About other houses, other priests. You should be proud to know so much." Irrelevantly enough, she decides that Monteagle must have been the one who provided the map of Hindlip, Monteagle the maneuverer. "What about the home at Erith in Kent?" He keeps on asking salient bits of questions amidst his pornographic musings, almost like a man unable to restrain himself, allowing the gross to intrude on the pedantic, and responding with a frisson of pleasure to her tight-lipped shock, the defensive motions of her feet and arms. He must have led that drab wife of his a merry dance, she decides—wore her to death while with child. What a pigmy this is. She sketches in, vaguely enough, some travels of Catesby and Tom Wintour, Tresham and others, evoking in the blandest way the social intercourse of White Webbs, anxious to be seen as a grande dame of

Catholic society. Saint Winifred's Well comes up, and so does the name of Lady Digby, along with the Feast of All Saints meeting at Coughton. She steers away from Father Garnet, toward whom he is ever so gently prodding her, not that he needs fresh information. What she excels at, as she has had to, being involved with so many houses and families, is an illusive familiarity that makes him feel like a social outcast from the outset, as if his hectic, potent life has been a waste of time and all those bills from spies abroad need never have been paid. Anne Vaux has the sublime gift of making him feel too ugly to have been invited. In retaliation, Cecil quietly adds the name of Henry Garnet to every reunion she mentions, which means he is mostly right anyway; he was the leaven, the catalyst, the informal toastmaster (as Cecil sees it), ever welcome, always in and out of hiding, under one name or another.

Cecil ushers her now into the presence of the Privy Councillors, crammed together in a chamber reeking of old men's bones and stale sack, as if a befouled dispenser has been lit to perfume the table they sit at. Stoutly she maintains Father Garnet's already lost innocence, forever preaching stillness and patience, peace and duty. Duty sets them off, but almost anything will. What he insisted on, she tells them, was a solution to be gained only by prayer, "at God's hands, in whose hands are the hearts of princes." This moves them somewhat, as does her grave, affronted demeanor. At least in here, she thinks, her skirts are safe. She writes down a postscript, wishing for lemon juice, confirming her sorrow that Henry Garnet "should be any least privy to this wicked action, as he himself called it."

Now she is alone with Cecil again. Most men are slime, he

tells her with relish. They have to be kept on the straight and narrow. This strikes her as theological and she does not object. His cynicism and her version of original sin encounter and glance off each other jadedly. He informs her that Father Garnet will soon be tried, for the sake of what she calls his innocence, and would she care to attend. If so, will she be Mrs Perkins, with all the privileges appertaining thereto, or who? He has no intention of admitting her, but he says so many things for effect he might be a stage manager. She merely stares him out, not an easy feat as he has this skill, seeming to immobilize his eyes and freeze them for minutes on end while reading the mind in front of him.

"Oh no," she blurts.

"Oh yes," he answers. "We could compel you."

"Then do, sir, add me to your list of the lost."

This flash of fire excites him to snap, "Beware, woman."

"No, sir," she retorts, "beware *Woman,* come what may."

And she goes on. "In our family and our religion, we do not flinch before the merest onslaught of any upstart pigmy who never even finished at Cambridge, he was so eager to get out into the world to make trouble and destroy innocent lives." He smiles wetly, delighted to have something original to while away the time between this interview and Garnet's show trial. "Some of us are not as unlettered as you may think, sir, and your depredations affect us only only as the meanderings of a bed-louse lost in paradise. Forgive me, I mean a bed-louse with a broken back and a mind to match. You see: I have made my way in this world, among many friends, with tact and honesty."

"With honesty," he whispers, transfixed. "To be sure."

"Then hang me with him, sir, if you wish. There will be little left."

"No, madam, we do not do this for the *convenience* of others. You cannot order up execution like a pound of cheese. It takes some striving for, and an enormous amount of preliminary paperwork. You have no idea how much paper I have to bear from place to place each day, verifying and countermanding. All is written. What is not written does not exist." Was it not I, he muses in the wake of that salvo, who saved Shakespeare's patron, Southampton, from beheading after he had become involved in that damned rebellion? 1601, my lords, the year before the Bodleian Library opened at Oxford, Bodley's prudish tastes reflected in it. He delivers the smile of a man who has read her judicious, curbed letters to Henry Garnet, with the juicy parts made plain by heat. He knows her too well, winning a bet with himself about how soon she would explode. A fiery wench, he thinks; at the same moment, as if she has not been attending to evidence planked right in front of her like joints of raw beef, she recognizes that the Cecil who adores to build new homes to be lonely in is the same man who knew Hindlip inside out. This is the architect-*Meister* of the government, able to probe people in all their privacy because that is all he has that is his own. Her well-informed mind nearly touches an image of what she's been told about the headless trunks after execution (excepting those condemned for treason, who get quartered and dispersed). Trussed in sacks, they go by a wheelbarrow from the block on Tower Hill to the cellar of Saint Peter *Ad Vincula* chapel, where the wheeler dumps them down the steps, tossing a scoopful of lime after them like a bouquet. What a stench must afflict that chapel, she decides; but no one ever mentions it. Perhaps they all end up in the Thames like butchered sheep. Don't think of such, Father Garnet has told her. Somewhere in Africa, I forget where, they bury a warrior sitting up, carefully planting a straw from his head to the surface. The straw sticks up a foot or so. When the first maggot crawls out of it, the mourners go home. "Now, isn't that a providential way to go?" She shakes her head, warrior that she can sometimes be. Anyway, what is Africa to *this?*

21

BEMUSED AT BEING BROUGHT to trial, after repeated interrogation and torture, Father Garnet tells himself it is bound to be the same as these, but without originality or pain. If so, he distantly guesses, then how so? What on earth can I tell them that is new? Do they just want to have me sing once more, a favorite old song chanting itself for a last time? Perhaps the whole event will be conducted in Latin, as is fitting among educated men. If only, he laments, he still had his linguistic wits about him so as to be sharp and caustic in riposte, especially with Coke and Cecil. If only it were not the 28th of March and not the Guildhall; every day has a date and a place, but what he wants is a dateless nowhere, and all he says ultimately unfindable, known only to God.

In any case, how will he ever get as far as the Guildhall? Suffering and deprivation have weakened him profoundly; he can hardly walk, and is unequal to that obligatory humiliation, the trudge to the final Star Chamber, through streets crowded with jeerers. Waad, however, has anticipated the problem by providing a coach; so this inconspicuous Jesuit rides in style, unlike other so-called conspirators who have walked amid a hail of spit and rotten vegetables.

"Better, sir," he whispers to Waad and Waad's lady, she
there to spectate as almost ever, touched by the cruel bitter-
sweet among so much personal refinement.

"I must *deliver* you, Father, in prime condition. Fine gentlemen would not like to see a bedraggled cockerel coming
into view for the last rites. Be at ease, Father. You are no good
as a footman these days."

Once the mob realizes who is in the coach (8:45 for a 9:30
appointment), they jeer away, confident the Jesuit has finagled
this luxury and half-expecting him to have a human mouth-
piece with him (not that they will be admitted to the trial). All
they want, Father Garnet keeps telling himself, meaning Cecil
and his ilk, is duplication, repetition, all the crass variants of
blame. He wishes his mouth and voice were as nimble as his
mind. The coach keeps lulling him as the Tower never did.

"Who's within?"

"Garnet the Jez-wit, going to trial."

On goes the tale, convincing all that the Jesuit has pull,
even at this late stage, yet another proof of the king's latent
tolerance for the Society of Jesus and its hangers-on. Little do
they know how much James wobbles, how evenly a Jez-wit
and a greyhound, a recusant and a goshawk, balance out on his
scale of interests. Going grandly, Father Garnet tells himself:
my first touch of pomp in a while. I wonder when the next will
be, and what. Thank God for a little weakness that gets a man
some ease before yet another ordeal.

He lapses into a dozing man's Latin, half-praying, half-
quoting, in a medley of Jesuitical Cicero, memorizing what to
say by the passing architecture, setting huge buildings amid
his ingenious bleats. Let a tavern stand for honor, a small

palace for lies. Have I had breakfast? What building corresponds to breakfast? Yes. A breaded slop with a rank rabbit kidney therein, or was it—for courage—a lion's eye? Globe slime. He cannot finish the figure, he can only just begin. It will go on all day like this, with King James once again hidden behind a tapestry, others present including Lady Arabella Stuart and Cecil's doxy, Catherine Countess of Suffolk. But no pregnant, pro-Popish Queen Anne, perhaps out of delicacy and finesse. Like it or not, Father Garnet is the cause of a social occasion, obliged to stand in an oaken pulpit, a mild, balding, bespectacled monster for all to see: Messrs Meaze, Whalley, Darcy, Roberts, Farmer, Philips and Perkins rolled into one. The nearer the coach gets, the faster it seems, drawn thither by eagerness to disgorge him.

Intent on duplicity, Coke cites multiples. Father Garnet, he rants, is a compound ghost, ever slipping away, a will-o'-the-wisp plotter. Why, even a *voluntarius daemon,* he cries, harnessing a phrase he himself has concocted to show how a drunkard may drink himself into madness, as it were volunteering to become a demon unto himself, except that *daemon* implies a mighty, twisted self. But even that might apply to this Jezzy-wit. They rumble, cough, and titter. Garnet is a dozen demons fused. No decent man, Coke argues, need be a Proteus; was ever Proteus renowned for decency? Oh to sleep in God's pocket, Father Garnet thinks: tucked in tight while yawning. On goes Coke, decrying this "clerk, of the profession of Jezzy-wits, conspiring to blow up the beloved king, God bless him wherever he may be this day, his family with him. To blow up Prince Henry, the Lords, the Commons."

Coke, with one of the pointiest faces in England, hacks and

coughs, summoning up and managing to trap, then swallows a nugget of phlegm provoked into being by that dank and shivery chamber. "Now does this Jezzy-wit plead? Not guilty, of course. A Jezzy-wit is a law unto himself, just as the Powder Treason is a conspiracy unto itself. They respect naught. I name it the *Powder Treason* but might just as well call it the *Jesuit* Treason for king-killing and queen-killing, a butchery shop where only Italian is heard. Lest"—he pauses, views the ceiling with abstracted eyes, finds God at last, and sighs—"this devil has had his placket-teasing finger in every treason since 1586, and God knows, as Mister Perkins and several other gentlemen. Well, we have a place for him ready, remarkable for lack of gunpowder."

Cecil, who has so far not spoken, but as it were trembled with Coke's slanderous resolve, fidgets at the prospect of a day's inflated orotundity and makes a mental note to ply Coke with more paperwork, to cut him down, to shut him occasionally up, little realizing that part of Coke's mind is already on a treatise of his own, *Third Part of the Laws,* much as Cecil's is on his own *An Answere to Certain Scandalous Papers.* Bookish men, they do not yield all of their being to rituals of scheming hate. Why, Ben Jonson did the Latin version of Cecil's opus. Father Garnet is a just a peg to dangle self-promotion from; Cecil and Coke have better fish to fry.

"Lest," he resumes his resuming, while shifting his aim a bit, "we think of him as a mere designer of deviltry, not a bloody-handed butcher of royal children, let us lay misprision of conspiracy at his doorstep, which is knowing of it without revealing it. He is the *author* of the plot." (Coke never seems to realize that Father Garnet is the author too of the much-

quoted treatise on prevarication.) "A fire-angel hath descended from the empyrean to vouchsafe us this." Cecil
squirms as if the prose style of the Monteagle letter has caught
on, converting all prose to fungus. "My lords and ladies," Coke
drones on, "go to *Genesis,* its very self, and behold how yonder
serpent receives *three* punishments for harboring the idea, and
Eve only two as being mediate procurer, and our Adam fellow
just the one as the party seduced. Now, most of your parties
seduced, our Adams, we have hanged, drawn, and quartered.
Here then is our serpent, free still to this day. Shall we top him
thrice, as Scripture says? What about *his* Eve, Mistress Vaux,
or Perkins? A dozen punishments would not suffice. Now,
hear me out. It worsens."

It is only when Coke, in some fit of rhetorical dissatisfaction, starts to alliterate that Father Garnet realizes what has
gone wrong in his life, what has changed it for the worse.
Even as Coke charges at him with not so much fresh facts as
stylish rearrangement, he musters his weary intellect and recognizes his main mistake. Plots abound, Coke says, like foxes
joined by their tails, "however severed in their heads." Father
Garnet has been involved in them all, certainly from 1603 on,
"a doctor of the Five *D's*," as Coke dubs him: Dissimulation,
Deposing of Princes, Disposing of Kingdoms, Daunting and
Deceiving of Subjects, and of Destruction. It is a feeble
enough figure, improvised in the wake of an earlier speech at
another trial, and it might with conciser grandeur have joined
with Dereliction, Depravity, Deviltry and Death, not to mention Diabolism and Disputation, but Coke is not Cecil, who
would have couched this five-pronged onslaught in Latin, at
least to begin with, even if only to get Father Garnet's learned

attention. Coke now works his way back and forward from Dissimulation to Destruction, wondering at the quintuple doctor's apparent boredom with the indictment.

"This devil's doctor," Coke is going on, "took it upon himself to send Sir Edward Baynham to Rome to seek the Pope's approval of their loathsome plot." The reverse was true: Garnet had asked the Pope's support for a pacific, do-nothing stance. "Always he was praying for Catesby's success in this benighted, treacherous endeavor, hearing him out in confession—the whole hatching of the conspiracy—and praying for his filthy soul. Prayer *for,* mark you, implies agreement, does it not?" Now he reverts to his alliterative onset. "Duty does not daunt the devil." What is he driving at? The timbre, as Ben Jonson might dub it, is accusatory, as if the same dentals, repeated, conferred guilt, but his matter is obscure, more iterative tantrum than evidence. He carries his listeners along through simplistic consonantal insistence, Colorful Coke as they call him, quite numbing their analytical faculties. Soon, no doubt, the two D's that have become five will be seven deadlies in a rhetorical climax they can hardly bear to wait for. This is a day out for gentlemen and some of their ladies; God forbid it degenerate into an affair of serious, primed logic or something as mere as principled investigation tainted with fairness. Let there be merriment or at least a mild scurry of delight.

There is a ripple among them at some precious figure, a semi-musical libel inflicted on the five-pronged Jezzy-wit. But Father Garnet is miles away, subdued by low-caliber oral artifice into a diagnostic reverie in which he realizes for the first time that an old belief of his, ripe from Winchester days to now, has just bitten the dust. He loves that expression.

Hitherto he has always felt that the mind, unlike the body, cannot be harmed, that whatever it is subjected to only makes it more flexible, lissome, nimble, resilient—all the things it is supposed to be: skeins of limber quicksilver responding to light, vibrating and adapting in blithe consort. (A touch of Byrd in this.) No matter what appalling fodder passed into a mind, it survived, or so he used to think: changed, of course, but ever-ready for more because, so went his old belief, the mind is the soul and shares in God's suppleness, never harmed by what it, He, passes through.

Coke is rambling on about prevarication again, as "an offence against chastity," but Father Garnet is succumbing to a different assault, from corruptibility, now converted to the belief that the mind is only too vulnerable, no more the transcendent armature but the fallible arena, not to be meddled with and, like the dyer's hand, soaked in what it lives among, changed forever by that immersion and perhaps the less able to cope with both adversity and joy. It has not always been so for him; his faith has kept him agile, but now he feels the gradual incessant uproar of peevish to savage ideas has weakened him exactly as torture has. The mind/soul, he tells himself, does not always heal, even though intimately joined to God. Those enraptured by the deity cannot always pass clear through their hindrances, but bear them for ever after as patches or bruises inside, blurring any light that once might have purged them into becoming mere abstracts or records of an ordeal: one of Satan's better fumbles.

Coke has not finished (he has hours to go and several ladies have already bestirred themselves for the closed-stool hidden away behind a temperate screen of fauns and dogs—mostly

Dalmatians, carriage dogs these, the cheetahs of the rutted streets). This being his day for recognitions, Father Garnet acknowledges that the winter half of his life has not been worth living, certainly not worth dying for. If only all were Italy, April to October. Yes, pushed, he will take March and November too, the one's winds, the other's mud, but only Italian ones. At his most Cecilian in this, which he does not heed, he studies pointy-chinned Coke fawning on himself in an imaginary looking glass, sibilantly saying, "Chastity—meaning tongue and heart in sacred union, speech and sentiment too. With no bastard utterances to soil that harmony. Lies are bastard children, interruptions of a noble bond. Not for our Jezzwit, though, whose own view of chastity may best be seen—his humble priestly vow—in his proximities with yonder Missus Vaux. Our priest is a fornicating prevaricant. God forbid such a man! What shall his temporal and eternal ally in Rome make of *that?* When he crouches, does he leave a curled snake of soil beneath him like a dog? He does. It is divinely decreed. But need he cater to his proscribed *member* like any ploughman in a hedge with his befouled doxy? Is *that* a given? Is it or is it not?" Stung to life by the sound of her name, Father Garnet raises a vowel from his stilled, clogged voice, but Coke's arm halts him, raised aloft to intercept God's intervening lightning bolt. "What a fault," Coke cries, limping into French for unknown reasons. *"Quelle faute."* Father Garnet subsides, mind quelled by occasion. *Witness Mrs Vaux,* he murmurs. Attorney-General Coke is quite right, he decides: he, Garnet, has corrupted himself, or as nearly as makes no difference, harboring thoughts—posing questions, coveting lewd views—that change him at once into a peep. A Tom. The first ogling Jezzy-wit? He wonders. Surely not. In which case, why on earth—

"A very obstinate woman," Coke is off again, "forever consorting with priests, hiding them, squandering her family's fortune on rented country houses in which to have proscribed services. Ever defying her monarch and his laws. For what? *To be with her leman,* to whom she writes in lemon juice or other juices prevalent in her body. *To defy.* Dissimulation. Deposing. Disposing. Daunting and Deterring. Destroying. And Defying!" *Six,* Cecil notes on a scrap. Get rid of this greased cuckoo. But how?

This little bout of impromptu scorn is enough to distract Cecil from the Jesuit on trial and set him brooding on his son William, who takes after his mother and is wholly without intellectual distinction. This dismal fact notwithstanding, William will go off to Cambridge (St John's College, his father's) in the fashion of the day and so must acquire Latin somehow, which he at present does while riding. Alas, the clamor of hounds drowns out the Latin spouted by his tutor and him, and Cecil senior has been unable to come up with a Latin-speaking horse. In fantasies Cecil has read, there have been Latin-speaking griffons and unicorns, but never in London. The boy, a mere nine, vexes him, having social graces for brains, yet cannot even fold a letter as a gentleman should. All he can do is send the lad off to the Cam at eleven for a final proof, so to speak, then whisk him away to Europe for posthumous polishing. This grand tour Cecil has already worked out, even to the point of selecting a personal brewer to accompany the boy and keep him supplied in his early teens with acceptable ales. He has even picked a tutor, John Finet, translator of a

French text entitled "The Beginning, Continuance, and Decay of Estates," as if to ready the child for apocalypse, theorizing in his way that, where a son lacks Latin, logic, and brains in general, but dotes on ale, horses, and hounds, he might as well learn about property and death, for he will inherit both. Whether Cecil finds all this fussing ridiculous, he never says, but it occupies him like a boil in the groin. His one hope is that William will form some passion for music, in which he shows an average interest. Perhaps a certain Byrd can be persuaded . . .

Once again, Cecil looks to Father Garnet and Coke, the former sagging in his pulpit, the latter still in full flight, raving on about lying as if it were the Neapolitan bone ache, quite reducing weary Garnet to a series of faltering assents: "It may be so, my lord, it may be so." Time has melted; Father Garnet knows only that midnight is ahead of him, his past must seem a rack of years numberless, blurring into one. These, the years he is living now, are the ones before midnight; that is all. Looking at his copy of Coke's brief, Cecil notes the deleted name of Monteagle, hero of the hour, even of the month, and smiles inwardly, knowing as few do that, for the mere suck of a Cecilian toe, Monteagle became the butt of a worldly stratagem engineered for him by the spy, forger, and cryptographer Thomas Phelippes, a man so redundantly complex he is bound to end up in the Gatehouse or even the Tower. Cecil has an astonishing satisfied sense of being wholly in charge of his world: right names expunged, right heads off, right rascals detained and shut away, right children aimed outward at Europe like clowns fired from a circus cannon, right priests tied in knots on public show. It will all *do*, he thinks, not perfect, but fair. Why must Coke go on so, a man who thinks his rhetoric supreme ? In truth he is no more than a literate Airedale, reading statements aloud and listing all plots while the priest sucks on his teeth, quoting Christ about Judgment Day. Here he goes again, Monsieur Garnet, claiming confession is inviolable unless the penitent give permission. Cecil can stand it no longer. Up he gets, in his mind's eye *rearing* up, and shatters the moribund calm with, "No such thing, my masters, as a seal of the confessional! 'Tis arbitrary as the taint of ancient haddock. Who is to say when a matter of degree is absolute? Try harder, Father, you have a guilty sound to me. As you would to His Majesty, were he here. A walk in the garden is not sealed by anything save an aroma of roses. Only horticulture is final there. Perhaps a rose is privileged, but who is to confer with it? In Latin, *sub rosa*, we say, for secret. Is there some rose-bower akin to the confessional? They talk with their scents, these roses, but our not hearing them does not mean they insist on secrecy. 'Tis said, by a former secretary to the Keeper of the Great Privy seal, that our Cecil in his time challenged the Earl of Hertford to a duel over a lawsuit. 'Tis *said*. Now, what seals that? There are three needed components for a Catholic confession: satisfaction, contrition, and repentance. 'Tis said. Where, as with Catesby to Father Tesimond, who relayed this to Father Garnet, there is no repentance, even in advance, the so-called confession is not valid, sires. The priests may consider themselves released. Catesby never promised *not* to go through with his revolting plan. Now, where is the repentance in that? I rather call it a prevaricate obstinancy, or an arrant promise. He tells only to be sympathized with, not to be cleansed. No priest is obligated to him, sealed in with him."

This conjuror's voluntary makes an impact of sorts, but Cecil has not finished. As often, he starts out not to make a speech, but, gathering momentum, converts an interjection into oratory, in which cleverness and sheer idiosyncrasy take him far beyond the matter at hand, to which, however, he always returns garlanded with newly improvised flowers: his majesty's pride and joy, whereas Coke is a mere journeyman, a loud mouth serving a loud mind.

"I add only," Cecil resumes, "that Father Garnet could have reported Catesby the malefactor simply from his general knowledge of the man, his obsessions and tendencies. *He does tend,* would have sufficed: that ordinary statement, enabling us to proceed. Such is not betrayal but informal admission, easily and cheaply paraphrased, as if to tell us this gentleman prefers sherris-sack to wine. Not a complex matter at all, Father Garnet. What do you say to that, Father?"

Unslept, unfed, aching in every bone, Garnet fudges up the best answer he can: "I did not understand this at the time. Perhaps at the time of anything I never quite understand what is implicit." A piece of non-sequitur suet, this, and Cecil knows it. Then why goad the old goat, why hound him? For practice? Because King James himself has personally interviewed Father Garnet, trying him in private beforehand, and still finding fascinating the watershed between seal and leakage. When, the king asked on that occasion, must something remain accessible only to God? Riddled with ambivalences sexual and national (a bisexual Scot ruling England), James is too sensitive to the modish word *equivocate* to use it, but he uses *prevaricate* in what he calls the Scottish sense, meaning *evade the issue,* much as Scots use "next" in "next Sunday" to mean the Sunday after the one coming up, which does not wash in England at all.

Nextness, north of the border, is a distant, foggy thing.

Oddly enough, Father Garnet, expert on temporizing (another word in vogue at that time) uses words in the same broad, rough way as the king, perhaps because the North of England is not far from Scotland. Call it the rustic use of words. Is this what attracts James to Garnet, who seems to be saying one thing while intending another based on sophistical attention to the faded meaning of something said, the lost ancestry of a word broken up into its component parts? *Praevaric-et cetera* recall the variants in the word's history, in the history of other words too, such as the bizarre changeling *tulilatum* that irrupted as the routine conjugation of *fero-ferre* when Father Garnet was first learning Latin, this forever transfixing him with etymological magic, akin to that of the Resurrection, something irrevocably changed. Now Cecil reiterates what is essentially the king's question: "Whether a priest is bound to reveal a treason dangerous to king and state if discovered unto him in confession, the party signifying his resolution to persist." It is the meat-and-potatoes question and they do not let Father Garnet avoid it.

22

A S COKE TAKES OVER again for more drubbing, from a Cecil lapsing bemused into antagonistic reverie, Father Garnet recognizes they will pester him with this issue until his last breath. Is the question even answerable? By anyone? He thinks not. What is the meaning of "bound"? What are all its meanings? Themselves bound together (he winces), do they make one superlative, absolute *bound?* No, they do not, any more than washing flapping on a clothes line becomes one shirt. What choice could there ever be between God and Mammon? These are false alternatives, he knows, since all kings answer to God. A Jesuit is not a courtier but a bride. All he can do is be chastely silent or, like a courtier, just rattle on in pointless debate until they tire of it. All he offers them is that a confessor is free to hinder, obstruct, discourage whatever plot he hears about, and this he did, with the Pope's backing.

"Not enough," Coke ambiguously blusters. "Tell your king, you Derbyshire-born Englishman. Were you not born a subject of the realm?" One day there will be a Prevention of Terrorism Act, with only lawyers exempt from it. "What you do not stop," Coke tells him in ringing tones, "when you can *is your fault.* Passivity is no defence." This stings Father Garnet and makes his eyes pool.

The cutting edge of his mind has long since vanished into a drawer of ill-matched, unused cutlery, its only charm a bone handle epitomizing the body. What, he lamely wonders, would I feel if the plot had succeeded? Guilt at all those deaths, king and children in pieces toppling back down from the top of the explosion like Sunday joints of beef. Beeves plural? Would I have gone my way oblivious? Would I have rejoiced? I would have been ashamed merely for knowing about the plot. Ergo, what? Are they right to condemn me then? He who knows should tell, unless . . . he who does not need not worry. But did I know enough? After all. God stopped it. All is well. All that happens is God's doing, is it not? A spectator I am, but no participant. Killer, marauder, plotter, incendiary, footpad—I am none of these, but rather a devout pietist who devises no earthquakes for others. Yet to be dove-like is some pain since no one hates a contemplative more than a man besotted with the active life. All along, these wealthy Londoners have been asking why I did not intervene. In my own fashion, I did. I am not Alexander the Great, I am Henry the Gentle, take it or leave it, burghers of unblown-up London.

Garnet feels cold with an unnerving sense of having failed some public or other. Why, they seem to have been asking him, can you not prove your innocence? Why can you not *im*-prove your situation? Is it we who have rendered you weary, flaccid, sleepy, tortured in every joint? Father, have we not been your enthralled watchers, intent on your average deed, eager to peel you off the hook you impaled yourself upon like Father Oldcorne with his tongue? I should have mustered my best strengths, he chides himself, my most strenuous self-analysis, and spelled all things out defiantly, a man on his mettle, rising to the occasion with better than Cecilian metaphor, a sea-beast at last unchained from the ocean floor. I should have dominated the proceedings with sheer mind, invoking the panoply of my worldly experience, swapping Latin for Latin (author, locus, date), not being more of a Jesuit, wilting or surrendering, shifting from foot to foot, squinting at them and cupping my ear to hear the churn of the sea, like an idiot in a primer. To those acting innocent, I believe, shall innocence be given. Who, then, is the keeper of innocence? Where is it stacked up, like gunpowder? In whose cellars?

So: all that dung-caked hiding has come to this. I am being worsted by Latinists from the other side of the fence. Hebrew has not come into play at all, as it never does. How forlorn life becomes when men of mind turn against one another in the interests of their own careers. I was physically reduced, so as to cut a pitiful figure in this midden of a court. Their interest in me is abstract. Not in what I say, but how I look. Behold the demon, fellow-tapsters. Their very effrontery swells their self-importance. The theologically-minded barbaric king soon loses interest, having encountered a soul that communicates only with God, having nothing to do with him who, ironically, claims divine right. Such pomp. Had I to say Away with Popes to say Away with kings, I'd do it, my masters. Away with all potentates. Let the meek, the few there are, judge the meek, run the world, even if, in the end, the strong inherit them. These judges do not like it that I lapse into a dullard's unbreakable silence. They prefer affable victims, hair combed, eyes ashine, lips pliant and obedient. I'm not such a monster after all, yet that most *dangerous* beast is the mild man who will not do violence to himself. Does that make me horned with poison, and swathed in a foul sulfurous vapor won from hell?

A pox on hypocrisy, he decides, as Cecil rises to add courtly trimming to the indictment. Have I aught I would like to say? "I would like to pray if you do not mind." He falls quiet as if before a vast deep he dare not tickle with his finger. I put myself back in God's hands, where I began. Should judgment not be passed? Are they asking me? Oh it should, I tell them. You have all worked so hard to reach this point. Even wealthy gentlemen must not waste their time, not on the penultimates of one who turned his back on his native heath and then returned in the service of a foreign power. Oh, I will not bandy words with them at this juncture, of course not. It occurs to him that, if they manage to wipe out the English Jesuits, then they will have only doctors and lawyers to chop at, to bandy Latin with. So, they will wipe out the doctors next and then fall out amongst themselves like thieves, spouting Latin at one another with desperate formality, sentencing one another to death until there is nobody left.

After a mere quarter-hour, the judges sentence him to be hanged, then drawn and quartered (coincidence of fractions, he notes absently), as if he were a mince-pie from Rome. The mob will view his traitorous organs and feel freer for the end of his malicious, Papish reign. He almost totters, twitches sideways with a mischievous sickened look (singled out yet again for bad behavior), then regains his composure, indefinably shorter in stature, his mind seeming to clank within his head, fixed on the few certainties left to him. No more Vaux. No more books. Those observing him (connoisseurs of this deathly moment as a man's world crumbles and ends before him) eye him for last-ditch ambivalence. Will he strut, giggle, or smirk? Does the multiple sentence somehow please him, take the guesswork out of his remaining days? "Ah," one of them whispers, "he will be hanged, without equivocation." London has a buzz-word, meaningless except to extremist hair-splitters or the nearest Jesuit. Only he and Oldcorne are left, he thinks, and soon the galloping monarchists will have made a clean sweep of the priests. Back in the Tower, again by carriage through an even more triumphant torchlit mob braving the smeary downpour of April, with a stark north wind lurking in the dusk, Father Garnet stays dry, legs almost molten, his every thought now aimed through Anne Vaux to God. Now he will have to be heroic and put up with his newly acquired grandeur, not fobbing it off as an undeserved honor but embracing it with vindicated fervor.

There are new problems for him to ponder: is this God's or man's finality? There are two, he decides, one fatuous because trumped-up, the other glorious because eternal. The wonderful thing about the afterlife, he knows (at least the secular side of him does), is that if it exists you find out. If it does not, then you don't. What could be more perfect than that? It's all arranged, he says, so as never to disappoint. God is ingenious, is He not? Communication thence, and thither, seems to him the main problem, but he reasons that angels are not for nothing and there are always the well-known harmless bolts of learned lightning that enliven mystics. Electric Latin: he looks forward to it, murmuring I am so innocent. If they will hang the likes of me, they might as well hang the sisters of Louvain, if they could only get their hands on them. He wonders if Cecil is now satisfied;

after all, this is the result he coveted, that only he could bring about. Or does his blood-lust continue as part of his power-mania, aiming to dominate the world that so disfigured him? In fact, Cecil's mind is no longer on Father Garnet, nor the king's. England saved rolls on toward the next plot, Cecil's brain under his body's thumb.

With fascinated revulsion, Father Garnet tests the hopelessness of his next few days: he need do nothing whatever, and the law will pursue its ghastly course. Let him scream, plead, wriggle, run, go utterly still, and nothing shall change. He has never been in such a situation, and its affinity with his wholly belonging to God offends him. What a poor way to end your days, pawn to Robert Cecil, James's master cripple whose passion himself is to deform. If Father Garnet knew how little, apart from matters of procedure, he entered Cecil's mind, he would be astonished. The most important thing in the world to him, to Anne Vaux, is a triviality. Certainly to be the centrepiece of a ghoulish show gives you importance of a lurid kind, but Father Garnet knows it is his church, his Society of Jesus, that has centre stage. He is only one among the many already tipped off the ladder to the crowd's big *Oo*. And none of them in the Tower are counselling him how best to approach this feat.

Among so many abominable things there is the chance of obscenity: his shirt floating up in the wind and flaring out (it is still a wild, windy spring with westerly gales howling across England and even Italy). He does not want his private parts exposed during his last moments, so he calls for needle and thread (an amazing privilege he cannot fathom), Carey the jailer obliging, bringing him some of Mrs Carey's best. With untutored care, Father Garnet sews up the side gaps in his long undershirt, to be sure making the garment harder to put on, to tug down. No matter. The Latin tag for this occasion will not come, does not exist: threat of death does not so much clear a man's mind as numb and void it. Surely it should run Last Things better than this, but the reverse has happened; the unruly aspect of his mind fudges up phrases the Romans did not need. His mind is going, sooner gone. Father Garnet knows now how the condemned man remains the same each hour but develops fresh tics, tremors, lapses of memory and skill. To this extent he is even more Cecil's toy now, both conquered and abject, a toy broken by a spiteful child. Does he need a priest? Are there any left? Is he the last? Waad lies to him that Tesimond, son of a bricklayer and a devout mother, choleric Yorkshireman with black hair and beard, has been hanged in his early forties, retrieved, Garnet surmises, from a boatload of rat-infested pig carcasses, but where and how? And Gerard, already abroad in Italy, is gone too, they say. Soon England will be Jesuitless, thank God. Father Garnet tends his suspicion with tender gratitude, realizing they are trying to break him down before the event, which torture, lack of sleep, and starvation failed to accomplish. Wary now of sack or wine, he seeks to purge and purify his being, grouping what is left of him around the image of a hanged man's soul ascending past the sun—in his case the soul will have ascended, preferably, beforehand: *taken care of,* he likes to think. He is a man no longer of any heft, no longer disposed to cringe or yelp, the body being the remainder husk and welcome to its low-caliber yearnings: not to suffer, not to disgrace him, not to disgust onlookers. Verily, he tells himself, I have already gone

up. I have quit these infernal premises like an infuriated tenant, eager only for a last meal at dawn, which they will not
provide, of pasta and Italian tomatoes.

So where is Anne? Denied access, he supposes, yet in the
Tower too, as if they were still immured in some old tale out
of Boccaccio, crying out for each other to the dry amusement
of the Waads, who have heard it all before with inert compassion (after all, Waad loves Lady Waad, so how would *they* feel
situated thus?). Anne pleads daily to see him; but, at the end
of a long chain of false promises and maybes, Cecil forbids it,
at his most unrelenting, and always vexed by that unpromising
son of his. Am I to be pander to this Jezzy-wit, he whispers, to
him of so many names, she of so many insults, they of so many
seditious maneuvers? Am *I* to be their go-between? His body
pains him, especially his stomach, though his fare is plain.
Something other than loathing eats him up; a devil at breakfast time, a rat over dinner. He is intermittently ailing, no
longer hale, in his stunted compass, or hearty. Father Garnet
has at least accomplished that, turned his sporting into spite.

No longer dreaming of escape (escape is merely to come *out*
of your *cape,* he recalls), Father Garnet would like to cut a
good figure, somehow, as they say, at the last, but he has no
idea how to do this, recognizing that at such extremes the impromptu rules all, few are gifted with the aplomb of Sir Everard Digby ("Thou liest" as they held up his heart on high).
Priests have been burned and hanged before, by the dozen, but
Father Garnet no longer regards himself as one of a team, a
set; rather, he does a grandiose reading of his loneliness, cast-
ing himself as an epic nonentity. No matter how trivial a man's
life, he reckons, when you rob him of it he becomes a Jesus.

Or, if not Jesus, then Little John Owen, one of him, already only vaguely lamented except by those he saved. Father Garnet no longer wishes for earthly life; he has chomped on the bitter pill to come on May the First (a day of national rejoicing and merriment year after year) and swallowed. He would like some guarantee that his end will be observed by a reputable authority: a priest, a recusant, and found seemly. Otherwise, he thinks, a death is worth nothing, a portentous bauble for a king to cart off to his political nursery, there to be toyed with till boredom sets in.

Now he suffers a long vale of interruptions, from Waad proffering sack and a promise from Lady Waad "to pray for you, good Father Garnet," to Carey who comes unbidden to report that he brings no news except that Father Oldcorne has gone off the ladder up in Worcestershire, one of several, crying the name of St Winifred, then grunting like a plebeian, "Eigh-up!" as a warning cry, perhaps, a noise of solidarity with the delighted rabble, reminding one of that other Yorkshireman Fawkes and the rest of them. Defiant to the last with tongue still impaled on its nail, Father Oldcorne remains Father Garnet's old comrade of the Stinkums. The world is emptier now, and he wishes it emptier. What can hangmen be that they would do this to their fellow-men just like plucking a flea from their ear? Trained for it? No, just naturally inclined that way, a kind of zealous exterminator thinning the vile human crop. Clearly, Father Garnet tells himself, we will have to train more Jesuits how to be hanged; the wastage is monstrous, but save them for Europe, keep them in Europe for God's sake. Keep them most of all from this barren, rigid, Scottish appendage of a country, rein them in straight off.

Never one to dote on the insect world, he now turns against it, not least for its way of ignoring him, as if he were a timber or a joist—no, he revises, ants and termites would love that. What do I mean? He has heard of long-term prisoners who form abiding tender relationships with mice, flies, roaches, and spiders: too tiny for him, he thinks, but he respects the impulse to revere creatures small and smaller, half-wondering how he would feel if obliged to share his cell with a lion or a tiger. What is the role of the minuscule in a cell? He cares not, not since the last three seconds, disdaining silverfish, caterpillars, wireworms, earwigs and the rest of the little team that patrols his hovel, thriving there not so much on crumbly stone as on the soil that graces it. Not far away, behold Anne Vaux, openly derided in the world of London, ever since his trial, a scorned celebrity who owns too many country houses. He hates all creatures that will survive him, almost all of them; they will never have known him. He will be gone, dismembered, and they will be quietly going about their time-honored patrols from crumb to crumb, all but the mice soundless, more expert denizens of the Tower than he would ever be. His hands have become rough, not that he was ever one for manicure, but torture, he concedes, is a great coarsener, and he wonders, not as if she is a separate being but a part of himself, if Anne Vaux has been subjected to manacles. Where is the point, he wonders, in torturing supposed plotters to get evidence on the dead? He understands Cecil's lust for completeness, the cipher/annal side of his nature embodied in all the paperwork he curses yet adores, without which his life would be just an uncoordinated scuffle: no text, no documentation, no bill of lading, no proof, no death warrants. Cecil the meticulous secretary is the opposite of Garnet the inspired listener. To Cecil no one is real without inscription; to Garnet the confessional has no daybook. The difference is between clerk and cleric, hardly a difference at all to anyone concerned with cast of mind—cerebral, aloof, private—but to a king, say, that between chalk and cheese. Cecil knows nothing of a million confessions floated unrecorded into the infinite, but Father Garnet understands them as thickening up the notion of heaven.

Anne Vaux has become a pest, demanding to see Garnet, forever troubling Waad and the rest with courteous but emphatic entreaties, harping on her needs as a penitent, only to hear Waad's jocose ridicule: "What monkey-business can you get up to in here, madam? What to confess? You should have been in here all through your life. A woman as devout as you claim to be has no business meddling with lecherous priests, whatever your placket says." Lady Waad disdains her, even though recognizing her as a woman of quality suitably ensconced in the Beaufort Tower with actual daylight pouring in.

"When, then?" has become Anne Vaux's incessant question.

"Not yet, madam." Waad has promised to let her see Garnet before—to see his execution, but remains unspecific about time and place. She will gladly join him on the scaffold, but Cecil, more eager to frustrate her than to wipe her out, continues to balk, since his wife's death a little squeamish about women. His wife died of social stress, yes; no more of that, he resolves. He will keep Anne Vaux in reserve against a rainy day, when a spectacle may require a specimen such as she. As it is, in the low-ceilinged chamber that has known the terminal headsweats of many doomed royals, she forms a new habit, falls into it: keeps bumping her head when rising from a crouch, as if she is being knighted in a grave. They refuse to let her confess, thus encumbering her with sundry guilts for blaming him, forgetting him, loving him indeed, none of these robust transgressions but fretting her almost to death. The regular rhythm of her days has broken down; the animus piled up, then shed, then built again, with the secular part of her ousting the devout one, at least in the sniffy realm of speculation. Love she easily defines as the complementary being without whom one never feels intact or complete; hence love of God or Jesus as being the true form of it, and love of a priest, so long as left spiritual, comparable, forbidden but soulful. For it is, is it not, his *soul* that she loves? She will never be sure. He will soon be soul only anyway, and she schools her mind for that sea change, deciding it will make no difference to her or even his sisters in Louvain. For the imminent shift in him, she is almost ready, at bottom even unwilling to see him ever again lest doing so impede the migration of his soul—metempsychosis to some. Waad never gives her a straight answer about the execution, badgered to death and always hinting at inconceivable obstacles, at times vaguely alluding to Redhill, Worcestershire, and Tyburn as other possible venues. Her brain goes numb and can find only the solace that all things end, except the goodness of . . .

Talking to herself, she develops an elocution of yawn, mispronouncing words with slackened mouth as if renouncing clear speech altogether, hoping to infect dread events with the same imprecision, blurring and muddling them so much that the hangman fails to arrive, the rope breaks, the knives go blunt, the brazier's coals go out, the hot water evaporates away . . . the sentence gets quashed. All this by way of interference from a gentlewoman still in waiting, a spinster of extraordinary prowess. Anne Vaux is not quite Cecil's yet, nor ever will be, though in her time, over the past twenty years, she has committed capital offenses galore. Can it be he fancies her, he so maladroit with educated women?

Just before he "goes," Father Garnet feels, he will have achieved fame as well as infamy: the top Jezzy-wit plotter, he will also be the man who invented lying—equivocation or prevarication—and turned it into an anti-government technique, an Italian perversion akin to sexual use of a so-called unfit orifice. So he ranks as yet another of Coke's demons, born to upset the realm, a man so habituated to lying he cannot quite believe his death sentence. Surely they intended its opposite, they themselves lying only to lure him into yet another lie. Who am *I*, he says in rhyming caricature, to lie? It is not irony I seek, but repose in the mind of God, with all my thinking done for me.

23

H E HAS BECOME a troubled author afraid he will not live long enough to put final touches to the last pages of a book. The closer he gets to the end, the worse he feels, bound to imagine, in self-aimed torment, the difference between not living through the last envisioned pages or the last five lines: sudden death in mid-sentence, say, or stroke, paralysis, or a fit of uncontrollable literary aversion that leaves his opus, even a treatise on mendacity, afloat on the wind for all to guess at—relegated in the end, if lucky, to the same questionable bin as someone's unfinished symphony or severed ballad, say, of how someone brought the news from London to Derby, all such amputated works famous for enacting in their very incompleteness the nature of life itself, the work in question that much nobler because it accommodates itself to chaos more than works of exquisitely carpentered conclusions. You were cut off in midflow, midstream, almost without realizing the ax could be so swift, although the mind may harbor one last image that never makes it into the work proper but initiates a new art form of penultimate prettiness. Now he squats, pulling his arms upward, and plasters his hands over his face, in the same movement retracting his knees until they touch his trunk, compressing himself at the last, but also, it has to be said, impeding the hangman. He will stay like this, he resolves, until they pry him loose.

But hold, though, he rebukes himself, it will not be a matter of a sudden chop, the monarch's fate, but rather a drawn-out series of gruesome inflictions grievous enough to halt all comely phrasemaking in any language, yet not altogether still-ing the conjurative mind (they are skilled at this), so it may be possible even in protracted extremis to conceive of master-strokes never penned but just sayable enough (after Digby) to extend the text beyond death, thus creating The Last Word of the Dying, or the Dying word at last. Whatever comes, he decides, the end, *his* end, will be untidy; he is so glad he is not involved in another treatise, only a dozen words into it, now, forever like a tiro addicted to the second or third act. No, did he not once pen a tract on the responsibility of Catholic women married to Protestants? How dare he forget his own works? Funny how people seeing you read a book assume you did not write it, so perhaps, seeing you write it, they assume you need not read it. Authorship merges itself back into the tumult of humanity.

So be it. London is aflame with lies and lying, less with gun-powder and treason, almost as if Londoners have at long last recognised what they have always been doing. It takes a Jesuit to pin it down for them, and so to an extent I have invented the English people, holding the mirror up to them. They should thank me. Perhaps in time I will become a verb, *to garnet*, say, or *garnetize*, and my treatise on lying will make its way into the curricula of Oxford and Cambridge. I will "go up" at long last, already a doctor (= teacher) of mendacity, belated bachelor of arts, there encountering the feeble, Latinless son of Cecil, duffer coached into admission by his bloodthirsty sire.

No: he is to be hanged, they tell him, on the First of May, that traditional day of national pomp, almost a pagan festival with Maypoles beribboned and spring serenaded with drunken chanties. How could I forget such a thing? As Cecil also puts it, damning himself for assuming Father Garnet has already gone the way of Father Oldcorne, John Wintour, Humphrey Littleton and Ralph Ashley (Redhill in Worcestershire, the 7th of April). It has been a stern, blustery winter. The people will want a riotous celebration, amid which the despatching of the top Jesuit will provoke an uproar of heathen delight. Why, even Father Garnet himself objects to this befouling of a gala day, far from feebly clutching at an extra hour or two of life, which is all humans ever do anyway. "What," he cries, "will they make a May game of *me*? Even if Mayday be a day of weighty delight, an ancient feast day of gathered green boughs and newborn bluebells, let them not soil it."

Then the Third, Cecil tells himself, after the plebs have calmed down, bring them up again with a garnished Garnet. He wishes the whole mess were done with, dreading an ultimate scandal on the scaffold as a man of firm presence and firmer faith quits his mortal role. A Garnet too near the pagan fire festival of Beltane could be explosive. Yet why fear a nearly dead man? Can it be because he stands for something huge? Cecil cannot control everything, he knows, but surely a statesman committed to public mutilation of a high priest, never mind how alien a sect, must expect some riotous show from those watching. His simultaneous passion for diplomatic finesse and decisive disposal grieves him; how can he be both Cicero and Attila? A genius such as he fancies he is not would spare Father Garnet and urge James to give full rein to his lurking tendency to tact. *Let* them glut themselves with their imagined gods. Then, he asks, what harm would moderation do but endear the king to his people? Could not the Catholics, such an alien minority, be calmed? Of course. Why then, Cecil asks himself, do I choose the bloodiest remedy, the most loathsome gesture? To keep the king in place and keep him from maneuvering against *me*.

In the end, Cecil blames his Council for engineering him into this or that, severely aware of times past when he has gone to compassionate lengths on behalf of a pleading rascal, an infirm child. Why does his honorable streak peter out so often? The Council chooses the Third of May, 1606, ignorant of the fact that this very day commemorates the Feast of the Invention of the Holy Cross by the Ancient British queen Helena, a coincidence not lost on the incredulous Garnet, to whom Invention remains to *discover,* to *happen upon.* For complex reasons having to do with the power of a word to emblazon an historic feat ("inventing" the Cross), his tumbling mind manages to bring together the twin but severed notions of the word as something stumbled upon, found by accident, and as something devised, thought up. For a keen moment, his weary head joins the two, viewing all invention as discovery of something holy, already planted in the manger of Creation, so that, he dimly sees, the infant Jesus does not exist until the person who concocts him happens upon him in the richness of imagination. This paradox is worthy of a rabbi, he thinks. He wants to hasten to Rome to pursue, on a meager diet of pasta and preserves, the holiness of language.

Alas for his ruminations, Cecil decides to make him guiltier still through incessant further questioning. They dupe him into a long letter to Tesimond, whom they claim captured, and he also writes to the king, unavailingly, in mellow plea. They want to see what he has left, making him relive his garden conversation with Tesimond at that secret house in Essex, which he always recalls as a great relief from kneeling (a painful posture). They get nowhere with him; weariness and despair have made him salubriously obtuse. How can he damage himself further? If he cannot do it to himself, then by all means let them try, foisting on the ancient Romans a verb they never had. When Waad charges that his confession is too little and too late, hardly an admission at all, Father Garnet persists, revising his testimony now to include matters he initially left out. "I took it as confession," he tells them about one incident, "even if wrongly." They no sooner pin something down, saying, "Here is an example of treason, sir," than he reels it away from them into a holier zone of intense privacy, contending that there is formal confession—a matter of furnishing and cabinets, seats, upholstery, screens, and sore knees —and what he now, to their fury, calls *invented privacy*, which sounds spurious but is actually, after the "invented cross," confession new-fangled and linked to the formal kind, as impulsive decency is to behavior by the book.

This stuns them, making Cecil wish he could send the doomed man off to Cambridge to await the arrival of his fathead son.

"Goodness to the good," Father Garnet tells them, seized by the threat of more torture. Does he cherish what is left of his creature comfort or not? He does. Deciding to live out the rest of his days in honorable confusion, he begins his last letter to Anne Vaux, though he has already said goodbye in the previous

347

one. As best he can, he has advised her how to look after herself, assuming she will be released, and this letter amounts to a
bit of ritual such as they have both enjoyed. "It pleaseth God,"
he writes, not in lemon or orange juice, "daily to multiply my
crosses." He likes the way this statement interposes between
them no Cecils, Waads, or Cokes, or between himself and
God. Summing up the calamities of his recent life—Hindlip,
his overheard confession to Father Oldcorne, the seizing of
Tesimond (as he thinks)—he mentions the vicious slander visited on them both. *Virginibus puerisque* (For Virgins and Boys)
is the phrase he unearths, although he does not write it down.
He is sorry, he tells her. Will she ever receive this? He doubts it,
with Cecil prowling. Still thinking in Latin (as if another language exempts him from this country's decree), he ends with a
few lines about the trials of Job, and signs himself, Yours *in eter-
num,* as I hope, HG." Below his initials he sketches in rough a
cross and the letters IHS for Jesus. Father Garnet has made his
mark, not so much carving a scar on the universe as being
scarred by it in all innocence and some guilt. It is 21st April
1606. He has twelve more days in which to compose himself.
Where is his old friend Byrd, he wonders, so wrapped in defensive prudence as not to remember a singing friend up against it
or even his voice. Or is Byrd trapped in ambiguous luxury in
some lavish palace, paralyzed by the plotters' fate? But still
publishing his masses without title-page, date, or printer's
name? It always said his own name, though, plain as a pikestaff.
What did he once say? *I skulk in the open.* I wish he would come
and try it in the Tower. Does he still come up with evasive titles
that run forward while retreating? Such as "Songs, which by
their argument are called sacred." Now, what is wrong with

that? If only he were in the gyves alongside me, we'd get good ideas for songs. Father Garnet meekly salutes him (he can hardly envision him on a scaffold) and other absent friends, especially those who have already given up the ghost, an act he thinks of physically: some phantasmal doll vaulted into heaven weightless and oblique on a Saturday morning.

When the Third of May comes, Father Garnet is ahead of himself. King James has already left London for Newmarket in Suffolk, his theological mania briefly extinguished by the crude facts of Garnet's case: hyper-refined argument lofting the priest to a scaffold. The king rides north while Waad reviews arrangements for producing the condemned, always a trial for him, not least for having had to do it so often and learned from it only to await the unexpected. No man of sentiment, he is not callous either and thus willingly brings Garnet Lady Waad's pious farewell even as the priest receives "Farewell, good sir" from one of the Tower's cooks, who could surely have killed him with his cooking by overfeeding him. What he hears in return strikes him as the epitome of gentry, a riposte worthy of the priest he has come to know over the last three months: "Farewell, good sir," Garnet says huskily, "Farewell, good friend Tom, this day I will save thee a labor to provide my dinner." Dissonance creeps into Father Garnet's mind where he has been hoping for harmony, his soul ready and stabilized for one last travesty. With some pride, he gives himself over limply to those who see only the day's entertainment getting under way, a trembling semblance of a hero wearing a black cloak over his modified long white shirt, and a clerical-looking hat soon to be cast aside.

This clerkly fellow they strap upside down to the hurdle that will tow him through tumultuous streets, his head vilely abased to the level of dog droppings, offal, mud, and garbage, to denote the foul level he has sunk to as a conspirator. It is going well, at least without protest from the humiliated Garnet, until, with a shriek and an almost construable cry seeming to need no air to fuel it, a woman plays chase in the courtyard, briefly eludes warders and bursts toward the inverted Garnet only to be unceremoniously grabbed by loins and throat to be removed to where she belongs. This is all Waad's fault, he having instructed his deputies to allow Anne Vaux (*Mistress* Anne Vaux, he said) to observe Father Garnet's departure at a distance, as she could from the Beaufort Tower, that obelisk of lonely spectatorship where one chop down on the green closes the present and blacks out future. Father Garnet, however, is going elsewhere behind three horses, an upside-down wretch for popular consumption. "Mistress Anne Vaux to the window," Waad had said, but her keeper, heart softened by gold, releases her down the steps into the courtyard, aerial anteroom to an ignominious ride. She goes back so fast—no word with him, no prayer, no touch—she might have been keelhauled by the hefty jailers, but her awful yell persists until a rag gray with donkeystone (for whitening windowsills) blocks her mouth so violently they want to hang her too, right there, for having marred a quiet-enough going-on, and she would not have called out. She has not been handled so roughly since being grabbed by the guards at the Newgate.

No carriage this time, Henry, Father Garnet is thinking: anything to shut out her combustible, almost infantile cry, her last contribution to their twenty-year reign. She has nerves of

rock, he tells himself, but not for this, which I can abide if only
nothing poignant—*daggery*—unmans me. He knows of money
changing hands for imminent widows to utter one last vow of
love and faith as their upturned beloved clatters by on his way
to the mob. Is it possible that, with Anne Vaux smothered
back into the vanished Tower, his last glimpse of her would be
a wimple enclosing a face white as cuttlefish bone? He is now
bouncing his way to St Paul's sacred churchyard; is he to be
tried yet again? Some scrupulous souls have opposed this
venue, claiming Saint Paul's is holy to the memory of Queen
Elizabeth, but Cecil has quashed them: he wants religious revenge in a sacred place, and no sentimental dithering.

So there is none. Fatter Garnet sets his hands together and
squeezes his eyes shut—enough, he thinks, to deform the balls
forever. Those watching see a forlorn man deep in contemplation, so much turned inward away from this world as to not
need hanging at all. He will fall away from this world like sawdust from the creases in Little John Owens's work-clothes, as if
he were anointed with pollen. At the churchyard there waits
the biggest congregation of his life, abuzz with Jezzy-wit
frenzy, the scaffold erected in the west with wooden stands all
around it. Windows full of heads have for Father Garnet a
gruesome look, as if a many-eyed giant is taunting him. Can I
pick out the de-rigueur observing priests, he wonders, or Francis Bacon, that scheming connoisseur of shows, the aphorist of
the drop? I will try to perform some last rites on this day of
days. The watching priest will try to do likewise on my
butchered carcass. Father Garnet himself has rendered this
ugly service, his heart almost halted, his chest burning. He has
been here before, to no great advantage—twelve pence for a seat

in hell, though quaking with premonitions now come true.

Unstrapped from the hurdle and feeling weaker than ever, Father Garnet comes to, amid the uproar, with a shrug, a headshake, a nod, and then a raising of both arms aloft. He would like to pray, he explains, but they want no prayers. He pleads with those in attendance–Dr George Abbot, Dean of Winchester; Dr John Overall, Dean of St Paul's; Henry Morgan the Recorder of London: and the Sheriff of London, all intent on suborning him to further admissions of guilt even here on the rim–but they heed him not, as if they believed last-minute confession sank the condemned even deeper into the mire. Only later on are they willing to strike a bargain with him: a refuge for a *mea culpa*. Offer him his life to renounce Rome! Such is the slogan bandied about among the crowd. It will never work with Father Garnet. What is it that vexes him about this offering that sounds almost scholarly? Their church, wanting a convert brutally, does not deserve a roof. "Further treasons?" Garnet repeats the Recorder's question, then snaps, "*Never any*," and robustly interrupts the two Deans' harangue about the ideals of Protestantism: "They may grace executioners, my lords, but they offend Catholics like a drink of neatsfoot oil. Pray let me . . . turn the other cheek."

Keepers of a mystery often lose heart, but not Father Garnet who, because his heart of mystery is so remote from everyone else, even from other Catholics, revels in its secrecy, convinced it has nothing to do with language, time, signs, gestures, but trembles in his core's quick like a brain flame, unique to him, leaving him not alone with God but God and him alone together amid the universe. If this be arrogance, he does not know but sails forward, almost relieved to be beyond vexation, naked in what later thinkers will come to call an electric no-man's-land where all is lightning and yonder.

These, he thinks, are the irreversible changes people make on giving up the world, on having the universe snatched from them, if they only get a chance. Many die without it, but Father Garnet is going to die, he now knows, having denied what an eternity-bound man does not need, and no amount of chivvying and pestering on the scaffold by Protestant prelates is going to sway him. He is all direction, and speed, not theirs, not his, not hers, but a mote hieing.

The priest in the twelve-penny seat sees much, but not all, of what follows: the shuffle to confront "a going soul," the impromptu quizzing to see what he still has in him to own up to, the way he shuts up the dignitaries delaying him on his way to the ladder. "I am prepared," they hear, "and resolved. Trouble me no further." But they do, reluctant to let him go without another apology to stimulate the groundlings, or a plea to be at last excused by the hunting king: forgiven before death. So long as they can squeeze a syllable out of him, they keep him from going, turning and tweaking him as if irresolutely trying to present him, as a vase or a sculpture. The Recorder calls out to the crowd, "Attention, attention, the Jezzy-wit has just asked the king's forgiveness."

"I did no such thing," Garnet tells them. An argument ensues under these horrific auspices.

"You do but equivocate, sir," one of the notables says, "and if you deny it, after your death we will publish your own hand, that the world may see your false dealing."

Energetically, considering his circumstances, Father Garnet springs into action: "This is not the time to talk of equivocation. Neither do I equivocate. But *in troth*" (he runs out of air) "you shall not find my hand otherwise than what I have said." He means it, some of the watchers are muttering. "He would not lie *now*." Garnet is addressing them again, as if playing chess on the brink of a volcano. "Show me the paper in question, sir. I defy you to produce any such thing."

Montague has to confess he has left it at home. If it exists. Garnet changes themes, weirdly exhilarated by this last-ditch encounter, and apologizes for the weariness of his usually firm voice. "Upon this day," he tells them in a valiant fit of calendrical allusion, "is recorded the invention" (word he loves) "of the Cross of Christ, and upon this day I thank God I have found a cross of mine own." He denies any guilt, expresses horror at the plot, and exhorts Catholics to live quietly. "God," he announces to all and sundry, "will not be unheedful of you." A closing threat? Some think so.

Are they listening at all, eager for the spectacle of a priest's body being dismantled? One shouts, a final rib, "But, Mr Garnet, were you not married to Mrs Anne Vaux, you a priest?" They love it. He flushes away his pallor, musters uncanny indignant vitality, as if she were present, which of course she is not. They have piqued him at the last, with secular insult born of spite; his legendary sexual aberrations have spurred them all to a new prurience. He is their temporary toy.

"That honorable gentlewoman," he begins, hoarse with fury, "hath undergone great wrong by such false reports. For it is suspected and said that I should be married to her and worse. But I protest the contrary. She is a virtuous good gentlewoman and therefore to impute any such thing unto her cannot proceed but of malice." It is the lingo of the seminar; on so lewd a matter, he is lecturing them *in extremis* as if he has hours and weeks before him, choking on the indignity offered, finding his memory of her and hers of him fused in a bright ingot the sun has offered to his mind, the May sun. Is he at last in Italy again? Soon.

After at last being able to pray in peace to the swarming blank of heaven, he strips down to his sewn-up bedshirt, his makeshift shift, ignoring one last Protestant come to badger his last inch. He mounts the ladder as if going to paint, with just a flicker in his mind of being a bricklayer, pauses, makes the sign of the Cross with steady hand, and then, as if this event will never begin or end, gets into verbal palaver yet again, hounded to the end by his own sheriffs of vocabulary.

On the ladder, and relieved that the May breeze does not waft his shirt revealingly upward, he makes the sign of the cross once more and asks good Catholics present to pray for him; but he is reckoning on a London crowd crammed into a churchyard reluctant, having got him, to let him go.

24

M R GARNET," SHOUTS one wag, "it is expected of you to *recant*. It is *expected*." Father Garnet is hardly in the mood, although no mood would describe him; he just wonders why Londoners are never satisfied.

"God forbid," he says, "I never meant to do wrong, but ever strove to be a true and perfect Catholic. As you shall see." To himself, he thinks: We Catholics are always attentive to the dying we do, from day to day, then at the end.

Dr Overall protests, but Garnet waves him aside, a pedantic ignoramus who thinks *moriturus* means ready to discuss. Father Garnet resumes his prayers, shifting from English to Latin, then hears the hangman is ready, as if he has finished his own prayers, as if they are all going out somewhere festive, Greenwich perhaps, in a coach. He crosses his unbound arms over his chest and is shoved off the rung, forming yet not voicing an uncouth cry of alarm and surprise rolled into one, that sudden, acrid smother brought on by the rope, an untoward turn of events. Father Garnet dangles briefly, the hangman prepares to cut him down alive for the next ordeal, but several spectators, animated to interfere, cry "Hold! Hold!" and, lunging forward to curb the hangman, tug on Father Garnet's legs heedless of what drips down from within the shirt. All of a sudden, the mob sides with the Jezzy-wit, for once not eager to watch the drawing and quartering done on a still living, responding body. It is usually the hanged's relatives who pull on the legs to effect a perfect strangulation, a swift demise, but something has altered the mood of this querulous crowd that has already had more than its way with Father Garnet. His dignity, his denials, his indignation, his candor, his hoarse voice have touched them somehow. He goes to the chopping block dead, and when his heart is lofted on high with the vindicated redundant yell of "Behold the heart of a traitor!" nobody stirs, cheers, applauds, or answers with a "God save the king." There is just a diffuse, insensate murmuring, a sheepish drift into shame as they begin to move away somehow deprived, debased. Perhaps too much preliminary talk has sapped the event of its drama. Father Garnet spoke unexpected lines and so became more of a person than most condemned, like Sir Everard Digby, and Garnet's spell still slows them down.

This very day, Father Gerard sneaks away to Europe, crossing the Channel in the retinue of two envoys, Baron Hoboken and the Marquis de Germain, who first turn him down—"Too dangerous, Father, to have you in *our* escort"—but suddenly relent having heard of Father Garnet's vivid end. Into de Germain's livery he wriggles, praying with each twist for Father Garnet, to whom he thinks he owes this change of heart. At least, he notes in a soon-to-be-famous manuscript, I have not crossed the Channel in the hide of a slaughtered hog. But here I am. I have re-entered the realm of freedom along the trajectory of a great soul going upward, the stick of his rocket I was, a life subordinate to his, could he not have escaped too? Did he even try? Or was it his duty as our Superior to die in front of them, just to show them up? Father Gerard, budding historian of the English Jesuits, will survive another thirty years, as will Anne Vaux, released from the Tower in August. Squinting with cataracts which St. Winifred has not helped, and aching with female disorders of long standing, she lives on in London with her sister-in-law, Eliza, still rebellious and devoutly sure she should have been hanged too. She keeps and nourishes not only her recusant intensity but also the mystical side that revered the sawdust in the creases of Little John's tunic when he stood groaning: God's droppings, he said. She does not comprehend her own death or any other transitory doorway, and she believes she has earned the right to continue to—she knows the word from Garnet—*transmogrify* secular events as if dispensing magic. The "gift" has come to her.

"No," says ebullient Eliza, "Don't overstep your bounds. We are safe in Leicestershire, safer. You have been bleakly honored in Lessius's *The Treasure of Vowed Chastity.* Enough—"

"Is never enough, Eliza. The work goes on, apace. He said I had to. I do. They will always be after me. My destiny, dear woman, is to be always sought out by *inferiors,* whom I tolerate with uncommon grace because I have been well brought up. I will always have customers. Be sure of that. One day with my white head I'll still hide bodies, if you see."

Eliza does not, nor does she wish to be involved in the devious toils of her restive junior who is only too familiar with the various separate towers within the Tower, the blood spilled at the execution site on Tower Hill, the ominous little room at the bottom of the White Tower where manacles and rack order the day's doings, and Tower Green where the Tower's captives are buried under the greensward when they have served their sentence. The women's next move, bitterly debated until Eliza gives in, will be to Stanley Grange near Derby. Back in Father Garnet's terrain, Eliza thinks Anne will be wilder than ever, an easy catch inspired by topography and the yearning to join her priest in punishment. *Fervor mortis,* she says, cattily. She knows. "Why do we not go to St Monica's in Louvain, or St Omer, and leave the English to their folly? Now you want to found a Jesuit school for young Catholic gentlemen? The Father Garnet seminary? I wonder at you. House arrest has only strengthened you. Loss has only enriched you. Truly a diligent demon, you could be Pope, dear Anne. Be soft."

With Father Garnet dead, efforts begin to keep him from being gone. At the request of a tailor's wife, a Mrs Griffin, a youth named John Wilkinson stationed himself in grisly altruism near the hangman as he dropped Father Garnet's head into the standard bucket lined with straw. John Wilkinson is to find for Mrs Griffin a relic on which to dote, though it is hard to imagine what, since pieces and splinters, specks and iotas, do not readily offer themselves to snappers-up of hitherto unconsidered trifles. A tooth, then, or a hair? God knows what such a woman has in mind, although of her zeal to come up with something there is no doubt. Entire religious regimes have emanated from such crumbs and will continue to do so, much as empty shrines will sometimes tempt a deity in.

So Wilkinson of strong stomach hears the plop sound as of a heavy cabbage dropped only to cast a previously unnoticed empty husk of corn into his hand, and stained with blood. Mrs

Griffin, on receiving this find, is overjoyed. A few days later, the blood on the husk has arranged itself into the countenance of Father Garnet, precisely his drained, anxious, emaciated face: eyes tight, beard bloody and around his neck a crimson weal. There in the crystal reliquary in which Mrs Griffin has cached it, the husk begins to exert uncanny power, an exact image of Henry Garnet becoming more exact the more people peer at it and wonder, as if the husk has become inspired. Other witnesses, of preposterous long-range discernment regarding all manner of things, claim the husk blanches and becomes a physiognomy the instant Father Garnet's parboiled, tarred head appears impaled on a pike on London Bridge. Perhaps they mean the head itself blanched, and this is why six weeks later a press of fascinated spectators causes the authorities (Cecil) to turn the face away from the curious mob, as if putting the clock back. Even in death, Father Garnet holds court with pagans who let a tiny husk reflect a head-sized one which, in turn, perhaps matches the head of God: a white all-encompassing effigy that, as one watching recusant says in ungrammatical ardor, "seemeth to gleameth."

When Anne Vaux first sees the Griffin husk after being released, she vindicates whoever branded her "sometimes too ardent, in divine things," discerning in it the visage of none other than her mentor: "He in any one of his various forms come home at last like a sheaf of maltreated wheat." Heedless of Belgian imitations sold not cheaply and a suppressed worshipful book on the husk, she rations out immortality to Father Garnet, even though the relic, after being peeped at (for a fee) by Zuniga the Spanish ambassador, remains hidden in

the Embassy before being whisked away to the coffers of the
Society of Jesus, ultimately a mere straw amid the hullabaloo
and the mayhem.

Mere memory of the husk's pallor incites her back to succoring priests at which she so excels she reckons it an artform
outdoing even Byrd, not heard from since the early days of the
plot when Guido Fawkes returned from Europe to get things
going. Two weeks after Henry Garnet's execution, Cecil is
made a Knight of the Garter and sports a new blue ribbon. *She*
is strong, she thinks, and durable because she too has been
parboiled whereas her leman (she shudders at this word) has
been converted to lovingly unfindable straw: Father Henry
Garnet once more invulnerable, armored in metaphor, returned to maker unused.